The Isle of Hast
NaHuk

ORANU

I

II

The Tower of Dragon

REY WICKS

THE KING OF EVERYTHING

The Legend of Chaos

The King Of Everything by Rey Wicks
© 2024, Rey Wicks
All rights reserved.
Published in the United States by Curious Corvid Publishing, LLC, Ohio.

No part of this publication may be reproduced, stored in a retrieval system, stored in a database and/or published in any form or by any means, electronic, mechanical, photocopying, recording or otherwise, without the prior written permission of the publisher, except as permitted by U.S. copyright law.
ISBN: 978-1-959860-50-1
978-1-959860-51-8

Cover Design by: Emily's World of Design

Printed in the United States of America
Curious Corvid Publishing, LLC
PO Box 204
Geneva, OH 44041

This is a work of fiction. Unless otherwise indicated, all the names, characters, businesses, places, events and incidents in this book are either the product of the author's imagination or used in a fictitious manner. Any resemblance to actual persons, living or dead, or actual events is purely coincidental.

curiouscorvidpublishing@gmail.com

TRIGGER WARNINGS:
Includes acts of violence, bloodshed, and death

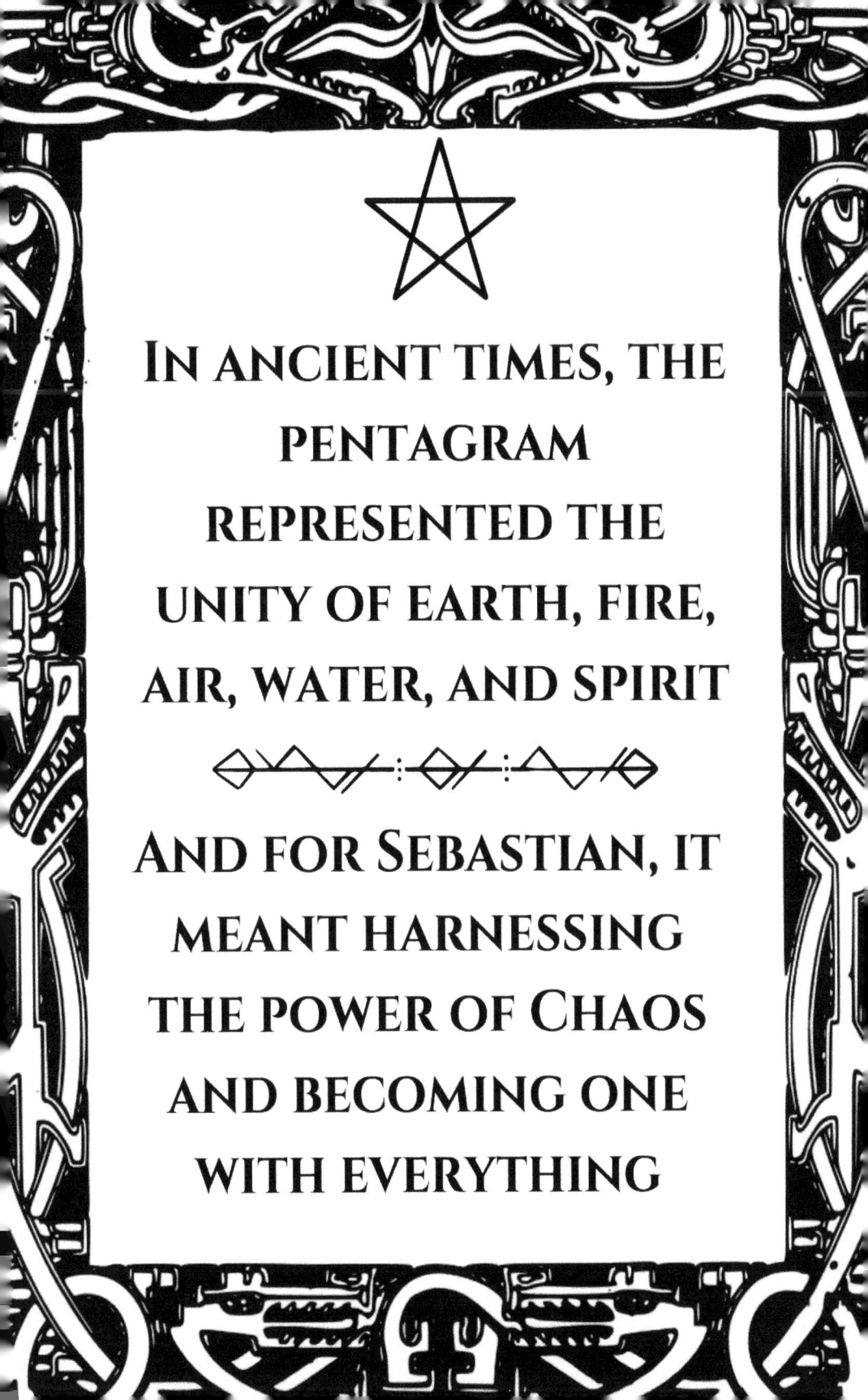

Chapter One
A Certain Evil

Snow and ice crunched under thick leather boots as Maxen, King of Men, wandered across the shoreline in Torrdale. As he made his way across castle grounds and into the plains, the sight began to haunt him. Men and women of both Midrel Istan and Erras had been slaughtered and lay soaked in blood, some with their eyes still open wide, staring at him with judgment. After the onslaught, and as the lands fell quiet from the eerie whispers of death, he stood and watched over the land that had been home to his bloodline since its birth. He stared at the blackness of the sea, waiting for his ship to come to save him from the place where his brother had once ruled.

Centuries before, in the time of Dragon's rule, Ansel Bolin was the only world leader not born of magic. Rejected by the gods, his own father, and the Order of Sorcery, Ansel made it his life mission to end the lineage of gods and to allow man to thrive in the lands they built. A place where non-magic folks could live in a world that rejected anyone who could wield magic. Ansel outlawed all forms of craft in his lands and brought forth the ideals of the Bolin family and their hatred toward any who could challenge them. But, as time passed, the Bolin bloodline shifted back to its magical roots, and Maxen and Valirus's father, the king, and their mother, the queen, birthed two boys, both gifted with the art of magic.

Their father was disgusted with his sons and exiled them to the land of Erras. At the age of nine, Maxen relied heavily on his older brother, Valirus to shelter him from the harshness of the new lands they had named Torrdale, which meant "hope." As the brothers got older, there was an imbalance between them that forced Maxen to flee south to the new kingdom he constructed on the backs of the thousands of natives he had found living on the banks of Alta Prime. But Maxen's rule in Erras fell short when his rise to power was consumed by greed and retaliation against the man who had rejected him.

Maxen sailed to Midrel Istan, leaving his newfound kingdom without a ruler. When he arrived in Altania a mere fifteen years later, Maxen marched into the grand halls of the Altanian castle built on the edge of a rocky cliffside. He brandished his staff in one hand and shouted his father's name as guards hurried to barricade the throne room doors. The jewel in his staff glowed a deep crimson, and a loud shriek was heard as a force of wind blew so powerfully that it sliced the guards in two. Maxen wandered into the place where he would see his father looking old and tired, sitting on his throne with a golden crown upon his head.

The youngest child of the Bolin king tilted his head to the side and raised one eyebrow. "I am home, father. I have come to claim my rightful place on the throne."

"You are an abomination." The Bolin king hissed. "An exile. You are not welcome here."

"And this abomination will rule over all as King of Kings." Maxen stood close to his father and raised his staff as the stone shined once more. "It is time you stepped aside, Father, or die defending your own prejudices."

The Bolin king laughed. "You will never truly rule as King of Kings until you fulfill the destiny that your great-great-grandfather started."

Maxen lowered his staff and stepped back a few paces. "There are no more gods in these lands."

"Are there not?" The Bolin king smirked. "Twins." He leaned back on the throne. "Born of the gods Dragon and Litha, and to one of the most powerful kings in the world, these twins must be dealt with in order for you to even think you are good enough to wear a crown upon your head." The Bolin king shook his head and growled. "You cannot defeat them. You are not strong enough."

"You are wrong, Father." Maxen brandished his staff again and jammed its jewel into his father's chest. He took a deep breath and whispered an enchantment until the stone turned from red to white. "I will be King of Kings, and I will end the line of gods in this world. It's too bad you will not be alive to see it." And, with a fatal conjuring of magic, the Bolin king slumped into a hollowed somber.

In the dungeons of Castle Drake, after the Order left for The Far North, there was a stir in the quiet halls. As he opened his eyes, the darkness startled him. His hands stroked the tight crypt that surrounded his entire body. He lay back, breathing heavily until a cold calm washed over his body, drowning him in the memory of the day he died on his knees in the cold, with King Maxen's grip on his hair. His eyes connected to the man who was identical to him in almost every way. "Sebastian." Tomas's lip trembled. Then, the cold returned as the image of a young Blackbird with blue eyes stood over him before he was taken to the priory where the others slept. "Chaos." He gritted his teeth and slapped his hand against his tomb, freezing the walls around him.

The shattering of stone and wood echoed through the corridor, but no one inside the walls of Castle Drake seemed to take any notice. A pale hand pushed through the rubble and reached for something, anything, it could grasp. A puddle on the floor of the dungeon reflected a beautiful brown-haired man with bright blue eyes. He turned to view the plaque on the wall that read "Prince Tomas Ivan Drake." He dusted off his coat and stared at the slumber of the tombs with confusion, yet the familiarity of it all made him flash a half-smile. "I am no longer Prince Tomas. I am Hydros, God of Water."

He wandered through the castle without fear of being seen, but seamlessly avoided guards as he slipped through the halls. It was night, and all was quiet in the kitchens. No guard on duty patrolling nor blocking the door into the courtyard.

As the darkest of night set in, he snuck away from the snowy castle in the mountains and wandered aimlessly through the blizzard until the sound of wind snapping a ship's sails became evident from the near distance. The snowfall was too heavy to see through, but a bright white light guided his path. Soon after climbing a rickety plank onto a ship's deck, he found himself face-to-face with a tall, bearded man with a square jaw and muscular shoulders.

"What is this?" Hydros asked.

"Do not fear," the bearded man said. "You and I need to discuss a significant problem that I believe you can help me with."

"Who are you?"

"The King of Kings." His voice was low and heavy.

"You don't look like a Drake."

The man laughed. "That is because my name is King Maxen Bolin, and my family has been sitting on the throne since my great-great-grandfather seized it from a mad king." Maxen paced across the deck, his boots thumping loudly with each step.

"But the man who wears the crown is the god Chaos."

Maxen's face turned as red as the crimson cape that adorned his shoulders. "Chaos is merely a man. A weak child who in no way should ever be allowed to rule in this world."

"Why am I here?"

"Because I need you in order to control him...to stop him." Maxen stopped pacing and put his finger over his lips. "And once we seize the power of the fire gods, we will be unstoppable."

"We?" Hydros laughed. "Oh, no...There is no we, King Maxen. There is you, the King of Men, a sorcerer, and me, the only one who can stop Chaos from ending all of time."

Maxen twirled his mustache. "I believe you. But I have revenge of my own to get on our mutual enemy." He stopped in front of the man he had invited onto his ship. "For too long, my family has been forced to fight tooth and nail against the wrath of the Drakes in order to save our bloodline. For too long, my family has remained in the shadows of a land once bleeding with gods who knew nothing but violence. For too long, my family has fought to create a kingdom where man can live free from the bounds of a force they cannot defend themselves against—"

"I get it." Hydros held up his hand. "You hate the gods. Why do you want me, then?"

"You," Maxen said, "are very special. Even if you are one of them."

"And you want me to kill Chaos? Why would I do that? He is technically my brother. My twin."

"I only need you to do one thing: distract him while I use the Oscura to kill him."

Hydros narrowed his eyes. "The Oscura? How do you intend to get it from him?"

"I have someone working on that as we speak."

"Why should I help you?"

Maxen rested his palms on the man's shoulders. "Allow me to end the apocalypse and restore what is rightfully mine, and you will get to live however you wish, anywhere you wish, and rule your own kingdom."

"That seems hardly worth my time and energy. I could just kill you and Chaos and rule over all. Over everything."

Maxen's face turned hallowed and ghostly. "If Chaos is allowed to live, the world will end. It is up to us to keep it alive."

"Don't lie to me." The man began to pace. "You don't want him dead to save the people of earth. You want him dead because, if he is left alive, then you will never be respected as King of Kings." He stood still. "What is stopping me from killing you and taking the crown for myself?"

"Because I can control the only one who can kill you." Maxen grinned. "If you help me, I will keep the Blackbird of Death under my thumb until Chaos is destroyed."

Winter lingered late into the new year in Icefall. Sebastian and Dom sat in the warm atrium garden inside the Alcala-Sage Manor. The Order of Thieves trained day and night alongside the Sinook warriors. All, even Dani, joined the others each day, often against Sebastian's wishes. It came into spring, yet the snow was still stacked high across the plains. The rivers were frozen, but the lakes began to weaken. Dom and his daughter, Torra, sat before the fire. Torra was an adolescent girl preparing to cross into womanhood. There was to be a party planned for her once the first flower bloomed in the fields.

Sebastian sipped his wine while twirling a chess piece between his fingers. He hadn't spoken much since arriving in The Far North. Often, his days consisted of riding to the borderlands in the morning, then resting in the atrium during midday, then joining the others for dinner before retreating to the watchtower that overlooked the icy seas. Sebastian's heart ached for Tomas. The guilt from ending Cyrus ate at him every day, forcing him to push away everyone who cared about him, including Dani.

"Don't look so sad," Torra said. Her brown eyes made Sebastian smile. She was turning into a beautiful young lady, and Dom was happier than he had ever seen. Sebastian's heart grew warm watching the little family grow. Torra's mother came to visit when the weather permitted, but as a seer, she was an important member of the tribe in Sedda.

Torra knelt before Sebastian. "His Majesty is so quiet these days. It breaks my heart to see. You have so much to be happy about." She smiled, then turned back to her father. "So, about the dress I want to be made for my birthday."

"I promised you," Dom said. "Anything you want, my sweet girl."

Sebastian stood and put on his coat. "This is too cute for me." He laughed. "I am going to go for a walk to see if I can find any flowers blooming." Sebastian winked at Torra, then left the atrium.

The sunshine glistened against the snow. The sounds of cracking ice echoed across the grounds, making him wince with each crumble of falling snow. Sebastian wandered off toward the archery range to watch the daily practice, remembering the day he was laughed at by the Sinook for missing the bullseye when he was trying too hard to impress Dom.

He followed a trail to the stadium and stood on a balcony that overlooked the shooter's marks. Sebastian saw one of Dom's brothers stand side by side with Meecah, and they readied their bows. The archers pulled back the bowstrings and aimed. Meecah glanced up to meet Sebastian's eyes. She grinned and returned her attention to the target. Her jaw tightened, and the muscles on her chest flexed under her sweat as the sun beat down. There was a whoosh of wind and a familiar thud. Dom's brother shot an arrow through the head of a dummy soldier, while Meecah's arrow went through the dummy's groin.

Sebastian covered his face while stifling back a laugh. "Scary, but excellent shot. Both of you!"

Meecah came to stand by his side. She rested her arm on his shoulder and watched the next set of archers go up to the line. "You watch the seas day and night. There are people that are paid to do that, Your Majesty." She brushed his hair back. "You look tired."

Sebastian stared across the field, where the ocean lay beyond an icy cliff. "I can't wait for a guard to come tell me our enemies are breaching the city." His attention turned back to the archers. Dani stepped up to the line against Dom's mother.

Vinita spent her time in her atrium with her spell books spread out on a metal table, but after lunch, she joined the warriors in combat training. As one of the last enchantresses in The Far North, she was in charge of the safety of Icefall. When she first met Dani, her eyes locked onto his like she was absorbing his soul, and Dani accepted her love as if she were his own mother.

Dani picked up his bow and looked up to see Sebastian watching him from the stage above the target. His face blushed and he grinned bashfully as his hand reached for an arrow. He nodded at Vinita, then strung his arrow.

Sebastian admired Dani's glistening sapphire eyes. The archers both aimed at the same time, then the whoosh of arrow fire and the thump of a target being pierced filled the air. The arrows were centered perfectly, with the arrowheads touching the same place on the bullseye. Sebastian stared at the target, then at Dani. He didn't speak. Instead, he jerked his head to one side and turned to walk away, leaving Meecah to watch the next archers alone.

He walked toward the watchtower quickly, staring at the ground with each step. The sounds of footsteps crunching in the snow came abruptly, then arms wrapped around his shoulders. He turned and leaned forward, resting his lips against Dani's.

"I'm happy to see that you are in a good mood." Dani bit his lip.

Sebastian smiled and grabbed his hand before stepping through the watchtower's doors. "My mood is about to get a lot better."

Dani's face turned red and his mouth turned into a wide smile. "You are so bad." He slammed the door closed and pushed Sebastian into a chair next to the fire. "I love it when you're bad," Dani whispered in Sebastian's ear. He lightly kissed his neck, then slipped off his coat and shirt.

Sebastian watched in silence. His eyes glanced over every inch of Dani's flesh as he stripped off his clothes. Dani contorted against the rough caresses on his back and hips, his muscles flexing on his petite frame. Sebastian let out a hum when Dani's hand slipped down his pants.

"Do you want me?" Dani kissed his lips. Sebastian nodded.

After the afternoon had passed, Sebastian lay before the fire, gasping to catch his breath. Dani dressed and left to fetch a maiden to bring them food. Sebastian climbed to his feet and donned his clothing before climbing to the top of the tower. When he returned, Dani was sitting at the top of the stairs, peering through a looking glass. "My father won't be bobbing on a boat somewhere. There is no place he could be other than Safareen. That is the only place our scouts haven't traveled."

"Unless he left Erras," Sebastian said.

"He didn't." Dani hurried down the stairs and returned with a tray in his hands. He set it on a table and went to Sebastian. "Come eat, my love. You must be hungry."

"I am." Sebastian took another glimpse at the sea. "Perhaps I am watching for my brother as well."

"Kristoff is out there somewhere on his own little adventure, finding new lands, new people... but regardless, he will come home when he is ready." Dani pulled on his arm. "Come eat."

They enjoyed their meal of crusty bread, carrots, and roasted pork. Sebastian sipped his wine and tried to resist the urge to go back to his telescope. Dani took out a book that Vinita had given him called *Guardians of Sedda*. It was about the ancient magic of the Sinook, which was said to be linked to the Blackbird gene. Sebastian watched him read aloud for quite some time before finally speaking:

"I noticed Valirus backed off on your training recently. What is that about?"

"I think he is a little jealous of Vinita." Dani let out a laugh. "The two of them argue like an old married couple."

"Please apologize to him or something," Sebastian said. "If you don't, he will revert to torturing me again, and I finally got him to leave me alone."

Dani burst out laughing. He put his hands on his hips. "But you still need more training, Your Majesty," Dani said in a mocking voice, imitating Valirus.

"Oh, dear gods." Sebastian shivered. "Don't ever do that again."

***

A week passed with little difference from day to day. Sebastian walked toward the southern border of Icefall where the forest covered the land. The sun showered a rainbow on the snowy ground from the icy trees bordering the forest. As he touched the branches of the frozen brush, his fingertips turned pale and ice formed on his skin. He found a log on the ground that was clear of any evidence of winter. Sebastian knelt, rested his hands against the wood, and closed his eyes. "Tomas," he whispered. "Can you hear me, Brother? I need you right now. Help me understand how to control this."

He let out a heavy breath, and the log began to crack and split under the pressure of the ice that formed from Sebastian's hands. His chest burned and his heart raced. He let out a painful growl and smoke escaped his mouth. Sebastian's skin was etched in glowing amber scales. He rolled back his sleeves, seeing the pattern run up above his elbows. When he pulled open his shirt, he saw the scales forming across his chest. He let out an echoing cry when his head began searing like it was filled with lava, and Sebastian roared until an ignition of fire shot from his throat.

The log burst into flames and the ground around him melted into a wet mess of dead grass. He heard branches cracking in the distance and turned fast to see his mentor approach.

"For someone who doesn't want to be called Dragon, you sure embrace the power." Valirus popped Sebastian on the arm with his staff.

"Ouch." Sebastian held his bicep. "Since when is it acceptable to strike a king?"

"When the king deserves to be struck." Valirus smacked him again.

"What did I do now?"

Valirus rolled his eyes. "Stupid boy. You are not only ignoring everyone day after day, but also sitting in your tower sulking like a child. Grow up, Your Majesty. Your brother is dead. Your lover is gone. My heart is with you, but you are a king, and all those people you keep hiding from need you. They depend on you. I depend on you."

Sebastian climbed to his feet and headed back toward Icefall. Before he reached the forest's end, his boot caught on a tree root, and he crashed onto the ground. He tasted blood in his mouth and his body burned with pins and needles. He growled and punched the ground, causing the land to shift and the trees to shake. Ice crashed down around him and Valirus. Sebastian covered his head until it finished. When he sat up, his eyes still fixed on the ground, he laughed so hard his belly hurt. "Look, old man." He pointed to the ground. "The first flower of spring."

Chapter Two

Torra's Dance

"Dom!" Sebastian shouted as he ran into the atrium. "Dom?" He looked around. "Torra?"

Sebastian walked the halls and peeked into rooms. Finally, he passed one of the two war rooms, where he heard Dom and Jon having a heated argument. Sebastian set his back against the wall and listened.

"We need to move the king back to NorthBrekka," Jon said. "Him being here is putting the north in danger."

Sebastian felt a sharp pain in his chest.

"Don't be daft," Dom snapped. "Our enemy will not dare march on these lands."

"You don't know King Maxen." Jon's voice was deep and hoarse.

"I know you are afraid—"

"I'm not afraid," Jon shouted. "Our king should be defending his homeland. My wife . . ." Jon put his hand on his forehead.

"I know," Dom said. "Your wife and children are in Castle Drake while Sebastian and his legion are here. Maxen could strike either city at any minute."

Sebastian clenched his jaw and took a deep breath. He spun around and kicked open the door. "I absolutely agree with you, Jon." He walked in and sat on the edge of the table. "I have sat still long enough. Winter has come and gone. Now I must return home."

"Your Majesty," Dom said. "Your men . . . their training."

"I ask for a few Sinook to return to NorthBrekka to resume training." Sebastian reached for Dom's hand. "And I hope you will be one of them."

Dom's porcelain skin shimmered like diamonds under the sunlight, making it appear opaque and otherworldly, with the exception of the hint of red covering his cheeks. He raised one eyebrow. "Whatever you need."

Sebastian stood and held Dom's hand open, exposing his palm. "I found something today." He smiled and reached into his coat pocket. He pulled out a small pink flower with a tiny stem and single leaf holding the small bud and placed it in Dom's open hand.

Dom's blue eyes sparkled. His smile revealed a row of perfectly white teeth. "The first flower of spring." His voice was light. "Thank you, my friend."

The ballroom was decorated with colorful pastel pottery and ribbons lining the ceiling. The tables were lined with the finest flatware and dishes, with flagons of ale and wine set for serving. The smell of meat cooking from the firepits made Sebastian dizzy, and he realized how hungry he was. The young women and men of The Far North gathered and sat at the front of the room. Sebastian had changed into his finest furs and leathers for the celebration of Torra's womanhood. With his crown upon his head, he marched to the head table and sat facing the growing crowd.

Dani joined his side, followed by Dom, with Torra and her mother sitting at the front table across from the king. As the ballroom filled and others began to eat, Sebastian watched his friends and family with admiration. Dani nudged his arm and then pointed to the plate of beef and potatoes in front of him. "Eat, my love."

"Yes, darling." Sebastian's body tingled excitedly as he quickly looked away from Dani.

"You are so shy," Dani said.

"You make me blush." Sebastian took a bite of his food. "Wow, this is good." He shoved another piece in his mouth. He cleared his throat and swallowed. "We will be returning home soon."

Dani's head turned fast. "But they said the snow is too deep."

"I have to return to my homeland. My family needs me there." Sebastian took a bite of his potato. "And I need to prepare to hunt down your father."

"Hunt him down? Sebastian. . ."

"Dani, I cannot wait for him to find me. I have a duty to my people."

Dani held his hand. "I understand." His eyes looked Sebastian up and down. "Let me help you."

Sebastian bit his lip. "I want to say no, but the truth is, I need your help."

"I know you do." Dani squeezed his hand and then returned to eating his meat. "This is so good."

After everyone had eaten their fill, Dom rose from his chair and stood between his daughter's table and Sebastian's. He held up his hands and waved for everyone to quiet down. "Thank you." He paced across the floor. "Any father's greatest time of fear is when their child has crossed into adulthood. This means they will marry, start a family of their own, and no longer call for Daddy when they need his help. My beautiful little girl has become a fine young lady. This night is for her, and she will stand before her peers and choose the one whom she will love for the rest of her days. My daughter, sweet Torra, rise." Dom reached his hand to Torra.

She stood and curtsied to her father, then to her mother, and again to Sebastian. Torra walked in front of the line of boys and girls who were prepared to cross into adulthood themselves. She looked at their faces as she passed and stroked the cheek of a lovely young woman as she walked by. "To my family and the Sinook, and to my king and his kind, I stand before you." Torra touched the hands of several boys and girls who reached for her hair, face, and arms as she sauntered down the line. "My heart leads me to he or she who calls to my spirit."

Sebastian looked at Dom, then at Dani. Both were fixed on Torra's movements. The others gripped their hands in anticipation. "She is still a child," he said quietly to Jon.

Jon leaned over. "She is only picking her future husband or wife. They don't marry until they are finished courting."

Torra stopped. She turned and stared at one of the waiting faces closely. "I choose," she said, "Elkho. I have watched him from the day my father took him under his wings. He will be a fine man." She kissed the blonde-haired, angel-faced young man, whose face turned bright pink.

"I agree," Dom said. "Elkho is one of my finest new cadets. Welcome to the family, young warrior."

Everyone stood, pounded twice on their chests, and grunted. The music carried from the bandstand, and people from the north, The

Far North, and Midrel Istan joined on the floor to dance around Torra and Elkho. Sebastian held his hand out for Dani to take. "You said you wanted me to come back." He stood and pulled Dani into his arms. "Dance with me, my darling."

They joined the others on the floor to stand next to Dom and Ketya, and all danced the ceremonial waltz. Dani's eyes were wide, and his jaw trembled. "I don't know this dance," he said.

Sebastian leaned closer. "Neither do I." He kissed Dani's cheek. "Just follow my lead."

They danced and moved in a rhythm that flowed with the sounds and singing that were meant for lovers and peace.

As the night became late, Dom stepped onto the stage and waved the band away. "Tonight was a success. But the journey is not over. Torra will be leaving for her quest to find her powers. The daughter of a seer and a listener will discover her strength somewhere far, far away." Dom took Torra's hand. "My sweet girl. You will not return home until your powers come to light. You may take your warm clothes but nothing more. Let your pain bring forth your magic. I will wait for you."

Torra nodded, hugged Dom and Ketya, and left to change into her warm winter clothing. The crowd cheered as she donned her bow and marched from the grand city. Dom's face was pale as he held Ketya securely against his chest.

"Take all the time you need, Dom." Sebastian said, patting his back. "Come to NorthBrekka when you are ready."

"Are you leaving so soon?" Dom reached for Sebastian's arm. "Can you not stay a little longer?"

Sebastian smiled. "I must get home, Dom. I will depart on the night after the full moon."

"I will join you after the full moon," Dom said. "Ketya has asked if she and Torra may come as well. That is, if Torra has discovered her powers by then."

"Of course. I would be honored." Sebastian patted Dom's back again. "You should consider reconciling with your former wife. I think she still loves you." Sebastian stared at Ketya. "Imagine the three of you roaming all of Erras. You as my high priest will never stand down to any man. You are a better man than me, Dom. This is the way I show that to you."

"Sebastian." Dom put his hand on Sebastian's chest. "My heart belongs to you. But... I love my daughter and Ketya very much. Our family needs to be together. I thank you for your belief in me."

Days had come and gone. Sebastian's people trained hard with the Sinook, and he sent letters to NorthBrekka and with a Sedda fishing ship in case they were to find Kristoff at sea. The full moon rose in the sky. Icefall was dead silent. The only noise came from soldiers walking the city borders in the snow.

Sebastian sat in his watchtower alone. He peered through the looking glass at the sea and toward The Break. He got frustrated, letting out bursts of fire in his fists. He set his back against the wall and closed his eyes, allowing the silence to fill the air. The peacefulness of twilight made his heart skip. Sebastian smiled and breathed in the cold, fresh air.

He lay in the euphoria of the perfect starry sky balanced by a glowing moon that peered down from high above. He could see the forest, and the mountain's silhouette stroked gently over the horizon. The ocean shimmered with the reflection of constellations. The sea was like a siren, inviting one in with its beauty and seducing even the strongest of sailors.

The morning after the full moon was bitter cold, but the sun quickly melted away the ice from trees, causing loud sounds as it broke and fell from the trees. Sebastian took Ossian and rode along the trail that ended in the forest. A running stream split the road. He stopped and let Ossian drink while he strolled along the water's edge. He stepped into the stream and hopped to the opposite side. The southern border of the forest was near. Sebastian turned to head back to Ossian. When he passed a fallen pile of boulders, something caught his eye. He bent down and shook his head. "What the hell?" Sebastian took a big step forward, then stopped. "Blood?"

Chapter Three

When the Ice Fell

The melting snow made the road slippery, but Sebastian urged Ossian to gallop faster. He saw flashes of light and heard a boom that he thought could only be one thing. "Cannons." He patted Ossian's neck. "We have to push harder, my friend. Give it everything you've got!" Sebastian struck his horse on the hip. He reached behind him, outstretching his hand as if he wanted the air to grasp his open fist. Then, he threw his hand forward, and with a cold blast, the wind stung his back and they moved faster.

As the city of Icefall came clear on the horizon, the vision of what had taken hold became clear. Sebastian took calm, even breaths and kept his head low as Ossian dashed through the snowy meadow. The sight of white sails whipping in the wind offshore forced Sebastian to yank back on the reins, causing Ossian to slip and tumble to the ground. He looked up and saw the broadside of the ship breach the fog and the bright blasts of cannons firing on the city. Sebastian jumped to his feet and ran. Thunder cracked and lightning struck as he screamed for Maxen. He slammed through the fortress side of the

Sage-Alcala manor, where the Sinook warriors waited alongside the men of Erras and Midrel Istan.

"Where is he?" Sebastian's tone was silky but serious.

"Your Majesty," Jon said. "Maxen has been taken captive."

Sebastian's eyes grew wide and his mouth dropped open a little.

Jon leaned closer. "You're never going to believe who captured him." He nodded. "Follow me."

They walked into a poorly lit chamber in a damp corner of the fortress dungeon. A deep voice carried through the air. Sebastian walked faster until he turned a corner and saw the tall, dark-haired, broad-shouldered sorcerer sitting with his arms secured behind his back. They locked eyes, and Maxen crested a slight grin.

"There you are. Out for a stroll?" Maxen tilted his head. "You look tired." He glared at Dani. "But, if I shared a bed with that creature, I wouldn't sleep a wink knowing he could just take your life so easily."

"Stop, Father."

Sebastian hurried forward. "Dani? You did this?"

Dani shook his head. "Someone's been working on her powers." He nodded to the opposite corner of the cell.

"Of course." Sebastian rolled his eyes. "I thought you liked not having power, Petra?"

"You have to admit, they are useful." Petra's voice was smooth and relaxed, which Sebastian was grateful for.

"My father was spotted walking from the forest," Dani said. "Petra and I went after him. That's when the cannons fired."

Sebastian looked around quickly. "Cannons. Right. Where is Dom?"

"Right here, Your Majesty." Dom stood by his side.

Sebastian sighed. "Is everyone alright? How bad was the damage?"

"We're not sure yet." Dom shook his head and closed his eyes. "This is all my f—"

"No, My King." Dom grabbed his shoulder. "It is not your fault."

Sebastian unsheathed his sword. Without a word, he turned and marched to Maxen and held the blade to his throat. He gripped the hilt of his sword tight. "I am going to kill you now."

"No," Dani said. "You are not. Not yet, anyway."

Sebastian felt his face get hot. "Excuse me, darling?"

"Because we are not done with him yet." Dani's voice turned eerily cold.

"I do not need him, Dani. He needs to pay for what he has done to my family, to you."

Dani's face turned from bright red to ghost white. He wrapped his hand around Maxen's throat. "I want him to feel everything I have ever felt." Dani smiled. "He deserves to suffer."

Maxen's eyes flickered and he choked up blood. Just as Sebastian reached his hand out to Dani, the wall exploded. A militia of Altanian soldiers flooded the dust-filled room. Sebastian pulled Dani to his chest, then felt a sharp, stinging pain fill his body. He squeezed his eyes shut, and when he opened them, he was sitting in Castle Drake with Dani still clung to his body and Petra holding his other arm. She disappeared suddenly, then returned, looking exhausted.

"I'm sorry," she said. "They would have killed you." Petra was gasping for breath. "It never used to drain me before." She clenched her chest.

"The others!" Sebastian said.

"They're fine." Petra sat down and held her head. "I put my father on his ship. His soldiers left Icefall and sailed away. Then I came back here."

"She had to let him go, Sebastian." Dani held onto him tight.

"All I had to do was drive my blade through his neck and he would have been dead." Sebastian's voice grew louder. "Why did you stop me, Dani?"

Dani jerked himself free. "Don't yell at me!"

Sebastian scooped Dani into his arms again. "Everything's going to be fine, my sweet darling. I didn't mean to frighten you." He turned to Petra. "I have to get back to Icefall."

"It will have to wait until morning." Petra leaned back. "I told you. My powers aren't what they were."

Sebastian paused for a moment and then looked at Petra with narrowed eyes. "Why did you take us away from Icefall to begin with? Why not just to the next room?"

Petra opened her mouth and then closed it. She glanced at Dani and shrugged. "It is like Dani said, we had to let my father go. I had to get you far away from him."

"Why did we need to let him go?" Sebastian raised his voice. "I could have ended all of this. Everything."

"Yes, everything." Petra stepped closer to Sebastian. "You can end everything. That is the problem. That is why my father is out for your head. It is a Bolin tradition to hunt the dragon gods and kill them. Ansel Bolin, the one who faced Dragon, failed our ancestors before. Every dragon god in history has been killed by a Bolin, besides Dragon himself."

"Well." Sebastian looked at the Oscura. "He will have a hell of a time doing so without this."

The next morning, Sebastian hurried down the stairs and turned quickly through the massive doors into the great hall.

Petra rolled her eyes. "For a man who says he is in a hurry, you sure are taking your time, Your Majesty."

Sebastian smirked. "Don't act like you have somewhere to be, Petra."

Dani sighed and grabbed Sebastian's hand. "Let's go. Jace and Kristoff have surely arrived by now."

Sebastian's eyes grew wide, but then, the pinching and pulling feeling of Petra's touch made his head spin. There was a pop, and he stumbled and fell face-first into the snow.

"What was that, Petra?" Dani yelled from across a snowy field.

"Ouch." Petra grimaced. "I told you I am not as good as I was before" Her face turned dark red.

Sebastian shook his head and stood. He stretched his neck and looked around quickly. "We're near the southern forest." He sniffed the air. "That's odd." Sebastian clenched his jaw and walked toward the woods.

"Sebastian?" Dani jogged after him.

Sebastian sniffed again. He stepped across a narrow stream that passed through the forest's edge, then the smell overtook him. He threw his hand over his mouth and nose. "Dani, don't come over here." Sebastian inched forward until he fell to his knees. His stomach burned, his heart ached, and his entire body felt as if it was about to burst. Golden lines formed across his hands and neck. He felt the hot tingle of scales forming on his face as he stared at the icy, lifeless gaze of a sweet girl who had just become a woman.

Dani gasped and dropped to his knees next to Sebastian.

"Petra," Sebastian said. "Fetch Dom." His voice cracked.

There was a popping sound behind him and he felt a breeze across his face.

"She was still a child." Sebastian brushed the flurries from her face. He looked over his shoulder. "What is taking Petra so long?"

"You don't listen very well, do you? She can't use her powers well." Dani grimaced. "Torra was so pure. So innocent." Dani climbed to his feet. "My father did this."

"And we let him go." Sebastian's voice was deep but carried through the forest. The wind whistled through the crackling branches and piles of snow swirled across the ground.

Sebastian picked Torra up into his arms and set off for the Sage-Alcala manor. "We can't wait for Petra any longer."

Screams cut through the city of Icefall late into the night. Sebastian dragged Dom down the corridor and into a small chamber at the end. Dom's knuckles were bloody from punching the wall. Torra's body rested gracefully in her bed as the people came to pay respects. Dom gripped his collar and cried into Sebastian's shoulder. "Why did this happen?" His voice was high-pitched and desperate. "Why her?"

Sebastian said nothing. He tightened his hold as Dom began to slip to the floor. "I'm sorry, Dom, I—"

Dom shoved Sebastian away, knocking him onto his back. "You brought him here!" He stood and leaned over Sebastian. "He came here for you and took my little girl instead. Why, Sebastian? Why does death follow you everywhere you go?" Dom's face was hollow and sweaty.

Sebastian sat up and put his back against the wall. He did not speak a word and held his forehead in his hands. He looked into Dom's angry blue eyes. "I am trying, Dom."

"I want you to leave my lands," Dom said. "Don't ever come back here . . . Dragon."

Sebastian's head jerked up. He felt his eyes fill with tears and his nose burn.

"I said leave!" Dom stormed out of the room.

Chapter Four

A Man Arrives from the Land of Hast

Sebastian, soaked in sweat, jerked awake and tumbled out of bed. He kicked backward until his back hit the corner of a table.

"My love?" The groggy voice of Dani came to Sebastian's ears.

"A nightmare, darling. Go back to sleep." Sebastian sat quietly, trying to catch his breath. His heart pounded in his chest and he felt the vein in his neck stick out.

The bed creaked and the blanket flipped over. Dani's feet touched the floor. Sebastian waited for him to sit on the floor and comfort him, but instead Dani walked to the fireplace and sat down. "It's cold tonight."

Sebastian smiled. "It always gets cold one last time before summer in NorthBrekka." He crawled over to Dani and wrapped his arms around his chest. "Let me get the fire." He kissed Dani's neck. "My Dani," Sebastian whispered.

Dani pushed Sebastian back and straddled his hips. "You really should try to sleep." He kissed Sebastian's lips.

"Are you saying you would rather sleep than make love to me?" Sebastian rolled on top of Dani. He cupped his cheek and kissed down his neck to his collarbone. Sebastian tore away the blanket that covered Dani's naked body. As he indulged himself in mind-numbing pleasure, Dom's voice echoed in his head from that day in Icefall: "Don't ever come back here, Dragon." Sebastian pushed himself backward. He struggled to catch his breath. His eyes were fixed on the wall across the room as his head twitched back and forth.

Dani held him in his arms. "It's alright, Sebastian. You are here with me." Dani kissed his cheek. "You are safe," he whispered.

"Dom was right. She died because of me."

The following morning, Sebastian made his way down to the throne room, expecting no one to be awake yet. He walked through the doorway and held his hand out. Fireplace logs engulfed in flames and the candles in the chandeliers flicked to life. There was a man standing across the room near the throne. Sebastian halted and tilted his head as he lit a fireball in his fist. "Who are you?"

The man held his hands up. "No need to fear, Your Majesty."

"I do not fear you," Sebastian said. "But I will burn you alive if you do not explain how you got into my castle without being escorted by my guards." He walked closer.

The man's soft lips and hazel eyes glistened in the candlelight. He was a little taller than Sebastian and old enough to be his father, with dark blonde and gray hair that hung below his ears. He stared

Sebastian up and down. "My name is Candor." He outstretched his hand. "I come from the Isle of Hast."

Sebastian's eyes squinted. "Hast?"

"It's alright, Sebastian." Kristoff ran into the room. "He is—"

"Hast?" Sebastian asked Kristoff.

Kristoff laughed. "Yes, Hast. It is east of Erras. A long way."

"Why is he here?" Sebastian pointed to Candor. "How did the two of you meet?"

Kristoff gestured to Candor. "We met at sea, but seriously, let him explain."

Sebastian sat on his throne and looked at the new visitor's odd attire. He wore a dark blue cuffed jacket with a thin white shirt underneath, form-fitting wool pants, and dainty black shoes. "Well . . . explain." Sebastian nodded.

Candor tilted his chin down and bit his bottom lip. "Your Majesty." He fell to one knee. "The legendary Chaos. The Heir of Dragon." His eyes locked on Sebastian's. "There is an entire world out there that you cannot even begin to imagine."

"Get to the point," Sebastian said.

"No, listen to him." Kristoff hurried to stand by his brother.

Candor smiled. "It's fine, Kristoff. Chaos is supposed to be blunt. He doesn't have time for a simple conversation."

Sebastian straightened his back. "Continue . . . please."

"On Hast, we have archives larger than any place on earth. History, prophecies—"

Sebastian held his hand up. "What brings you to NorthBrekka?"

Candor grinned and blushed a bit. "Dear boy, I am your uncle."

The fires dampened from blazing to deep orange embers. Smoke wafted through the air as Sebastian slowly stepped toward Candor. "You're lying." His skin tingled as the shimmering scales graced his hands and neck. "My father had one brother, and he died when I was nine."

"Did you forget you had a mother?" Candor interrupted. "Oh, right. You never knew your mother. It's a shame. But I see her in you just as I did when you were a baby."

Sebastian opened his mouth and took a deep breath. His eyes teared as he tried to speak, but his throat tightened. A maiden slipped through the doorway to announce that breakfast was served. Sebastian clenched his jaw and pushed his way past Kristoff and Candor toward the open doors to the great hall. The sound of light chatter came from the hall, and the smell of sausages made Sebastian's stomach growl.

As he entered the room, Sebastian saw Nadya's eyes meet his. Her laughter and smile turned into a straight, solemn expression. He marched over and embraced her gently, then kissed her forehead. "Sister," he whispered.

"I am so happy you are home, Brother. We have to talk. Now!" She held him tight, then stepped back. "Listen to me." She pushed him away from the others. "Tomas's tomb was raided—destroyed. We don't know how or why, but he is gone."

Sebastian stood with his mouth dropped open. "Who would do this?" He watched as others entered the hall, along with Jon and his and Nadya's children. Jon turned to meet Sebastian's gaze and gently nodded his head. Sebastian tried to remain composed. "What the hell do you mean his body is missing?"

"I have been sending out soldiers for weeks." She paused to smile and nod as people greeted her in passing. "I don't know how no one has heard anything. It's frightening that someone is robbing our family's tombs."

Sebastian's jaw clenched tight. "Another thing to worry about." He groaned. "I can't believe this. How am I going to tell the others?"

"The same way I had to tell everyone here, including Amara, who is a wreck." She closed her eyes and took a deep breath. "I heard about Torra."

Sebastian sighed. "Dom blames me for bringing Maxen to Icefall—"

"Well," Nadya interrupted. "Maxen would not have gone there if he wouldn't have found you there."

"Please don't blame me for Torra's death. My blood boils with vengeance already. I don't need this from you."

"I don't blame you." Nadya held his hand for a moment. "Go and eat. You are obviously hungry."

Dani sat at the king's table and shifted in his seat until Sebastian sat by his side. "You look upset." He reached his hand toward Sebastian's. "Tell me what happened."

"I, umm—"

Barron dropped a stack of books on the table and began flipping through them page after page, with beads of sweat forming on his forehead. He would curse when he didn't find the right journal and toss it across the table. One book knocked over a pitcher of milk. Barron watched the spill run until it poured over the other end of the table. He glanced at Sebastian. "What did that man tell you?"

"Oh, nothing, except that he is our uncle." Sebastian paused. "Are you not going to welcome home your king?" He raised an eyebrow.

"I'm busy trying to find out if he is who he says he is . . . Welcome home, Brother." Barron rolled his eyes.

"Are you finding anything?"

"No." Barron kept sifting through the pages. "Why is there nothing about our mother in any of our father's diaries?" He sat down in defeat and snatched a muffin from the tray.

"Wow," Sebastian sighed. He reached for a pork sausage from the plate where the milk had spilled. "You are overly dramatic, Brother." Sebastian sunk his teeth into the meat. He pointed at Barron as he chewed. "If you will calm down, he will tell us what the hell is going on."

Candor walked through the doors into the hall and looked around with a grin on his face. He made his way toward the king's table, then stopped and bowed. "It suits you well, the crown."

Sebastian stared at nothing in particular while playing over his thoughts in his head. Dani squeezed his hand.

"You'll have to forgive my brother," Barron said. "His mind has been quiet since he lost—"

"That's enough, Barron." Sebastian's voice was low and cracked. He touched his fingertips to the onyx and ruby crown on his head. "Why is there no mention of you in the records?" He sat up straight. "Or, better question: Why is there no mention of my mother?"

"Yes, Your Majesty." Candor bowed his head. "Your mother and I did not belong in NorthBrekka—"

Sebastian interrupted. "Did not belong?"

"Nephew, your mother and I are from Safareen. My sister—your mother, Shauni—was a witch, just as I am."

Sebastian furrowed his eyebrows "What are you speaking of?"

"It explains why Barron was born a Blackbird." He stared into Sebastian's eyes. "Your eyes—"

"Yes, they are always red now," Sebastian said. "Continue."

"You are half Safar, Sebastian." He examined Barron's face. "Both of you, born of a twisted fate. Sebastian, inheriting the Dragon blood from the Drake line, and Barron, a Blackbird with ancient ties that lead back to Safareen, and beyond that." He looked around the room. "There are two more children born from Shauni. A boy and a girl."

Nadya and Viktor stood.

"Just as I thought. The two of you look just like your father, but it is possible you are very special as well," Candor said before spinning back toward Sebastian. "Ivan and Shauni wanted to be married, but with the distrust between the north and south, it was not allowed. But Ivan was in love, and Shauni was pregnant with Barron. So, they married without approval. The kings of the north and south feuded in their own way until the day twins were born." He paced across the floor. "Your father locked down the castle. He hid the twins from everyone. Handmaidens, nurses, and even their siblings. It was a dark time in Castle Drake. Ivan was afraid. No one knew when the Dragon curse would resurface, and the king never imagined it would be his own little boys. Erras was on the hinges of war. Shauni gave birth to her youngest son just two years later, and then she died."

The room was dead silent. Sebastian realized his grip was hurting Dani's hand. He clenched his jaw and looked over at Viktor, who hung his head low. "Please, go on."

Candor nodded and began to pace again. "Ivan was broken. He lost touch with everyone and everything. Then, one day when the twins were five, they were leaving their classes when Barron tripped Sebastian on purpose. I remember your face, Your Majesty." He paused and grinned. "Your face turned so red you could compete with an apple. But . . . then it happened. Your father arrived just in time to see fire explode from your fists. Everyone was afraid. They didn't know if you would attack someone. The Dragon curse had started to show so soon." He held his hand to his chest. "I was a coward. I feared the anger in Ivan as I watched that man lock you in a room in a quiet hall away from everyone. You poor thing. Seeing you like this now is—"

"Stop." Sebastian stood quickly. "Do not make this about me." A tear ran down his cheek. "Whatever my father did to me is in the past. I broke free a long time ago, and he realized he could not stop me, so he chose to end his life."

"I ran," Candor continued. "I went to the King of Kings and told him about you. Why? I don't know. I guess I feared for your life. Your father went mad, Your Majesty. And I wanted to protect you as your mother would."

Sebastian's face burned. His eyebrows furrowed and he felt a burning sensation fill his chest.

Candor reached his hand out toward the king's table and placed it on Sebastian's. "I was banished for betraying your father. King Roman adored you . . . so much. He was there just after your birth. He begged your father to let him take you and your brother somewhere where no one would hurt you, but Ivan refused."

"Where did he want to send us?" Sebastian's voice was deep and low.

"He wanted to adopt you, Your Majesty. To raise you in the capital city where no one could possibly reach you without first passing through legions of soldiers." He stepped back and shook his head. "I never said my condolences for Tomas's death. Kristoff told me everything."

Sebastian took a deep breath. "Is there anything else I should know?"

"I will not waste any more of your time for now, Nephew."

Sebastian hurried out of the hall and marched out the castle doors to the stables. His horse, Ossian was due to be retired as his age began to show in battle. "We have been through a lot, my friend." He sat in the corner of Ossian's stall. "You are lucky, though. You get to stay here and rest." Sebastian smiled and laughed. "You get to run down the mountain and prance around and chase girls in the forest. Meanwhile, I will still be busy saving the damned world from myself. I will miss our rides through these mountains, though."

Sebastian sat in the stables until a storm rumbled across the mountains. What he had just heard from Candor dismantled nearly everything Sebastian's father had taught him about the world. He wondered why there were so many lies, so much betrayal, and why his father was so afraid. Sebastian knew that if he wanted answers, he would have to trust Candor—for now. He reached up and patted Ossian. "Enjoy your freedom, old man." Sebastian climbed to his feet and kissed Ossian on the nose. "You have been the best horse a king could ask for. I wish you peace."

Chapter Five

I Am a God

Spring was gone and summer had arrived upon the mountains. It was stormy and the rain poured, flooding the castle grounds. Stormfire Lake threatened to overtake the streets of the little NorthBrekkian village that covered much of the valley at the base of the mountains. Sebastian rode his new horse, Babo, through the forest and into town. The shopkeepers stood at their doors and bowed as he passed. Valirus, Dani, and Jace joined him as he eventually came to the edge of the water.

Sebastian dismounted and walked to the water's edge. He let out a heavy sigh and felt his face, lips, and fingers tingle. His chest burned and the hairs on the back of his neck stood. There was a rumble in his voice when he exhaled, and he felt the fire in the back of his throat. For a moment, his heart skipped a beat, and he stumbled. His eyes locked on the water droplets splashing into the lake. Smoke gently escaped his mouth.

"I am going to Safareen." He paused and turned to his men. "King Lucian and I have words to exchange. I must ask all of you to join me, along with the remainder of the Order."

"We would demand to come," Dani said. "Did you have to drag us out into this miserable rain to tell us that?" He smiled and climbed down from his horse.

"Right," Sebastian said. "The rain." He reached his hand into the sky and locked his gaze on the storm clouds. Lightning cracked across his fingers. Sebastian snarled as a bright flash left his hand and crashed into the sky. The clouds began to drift away slowly, and the rain stopped. He turned to the others. "No, Dani. That is not all I have to say. I don't know what will happen in Safareen. I have never been there. It is forbidden for others to enter the borders without permission. I will send my crows with a message this evening telling Lucian we are coming and to be expect us at the door."

Jace laughed. "He is going to have men waiting in line to kill us."

"That is why..." Sebastian paused. He reached his palm to Valirus and raised an eyebrow. "This is your line."

"You need more practice." Valirus shook his head. "Smart-ass."

"Alright Valirus," Sebastian said. "Do your job and teach me how to do something extraordinary."

Valirus stepped toward the lake and stopped at the water's edge and removed his shoes. He dipped his feet into the water and waded out to his knees. "Come, Your Majesty. I want to see something. After all, Safareen is on the sea ... If they attack, you will want to use water to your advantage." He continued to walk into the water and turned when it was waist-deep.

"Where are you going?" Sebastian put his hands on his hips.

"Come with me."

"I don't feel like swimming." Sebastian tilted his head. "And you can't swim."

"Then you better save me." Valirus stepped backward.

"Stop!" Sebastian stepped forward. "I am your king. Listen to me!"

"Oh boy, the attitude starts already." Valirus inched back.

"If I have to come in there and get wet to save you, I will kill you when we get back to shore!"

"No, you won't." Valirus moved again. "You will come out here, but you don't have to get wet."

Sebastian scrunched his nose and narrowed his eyes. He opened his mouth and let out a sound, then shook his head, stood straight, and focused on the water. He reached his hand toward the lake and took a step forward as the water under his foot froze. "Valirus, if you go any further, I will freeze this whole lake with you in it. Understand?"

"You are terrible at saving people." Valirus stepped back, but slipped and went under the water.

Sebastian stood tall and took a deep breath. "Damn you." His voice was still and calm. He started forward, turning the water into ice with each step. "This is too slow." Sebastian looked at the water where Valirus splashed to the surface before going back under. He stepped fast, getting to Valirus just as he surfaced again. Sebastian held onto his collar to keep his head above the water.

Valirus choked and caught his breath, but suddenly stopped and stared at Sebastian with awe. "Well, look at you." He gripped Sebastian's hand and looked him up and down. "That is a very unusual thing for anyone to do."

Sebastian was down on one knee on the water's surface. He looked over his shoulder only to realize how far he had walked past where the ice had stopped. He turned to Valirus and pulled on his arm. "Come on, swim forward until you can reach. I've got ahold of you." He walked slowly across the lake's surface, each foot shaking as it lifted and stepped down. "Was this your intention? For me to walk on water?"

Valirus breathed heavily as he came to chest level in the lake. "I will admit, I was curious, especially after seeing how terrible you are at using your water powers. But I wanted to teach you to use your powers to save someone you care about. To frighten you into doing something... extraordinary."

"It's bold of you to think that I care about you." Sebastian kept a straight face and darted his eyes down to Valirus. A grin stretched across his lips, then he burst into laughter.

Valirus snorted out a laugh. "Actually, yes. I did want to know if you could do it. This is an old test that the most powerful of sorcerers would do to prove they were worthy to sit on a throne."

"Has anyone done it?" Sebastian said.

"Not until today, Your Majesty.

Sebastian saw Dani standing on the shore. The gentle breeze waved his black hair across his cheek.

"You are walking on water, my love." Dani's hands were over his mouth. "How are you doing that? No sorcerer has been able to cross water on foot."

"That's easy, Dani." Sebastian helped Valirus secure his footing on the beach. "I am not a sorcerer." He stopped and kissed Dani's lips. "I am a god."

"Well," Dani said. "Your mother was a witch. Perhaps you inherited a tiny bit of her magic as well."

Sebastian paused, then burst into laughter. "You are always the optimist, Dani." He turned to the sorcerer. "Valirus, what was the point of that?"

"To teach you to use your most significant elemental weakness without thinking." Valirus nodded. "You could have saved me in a million ways. You could have had a wave wash me back on shore, or you could have sent the water away, but you chose to walk on water... I am impressed, Your Majesty."

That afternoon in Castle Drake, Sebastian disappeared into a hot bath. The tub sat before a massive window that overlooked the mountains toward East Bay. He slipped off his clothes and set the Oscura on the table next to the fire. Sebastian eased his body below the steaming water. The sun periodically drifted behind dark rain clouds that rolled in over The Break, and a gentle rumble of thunder echoed across the castle from the clouds above. Sebastian grinned and sat up a little more in the water. He watched it start to rain, enjoying the sounds of droplets tapping against the glass. He sunk his head under the water for a moment. A sharp *pop* echoed oddly under the water. He surfaced quickly but saw nothing that wasn't there before.

Sebastian shook his head and sat back in the tub. His focus got lost in the enchantment of the growing storm. His mind began to wander into its own story until he felt something run across his back. Sebastian turned and lunged, gripping the throat of whoever had disturbed his bath.

"Sebastian!"

"Dani." Sebastian fell back into the water. "I'm so sorry, my darling. I didn't know where I was for a moment." He looked around quickly.

Dani sat up and grinned, then stood and disrobed. He stepped down into the tub and climbed onto Sebastian's lap. "Does that happen often?"

Sebastian gazed into Dani's sky-blue eyes, then nodded.

"Well, I need you to be here." He kissed Sebastian's lips. "I know you are hurt." Dani ran his mouth along Sebastian's jawline. "I understand that you are angry. But it is time you came back to me. It has been a long time since anyone has seen my father. It is time we find answers."

Sebastian gripped Dani's upper arms and pushed him back. "That is why we are heading south. My darling, forgive me, but I don't want to talk about this right now."

Dani smiled and held Sebastian's cheeks in his palms. "You are right." He shifted his weight and moaned when he straightened himself up on Sebastian's lap. Dani grasped two fistfuls of Sebastian's hair and bit onto his shoulder.

"I am always here for you, darling. I will never leave you." Sebastian picked Dani up out of the water and laid him on the stone floor.

Dani winced. "It's cold!"

Sebastian put his lips to Dani's ear. "I will warm you."

The water in the tub was cold by the time Sebastian and Dani finished making love on the frigid castle floor. They lay in each other's arms, wrapped in linens from the old chest in the corner of the room. Sebastian stirred the embers in the fireplace, then crawled back over to Dani. "I love you," he whispered.

Dani pecked Sebastian's lips and blushed. He sat up and reached for his clothes. "When do we depart?"

"In a few days. I need to get some of my affairs in order first. I must impose upon you to inform the Order to prepare to ride south soon." Sebastian watched out the window in a daze as he slipped his pants on.

Dani dressed quickly, as usual, then joined Sebastian at his side. "What do you expect to happen when we arrive in Safareen?" He cuffed Sebastian's bicep and kissed his shoulder. "I don't want to see you lose your head if something bad happens."

Sebastian let out a laugh, then rubbed his face. "I don't even know at this point." He stopped Dani from opening the door. "Please don't tell anyone. They all expect me to have all the answers, and right now, I am as clueless as I was when I first wore the crown."

Dani embraced him. "You worry too much." He kissed Sebastian's lips. "Come on. I'm hungry."

The next morning, Sebastian sat in the letter room and wrote a message to Dom, then another to Vinita in case Dom were to discard his. He held his face in his hands for a moment and rubbed his forehead with his fingertips. "Dom, please forgive me."

"He will." A deep voice came from the doorway. "After all, it was his birthright to be on your side. The two of you are bound."

"Barron," Sebastian said. "I haven't seen much of you lately. Not that I am complaining."

Barron huffed and then cleared his throat. "Are we ever going to talk about our supposed uncle who has been roaming the halls of our family home."

Sebastian stared at the floor for a moment. Without breaking his gaze, the corner of his upper lip flashed a smile. "We will find out if he tells the truth soon enough." He turned his attention to Barron. "If he is a liar, we will burn the bastard to ash. But if he is our kin, he can help us pass through the borders." Sebastian paused and darted his eyes to his coat. He patted the pockets, then pulled out a rolled parchment. "I found this the other day. It was in one of Father's coat pockets for some odd reason. I have no idea how it got back here to NorthBrekka." He passed the letter to Barron.

Barron opened it and read partially to himself, with only a few words audible. "Wait." He pulled his head back then returned to mumbling the words quickly.

"Our mother was royalty." Sebastian interrupted. "She was Lorna's sister." He sat up straight. "That man told us a lie."

Barron's head shot up to see Sebastian's smirk. "So, he is not our uncle."

"No, I believe he is," Sebastian said. "But he lied about their upbringing." He stood and walked past Barron. "I am going to speak with him now if you would like to join me."

They moved hastily from the throne room and down the corridor to the front of the keep where Candor was sitting by the fire, speaking to Nadya and Jon. Sebastian sped up and stepped between them. "You." He grasped Candor by the collar. "Who are you? Don't lie to me again."

"Your Majesty," Candor said. "I never lied to you."

Sebastian held up the letter. "My mother wrote this letter when she first arrived in NorthBrekka. She spoke about her father, the King of Safareen." He pushed the parchment against Candor's chest. "Why did you lie to us?"

Nadya grabbed Sebastian's arm. "Is it true? Our mother was the Princess of Safareen? But... we are enemies. Their king declared war, and—"

Candor sighed. "Their king is not the reason Safareen is isolated from the rest of Erras. It is because your mother brought down the entire monarchy when she sent NorthBrekkian armies south to decimate the Safar." He paused and looked back and forth from Nadya to Sebastian. The room began to fill with others. "She was a woman desperately in love. Our father refused her marriage request. He claimed the Drakes to be a cursed bloodline and said no man or woman of Safareen should ever be kind to any from NorthBrekka. But Shauni and Ivan were inseparable. Therefore, she made a choice. Then my father screamed war, but before the Safar could leave the desert, they were ambushed. NorthBrekka dismantled one of the most powerful armies in the world in one strike. It showed my father who held the true power in Erras. Now, my brother Lucian sits on the throne and upholds the laws set down by our kin before us. Although, he is nothing like my father."

Sebastian held up his hand. "Enough." He came face-to-face with Candor. "Why did you claim my mother was a witch before? Why not tell the truth?"

"Nephew, she was a witch. She denounced our family name years before meeting your father. She ran away to live with the coven, and I went along with her as soon as I was old enough."

Sebastian smiled and shook his head. "This family is getting more fucked by the day. So are you telling me you can gain me an audience with Lucian, or not?"

Candor put his hand on Sebastian's shoulder. "Oh, I can. Trust me on that."

"Good. Because we leave tomorrow."

Chapter Six

Witches

The sunrise sent light bouncing from the valley below through The Break and onto the castle grounds. The sky was cloudless, and it was cool and breezy. Sebastian stood alone in the middle of the muster field and watched the sun rise over East Bay. He heard someone make a shush sound and turned to see Meecah, Samir, Meecah's lover and leader of the town of Dunebar, Viktor, and Valirus tiptoeing from the servants' entrance.

"Your Majesty—" Meecah started.

Sebastian held up his hand, not breaking his attention away from the sunrise. He took a deep breath, enjoying the warmth on his face. "Never spoil a perfect moment." He turned and smiled. "Good morning, Meecah."

"You are something special." She kissed his cheek.

"Shall we get moving?" Sebastian grinned and headed toward the horses; his attention turned toward the stables. He missed seeing Ossian saddled and waiting. Now he trusted in his large, muscular horse with its deep brown coat and black braided mane, Babo.

Sebastian climbed into his saddle and walked before the others as the Order of Thieves arrived on the field. Meecah, the Padora warrior princess, Barron, Sebastian's traitorous but useful brother, Jon, the future king of NorthBrekka, Dom, the High Priest of Erras, Jace, Sebastian's advisor and captain of Sebastian's armies, and six of the highest-ranking soldiers in NorthBrekka hopped onto their horses and waited for Sebastian's guidance.

Dani came riding from the stables to join him, along with Valirus.

"We are ready, Your Majesty." Valirus brought his horse to follow Sebastian.

"Candor," Sebastian said. "You, here." He pointed to the ground next to him.

Candor rode up, stopped by Sebastian's side, and nodded.

Sebastian led the army from the castle's east side and down through the forest to the village near the lake. The people bowed as the king passed, some cheering for his safe return while others offered prayers to the gods. The legion pushed south until the sun no longer lit the sky. They prepared to make camp in a small village near a wide stream on the edge of a hilly landscape.

"I'm starving," Dani said.

"Perhaps they have a tavern where we can get a meal and a drink." Sebastian hurried his horse along. As they came over the last hill, Sebastian smelled a hint of wet soot in the breeze. They passed over the stream and found a village that was as quiet as the darkest part of night. The smell of rot and char filled his nose. The shops were tattered and blackened. The homes creaked with every passing gust of wind. Sebastian stopped for a moment. "We shouldn't be here." His eyes darted from broken window to broken window and then to the skeletons that littered the ground.

Dani gasped and squeezed his eyes shut. His hands trembled on the horn of his saddle, which he gripped so tight his knuckles were white. "Get me out of here." His voice cracked and tears streamed down his cheeks. "Sebastian, please."

Sebastian reached out and took his hand. "Let's move!"

They left the village and moved beyond its sight into a green pasture where the men found deer to hunt. Sebastian pulled Dani from his saddle and cradled him against the warm grass.

"They're all dead because of me," Dani choked out. "When my father kidnapped me and took me to Torrdale, we came through here. I lost control of my power." He buried his face in Sebastian's chest and did not move until they went to get some sleep. Sebastian kissed his forehead and held him all night while Dani restlessly cried in his sleep.

The next few days brought warmer weather and more sun as they finally reached The Wall. It was a stone structure that stood as high as any castle wall, and it divided the north from the south. Soldiers of both regions stood watch and walked to passages that went from east to west and from the sea to the mountains of Torrdale. Sebastian led his accompaniment to one of the few gateways that lay along The Wall. Northern soldiers approached in a hustle, then stopped and bowed suddenly upon noticing King Sebastian leading the pack.

"Open the gates for the King of Kings!" The soldier bowed again and stepped aside as the massive oak doors popped and clanked until the passageway was clear. Southern soldiers bowed as the group passed and the gates closed behind them. Sebastian stopped and turned, remembering many years ago when he had looked back on the mountains of NorthBrekka in the distance and felt homesick for the first time until Cyrus joined his side. He turned to where Cyrus stood that night: on the grassy slope near a stream where he was once afraid and naïve, and where his whole reason for fighting was to save his Cyrus. Sebastian closed his eyes and clutched his chest as tears rolled down his cheeks. He shook his head, turned back south, and marched on.

The next day, Sebastian rode quietly, as the endless grasslands made it easy for southern armies to spot an arrival. They rode along the edge of Blackport Bay and spoke to some fishermen in passing.

Jace hurried ahead to ride along Sebastian's side. "You have been quiet. Although, that's not unusual for you these days."

Sebastian frowned and kept his focus on the road ahead. "I don't have a lot to say." Sebastian took a deep breath and turned to see Jace staring back at him. "I failed, Jace."

"What?"

"People around me keep dying—"

Jace let out a groan. "Why does your mind always immediately assume that you have somehow doomed the world?"

Sebastian let out a laugh. "Isn't that what I was born to do? Destroy things."

Jace nudged him. "Did you really expect to bring down King Maxen, the most powerful sorcerer in the known world, that easily?"

"You call that easy?" Sebastian felt a stabbing pain in his chest and stomach. "We lost so much." His voice trailed off. He felt a hand squeeze his thigh and turned to see Dani watching him, the sun bouncing off his face. His eyes shined like cut gems, and a grin crossed his lips.

"Apologies, Sebastian." Jace's voice trembled. He cleared his throat. "I meant nothing by that."

"I know, Jace." Sebastian patted his shoulder. "Forget it. Let's focus on right now." He tapped his horse's ribs with his boot and sped ahead of the others. He heard Jace whisper, "Has he gone mad?"

"Give it a rest, gentlemen." Candor's voice traveled with the wind. "The king just discovered he is half Safarian. He is going to meet his other uncle, King Lucian. For some reason, I do not see it going well."

Sebastian kicked his horse again to move forward and escape the noise. He wanted to be alone in his thoughts. He was angry with his father for not telling him about his mother. He realized he had never learned any stories, and he couldn't remember her voice. Sebastian wondered why Lorna never mentioned it, or Roman. He sat up straight when he thought of Cyrus and shifted uncomfortably until he could put the thought out of his mind.

The land turned from rolling hills and grassy plains to flat fields of compacted dirt and small bushes. Night fell over the desert where Sebastian stopped to set up camp. "There is no point in hunting tonight. There is nothing more than wolves in these lands. It's best we all get some sleep."

"That means you, Sebastian." Jace stood and took Petra's hand before excusing himself to his tent.

Sebastian shivered. "That sight is going to give me nightmares."

"Don't be jealous," Petra said. "I offered myself to you once. We took a bath together—"

"Excuse me!" Dani's face turned red. He grabbed Petra by the arm. "You're lying."

"She's not lying." Sebastian let out a deep breath and he stared at the ground. "But nothing else happened. I would have never."

Jace stepped between them. "Stop arguing. I thought the two of you were getting along."

"Ehhh." Sebastian shrugged. "Go to bed. Both of you."

Dani stormed away. Sebastian watched him disappear into their tent. He leaned his head back and growled before slowly making his way to his bed where his angry husband would be waiting to argue.

He approached the bed slowly. Dani sat with his arms crossed and eyes locked across the tent. Sebastian kissed his shoulder, then his neck.

"You have nothing to worry about, my darling." Sebastian kissed Dani's ear. "I have always been in love with you. Ever since you saved my life, I have thought about you and only you."

"Why do you keep secrets from me?" Dani turned to face him. "I know there are so many more."

"I don't want to hurt you," Sebastian whispered. "Please don't make me."

Dani sat up straight. "Did you make love to my sister?"

"No." Sebastian shook his head and laughed. "Nor have I ever wanted to."

Dani stared at him and clenched his jaw. "Have you been with Cyrus since we met?"

Sebastian bit his lip. "Yes. Only once."

A tear rolled down Dani's cheek. He started to speak but rolled onto his side and pulled the blanket over himself. Sebastian watched him try to hide his tears. He wanted to hold Dani in his arms and beg for forgiveness, but he stood there, frozen. He took off his jacket and boots, then slipped into the bed and wrapped his arms tight around Dani.

"Please, don't cry, my sweet love." Sebastian's voice was soft.

"Just let me deal with this, Sebastian. I knew you would when you saw him. I thought it wouldn't hurt, but it does."

Sebastian held Dani in his arms all night. He slept until he was startled awake at the sound of howling. He kissed Dani's cheek and slipped out of bed. He felt a hand touch his back and heard Dani's voice say, "Where are you going, my love?"

"Wolves. I need to run them off before they hurt someone."

"There are people to do that," Dani said. "Come here." He slipped off his shirt, cuffed his hand around Sebastian's neck, and nipped at his ear. "I want you."

Sebastian slipped his arms around Dani's back and brushed his lips against his neck. "You're right. I have people to handle wolves." He tossed his boots aside and turned to push Dani onto the bed.

"Time to wake up, my love."

Sebastian snapped awake and sat up too quickly. His head spun and his eyes burned.

"We have a long ride today." Dani kissed him.

They gathered on the road and Sebastian led the way once again. As the afternoon came, they arrived at a split in the road. One path leads east to Alta Prime, and one lead west to Safareen. Sebastian stared east for a moment, then shook his head and turned toward the vast, empty lands that awaited him. As night approached, the desert was no different from before, only there was a shallow river that cut across the path. They set camp again, and as the others began to disappear to bed, Sebastian heard howling in the distance.

"Want us to take care of it, Brother?" Viktor arrived at Sebastian's side with Barron close behind.

"Both of you, with me. These wolves are hunting us. Let's take care of it before it becomes a problem." Sebastian untied his horse and hopped into his saddle.

Dani grabbed Sebastian's reins. "What do you think you are doing?"

"Dani, stay here. I won't be long." Sebastian brushed Dani's cheek with his fingertips and took the reins back. He tapped his horse and hurried away into the desert.

The howling became more frequent as Sebastian and his brothers reached the small brushy forest from where they couldn't see the glow of the camp anymore. In the near distance was a ridgeline of rocks that tailed over a tall hill. At the top were the ruins of a watchtower. "I wonder if that was destroyed when our father went to war with the Safar." Sebastian climbed down from his horse and walked toward the ridge.

"Are you going up there?" Viktor caught up to him quickly.

Sebastian grinned and picked up his pace. They began to ascend through the boulders and cacti until they topped the peak of the hill where a narrow path was carved on the hard ground. They followed it to the rickety rock tower. Viktor was first to go inside, but Sebastian felt a yank at his arm before he stepped through the door. His eyebrows furrowed and he tilted his head at Barron.

"Look." Barron pointed.

"Sebastian," Viktor shouted from the top of the tower. "The wolves are here."

"I know," Sebastian said. He was inches from a wolf's staring gaze. He looked at it closely and reached his hand out. The wolf growled, then placed her head in his hand. "Widow." He patted her head. "You are Dom's wolf. Why are you here?"

A snarky voice came from around the tower. "I have come to fight you one-on-one, once and for all."

"Dom!" Sebastian's stomach felt as if it were twisting. "Wait, what do you mean? Dom—" Sebastian reached for his hilt.

Dom gripped his knife tight in his fist, then burst out laughing. "I can't do this." He slipped the knife into his belt. "How could I blame you for what happened?" Dom reached his hand out and rested it on Sebastian's chest. "I am sorry for my behavior."

"Do not apologize to me, Dom." He grabbed Dom's shoulders. "I am so happy you are here."

"I brought reinforcements just in case things go upside down." Dom turned and whistled. A small group of Sinook came out from behind boulders.

Sebastian tilted his head. "Vinita?"

"Yes," Dom said. "My mother insisted on being here."

Sebastian felt his face burn when Vinita pecked a kiss on his cheek before greeting Viktor and Barron. Sebastian knelt before the alpha wolf and held out his palm. "Hello, Sky." The wolf slowly leaned closer until her nose was near the tips of his fingers. Sebastian was calm, with his soft smile and heavy eyes resting on her cautious face. She stepped forward and rested her head against Sebastian's forearm.

Dom knelt before them. "She likes you." He patted her neck. "She sees what you really are."

"Enough about that." Sebastian stood quickly, startling the wolf. "We need to get back to camp before Dani sends a search party out for us."

Sebastian hopped into his saddle and rode away. The camp was still awake and tending to fires as they tied their horses up. Sebastian led the way between the tents where the others were gathered around a fire. Dani wrapped his blanket around his bare chest and hurried over, but slowed upon seeing the wolves. Sebastian grinned and turned to the side just as Dom came from behind the crowd with Vinita on his arm.

Dani smiled and took Sebastian's arm. He nodded to Dom and Vinita. "So, you are the ones who have been hunting us. Welcome. It's good to see you all." He turned to Sebastian. "You. Explain."

Sebastian laughed and shrugged. "I knew there were wolves following us. I did not know they were Dom's wolves."

"We can cozy up on the trail tomorrow," Dani said. "We need sleep." He pulled Sebastian in the direction of their tent. Sebastian nodded his goodnight to Dom and the others and followed Dani to bed.

The morning was warm and the sun rose early in the desert highlands. Dani kissed Sebastian and hurried outside to shout at everyone to pack up camp.

"Shut up, Dani." Jace's voice echoed throughout the grounds. "Go back to sleep."

"The sun is up," Dani said. "We have a long way to go. Get up, Jace!"

Sebastian sat back on the bed and laughed at the argument taking place outside. "No one can sleep through that." He finished tying his boots and stepped out into the fresh morning air. He closed his eyes and took a deep breath, noticing a hint of salt in the air. A smile formed across his mouth and he slowly opened his eyes just as Dom joined his side.

"Is your husband always this crazy?" Dom raised his eyebrows and yawned.

Sebastian puffed his chest. "He used to be sweet and shy." He paused for a moment and nodded. "I love how strong he has become in such a short time. But sometimes, it's . . . a lot."

Dom nudged him. "I remember a young prince who used to stare anywhere but in a man's eyes to avoid the awkwardness of seeing someone's expressions." His cheeks turned a dusty shade of pink and he smiled. "But then you left." He stared at Sebastian. "Years passed with no word. I traveled to every town, every field, mountain, and forest trying to find something that would tell me that you were still alive. But my journey took me to Cyrus."

Sebastian looked up at Dom, his nose burning and his heart beating fast.

Dom tucked Sebastian's hair behind his ear. Sebastian gasped and shook. Dom squeezed his shoulder. "I promise, we tried everything to help him. Even after the curse was broken, he was too far gone, Sebastian. Even without the curse, Cyrus held so much pain in his heart. He would have never been happy, not even with you. I wanted to save him, Sebastian. For you."

"Cyrus and I could have never been." Sebastian huffed out a breath. "He was a Bolin. But I never wanted to take his life." Sebastian grasped his chest. "I hate myself, Dom. I wish it was me who died that night. Not Cyrus. He didn't deserve the life he was given. And Tomas." Sebastian's voice cracked and tears flooded his face. "Tomas. My perfect brother. He was everything I wanted to be. Pure, brilliant, good . . . and he died. You better run for your life, Dom. Before my curse takes your life too."

"Stop that, right now." Dom held his face in his hands. "You know better."

Dani stepped between them. "What's going on?" He jumped a little when he looked at Sebastian's face. "You're crying, my love."

Sebastian sniffed and wiped his face. "Just bad memories surfacing. We should get going."

Dani squeezed Sebastian's face in his hands, then let it go in defeat.

Sebastian smiled and kissed Dani's lips. "It's fine." He turned his attention to Dom. "It's going to be alright."

Candor came riding up fast to Sebastian's side. "Once we pass the rocky desert and go into the sand dunes, you need to let me lead the way. Understand?"

Sebastian nodded and let Candor take the lead. The horses began to slow as the sand got deeper. The sun was hot and the air was dry. Sebastian looked over at his people from Midrel Istan.

Meecah turned and winked. "Is it too hot for you, Your Majesty?"

"This is what hell feels like. I just know it." Sebastian squeezed his eyes shut.

"You will understand why the people of Safareen dress in very little," Candor said. "It is said that the sun gods hate the Safar, therefore they send their wrath upon our lands."

"The Safar are quite dramatic," Sebastian said.

"So that's where he gets it from," Valirus said. "His mother."

Sebastian threw his head back and growled.

"He definitely looks like her," Candor said. "The twins and Barron look exactly like their mother. It is uncanny."

Sebastian closed his eyes and hummed quietly to himself until they stopped talking. They rode through the late afternoon until they came to a narrow ravine that split the land in two.

"Candor," Sebastian shouted. "There is no bridge."

"That's because you have to go down there." Candor pointed into the gully.

Sebastian hopped off his horse and stepped to the edge. It was dimly lit, and rocks and trees protruded from canyon walls. He scanned the ravine for a trail. "How do you suppose we do that, Candor?"

"It's magic, Your Majesty. Give me a moment." Candor held up his hands and walked down the ridgeline, whistling an odd tune. He stopped and took a knee. His fingers gently stroked the ground and flicked away pebbles before drawing a symbol unlike anything Sebastian had ever seen. Candor pressed his palm against the sand and the symbol shined like the sun, then he mumbled something in a language Sebastian had never heard.

Sebastian watched the ground, his gut twisted at the thought of what was about to happen. There was a crack and a hiss, but then it was silent except for the echo passing through the canyon. Sebastian opened his mouth, but Candor held up his hand and said, "One more moment."

Sebastian felt a tap on his shoulder.

"Umm, Your Majesty." Meecah's voice was higher pitched than usual.

Sebastian turned. "What, Meecah?" Without a thought, Sebastian marched before his people and stood close to the group of men and women who were clutching maces, staffs, and batons. The people didn't speak or move. Their eyes were locked on Sebastian, following his every move.

A woman emerged from the crowd and stood before Sebastian. She slowly reached for his face but stopped when Sebastian tensed up and stood straighter. "You are Shauni's boy." She smiled. "The King of Kings. I wondered if I would ever meet you."

Candor joined Sebastian's side. "Magda, this is Sebastian." He turned. "Your Majesty, Magda was the woman who took your mother and me in when we ran away from the palace. These people are the coven I spoke about before."

"Come." Magda walked to the edge of the ravine and looked at the sand. "You almost had it, Candor." She wiped away Candor's drawing and made a new symbol in the dirt. She chanted the same odd language and the symbol lit up, only this time, the ground jerked and broke away. Sebastian walked toward the rocks that tumbled into the canyon, seeing a wide pathway breaking away from the rocky walls.

Candor shrugged. "I never said I was good at magic." He walked with Sebastian back to the horses and followed the coven into the canyon.

The trail led down below where the sun touched. It was much colder and smelled of mildew instead of sand. They passed under a massive tree that reached nearly all the way across the trail. Sebastian admired the thick, healthy branches and the bright green leaves. The smell of bark and foliage brushed across his face as a breeze whistled past. They reached the bottom of the trail and stepped into the ravine. Two massive oak trees sprouted from the soft, grassy ground. Sebastian and the others climbed of their horses and rested. Sebastian leaned against one of the large tree trunks.

Dani leaned next to him and said, "I don't understand this place."

"Legend says these trees were planted by the earth goddess herself," Magda said. "This is where they were meant to grow, therefore they do." She showed Sebastian her necklace. It was a silver amulet with an oak tree carved in the center. "The oak tree is the sigil of our people." She rested her hand on Sebastian's.

Sebastian nudged Dani. "Do you understand now?"

"No."

"Neither do I, but perhaps they can help us understand what we are up against in the city." Sebastian trailed the others as they followed the pathway cut along the hot desert above.

The sun no longer lit the ground below their feet, and the sky Sebastian saw above was a deep shade of orange. He felt a tap on his thigh. Candor walked alongside Sebastian's horse with an unlit torch in his grasp. Sebastian rolled his eyes and lit a fireball in his palm. The coven stopped and watched. They were quiet as if mesmerized until he relinquished the fire. The accompaniment led ahead, and they continued until Sebastian was struggling to hold his eyes open.

"My love." Dani grabbed his wrist and squeezed. "Look!" He jumped from his saddle and hurried toward a wall of oak trees.

The smell of meat cooking filled the air and firelight could be seen through the trunks. As they got closer, laughter and merry chatting could be heard. The coven passed through the trees, and Sebastian's people followed. He was last to walk through the woods. Sebastian passed the last oak and came into the warmth of bonfires lit along a path. There were small homes built against the canyon walls, all made of old shipwood with linens and sheets for windows and doors. There were gardens growing between homes and a horse stable near the middle. There was no marketplace, but craftsmen and women made wares and traded with others in the village.

Sebastian walked until he noticed that everyone had stopped and formed around him. "I know nothing of your world." Sebastian turned his attention to Magda. "But I want to learn. What can I give you to teach me the ways of the people of Safareen?"

Magda stepped forward. "You, sweet boy, are one of us. We all loved your mother very much."

"I . . ." Sebastian shook his head and turned to Viktor and Barron. He gestured for them to join his side. "We know nothing of our mother, but I think it is important we know now. If we are truly part Safarian, we must know how to behave as such."

Magda smiled and shook her head. "My King, you already behave as such. You are all angry, mean, and powerful men. That is the Safarian blood. No empathy, no mercy. Just blood."

Jace burst out laughing. "This explains everything. The great mystery of Sebastian is unlocked."

Sebastian took a deep breath. "Shut up, Jace." The others laughed.

"First," Magda said, "we need to feed you. You are too skinny."

Sebastian's cheeks burned and he stared at the ground for a moment before meeting Magda's eyes. "I am very hungry."

The cooks brought plate after plate, offering different meats, fruits, and pies to Sebastian and his people. Dani wanted to taste everything and ended up eating half of Sebastian's cobbler. Sebastian satisfied his hunger with a bowl of soup, a piece of bread, an orange, and half of a cobbler.

"My King, you should eat more," Magda said.

"I have had plenty, thank you." Sebastian patted his stomach. "Why do they stare at me?" He nodded toward the coven.

"In Safareen, they worship the gods more than in any other place. You will see." Magda paused and looked over to her people. "You are Chaos, God of Fire. You are part Safarian and King of Kings. They worship you, Your Majesty."

"Please don't," Sebastian said. "I don't think I can handle that right now. Can they help me prepare for what awaits me?"

"They will be honored." Magda stepped away and reached for his hand. "You and your brothers only. Follow me. He wants to meet you."

Sebastian kissed Dani and followed Magda, with Barron and Viktor in tow. They entered a little painted blue house on an intersection of two roads. Smoke from a pipe left wisps of clouds that blew away as they passed down a narrow hallway and into the warm and quaint sitting room. Sebastian sank into the couch and had to use Barron's knee to push himself into a sitting-up position. He stopped and stared at Barron's ghostly face. "What is wrong with you?"

"Don't worry about me, Brother."

"I didn't say I was worried, but you look unwell."

"Ahh" A voice came from behind some curtains. In came an old man carrying a goblet in one hand and a book in the other. He lit his pipe and took a puff. His head tilted to the side and a smile formed across his lips. "What do we have here?" He made a ticking sound with his tongue. "A Blackbird, a god ... and then you, the blonde one." The man reached out and touched Viktor's face. "Brilliant." He touched his chin and looked into Viktor's eyes. "Your mind is incredible."

Sebastian smiled. He always remembered Viktor being smart. He learned everything twice as fast as his brothers. He was also the brightest in their lessons, next to Tomas.

The man moved to Barron. As he placed his palm on Barron's chest, he gasped. "You poor child. Never seen. Born in fear. The child your mother betrayed her kin for. You are precious, dear boy, although something is wrong. Your powers, perhaps." The man moved to Sebastian.

Sebastian grabbed his hand. "Who are you?"

"Forgive me," the man said. "My name is Frey. I am Magda's husband. Some call me the Guardian of the Gates. No outsiders enter Safareen without my blessing." He reached out and grasped Sebastian by the shoulder. "Chaos!" His grip tightened. "Such power. Such force. But there is kindness within. It stems from the one who is just like you."

"My twin brother, Tomas." Sebastian swallowed. "He died."

"Are you sure?" Frey said. He sat back on the couch and kept his stare locked on Sebastian. "I feel his energy." He shrugged and took another puff from his pipe. "Either way. A god, you are. And I am at your service, Your Highness. You will learn that the people of Safareen are not as repulsive as you may have been taught. Your father truly despised our kind, but he loved your mother. Though gruff, we are a religious sect. You have nothing to worry about while walking the streets of the king's city. Though it may seem odd, they will bow to you."

"King Lucian tried to kill me," Sebastian said. "He sided with Maxen. Why would they bow to me?"

Frey grabbed both of Sebastian's hands. "You shall see. Remember, King Lucian is no fool." He stood and excused himself.

"What does that mean?" Sebastian looked at Viktor and Barron.

Barron patted his shoulder. "I think it means you will see when we get there."

Sebastian rolled his eyes and made his way to the door.

They went back to the others. Sebastian found Dani sitting in a circle with the Order. He laid his head on Dani's lap and stared at the fire. Dani stroked his hair and rubbed the tension from his neck. "Get some sleep, my love." Dani kissed his cheek and leaned his head back while holding Sebastian in his arms.

Chapter Seven
The Secret of Stormfire Lake

Sebastian woke to the sounds of cheerful chatting and the smell of meat cooking in the firepit. "I thought the coven was going to give you some kind of life-altering advice," Dani said. "He really only told you to wait and see?" He sat down with a heaping mound of eggs and bacon and started shoving whole pieces into his mouth until he saw Sebastian staring at him with raised eyebrows. Dani passed the plate over to share.

Sebastian laughed and took a piece of pork. "Yeah, apparently the coven has a way of giving you nothing and everything at the same time."

"But what did you learn that was so critical?"

"That I am a god and that in these lands, these people worship the gods." Sebastian's shoulders shook for a quick moment. "I am looking forward to passing through the gates even less."

After breakfast, he said goodbye to Magda and climbed into his saddle but saw the coven all coming quickly from their homes as Frey whistled from the end of the village. Sebastian took a deep breath, puffed his chest, and waited for the Order to join his side. He slowly guided his horse toward the villagers and then noticed they were carrying packs.

"Hurry along everyone," Frey said. "Do not be the one responsible for holding up the workings of a god." He helped the coven toss blankets, clothing, and jewelry into a wagon. "Chaos waits for no one, Millicent." Frey patted an elderly woman on the shoulder as she sat on the back of the cart.

"What is happening here?" Sebastian said.

"We're coming with ya." Frey clapped.

Sebastian shook his head. "Oh, no... I can't let you get involved."

Frey shooed along another family as they stumbled over their belongings. "Your Majesty, with all due respect, we are coming. You need me to get you inside the gateway and we have business in the marketplace, as you see. We were just waiting for you to arrive before we set off."

"Fine!" Sebastian rubbed his face. His skin glowed a slight hint of gold. Frey stopped and stared, and Sebastian saw the others watching him closely. He saw scales etching into his hand and felt the sensation of skin breaking across his neck and face. "Do not get in my way."

Frey bowed. "We only live to serve the gods."

"Easy." Dani put his hand on Sebastian's. "Save that for when you see my father again."

Frey cleared his throat. "And who is your father, dear boy?"

"King Maxen."

The coven gasped and turned their attention to Dani. It was eerily silent in the canyon. Sebastian narrowed his eyes, and his lip twitched into a snarl.

"So, you are a Blackbird too," Frey said. "The myths are true."

Barron came up to Dani's side.

"And there are two." Frey looked back and forth from Dani to Barron and laughed at his rhyme for a moment.

Dani snorted out in laughter. "I get it."

Okay that's enough." Sebastian laughed. "Frey, what lies ahead?"

"Nothing for a bit, and then a trading town. Well, it was when Alta Prime was still a populated and thriving capital. Now this town is dying."

"Yeah, that's my fault." Sebastian dropped his shoulders. "This should be interesting."

The canyon ended at the border of two crossing deserts. Where they came from was rocky with hard, compacted dirt, but the gates lay ahead, deep in the dunes of the sandy hills. It was past lunch by the time they passed from one desert to the other. The hot sun burned Sebastian's neck. The coven passed scarves to the members of the Order. Sebastian wrapped his around his mouth and nose, then pulled his hood over his head as the wind carried the sand into his hair and eyes. In the early evening, they arrived at a small market at the end of the road.

The coven set up camp and began to cook. Sebastian walked through the small township, realizing it reminded him a lot of Adurak. He found himself walking into a tavern called The Serpent's Lair. The two men standing behind the bar were tall, had enormous muscles, and both wore scowls that were not well-hidden by their beards and mustaches. Sebastian walked up to the bar, not taking his focus off the large brutes who were staring back at him.

One of the men stepped forward and leaned down to meet Sebastian's face, his nose inches away. He suddenly stood up straight before he and the other man dropped to one knee and, in unison, said, "Your Majesty. Chaos, God of Fire. It is our honor to serve you."

The tavern fell quiet. Sebastian looked at the unfamiliar faces that surrounded him. He realized he was without accompaniment, standing in a room filled with people whom he had been taught his whole life were his enemy. His hand wrapped around the hilt of his sword. The barmen hurried from behind the counter. Sebastian drew his sword and stood, prepared to fight.

The barmen stopped and knelt again. "No, you do not understand," one spoke. "My name is Hansu, and this is my brother Hinsu. We have never met a god before. This is truly the greatest day of our lives."

Sebastian stared in disbelief. He felt his hands tingle and his stomach flutter. He wasn't sure whether he was amused or afraid.

"Please," Hansu said quickly. "Let me get you a drink. We have some of the finest spiced meads here in Safareen. You will be impressed."

Hinsu jumped to his feet, making the floor shake dangerously. "And I will make you a feast."

"Umm," Sebastian said, but the brothers had already hurried off to the kitchen.

The tavern was still quiet. The people had migrated into one corner were watching Sebastian's every move. He walked over to a man with a pipe. Without a word, he took a draw at the tobacco, then handed the pipe back. Sebastian turned and walked over to a table in the middle of the room. The others still watched. He laughed and shook his head, then a mug was set down on the table, and Hansu sat in the chair across from him. Sebastian picked up the mead and gazed at Hansu as his lips touched the rim. Sebastian took in a drink and set the mug down.

He felt a cool and ambrosial feeling fill his chest as the liquid passed into his stomach. Sebastian took another drink. "This is amazing. Delicious."

"I make it myself." Hansu's face turned bright red. He slapped his hand on the table and laughed. "I'm so privileged to have the honor of serving my mead to the King of Kings and a god."

"Please." Sebastian set his cup down. "Don't. I do not wish to be worshiped." He turned and looked at the people still standing in the corner. "Or feared."

Hinsu sat in the other chair as he dropped a plate filled with the most diverse meats and vegetables he had ever seen. The brothers stared at him with widened eyes and wide, open-mouth smiles.

"I don't even know how to eat this." Sebastian picked up what appeared to be some sort of snake.

"Let me show you." Hinsu nearly knocked over the mead when he lunged forward. He grabbed the snake and squeezed until its skin popped open. He slid a piece of meat out and passed it to Sebastian. Hinsu's face returned to a beaming smile.

Sebastian clenched his jaw. "Why am I doing this?" he mumbled before popping the meat into his mouth. He closed his eyes and chewed. His eyebrows furrowed, and he swallowed quickly. "That's different."

Hindu cheered and yanked the skin off the snake's body in one rip. Sebastian took a sip of his mead and stared in slight fear. The door of the tavern swung open and revealed the bright blue eyes of his Dani, who was sweating and trying to catch his breath.

"My love."

Sebastian waved Dani over. "Come meet my new friends, darling."

"Are you alright?" Dani hugged him.

"These people are insane," Sebastian whispered into Dani's ear. "Get me out of here."

Dani set gold on the bar and waved as he pushed Sebastian through the door and into the street. "What were you doing in there? I was looking everyw—"

Sebastian put his finger over Dani's lips. "They fed me a snake."

"A snake?" Dani's concerned expression turned into an amused smile. "And you ate it?"

Sebastian took Dani's hand and hurried back to the witch camp where the Order was resting before a campfire. Jace jumped up and said, "Your Majesty, thank the gods."

Sebastian held up his hand. "I'm fine, Jace." He looked around at everyone. "The lot of you never leave me alone for a minute, but when I actually need you, I find myself alone among these... people." He turned and looked behind him where a small group had formed outside the tavern, including the brothers.

Meecah jumped to her feet. "Did they try to hurt you?"

"No," Sebastian said. His focus was still on the townspeople. "Actually, they fed me and said things like meeting me was the greatest day of their life."

Dani burst out laughing. "Frey warned you. Have you not been listening?"

"When does he ever listen?" Valirus said. "The Safar worship the gods. You are a god. How does this not make sense to you?"

"Don't start with me, old man."

After a restless night's sleep and when the sun peeked out over the dunes, Sebastian stood on the road and looked ahead at the closed gateway in the distance. Barron joined him by his side and said nothing, only set his hand on Sebastian's shoulder. They rode out of the little village with Sebastian out front, along with Jace, Candor, and Meecah by his side. It fell oddly quiet when they arrived before the gates. Sebastian looked along the wall, seeing no soldiers on patrol. He heard footsteps coming quickly from behind.

Frey ran past the horses and did not stop until he reached the doors. He ran his fingers across the iron in a pattern until a light glowed bright orange against the gate. After a loud bang, a dust cloud blew across Sebastian and his accompaniment, followed by the rumble of the gateway opening, revealing a massive desert city. Frey waved for the others to join him as his feet crossed the threshold. Sebastian brushed the sand off his jacket and moved forward.

The homes near the wall were tattered, some with broken doors and nothing more than a piece of cloth hanging over the windows. Sebastian saw the faces of children who hid behind chairs and tables upon seeing him pass. A group of young women crouched alongside a trough filled with water and linens. They bowed their heads and returned to their work. Sebastian looked into every home, every tavern, and the shops along the way as the city changed from poor to filth. The buildings blocked out the sun, the streets were littered with moldy food and feces, and the shops were a mix of pubs and brothels.

Sebastian caught the attention of a few young ladies standing in nothing more than a thin piece of silk to cover their midsection with their breasts bare to anyone that passed. One of the ladies winked as he approached. He felt a squeeze on his forearm and turned to see Dani's narrowed eyes.

Sebastian sighed. "I didn't do anything." He shook his head then turned and shouted, "Pick up the pace people, we are almost there." He tapped his horse and galloped along the main road through town.

They arrived at a massive marketplace that was strangely empty. Frey ran forward and shouted the names of merchants, but no one responded. "This is odd," Frey said. "The bazaar is the largest in all of Erras. People come from all over the world to buy, sell, and trade here, but this..."

Sebastian rode forward again, moving his head back and forth. The carts and wagons were empty, and the shops were dark inside. He sat up straight and continued down the road that eventually led to quaint shops with dresses and shoes in the window displays. The smell of freshly baked bread and cakes made Sebastian smile. He looked for the bakers and the shopkeepers but was again disappointed by the silence and naked streets.

At the peak of a hill along the pathway was the overlook of a golden palace glistening in the midday sun. Sebastian yanked back on his reins and stared in wonder. The view transitioned from weathered desert dwellings to fine-crafted stone and clay homes that stacked high along the maze of a city that rested against the outer wall of the palace. A breeze brushed through his hair, and the smell of salt was stronger than it had been before. Beyond the castle, he could see the sparkling teal of a shallow sea and yellow, sandy beaches.

"My love?" Dani said.

"Yes, darling." He refocused on moving forward. "Let's get this over with."

The streets remained clear, but sound started carrying across the town. As they approached the outer wall, the gate lifted and guards ran out with their weapons ready. Sebastian held up his hand and his company halted. The battle-ready soldiers stopped, then divided and fell to one knee, leaving an open path into the castle grounds. The sounds of cheering and laughter, boos, and scolding echoed against the wall as they passed under the gate. A young boy stood on the steps to the castle doors. He was dressed in a white linen skirt and a pleated wrap and wore a gold crown on his head.

The boy stepped forward. "Chaos. God of Fire. Welcome to Safareen." He gracefully bowed. "I am Prince Paolo. My father, the king, is waiting for you." Paolo did not wait for a response. He turned and climbed the steps, but stopped suddenly. "Leave the horses here. Someone will tend to them. The rest of you may follow."

Sebastian was the first to climb the stairs with Dani on his arm and Barron by his other side. Roaring noise burst through the castle doors, and then Sebastian saw what was happening in Safareen and why the people of the town were missing. As he passed through the castle doors, he saw steep descending stairs leading into an open-air arena that occupied the east side of the palace. Massive statues lined the gallery, with palm trees and ferns growing along the corridor. Ponds with brightly colored fish that caught Sebastian's eye sat on each side of the room. He followed the young prince into the stadium. As the sun beamed on his face, the powerful cheering fell to a silence.

King Lucian stood from his throne. Sebastian began his downward climb through a thick crowd of townspeople of all sorts. Some touched his arms, face, and hair as he passed. He saw many women taking a special interest in Meecah and Samir, and whispers of them coming from unknown lands crept through the crowd. "He's the only living god," a man said. "Is he here to kill us?" a little girl said to her mother. Lucian's stare did not leave Sebastian's face.

Sebastian stepped from the stadium and into the arena and led his people toward the king.

"Nephew!" Lucian held his hands out. "Imagine that. My own kin is a god." Lucian grinned and looked around at the arena. "Isn't it just beautiful?" His blonde hair danced with every movement of his head, and his dimples made his smile more annoying than attractive.

Sebastian stepped forward. "What is all this?"

Lucian stopped smiling and changed his posture. "Don't you know?" He hurried over to meet Sebastian face-to-face. Jace drew his sword and pointed it at Lucian's throat. Lucian pushed the sword away. "Isn't he well trained?"

Sebastian laughed. "I should let him cut your head off for what you did to me in Torrdale."

"Ahh, Sebastian." Lucian wrapped his arm around Sebastian's shoulders. "That is old news. But this." He waved at the crowd. They cheered loudly and whistled. "This is today, and we have been waiting a long time for you to come here."

"Why?"

Lucian whistled. Gates opened in the corners of the arena. Sebastian slowly turned and watched as a massive cat-like animal came slashing from its keep, its long and sharp teeth gnashing desperately. Then two men holding shields and clubs came from another space. Another person came out fast and ran straight at Sebastian. Her scream was deafening and her hand tightly gripped a broadsword that she held pointed to kill. She stopped inches from his face and stared deep into his eyes.

Sebastian backed away and turned back to Lucian. "What is the meaning of this?"

Lucian let out a laugh. "Do you still not understand?"

"It's a tournament," Sebastian said.

"Of course it is a tournament, Nephew. But that's not it at all." Lucian joined Sebastian in the dirt. "They are here ... for you, God of Fire."

Sebastian backed away and started toward his people but was stopped by the two men with clubs. He snarled, "Move out of my way."

"No, no," Lucian said. "You still don't get it, do you?"

Sebastian turned. "What game are you playing?"

"This tournament"—a twitch of a smile grew across Lucian's lips—"has not been seen in this world since the days of Dragon and the Stormfire battle arena that once stood in NorthBrekka, and it just happens to be on this day that the last tournament took place."

Sebastian's eyes narrowed.

"You really know nothing of your bloodline," Lucian said.

"My father had a lot of secrets." Sebastian stepped toward Lucian.

Lucian stepped forward and put his hands on Sebastian's shoulders. "Stormfire Lake was once a massive area, and every year, people from all over would come to see the gods face off against some of the finest men, women, and creatures. But when Dragon watched his little brother get slaughtered, he flooded the lake and left his body at the bottom." Lucian backed toward the platform. "Perhaps that is why your powers surfaced that night on Stormfire." He waved his hand, and the clatter of gates opening filled the stadium.

Men and women brandished weapons and took a stance. Sebastian instructed the Order to take a seat in the stands. He ran his fingers across the handles of his axes.

Lucian laughed and raised his arms. "Chaos, you are the only remaining god on earth." He nodded. "These champions have come to see if they can take down the God of Fire. Respectfully, of course. If they defeat you, they and their families are heavily rewarded."

"And if they lose?" Sebastian looked at the arena filled with acolytes.

"They will be dead." Lucian nodded. "I thought that would be clear."

Sebastian turned to Lucian. "Did Dragon compete in these tournaments?"

"Of course." Lucian's broad smile and white teeth twinkled in the sun. "He competed just as you will now."

Loud clapping came from the balcony at the top of the arena. Sebastian's head shot up. He squinted his eyes, then his heart began pounding. He felt blood rush through his veins, and his chest burned.

"They cannot defeat him," said an echoing voice from above. "Only I can."

Sebastian felt dizzy. He knew that voice, and it sent chills down his spine. His eyes watered, and his stomach bubbled. It was nearly silent. His chin quivered. "Hydros."

Chapter Eight
The Curse of the Blackbird

A fiery sensation shot down Sebastian's spine at the sound of his twin's voice. A broken growl filled his throat as he pulled his shoulder blades together and stood straight, staring his brother in the face. His head tipped low with a snarl across his lip as wisps of fire escaped through his balled fists. Out of the corner of his eye, he noticed the acolytes moving in on him, each brandishing their weapon.

The two men with clubs approached him silently, but Sebastian easily threw them back with a gust of wind. He marched over to the men with a fireball in between his enclosed hands. "Who wants it first?"

The two men pointed at each other. Sebastian laughed. "Very well." He caught his reflection in the shield of one of the fallen men. Fiery scales etched across his cheeks and down his chest. His skin felt as if it were being ripped from his bones as he screamed and reached his hand into the sky. A bolt of lightning crashed into his waiting grasp, which he used to strike down a man and woman who were inching forward to attack.

Dust from the sand spun and swirled with every maneuver. The dance of Sebastian's feet thumped on the shaking ground as he held the lightning in attack formation. He didn't see the faces of the audience, the Order, Lucian, or Hydros. He thought of nothing except the fire and lightning coming from his hands. A roar shook his eardrums. Sebastian winced and turned to see the massive creature slashing and snapping from a few yards away. He lowered his hands and stretched his fingers out wide.

Everything stopped moving and the dust cleared. The other opponents scurried away behind the beast. The winds subsided and the audience quieted. Sebastian stared at the animal with pity, admiring its beauty and strength, knowing he had to kill it in order to survive. A crack split open next to his foot. With another pop and crack, the floor of the arena broke apart. Sebastian stared at the creature blankly. He slowly lifted his arms and twitched his hand into a fist as his feet moved toward the angry beast that threatened to pounce. Sebastian hissed and the creature roared and crouched to the ground. Sand trickled across the ground into a swirling pool around the beast's paws. Sebastian stomped, and the crack in the ground jolted apart, swallowing the animal and the acolytes in one fatal maneuver. He clapped his hands together with a powerful force that shook the arena—the ground slammed together and the crack was gone.

A deep, haughty laugh came from the platform. "Incredible," Lucian said. "Just to think that the man who can do all of that is my kin."

Sebastian shoved Lucian out of his way and marched for the stairs, his eyes locked on Hydros. "You were dead," he shouted. "How are you here?"

"I can answer that." A familiar voice carried across the arena.

Sebastian stumbled to a stop. "Maxen," he whispered.

"Your Majesty," Maxen spoke loudly for all to hear. "I was... happy when I heard you were still alive. But your twin." Maxen turned his attention to Tomas. "There is only one way he stands here before us now." Maxen started to laugh and turned toward the audience. "Where is my extraordinarily talented son, Dani?"

Sebastian's mouth dropped. "Dani?" He sheathed his sword and made his way to the stands where the audience was watching. Some wore faces of terror as he pushed up the steps to where Dani waited. The townspeople gasped as Sebastian moved people out of his way. Some cowered at his presence while others ran away. He reached Dani and grabbed him by his wrists. "What did you do?"

Dani's body shook for a moment. He closed his eyes and took a long, deep breath. "When you were unconscious after the war." He paused and stared away for a moment before continuing. "I washed Tomas's body and dressed him. I was the last person to touch him before they closed his tomb." Dani started to sob.

Sebastian let him go but brushed his cheek with the back of his hand. "Did you just touch him, or did you do that thing where your eyes turn white and you go into this unexplainable state?"

Dani's eyes shot up to meet Sebastian's. "I couldn't stop looking at his face and seeing you. It frightened me that there was a chance I would see you the same way." He backed away. "I didn't know what I was doing, Sebastian, I swear it."

Sebastian didn't know what to say but tried to comfort Dani. He pulled him in for an embrace. "I don't blame you, but we need to understand your gifts so we know how to fix this."

"My father only taught me to use it to kill. Never the other way around." Dani sighed. "But I do know that if my emotions get out of control, I can sort of pass my energy into a dead body and revitalize it. The worst part is, the person will never be the same. There are consequences to bringing back the dead, and I want nothing to do with it." Tears continued to fall from the corners of his eyes.

"We will sort this out later." Sebastian looked around at the crowd. "But for now, I have to face the ghost standing before us." He left the stands and made his way back into the arena. Sebastian marched toward Hydros. "How did you escape that tomb?"

Hydros's face shined in the sun. His eyes were blue and his smile was soft, reminding him of Tomas in every way. It was the face that Sebastian had known as the sweet brother he grew up with, only, this Tomas was different. He possessed his god form, standing above all others with icy scales forming across his skin and his sapphire eyes shining so bright, even Dani's couldn't compare.

Sebastian made his way up the steps but stopped halfway. "Hydros, I—"

"You're sorry," Hydros said. "You are sorry you let me die. You are sorry you were never there for me when I needed you, and you are sorry that I was too weak to save myself." He stomped his foot, and the steps began to freeze. Every step cracked as the ice shattered under his feet. Hydros stopped on the same landing as his twin.

Sebastian's body seared as he ignited into his Chaos form. He barely got out before he felt a cold hand clamp his shoulder. Sebastian suddenly felt completely calm.

"Join me, Brother." Hydros's voice was calm. "It is time for you and me to unite as we were always meant to." He held out his hand, palm up. "Come with me."

Sebastian looked over his shoulder at the thinning crowd. His order was easily spottable among those who were still there. Lucian stood proudly on the king's platform and watched as if it were a part of the tournament. He turned back to Hydros. "I would never betray my people to join the likes of him." He nodded toward Maxen. "You betrayed your own people, and you betrayed me."

Hydros laughed and glanced at Maxen. "I will see you again in the place where the moon guides the way." And with a whoosh of wind and a loud pop, he was gone.

"Hydros!" Sebastian looked all around.

"Where did he go?" Dani came running up to meet him.

Footsteps came from the steps that lead to the upper balcony. "Don't look so surprised, Sebastian. You knew this day would come soon enough."

The voice made Sebastian's head hurt. He turned and took a step forward. "Countless nights have come and gone since the last time we crossed paths." He puffed his chest and stared up at Maxen as he descended to Sebastian's level until they were nearly nose-to-nose. Sebastian leaned over and whispered, "Why now?"

Maxen put his mouth to Sebastian's ear. "When you buried me in that cave, I vowed I would do everything in my power to dismantle the great Chaos, God of Fire." He tightened his fist around his staff and shoved his palm into Sebastian's chest.

Sebastian felt the wind get taken from his lungs. The sensation of pins and needles filled his chest and stomach as he fell through the air until he crashed into the sandy ground below. He struggled to get a breath and his eyes stung from sweat and dirt. His legs shook as he climbed to his feet. He tilted his head at Maxen's staff. "That's different," he whispered. The stone atop the staff was no longer a milky white opal, but now etched with black and gold.

"Sebastian!" Dani dove toward him and cupped his face in his hands.

Jace stepped into the sunlight, casting his shadow across Sebastian's face. "Your Majesty. Let me at him!"

Sebastian marched back toward the stairs where Maxen waited on the landing above. Sebastian dropped his hand to his side and spread his fingers apart. "Your turn." He balled his fists and waved his arms. He threw open his hands as they passed over the stairway. The rocks shifted into a flat slope. Maxen fell onto his back and tumbled down to the floor of the arena at Sebastian's feet.

Sebastian let out a laugh and unsheathed his sword. He pointed the blade to Maxen's throat. "I have more tricks than a silly old staff." He pulled back on the hilt and screamed before he plunged the sword forward. A bright flash of light filled the stadium and a hard blow to the face threw Sebastian back. He touched his fingertips to his bleeding lip, then reached for his sword again.

Maxen was on his feet and moving closer. The sound of iron slicing through air came from the sheath at Maxen's hip as he readied his sword. Sebastian climbed to his feet, grasped his sword in both hands, and charged forward. As their swords collided, an intense gust of wind pounded through the arena, knocking Dani and Jace into the barrier. Jon and Viktor shouted from the stands, but Sebastian couldn't hear their voices over the sound of metal ringing as he defended every swing of Maxen's sword. Safarian soldiers lined up and guided the remaining audience from the arena.

Lucian stood on his platform with a smile on his face while armed guards protected him with bows. Dani slipped between two soldiers and ran to the stage. Sebastian punched Maxen hard in the nose and screamed, "Dani, no!" The archers aimed their arrows at Dani's head, but Lucian waved them down. Dani nearly stumbled at Lucian's feet and spoke to him while watching Sebastian from over his shoulder.

Sebastian turned his head to see Valirus on the edge of the stadium with his staff in hand, the crystal still shining bright. Every footstep thumped as Sebastian walked, sword tight in his fist, toward the Altanian king. He ignited a fire in his hand and ran his palm along the blade. Maxen was on his knees, trying to catch his breath. Sebastian held the sword above his shoulders and stared into Maxen's eyes. "Your time is done." He shifted his arms and began to swing, but there was a sudden jolt that sent him crashing into the ground.

Dom leaned over. "I apologize, Your Majesty." He turned to Maxen. "But this vile piece of scum murdered my daughter. I made a promise that I would be the one who rips his heart out." He gripped Maxen's throat and held a dagger to his chest. "She was only a child." A tear fell down Dom's cheek.

A strange rumble filled the air, followed by a loud pop. Then, a shadow cast on the ground of the long hair of a woman, flowing in the breeze. Sebastian looked up to see the bright azure mane of Petra standing before him. She stared Sebastian down for a long moment as she slipped her hand on Maxen's shoulder.

Sebastian shouted and lunged forward only to crash into the dirt, hard, as a thunderous echo sounded, and Maxen and Petra were gone. His eyes darted over to Jace, whose face was as white as snow.

"Where did he go?" Dom's voice was loud and sharp, and filled with violent rage. "He was right here!"

"It was his daughter." Sebastian's voice overpowered Dom. "She has been tricking us this whole time. She was helping Maxen. Dom . . . I want him dead as much as you do, but I need you to calm down."

Dom's face was sweaty and his eyes manic. His beauty only made his anger that much more painful for Sebastian to see.

"Dom, please. I am sorry."

"And you trusted her?" Dom spat. "That blue-haired monster."

Jace marched forward. "Now hold on, Dom. That was not necessary."

"Gentlemen." Sebastian stepped between them. "Now is not the time. We have to find out where they have gone!"

Lucian cleared his throat. "Not so fast." He made his way into the arena and stood next to Sebastian. "We have a lot to talk about."

"I have nothing to say to the man who attacked me in Torrdale."

Lucian grinned. "You and your people can follow these lovely girls." He gestured to a row of women at the top of the arena. "They will have you washed and fed." He started toward the stage, then turned and stopped. "It's been a long journey. Take rest."

"We don't have time for this."

"Now, just a minute, Sebastian!" Dani interrupted. "We came all the way here to speak to King Lucian. The least you can do is take him up on his generous offer."

Sebastian watched the Order already starting their ascent up the stairs, with Dom joining them. He pulled Dani against his chest and kissed his forehead while keeping his focus on Lucian. "You are right, my love."

"Don't keep them waiting," Lucian said. "In Safareen, we dedicate an hour each day after lunch to praising the gods." He chuckled. "You must realize what your presence means here." Lucian softly bowed and made his way to the stairs.

"This is going to be weird," Dani said. He gripped Sebastian's hands and pulled him along.

They climbed the stairs until they were met by a woman who introduced herself as Kiya. She kept her composure and spoke clearly as they made their way through the castle. "Those were my great grandmother's vases over by the pond. She was proud of them." Kiya laughed a little. They walked through a narrow corridor where Kiya stopped and turned to face the men. "This is where I leave you." She pointed at Dani. Two ladies came from an open door and invited him inside.

"No," Sebastian said.

"You"—Kiya interrupted, completely ignoring Sebastian—"will stay with me. Come along."

Dani let go of Sebastian's arm and shrugged. "I could use a bath." He disappeared into the room and the door closed.

Kiya bowed. "King Sebastian. I am Lucian's wife. It is my honor to personally serve you this day." She bowed again and led the way through another door.

The room was warm with the windows open to a view of the sea. Sebastian gripped the windowsill and took a breath of the fresh salty breeze. "A queen should not be serving anyone. Not even me."

"You are a god." Kiya joined him at the window. "It is all of our duty to serve you. If you only understood your connection to Safareen. You are one of us."

Sebastian gazed at the ocean a little longer.

"You love the sea," Kiya said. "Not surprised. Your mother used to spend hours on the beach."

"You knew my mother?"

"No, but I have heard stories about her." Kiya handed Sebastian some clothing. "She was a kind woman who spent most of her time lying in the sand." She nodded at the beach near the harbor. "You can ask Lucian anything about your mother. There are all kinds of knowledge of her here in the castle." She set clothes on the stool next to the bath. "Now wash and put these on." She walked to the door but stopped. "You can wash yourself, can't you? I know how men in the north expect to be bathed."

Sebastian laughed. "I can handle it myself."

Kiya bowed and left the room.

Sebastian enjoyed the hot bath until he heard noises coming from the harbor. A bell rang continuously. He climbed out of the tub, walked over to the window, and stood naked, letting the warm air dry his body. Sebastian dressed, realizing the clothes were nothing more than long, thin, silken black pants and a matching shirt that had gold embroidery on the lining. The material was soft on his skin and would keep him cool in the hot desert sun. The door opened, and Kiya slipped inside.

"Oh good, you're ready." She waved for him to follow.

The great hall had no walls, just open air and a canopy above, much like Moonlight Castle in Adurak, but this one faced the sea. Palm plants of all shapes and sizes provided shade from the sun and places for lizards to hide. Two brightly colored birds screeched from a nearby branch, and a monkey trotted along the path next to Kiya. Sebastian heard Dani's voice in the distance and hurried along faster. The Safar were posted around the room and by the doors, watching the hall for intruders.

"They are surely on high alert after Maxen showed his face." Sebastian stopped in the doorway, seeing the faces of his order, his brothers, and Dani at the king's table with Lucian. As Sebastian approached the table, the hall silenced.

"The other one . . . Hydros." Kiya grasped Sebastian by the arm. "He was your twin."

"Was." Sebastian nodded. "He died in the battle in Torrdale. Only now—"

"Your lover brought him back to life." Niya looked him up and down. "You should go and join the others."

"Dani isn't to blame." Sebastian stopped her from leaving. "He is only learning what his powers do." He turned and marched toward the king's table.

The Safarian people dropped to their knees and rested their foreheads on the floor. Lucian stood and spread his arms wide. "Chaos. God of Fire. Welcome home."

Sebastian tilted his head and rolled his eyes, then made his way to his seat. "This is unnecessary, Lucian."

"Have you not listened to anything I said?" Lucian asked.

"Doubtfully." Viktor snickered.

"He doesn't listen to anyone." Dani rested his hand on Sebastian's arm.

Sebastian clenched his jaw. "My whole life, I was told your people were my enemy. Yet I realize I know nothing of the world, other than by my own discovery. My father refused to tell me about my mother. He always said that she was a lost soul and that she loved me very much. Nothing more."

"I was not born when your mother left Safareen, so I know only the stories I was told. But, if you would like to know them, I would be happy to tell you." Lucian sipped his wine.

Sebastian sat up and let out a deep breath. "Why did you attack me in Torrdale?"

"I wondered when you would ask," Lucian said. He looked past Sebastian. "I did what I did to save your life."

"What—"

"Let me finish." He drummed his fingers on the table. "Let's just say, back in Torrdale, Maxen and Lorna concocted some sort of stone that is similar to the Oscura. It is quite deadly, but they weren't sure if it would actually kill you. But, it would horribly disfigure you... like, unrecognizable, you would probably wish you were dead kind of thing."

"Was that the stone on his staff I saw in the arena?" Sebastian urged him to continue.

Lucian nodded. "My sister loved to gloat about her accomplishments. Lorna and Maxen planned to get you alone in the woods, but Lorna was killed by Barron, so Maxen led you on a trail where he was planning to perform the spell that would cast the stone against you. If you would have followed him, he would have done something awful. You wouldn't be with me today if I hadn't interfered."

"So now he has this stone in his staff." Sebastian fidgeted with his hand. "Wait. The Oscura. Why is the Oscura so significant again?"

Lucian's eyes widened.

Sebastian looked at his hand again and groaned. "I am an idiot."

"What do you mean?" Dani said.

"At Castle Drake, I was in the bath." Sebastian rubbed his finger where he wore the ring. "I took it off to bathe, and when I was underwater, I heard a strange noise. It just dawned on me that it was Petra and the sound that's made when she enters or leaves a space."

"So, you lost it." Dani grabbed his hand. "How could you not tell it was gone?"

"I guess my mind was on so many other things . . . So, Maxen sent Petra to fetch it." Sebastian turned away and rubbed his neck. "That stone . . ."

"Do you even know what it is?" Lucian asked. He glanced over at Dom. "You never told him, did you?"

Dom stared at the floor. "I was told it was the Dragon-killing stone." He looked at Sebastian. "My mother said it was made by Dragon's enemy to end his life in battle, but it didn't work and the stone broke. Although, rumors say that the broken stone only makes it even more volatile."

Sebastian sat back and peered at Dom. "Why did you give it to me?"

"Because you are the Heir of Dragon." Dom sighed. "And because I didn't want anyone to use it to hurt you, therefore I thought the safest place for it was with you."

Sebastian rubbed the index finger the ring usually sat on. "I can't believe I lost it. So, what does this mean, Lucian?"

"It means Maxen could very well have Dragon-killing powers." Lucian shrugged. "He was obsessed with trying to kill you. Even my sister, Lorna, became obsessed with the damn thing too. That is why she married Maxen. She wanted revenge on the Drakes just as much. She blamed your father for her sister's death."

"Is that why she took Cyrus from me?"

"Cyrus was never going to be yours." Lucian raised his voice. "He was a Bolin. And the Bolin bloodline is poison."

Sebastian's eyes shot to Valirus. Then to Dani, who was next to him.

"I already know." Lucian turned his attention toward the old man sitting with the Order. "The sorcerer is no more a Bolin than I, even if he possesses the name. And Dani was betrayed by the Bolins just as your ancestors were in the past." He stared at Sebastian for a long moment. "The Bolins tore our nations apart. Now is our chance to reunite as one people to defeat our enemy."

Sebastian nodded. "I will send word if need be, otherwise leave Maxen and Hydros to me. It is my responsibility."

Lucian smiled and reached his arm out. "Just be careful out there." He backed away. "So, you're not planning to take my throne, King of Kings?"

Sebastian laughed. "I already have a throne I never wanted."

"Two," Jace said from the closest table. "He has two thrones he doesn't want."

Sebastian narrowed his eyes. "Shut up, Jace."

That evening, Sebastian found Valirus sitting alone, watching the ships in the harbor. "May I join you?"

Valirus gestured for Sebastian to sit. "I used to get annoyed when you came and bothered me. Now, I hope for your company."

"I apologize," Sebastian said. "I haven't been very social since returning to Erras."

A young lady slipped through the door and set down a teapot and two cups. Her eyes were wide and her lip trembled as she locked eyes with Sebastian. She backed out of the door before he could speak.

Sebastian shook his head and turned back to Valirus. "I have not been easy to deal with since we returned."

Valirus waved his hand over the kettle and whispered something Sebastian could not understand. He took a deep breath. "No, you have not. But I understand. I never belonged here either." He brought the cup to his lips.

Sebastian looked at the tea, then at Valirus.

"It isn't hexed." Valirus took a sip. "I just checked."

Sebastian sighed. "Lucian wants the Bolin lineage wiped clean from the map." A teacup was placed in his outstretched hand. He laughed and took a drink. "I don't think he realizes that means you and Dani would have to die as well."

"I am old, and Dani isn't going to have babies to continue the name. Lucian will have his wish soon enough. The Bolins will all cease to exist in his lifetime. He will be a hero to his people."

"Valirus." Sebastian bit his lip. "What was the world like when you were King of Torrdale?"

"It was... quiet." Valirus took a moment and stared off into the harbor. "The King of Kings was too busy fighting with the Kuhar to care about NorthBrekka, and your grandfather was too busy building the wall that divides Erras."

Sebastian shook his head. "I'm confused."

"Your grandfather, Drakis, saw that the King of Kings was going mad." Valirus adjusted his back and leaned against a post. "After the war in Safareen, King Robert's thirst for blood had yet to be quenched. While he took the Hetta Horizon to Khan Khar, King Drakis closed the north and posted soldiers along the wall so that when Robert returned and turned his violence on NorthBrekka, he would be met with obstacles. But I was distracted with my brother and his rise to power in Midrel Istan." Valirus twiddled his thumbs. "I loved your grandfather and your grandmother like family. But, I had no choice but to leave Torrdale in the hands of my adolescent son, Roman. This is when Ivan and Roman became friends and the Bolin-Drake history changed."

Sebastian's stomach twisted. "So, you didn't know my mother either."

"Unfortunately, not many that are still alive knew your mother. The coven are your people. Lean on them to answer your questions. But for now, your focus has shifted."

"Tomas," Sebastian said. He put his head in his hands. "What am I supposed to do? I can't kill—" A tear fell down his cheek. "What happened to him?"

"The Curse of the Blackbird." Valirus sat back and crossed his arms. "Bringing one back from the dead is ungodly. Dani is dangerous. You are going to have to keep him close at all times. His power is rising, and he does not understand any of it. Dani brought Tomas back from the dead. Once the people of Erras find out, they will come for him as well. But for now, Tomas is no longer Tomas. He is a monster." He climbed to his feet and offered his hand to help Sebastian to his. "This is no time for you to sit around, lost in a daze. You cannot fall apart anymore, Sebastian. I will not allow it. You have had your time to grieve. Your brother is dead."

Sebastian stood and set the cup down. He took one last look at the harbor and nodded at Valirus before departing toward the gardens where elderly women were tending to weeds and flowers. Every breath of air was filled with unique flora that drew a smile across Sebastian's tired face. He felt a tap on his boot and looked down to see a woman shooing him away from the fern he was standing on. "Sorry." He moved away quickly. The woman bowed and returned to her work.

"Young man." A garbled light voice came from nearby.

Sebastian turned and saw a frail woman whose wrinkles drooped heavily. He smiled and nodded his head. "Madam."

"Can you assist me one moment?" she said. "My hands don't work as well as they used to." She handed him a pair of shears.

"What do I do?" Sebastian looked at the flowers.

The woman patted his arm. "Whatever feels natural. Just pick your favorite one."

Sebastian opened his mouth to speak but stopped and stared at the flowers again. He felt the heat rise in his face. He fumbled with a bright orange tiger lily, then his hands moved to some yellow honeysuckle.

"Relax," the woman said. "There is no wrong way to do it." She reached over and took Sebastian's hand in hers. She guided the shears to a flower's stem and held it tight. "Cut here." She smiled at the lily Sebastian handed her, then laid it in her basket. "In life, you have a choice. You can leave the flowers to grow and die on their own. There is no fault in that logic. But, if you want the plant to grow stronger, you have to clip away some of the blooms. Even if it makes you sad."

Sebastian stared into her eyes for a moment. He thought about Tomas and then turned back to the plants. His hand clasped the shears and he snipped a white orchid.

The woman winced and covered her mouth. "Even if it makes me sad." She took the flower and stared at it.

"I'm sorry." Sebastian put his hand on her back. "You said to cut anything I want. I just thought that flower was pretty."

"That orchid was fifteen years old." She gently stroked its petals. "I planted it myself."

Sebastian's cheeks burned.

"Don't worry, love." She took the orchid and handed it back to him. "It is a gift. Take it." She smiled and held his cheek for a moment.

"Thank you." Sebastian handed her the shears. "I don't think I should be cutting your flowers anymore."

"No," she said. "You have flowers of your own to cut." The woman patted her hand over her heart and returned her attention to the lilies.

Sebastian pulled the orchid to his nose and breathed in the scent of vanilla. He nodded at the woman. "Madam." Then bowed and took his leave.

He found Dani sitting alone by a fire, reading a book. The warmth was relaxing, even in the desert. Sebastian reached the flower toward Dani. "Here. This for you." He grimaced for a moment. "I may have hurt an old lady's feelings by cutting it."

"Sebastian!" Dani scolded but took the orchid and held it to his nose. He smiled and then narrowed his eyes. "You didn't steal it, did you?"

"She told me to cut a flower, so I cut a flower. It's for you, my darling."

"It's beautiful." Dani took a deep breath of its scent.

Sebastian kissed Dani and laid him back on the floor. They made love before the fire, then crawled into bed early. The night was cool and the land was peaceful. The only sounds were of the ocean and birds. Sebastian breathed in the scent of salt and lavender. A smile crested his lips and he closed his eyes.

Chapter Nine

The Ship with Wings for Sails

A pair of battleships departed from the harbor early the following morning. It was already warm and the people were hard at work around the castle. Sebastian stood alone on a terrace he stumbled upon by chance while trying to find his way to the great hall. The sounds of bells and seagulls drew his attention to the sea. He heard footsteps coming down the corridor, and then the door creaked open.

"My soldiers are headed out to search for Maxen and Tomas."

Sebastian still stared at the harbor. "Good morning, Lucian."

"Nephew."

"I need to go home." Sebastian turned to face Lucian. "I cannot let Hydros reach NorthBrekka before me."

Lucian slapped him on the shoulder. "What are you going to do about Maxen?"

"That's easy. I am going to run my blade through his skull... when I find him."

Lucian laughed. "What are you going to do about your brother?"

Sebastian paused for a moment. "He is not my brother anymore. He is Hydros. My brother will rest when I cast that monster from his body."

"That's the spirit. Calling your own kind a monster." Lucian reached out his forearm. "I will keep a watchful eye on the horizon. Send word the moment you need my help. Meanwhile, I will keep the seas safe." He backed away. "Don't get yourself killed out there. I would like to get to know my kin."

Sebastian smiled and nodded. "Me too."

Lucian left the room but quickly returned. "Actually, I ask a favor of you. Follow me." He marched through the door. "Hurry up, Nephew."

They made their way into the hall where the Order was waiting. Sebastian followed Lucian across the room, then stopped where a young man sat at the far corner of a table.

Lucian turned to Sebastian. "This one was found roaming the streets. He says he is from Midrel Istan. He was a captive on one of Maxen's ships. The guards caught him stealing a woman's coin purse."

Sebastian's eyebrows furrowed. "What are you asking of me?"

"Take him with you." Lucian smiled.

"No." Sebastian looked at the boy and then back to Lucian. "Absolutely not. Where are his parents?"

Lucian clenched his jaw. "I don't know. But he is a thief, and you are the King of Thieves. He cannot stay here. The Safarian army will torture the poor child."

"Lucian, I cannot guarantee his safety. In case you forgot, I am at war." Sebastian walked over to the boy and towered over him. "What is your name?"

The boy had copper hair and emerald eyes. His button nose scrunched, and he shivered as Sebastian got closer.

"Do not fear me." Sebastian rested his hand on the back of the boy's chair. "Who are you? Who are your parents?"

"I am—"

Dani's loud voice filled the room. "Move. Out of my way. I know who that is." He stormed over to Sebastian.

"Dani?" The boy's voice squeaked.

Dani's face was serious and his cheeks were red. "What the hell are you doing here, Boy? Where is your brother?"

"King Maxen came to the farm and took me." The boy sunk into the chair. "I think my father is dead. And Mom and Little Boy."

Sebastian watched Dani's jaw open and then close tight as he took a deep breath. He thought he saw a flash of a smile on Dani's lips. "Fenton," Sebastian said. "This boy is Fenton Paark's son."

"Yes." Dani closed his eyes.

Sebastian bit his fist. "What do we do with him?"

Dani's focus was only on the child. "We take him with us."

"He won't even make the trip to NorthBrekka. Look at him!" Sebastian put his hand over his face. He stepped over to the boy again. "What is your name?"

Dani grabbed Sebastian's arm. "Fenton didn't name his children. They call him Boy."

Sebastian felt his face get hot. "I am not calling him that. If he is going to be following me around, he needs a name." He grabbed the boy's collar and lifted him to his feet. He turned to Lucian. "If I am to take him, can we get him a bath and some clean clothes? He is a mess. And feed him." Sebastian backed away. "What do you want to be called, child?"

"Horse?" The boy said.

Sebastian shook his head. "That is not a name. That is an animal."

"Cat."

"Same answer as before." Sebastian rubbed his neck. "Let's call you..." He looked at Dani for help, but Dani shrugged and held his hands in the air. The Order stood around and watched. "Would you all back off?" Sebastian waved his hands.

"Your Majesty." The powerful yet soft voice of Meecah came across the room. "May I suggest something?"

"Please." Sebastian nodded.

"In Padora, the entire village names every newborn child." Meecah put her arm around the child's shoulders. "We will give him a name in time. Meanwhile, he is Boy."

"Fine. I have no will to argue with you." He winked at Meecah. "Go get him fed and cleaned up. We leave for NorthBrekka soon."

Jace came over and grabbed Sebastian by the arm. "I need to talk to you about Petra."

"She betrayed us, Jace." Sebastian put his hand on Jace's shoulder. "I know you loved her, but she was tricking us all along. Icefall... Her taking Dani and me back to NorthBrekka. Why? So she could help Maxen escape? She was fooling us all, Jace."

Jace stumbled back and leaned against a table. "How did I not notice anything?"

Sebastian reached over and rested his palm on Jace's shoulder. "She is an enchantress, Jace. She tricked us all."

Sebastian waited patiently and stared at the road ahead as the accompaniment was preparing to depart. The coven led them through the gate and across the canyon. They reached the end and stopped. Sebastian climbed off his horse and walked over to Candor.

"I would like to know more about my mother. But now is not the time."

"Come and visit us. We have a lot to tell you." Candor reached out his hand.

"You're not coming back to NorthBrekka, are you?"

Candor shook his head. "This is where I belong." He touched Sebastian's chin. "You look just like her."

Sebastian nodded. "Await my return."

"We will." Candor turned to Frey.

Frey bowed and hurried over to the wall of the ravine. He drew a symbol and pressed his hand against it. There was an enchantment, and the symbol turned sunny yellow and a trail appeared to the top. "Safe travels, Your Majesty. And remember, this place may not be much, but it is home to you and your kin."

"Thank you, Frey. I look forward to seeing you again." Sebastian nodded his head, then urged his horse to start the ascent into the outer desert of Safareen.

***

The accompaniment left the outer desert early the next morning. They rode through the day into the grassy plains of the midlands between the wall and the split in the road that headed to Alta Prime. They arrived at the fork and stopped. Sebastian jumped down from his horse and titled his head toward the path that headed east. His body tingled from his fingertips to his toes, and his heart began to beat faster.

"Your Majesty." Jace leaped from his horse and hurried over. "There is nothing good in Alta Prime." He took Sebastian by the arm. "I thought you said you had to reach north before Hyrdos."

"Hydros isn't headed for NorthBrekka. I can feel his energy." Sebastian jerked his arm free and took to his horse again. He thundered down the familiar road to the former capital city.

The day turned late and the green fields turned softer and sandy, with palm trees lining the way. The flutters in Sebastian's chest intensified when he arrived at the hill. He stopped and hopped down onto the thin patches of grass. His eyes scanned the massive city. Whispers erupted behind him.

"What happened here?" Meecah's voice sounded above all others. "Was this your doing, Your Majesty?"

Sebastian turned his head and looked over his shoulder. He clenched his jaw and returned his gaze to the shattered palace by the sea. "Yes. The last time I stood on this hill and stared down at that city, Cyrus was by my side. We came here because we thought Sacha was going to destroy the world, and we wanted to stop him." Sebastian stared at his feet for a moment and shook his head. "We were so naïve. Ignorant boys trying too hard to be mighty before they were even weaned from the pack."

"Sebastian." Dani wrapped his arm around Sebastian's waist.

"I did this." Sebastian interrupted. "All that time I blamed Sacha, but it was me who would destroy the world all along." He started down the hill. "I don't know how to stop myself from destroying everything." Sebastian stopped before passing through the city walls. His fingertips tingled and he felt cold as goosebumps covered his body.

The impoverished outer rim of Alta Prime was empty. Fires had not been lit in years and the air smelled of decay and rot. As they passed into the inner markets, the site of the road ahead halted the entire accompaniment. Sebastian walked into the town square and took a deep breath.

Dom rested his hand on Sebastian's shoulder. "Keep moving. There is nothing good that comes from bringing up the past."

"Dom." Sebastian pointed to the ground. "The past is literally blocking me from moving forward."

A pile of bones and skeletons was spread across the ground. Their arms stretched forward and their backs straight. "It looks like they were running away," Dani said.

The buildings that once stood a few stories high were broken and stones littered the streets. Carts and wagons were in pieces, and shards of wood impaled walls of homes. Trees were cracked at their lower trunks and the cobblestones that once neatly lined the road were scattered.

Boy tugged on Sebastian's sleeve. "There is another way to the palace."

"What?" Sebastian stopped and stared at Boy. "How would you know that?"

"Through the apothecary—"

"Answer me, child. How do you know about this place?"

Boy kicked a rock. "King Maxen brought us here."

"Maxen? Why would he . . . never mind. You said there is a path through the shop."

Boy smiled and nodded fast. "A tunnel. It comes up just inside the castle gates."

Sebastian shouted for Jace. "Stop the men. We will follow Boy." He saw Dani swing around.

Dani stormed across the cobblestones with grace. He grasped Sebastian's chin. "You are taking advice from a ten-year-old."

Sebastian smiled. "Why would Maxen come to Alta Prime?"

"My family ruled here before you destroyed it." Dani shrugged. "So, where do we need to go?"

The apothecary smelled of mildew and sage. Broken bottles that littered the floor crunched under every step they made. There was a narrow door with a black curtain draped over it. Sebastian passed into a cool, damp, and dark hallway. He lit a fire in his palm and saw mud on the walls and water dripping from cracks in the stone. His men lit torches as they walked long at a slow pace. The tunnel got cooler and more damp, and some places were more narrow than others.

Sebastian tilted his head as they approached spikes in the ceiling. "We must be passing into the castle grounds. Only a gate would have posts like that." He climbed out first; then a rumble came from the earth beneath their feet.

"Sebastian." Dani fell backward as the ground shook violently. "Was that you?"

"No." Sebastian stumbled to keep his balance.

The ground began to split. Rocks fell with a thundering force. Dani and the others fell back into the tunnel as a widening crevice split the land apart, all the way to the sea. Water flooded into the tunnels with a rapid, thundering whoosh. Sebastian spun around and shouted to the others, "Hurry! To the surface!"

The accompaniment desperately climbed the broken debris as the water turned the once-dark tunnels into a deep flowing river. As the sea rose above the debris, Sebastian grabbed Dani's arm and began to swim, as his feet could no longer touch any ground. The river soon filled the crevice to the tops where the others could easily climb to dry land. A loud rumble came from the broken castle and soon a large wooden ship appeared with the most unique sails Sebastian had ever seen. His mouth fell open as he turned to Valirus. "What is that thing?" Sebastian yelled.

Valirus quietly shook his head. "I don't have answers, Your Majesty."

A gust of wind blew the ship's sails wide open. "Wow," Sebastian whispered. "It looks like... wings." He squinted. "Wait, who is on that ship?" He stepped forward, and then his shoulders dropped and his heart burned. "Hydros."

Hydros smiled and nodded at Sebastian, then threw his arm in the air. Maxen stood by his side as the ship turned. A sharp gust of wind passed through the air and the sails erupted to life, forcing the ship down the river and to the harbor.

Sebastian ran across the grounds and into the palace. He crossed the great room, passed the throne room, and moved through the shattered end of the castle where the tower stood high above the rest. He climbed the stairs two at a time until he reached the platform where he and Tomas once faced Sacha in battle. He stood at the edge where there was once a wall and watched the ship pass into Blackport Harbor. Hydros stood on the aft.

Sebastian could just barely make out his eyes. His skin ignited into golden glowing scales and his belly burned with fury. He let out a scream, and a flash of lightning cracked across the sky and struck the tail of the ship. Sebastian locked eyes with Hydros for a moment, then sat down in defeat. Footsteps came from the stairway before someone sat down next to him. Sebastian took a deep breath. "Jace. Can I ask you something?"

Jace narrowed his eyes. "Sure."

"What are you going to do when the war is over?"

Jace furrowed his eyebrows and pursed his lips. "Excuse me, Your Majesty? What do you mean?"

"I mean, don't you want to take a wife and start a family one day?"

"Of course, but I could never leave you behind." Jace stared at the ship that was quickly disappearing into the sunlight. "You were my first real friend." He looked back at Sebastian. "Are you alright, Your Majesty?"

"I just watched my brother ... my dead brother." He corrected. "And my enemy sail away together, and I did nothing to stop them."

"What could you have done?" Jace shrugged.

A shadow cast over them.

"We need to talk." Barron stared at the sea.

Jace hopped up to leave but Sebastian reached out and wrapped his fingers around his forearm.

"He can stay." Barron sat on the edge of a boulder. He looked at Jace, then Sebastian. "What are you going to do about Hydros? He is sailing away. Where can he be going on such a contraption?"

Sebastian picked up a palm full of pebbles and threw them at the wall one by one. "Do you really think I already have some magical solution figured out, Barron? I have no idea where they are sailing. Hydros said, 'Come to the place where the moon guides the way.' What does that mean?"

The stairs led down into the hall behind the throne room. Sebastian felt a breeze pass across his face. His eyes turned to the hole in the wall of the castle. He set his foot on the opening and squinted his eyes over the bright sun that was starting to set over the sea.

"Your Highness!" A tiny voice came from down the hall.

Sebastian sighed and turned to see Boy standing in the doorway with a smile on his face.

"Look what I found!" Boy held out a gold, jeweled crown for Sebastian to take.

"This is..." Sebastian gripped it tight. "The crown of King Roman Bolin of Alta Prime. Former King of Kings." He clenched his jaw. "He died in his own house in unjust ways." Sebastian put his hand on Boy's shoulder. "This castle is filled with the ghosts of murdered kings. Do not linger here."

Boy bowed and followed Sebastian into the courtyard where the others had gathered. Sebastian guided Boy with his hand on his back, making sure he got over the debris without hurting himself.

Once Boy set off toward Dani, Sebastian focused on the crown as he approached Valirus. "This belonged to your son, Roman."

Valirus reached out and took the crown. His cheeks turned red and his eyes glazed as his hand ran across the emeralds and gold. "Thank you, Your Majesty. It means a lot to me."

Sebastian felt his face burn. "I wish I could have helped him. He was a good man. He believed in me when most others did not."

Valirus did not speak. He only nodded and held the crown against his chest.

Sebastian started toward his horse. "Let's ride before we lose the sun. We will make camp at the wall."

Chapter Ten

A Blackbird's Dark Magic

They arrived at the crossing at the north and south border. The rain was pouring down, soaking Sebastian to the bone. They took refuge in the guards' barracks as the storm thundered through the night. Sebastian enjoyed the sounds of nature as he tended to the fire. Most others slept, yet some sat quietly in their spaces.

"Why aren't you sleeping, Your Majesty?"

Sebastian jumped and clutched his chest. "Jon. You scared the hell out of me."

"I apologize." Jon took the fire stick from Sebastian's hands. "Go, sleep."

"I'm fine."

"Don't make me tell your sister." Jon raised an eyebrow. "You know how she is."

Sebastian laughed. "And you would tattle on me?"

"You are taking on too much. You need to rest between all your plotting."

"Plotting..." Sebastian shrugged. "I am losing my damn mind. First, I lose Maxen, and then, I lose him again. Now there is Tomas or Hydros or whatever. I don't know where either of them is or where they will strike again, but I'm supposed to find time to sleep?"

"Your Majesty..." Jon put his hand on Sebastian's shoulder. "Easy, Brother. This is what I mean. You take on too much blame for something you have no control over."

Sebastian's face burned and the familiar etching of scales danced across his hands. He held in a long, deep breath for a moment. "Perhaps you are right. I need sleep before I go completely mad."

"We are all going mad, Your Grace." Jon winked. "Goodnight."

Sebastian turned and then stopped. "Jon, I never thanked you for being there for my family all those years. I am proud to call you my brother. You are truly the best man to rule NorthBrekka when I leave for Adurak."

"I wish you would consider staying. Erras is your home."

The following morning was cool and calm. Sebastian stood on the northern side of the wall and watched the sun break just above the horizon. The smell of meat cooking over fire filled the air. Sebastian wandered through a field and heard the crickets out for their early morning serenade. Meecah sat over the spit, cooking a pair of rabbits. The smell made Sebastian's stomach growl, but his eyes were locked on the fire. His mind played images of Tomas's body, lifeless in the cart on the plains of Torrdale. It was the last time he'd seen his brother's face. He turned to see Dani sitting close to

Meecah, peering up with his sapphire eyes every so often. Dani's face was pale, and he didn't smile much on this return journey.

Sebastian watched Dani tend to Boy as much as he could, making Sebastian wonder what he was going to do with the child. He knew Boy would only be safe in NorthBrekka, and it was the best chance he had at a better life.

Sebastian knelt down next to his husband and wrapped his arms around his shoulders. He placed his mouth against Dani's earlobe. "I love you," he whispered.

Dani turned his body to face Sebastian. "Are you angry with me? For bringing Tomas back. I swear I didn't know."

"I know, my darling. I know. I am not angry with you. I fear for the way your heart must feel." He held Dani's cheeks in his palms. "I will fix this."

"No." Dani sat up straight. "Let me put Tomas back to rest. It is my fault."

"Dani—" Sebastian started, but was interrupted.

"Hungry?" Meecah pushed food into their hands. "Eat. Even gods and necromancers need nourishment."

Dani gasped. "I am not a—"

"Just eat." Meecah returned to passing food out to the others.

"Am I not?" Dani looked at Sebastian.

Sebastian shrugged. "Just eat." His eyes darted to Dani, then back to his plate. "No. You are a Blackbird. You were gifted with a peculiar gift. Now we have to figure out how to control it."

"We?" Dani let out a nervous laugh. "Me. I have to figure this out. Maybe Barron can help me. He seems to have figured his powers out."

Sebastian looked over his shoulder. "Yeah, he was always smarter than me." He watched Barron slowly make his way to a place to sit down. "He is not looking so well these days."

A few days passed as Sebastian made his way through the break and landed on the castle grounds. As Amara stood in the doorway, Sebastian clenched his jaw and thought about how to explain Tomas to her, but as he got close, a maiden appeared behind her, holding a little girl.

"Welcome home, Amara." Sebastian kissed her on the cheek and stared at the child with a smile growing across his mouth as her face reflected Tomas's.

"She looks just like you. Well, Tomas, but you know what I mean." Amara's cheeks turned bright red.

Sebastian felt the soft skin of the child's cheek. A tuft of dark hair twirled on the top of her head and her eyes were blue like Amara's. "She was born in Icefall. I waited until it was safe before I made the journey back here with her." She paused for a moment. "Her name is Liliana." Amara reached her hand up to Sebastian's chin.

Sebastian opened his mouth to speak, but saw Nadya burst through the door.

"This just came for you, Sebastian. The courier said it was urgent." Nadya handed him a roll of parchment, then scooped up baby Liliana in her arms. "You should rest, Amara." She ushered Amara inside, then stepped back down the steps. "The courier said a young man from Oyster Cove passed the letter on to him. They said it was from a massive ship with sails that looked like wings." She looked around at the others. "What was he talking about? Sebastian?"

Sebastian stared at the scroll until Dani took it from his hand. "Nadya. We need to talk about what has happened."

Nadya's jaw clenched. "This is about Tomas, isn't it?"

Sebastian looked at Dani, then back to Nadya, and opened his mouth, but Dani set his hand on his arm.

"It's my fault." Dani cleared his throat and spoke louder. "My powers..."

"Tomas isn't Tomas, anymore." Sebastian interrupted. "He is Hydros, his god form."

Nadya stared back and forth for a moment. "So Dani used his Blackbird powers to bring Tomas back to life?"

Sebastian bit his lip and nodded. "I am going to take care of this and bring our brother home once and for all."

Nadya stared at Dani without speaking as he explained how he was the last person alone with Tomas before the undertakers placed him in his tomb. She sighed at the end. "I am not upset with you, Dani. You are still learning. However, I feel like we shouldn't make this information public. The townspeople will fear him."

"They already fear him!" Sebastian's face got hot.

Dani cleared his throat even louder, broke the seal, and unrolled the page. "You can find all the answers you seek at the place where the blood moon brings the tide." Dani flipped the parchment over in his hand. "It doesn't say who it was from."

"Hydros," Sebastian mumbled. "Have everyone gather in the great hall." Sebastian took the parchment from Dani. He marched into the castle.

Maidens and guards hopped out of the way as Sebastian stormed across the hall and down the stairway that led to the burial tombs. He threw open the oaken doors, marched across a corridor, then stopped suddenly. He squeezed his eyes closed and touched the plaque that read *Cyrus Bolin*. His hand slid across the stone as he continued walking. Sebastian's steps slowed when he reached a pile of rocks scattered across the floor. He picked up something shiny in the rubble and turned it over in his hand. "His Royal Majesty, Prince Tomas Ivan Drake," he read aloud.

Sebastian bent over and stared into the void in the wall. The tomb still sat on its platform, yet the broken crypt was empty. He fell to his knees and stared at the hollow space, then glanced at the waiting space next to Tomas's. He turned to face his father's tomb. "I'm sorry, Father. One day, I will make this right." He looked up and down the corridor. "I have to make everything right."

He slowly ascended the stairs and pushed the door closed. Sebastian turned and stumbled backward. "Boy ... what are you doing?" He clutched his chest.

"Island." Boy stared at Sebastian.

"Island?"

Boy lowered his head. "King Maxen said something about finding the island..."

"Boy!" A voice echoed from the hall. "Boy!" Nadya came around the corner. "Oh, there you are. Don't bother the king. Go and sit down and have something to eat with the other children."

"Wait," Sebastian said. Boy disappeared around the corner. "He was trying to tell me something, Nadya." His face got hot. "I think he's telling me where to find Maxen."

"That child has been through a lot and needs rest. He has no idea what he is saying." Nadya adjusted Sebastian's coat buttons. "Everyone is waiting for your big announcement." She jerked her head toward the great hall. "Come on."

"Nadya." Sebastian stopped her. "I need to ask you a favor. I need you to care for Boy. Maybe try to find him a family. He has no one. He knows Dani as his brother, but his father was the man Dani was forced to live with when his father sold him." He paused for a moment. "Can you care for Boy, please?"

Nadya nodded. "Of course. He will be well cared for here. But do we really have to call him Boy?"

"Long story." Sebastian nudged her arm and led the way to the noise coming from ahead.

The great hall echoed with chatter and the shuffle of cooks hauling trays of food and treats from the kitchens. As Sebastian entered the room, the voices silenced and the cooks halted. Sebastian rolled his eyes when everyone bowed as he passed. Dani sat with a smirk next to Barron, who held his wine cup to his lips with an eyebrow raised as his gaze remained on Sebastian. Sebastian ran his hand across the king's table as he walked to his seat. The rough wood comforted Sebastian in a way he didn't understand.

The crowd was filled with solemn faces. Sebastian opened his mouth and then closed it again. He let out a deep sigh and rested his knuckles against the tabletop. "I don't really know how to explain what happened to Tomas—"

"Is he really alive?" Amara asked.

"He's not alive, so to speak." Sebastian glanced at Dani. "Tomas is no longer the Tomas we knew. He is Hydros, the Heir of Litha, and nothing more. He doesn't see us as his kin. He sees us as his enemy." Sebastian walked around the table and to the middle of the room. "Many years ago, I had a conversation with my father. It was just after I discovered my powers, and he begged me to never use them to harm my own brothers or sisters." He turned to Barron and then back to the crowd. "Once Tomas discovered his powers, my father told him the same thing. Tomas's intent in Safareen was to kill me. The Tomas I knew never would have lifted a hand in battle. But this man is not Tomas. He is not my brother. And I will face him in battle once I find where he is hiding."

"The island," Boy shouted.

Sebastian spun around and marched over to the child and grabbed him by the arm. He knelt down and put his hands on Boy's shoulders. "What island?"

Boy shrugged. "King Maxen called it Hast."

"How do you know Tomas is there?"

"Because," Boy said.

"They're working together." Sebastian rushed away from the hall.

"Sebastian!" Dani came running down the corridor. "Where are you going?"

Sebastian stopped and waited for Dani to catch up. "I don't really know. I just need to get out of there before anyone asks me questions I cannot answer."

"I'm afraid I have a question." Dani lowered his head.

"My darling." Sebastian lifted his chin.

"How do you know that island is where they went?"

Sebastian shook his head. "I don't. But if Boy learned about Hast by Maxen, then that could explain why no one in Erras has seen him. But either way, they were on that ship together."

"So this means you are going to sail to Hast."

"Yes, my love. I have to." He paused for a moment. "Only problem is, I have no idea where Hast is."

Over the next few weeks, Sebastian sent crow after crow to Candor, demanding his presence in NorthBrekka. He waited on castle grounds morning and night. He rode through the woods and mountain passes patiently waiting for a sign, a crow, or a person to come. One night, he stood in the courtyard and watched the stars in the clear night of the full moon. Bats circled above the tree line, catching bugs and fluttering their wings against the gentle breeze.

On an early summer morning, Sebastian marched to the stables to take his horse out for a run of the territory. The blacksmith, Mikhail, sat on a wooden bench, looking out towards the arena. His shoulders bounced with every laugh. Sebastian stepped softly along the freshly swept stable floors and past the forge to join Mikhail at the doorway. In the arena, Valirus waved his arms wildly and shouted at a red-faced Dani.

Mikhail's head turned up, then he jumped from his seat. "Your Majesty!"

Sebastian waved his hand and gestured to the bench. "Relax. What is going on over there?"

"Please have my seat, My King." Mikhail bowed.

Sebastian stepped closer to the rocky pathway that led to the arena. He looked back at Mikhail. "Come get a better look if you'd like." He jerked his head and started down the road. Mikhail rushed to catch up. They stopped at the ledge that looked over the archery arena where Dani was resting his forehead against a post while Valirus leaned against the wall next to him saying, "You are being lazy" and "If you don't practice, you will kill everyone."

Sebastian laughed and leaned over the rail. "He said the same thing to me, my darling. Don't let him get in your head."

Valirus's head shot up. "Quiet down or go away, Your Majesty."

"That is very rude." Sebastian crossed his arms. "How do you propose to train Dani how to kill people, Valirus?"

"Simple." Valirus pushed away from the wall and moved to the middle of the arena, letting out a trill from his lips. "While you have been losing your mind over the last few weeks, scanning maps, waiting for letters, and running dangerously through the mountains, you seemed to have missed a very important arrival."

From the tunnels across the arena, human forms appeared in the sunlight. A smile twitched across Sebastian's lips as he hurried down to the arena floor. "All this time"—he jaunted down the steps—"months of waiting"—he stamped across the grounds and reached his arm out in acceptance of another—"you couldn't return a letter, Uncle?"

"You should know that I am not one for writing." Candor wrapped his arms around Sebastian's shoulders.

Valirus appeared at Sebastian's side. "Candor and the coven are here for more than one reason. We need to find Hast, but also, we need their help teaching Dani."

Sebastian opened his mouth to speak, then closed it again. Valirus raised an eyebrow and Candor wore a smirk. Sebastian turned back to Dani. "Why am I always the last to know anything that happens around here?"

"Because you are always disappearing before anyone can talk to you." Dani made his way over to Sebastian and took his hand. "They arrived early this morning."

"I see that," Sebastian said. "I need to know how to find Hast. I fear Maxen and Tomas are working together."

"So I have heard, Nephew." Candor turned his sights on Dani. "As for you ... This will be challenging."

Valirus grasped Sebastian by the arm and pulled him away. "Let him work."

Candor reached into his satchel, and in his grip appeared a small yellow bird. The bird cheeped as it perched on the edge of Candor's index finger. He stretched his arm toward Dani. "I will not allow you to test your powers on humans."

"I am not going to kill that bird." Dani interrupted.

"Why do you worry?" Candor replied. "You are both death and life. With your powers, you could keep everyone you love alive for eternity if you want." His eyes flashed to Sebastian, then back to Dani.

"What I did to Tomas—"

"Was because you did not know what you were doing." Candor stroked the bird's head. "That is what this test is about. You will end the bird's life, then I will give you the chance to bring it back the right way."

Dani's jaw tightened as he focused on the bird. "I'm sorry," he whispered. He reached his hand outward until his fingers barely graced the bird's golden feathers. Sebastian's heart beat fast, but his eyes never broke away from seeing Dani clear his throat and squeeze his eyes closed before releasing a deep breath. Dani's skin turned pale as a ghost with a bluish-gray blush across his cheeks. The bird let out a peep and then fell backward into Candor's waiting hands.

The coven was quiet. Not one moved, and all their heads were aimed at the little bird who lay on its back, lifeless and waiting for Dani's touch again. His color returned and his eyes were blue once more.

"This time," Candor said, "I don't want you to think of anything sad. Think about what makes you the happiest. Something you want more than anything in the whole world. Pretend it is in arm's reach, only you cannot seem to get it, so you want it more and more until you tear yourself apart to hold it in your hands."

Sebastian lifted his chin slowly to see shimmering sapphire eyes staring back. Without a word escaping his lips, Sebastian mouthed, "I love you."

Dani gasped, then his skin turned white again. His gaze never left Sebastian as he turned his body back toward the bird. Even Dani's breaths were heavy and troubled, then rosiness returned to his cheeks, and he looked as if his mind had traveled to another world. Dani seemed lost in a trance, then he looked down at the bird. His fingers touched the tips of its beak and Dani closed his eyes while a smile rested on his face.

Sebastian stepped forward to see, waiting for a chirp and little feathery wings to pop open with life. The bird's mouth trembled and opened, and a foot twitched.

"Think, Dani." Candor chanted. "What do you want the most?"

Dani looked at Sebastian again. "You." He smiled. "It has always been you, Sebastian." A tear ran down his cheek.

There was a gasp from a lady in the witch camp. Sebastian's focus broke and he looked down at the yellow bird whose wings had suddenly begun turning black. "Dani," he said. But Dani did not answer. "Dani?" His head shot up. "Candor, what is happening?"

Blood ran from the bird's tiny eyes. There was a terrible squeak and the bird turned to ash in Candor's hands.

Dani fell to the ground and crawled into a ball. "I told you I did not want to do it!"

Sebastian pulled up him into his arms. "It's alright, my love. You can try again."

"I said I don't want to."

"Dani." Sebastian held him closer.

Valirus stood between them. "Stop this at once, Dani. Do not let it consume you."

Dani's eyes turned milky and his skin paled. "Why does everyone keep telling me what to do?" Dani's voice was monotonous and slow, almost eerie in the still air. Sebastian began to choke and fell to the ground. Dani squeaked, "My Sebastian!" He struggled to take a steady breath. "Did I hurt you?"

Valirus smacked Dani with his staff. "If you weren't my own kin, I would cast you out."

"I'm sorry!" Dani slipped out of Sebastian's grip. "I don't know why this keeps happening." His breaths became heavy again. Sebastian sat up and assured Dani he was alright.

Dani's shivered and he backed away shaking his head. "I can't do this, Sebastian. This power scares me. It is a horrible burden."

Sebastian stood and saw Candor making his way over. "Can you help him, Uncle?"

Candor shook his head. "I am not very good with dark magic, but I believe my Frey could do him justice." He turned and waved his hand at a maroon-painted wagon sitting behind the crowd.

Frey found his way to Sebastian's side. "I understand you are still focused on getting to Maxen and your twin first, but you have to prepare. It is a long journey ahead, and you and your armies cannot fathom what you will find in Hast. Understand that Dani's training is priority one. Maxen will have everything he needs to not only kill your soldiers, but Dani, and most importantly, you." Frey took Sebastian's hand in his. "He has the Oscura. It is the only thing that can kill you besides time itself."

"What about Hydros?" Sebastian clenched his jaw.

"There is more bad news." Frey shook his head and cleared his throat. "You must leave your twin to Dani. Dani brought him back, therefore Hydros is not living, nor dead. You, Your Majesty, cannot kill something that lingers in the in-between. Only Dani can. That is why his training is most important."

Dani blushed and the tip of his nose turned red before a heavy tear dripped down to his chin. His watery eyes flashed at Sebastian, then to Frey. "Whatever it takes. But when this is over, I will never use my powers again." His eyes darted back to Sebastian. "Never again. Do you understand?"

Sebastian simply nodded. He took a deep breath and looked around the arena. "Any more bad news while I am still standing here?"

Frey let out a hefty laugh. "Not for now."

Sebastian nodded, then kissed Dani's forehead before walking toward the steps. He grabbed the stable worker by the arm and climbed back toward the stables.

Chapter Eleven

The Return of a Witch

The summer solstice arrived and the morning was already unusually warm and bright without the sight of a single cloud in the sky. The sun barely poked over the East Bay Mountain Pass as Sebastian watched from the war room terrace. He planned to take Dani and ride out early before anyone else awoke, but Nadya was one step ahead. The night before, the people who remained living in Torrdale arrived at Castle Drake with fresh kills ready to prepare for the feast.

The people from The Far North had traveled the long journey to NorthBrekka the morning before, bringing musicians, dancers, and enchanters from Sedda. All the north was already awake and decorating the towns, the castle, and all in between with banners and announcements of a great celebration in the castle halls. A ball for all to come. Sebastian did not argue but refused to be any part of the mayhem that encompassed his home until he would be physically dragged to the great hall.

After breakfast, Sebastian made his way out into the gardens where the coven had set up camp. A loud racket came from the pond where men were working to repair the broken rocks. He smelled the sweet scent of cooked meat and heard the crunch of footsteps on the rocky ground.

"Tomas did that, a long time ago." Barron stopped next to Sebastian with a biscuit and a fistful of bacon. "He is very powerful. I don't know why it has taken them so long to fix it." Barron paused and watched the workers fight the fresh snow melt that overflowed from the pond and the shifting broken rocks. "And since he is no longer Tomas, he doesn't have emotion to keep him from using his full potential against you." Barron shook his head. "I recommend that you embrace becoming Chaos. Let Sebastian go and rest for a while."

Sebastian sighed deeply but did not speak. He kept his gaze on the pond as his feet carried him toward Candor and Frey, who were watering the flowers around the bench where Shauni had given birth to the twins. His fingers graced the iron back that was carefully crafted with intricate iron vines.

Frey's head shot up and a smile widened across his mouth. "My wonderful boys."

"I wouldn't say either of us could be considered wonderful." Barron sat down on the bench.

"On the contrary." Frey raised one finger in the air. "The two of you are quite perfect, in your own way."

Sebastian sat next to Barron, and Candor leaned on the nearby tree. Sebastian shifted in his seat. "Candor, tell me about Hast."

"No ordinary ship can sail to Hast, for it is surrounded by storm, raging sea, and jagged rocks." Candor's voice was soothing and melodic. "It is shaped like a serpent, with towns trickling across its body and a big tower right along the neck. The rest is too cold for anyone to live."

"If it's so dangerous and difficult to sail to and from, how did you return from there?" Sebastian interrupted. "You told me you came from Hast."

"Yes." Candor hung his head. "I was a prisoner there. I was at sea with a Safarian crew and we crash-landed into the rocks that surround the island. The people of Hast are odd, but very serious about their privacy. They will attack without asking questions. I stole a ship that was just finished loaded with supplies and waited for the right time, when the tide was high enough. I sailed in hopes of finding my way home one day. Took me a while, but I made it."

Music filled the castle as the sun began to fall below the mountains. Sebastian stood before a mirror, admiring the clothes the Sinook had tailor-made especially for him.

"Your Majesty." The tailor bowed. "May I suggest something?"

"Of course." Sebastian narrowed his eyes.

"Smile." The tailor lowered his head again. "The outfit is fierce. It is dark and intimidating, like you. But, a smile will show them that you are confident." The tailor backed away and left the room.

Sebastian spun around and stared at his reflection. His fingers ran across his braided hair and down his scruffy cheek. The collar of his coat was crisp and black, with thin, shining trim that coiled into dragons intricately stitched on the cuffs. Sebastian fidgeted with the devilish attire until the door creaked open. He watched Dani slip through the door, wearing deep blue silk that reflected silver in the candlelight. His heart thumped and butterflies filled Sebastian's stomach as he turned quickly and ran to meet Dani, kissing his lips without a word first.

Dani laughed and stepped back. "Sebastian, you look incredible." His face went serious. "Well, you always look incredible to me, but—"

"Thank you, my darling." Sebastian walked over to a box on the edge of the bed. "You look beautiful. Come here. I have a gift for you."

Dani blushed and approached the bed.

"You are my husband and you don't have a proper crown." Sebastian opened the box. "So I had one made for you. Together, Dani, we are more powerful than anyone on this earth." He pulled a silver-enlaced crown covered in shimmering gems. "There are over two thousand diamonds on this crown. I wanted it to reflect the perfect beauty of its intended owner."

Dani's mouth dropped open and his eyes darted to the crown, then back to Sebastian. A tear formed in the corner of his eye. His hand slowly reached out, shaking gently as it rested against the silver.

"Let me put it on you." Sebastian took the crown and walked Dani to the mirror. He reached the crown out and rested it on top of Dani's head. The diamonds twinkled under the chandelier's firelight.

"It's incredible." Dani reached up to touch the crown. His eyes darted to Sebastian. "When did you have time to do this? I mean, I love it, thank you, but you have been so . . ."

"Unbearable? Mean?"

"Distant." Dani touched Sebastian's cheek. "I started to wonder if you were happy."

Sebastian pulled Dani against him. "I will always be happy as long as I have you."

Music echoed down the corridors. There was a knock at the door and two guards entered the room. They stood aside and waited for Sebastian to make way to the great hall. The walk seemed to take longer than usual. Sebastian topped his crown upon his head and checked his hair again, but he couldn't help but take subtle glimpses at Dani. They settled before the door as the usher hurried inside and called for the attention of the room. The music silenced and the people moved to the side.

"His Royal Majesty, King of Kings, Sebastian Drake."

The doors opened wide and Sebastian led the way with Dani's arm locked with his. As he caught glances into the eyes of his people, he saw a tall blonde in a green gown running toward him, wearing a lovely smile on her face. "Nadya" was all he could say before she wrapped her arms tight around his neck.

"Happy birthday, Brother." She kissed Sebastian's cheek.

"As always, you did a wonderful job with the festivities."

"You deserve the best. Even if you hate it." She turned to Dani. "Your new crown is magnificent." She slipped back to Jon and her children at their seats near the king's table.

Viktor came quickly from behind and embraced Sebastian in a hug. "Happy birthday." He leaned in close. "I can make it more exciting if you want."

"More exciting?"

"Jace and I bought fireworks from a foreign trader in Oyster Cove. We have been saving them for a special occasion." Viktor winked.

Sebastian shrugged. "Don't let Nadya catch you."

Jace and Dom joined his side as Sebastian arrived in the ballroom to see that the coven's music had livened the room as people from all over Erras and Midrel Istan danced. Sebastian held Dani tight as they whisked across the ballroom floor. His gaze never left the sapphire of Dani's irises staring back at him.

Before the feast began, Sebastian stood at the front of the room with a goblet in his hand. "Ladies and gentlemen," his voice raised. "Good people of the north. I have some . . . news to share."

There was the sound of a gust of wind. The candles extinguished quickly, leaving the room dim. The doors opened and smoke filled the hall. Sebastian heard cackling creeping through the fog, and the *tap tap tap* of heeled shoes on stone made him wince. "I know that laugh," Sebastian mumbled as he met eyes with Dani.

"She's back." Dani let go of Sebastian's hand and rushed toward the intruder.

A hand gripped Sebastian's arm too tight. The clenched jaw and narrowed eyes Jace wore at that moment were hiding a scared and angry quiver that flicked across his chin.

"Jace . . ." Sebastian snapped in front of his face.

The room silenced and Dani stopped in time for the smoke to wisp away, revealing long and wavy blue hair and a menacing smile. Dani stared down at his sister. "How dare you come back here. He trusted you."

Petra's eyes shot from Dani to Sebastian. "Well, we have always had a special relationship."

Jace's fingers dug into Sebastian's bicep. "Tell me what's happening."

Sebastian ripped his arm free and marched across the hall. "How long have you been lying to us?" He stopped a mere foot from her position. "Answer me. Now." His body grew tense and a familiar burn filled his chest. Sebastian tilted his head and snarled. He thrust his arm forward and wrapped his hand around her throat. "How long?" His voice echoed down the corridors.

"The whole time," Petra whispered. "You didn't break my curse, Sebastian. My powers aren't a curse—I am a witch. I was born with my powers. You merely broke my father's hold."

"Why?" Sebastian loosened his grip. "We took care of you. We gave you a life free of Maxen's tyranny, and you betrayed us."

"Are you saying that you actually trusted me, my sweet king?" Petra turned her attention away. "Jacey, my sweet baby." She walked toward him slowly. "I really did love your beautiful face."

"Why are you here?" Sebastian interrupted.

"I'm delivering a message from my father." She reached into her satchel and pulled out a letter. Her eyes shifted to Jace. "I'm sorry Jace. You were wonderful while it lasted."

"Petra, wait!" Jace knocked over a chair and stumbled across the floor to where Sebastian stood. "There is no future for you with your father, nor Hydros. Please stay."

Petra frowned, then broke out in a giggle. "My handsome knight. You will be my greatest loss." She reached over to Sebastian. "Even more than losing this one."

"We?" Sebastian said. "We were never a thing."

"Sure, sure." Petra backed away. "Read the letter."

"You won't win. I will end your father, then Hydros. They cannot defeat me."

Petra's hand shot out in front of her, revealing a black jeweled ring. "I think they have the one thing they need to kill the Heir of Dragon."

"The Oscura." Dom clenched Sebastian's shoulder.

"Sebastian shouldn't leave something with this much power lying around while he is bathing." Petra stroked the ring. "The Dragon-killing stone." She cackled and walked backward.

"No! Don't let her leave," Sebastian shouted. Soldiers rushed into the great hall.

"Oh, that's cute." Petra taunted.

The men charged for her.

Petra laughed and blew a kiss at Sebastian. She clapped her hands twice. A bright glowing light filled the hall. Then Sebastian saw her silhouette disappear as a pop echoed in the hall. The candles relit and the fireplaces flicked with fires once more. The soldiers tumbled to the floor. Sebastian rubbed his forehead and stared at the letter. Dani reached for it, but Sebastian pulled it away.

"Not here." Sebastian looked at Jace. "Gather the Order in the war room. Bring Candor and Frey. Have word sent to King Lucian that we will set sail for Hast before the winter." He made his way over to Nadya. "I apologize. Please commence the ball. Begin the feast. We will be along after we discuss this letter."

"Don't worry about the people. Feed them and they will forget what just happened." She winked. "Is everything going to be alright?" Her eyes were soft and her lips pouted just a bit. "My whole world is in this castle. Everything. I know you are going to war. I know my brothers, my husband . . . they will follow you. I just have to know that you will do everything to make sure my whole world doesn't come to an end."

Sebastian's stomach wrenched and his heart thumped. He swallowed the lump in his throat. "You are not losing anyone else." He kissed Nadya's forehead and left the great hall with haste.

The war room filled with the Order. Dani's eyes were wide and he spoke fast. "Dom, how does that stone kill Sebastian? He used to wear it all the time and it never hurt him."

Dom sighed. "There is a spell that only the Heir of Litha can speak in order for it to be deadly. If Petra takes it back to Hydros, then he will be able to use it against you."

"The stone is cracked, therefore unpredictable." Sebastian paced back and forth.

Frey put his hand on Sebastian's shoulder. "That only means it is more dangerous." He took a seat. " It could only kill you, or it could wipe out an entire kingdom. Either way, you allowed it to get into the wrong hands."

"I was naïve to think that no one would steal it." Sebastian rubbed his forehead. He looked up at Valirus, who had his arms crossed and a scowl on his face. Sebastian sighed. "I know, I know. I am an idiot."

"Stupid, boy." Valirus smacked him on the forearm with his staff. "You just gave them everything they need to win this war."

"This war is not just Hydros and me. Maxen will have armies by the thousands at his disposal that will be ready to burn down every last man, woman, and child in the world." Sebastian looked around at all the staring faces in the room. "We are all at war. Everyone."

Dani slipped the letter from Sebastian's hand. "Let's begin with this." He popped open the seal and unfolded the parchment. His chest rose and fell with a deep breath. "Your Majesty, King Sebastian. I invite you to Hast to surrender yourself. On the night of the blood moon, the tide is high and any ship can sail the rigid path through the tower of broken statues. If you refuse, all you have fought to protect will be massacred. Don't be late." Dani folded the letter and dropped it onto the table. "He just gave you the key to sailing to Hast. Why would he do that?"

Sebastian stared at the letter. "It doesn't matter. I'm going."

"When is the blood moon?" Dani said.

"Two weeks before the winter solstice." Candor stood from his chair. "Maxen is right. The tide is unusually high on the blood moon. Sometimes the streets of Hast become flooded. Your Majesty, he has the Oscura. He is baiting you into a trap."

"I know what he is doing. He thinks the sight of Tomas will weaken me. Litha once tried to use the Oscura to kill Dragon, but she couldn't go through with it, so she hid it. Tomas and Sebastian, Hydros and Chaos. Either way, we are still twins, and I can feel Hydros in my heart. He fears the stone as much as Litha did."

"My father can control his mind." Dani's eyebrows raised. "He could be already."

Sebastian stared at every map of the world he could find, with none showing Hast. "I don't even know where to find this place."

"All you have to do is sail east," Candor said. "But if you want a map, you can find one in Oyster Cove. They have every map of the whole world you could ever want."

"That's true." Jace picked a large map from the pile and looked it over. "All ships eventually come through Oyster Cove at some point, from everywhere in the world. The Harbor Master always collects maps as new ships arrive."

"The Hetta is in Oyster Cove for repairs and the harbor master said it would take a few months to gather the wood to fix the hull" Sebastian backed away from the table and looked out over the valley. "Jace, once the fall passes, you will take a crew to East Bay. The lot of you will take the ghost ships to Oyster Cove. I will ride to the harbor and board the Hetta. Then we sail to Hast."

CHAPTER TWELVE

The Red Moon

The morning before his departure to Oyster Cove, Sebastian sat alone in his office while most of the others enjoyed a nice day before the winter came. The sound of a crying baby came from down the corridor before a knock rapped against the door.

Amara slipped through the door. "Can I talk to you?"

"You shouldn't need to ask." Sebastian stood and walked over to her. He stared at the baby and then back at Amara. Without a word, he pulled them into his chest and held Amara's head against him. "You don't deserve this life. You deserve better."

She pulled away and smiled. "We are exactly where we are supposed to be. Life will get better when you finish this nonsense." She sat on the couch and stroked the baby's head. "Why do men go to war?" Amara laughed and met Sebastian's stare. "Because men are like wolves. They only know how to hunt, make babies, and protect their territory. When you face him..." She held her baby close against her. "Just make it quick so we can mourn for him properly."

"I will. I promise. I won't let them get to you. To any of you." Sebastian stroked his fingers across the baby's cheek. "Can I hold her?"

Amara's eyes filled with tears as she passed the child over. "Careful."

"Do you think I have never held a baby?"

Amara tilted her head. "When have you held a baby?"

"I used to have siblings that were small children."

"Barron killed them." Amara's voice was low and remorseful for mentioning the little one's deaths.

Sebastian clenched his jaw. "He ordered men to do it. But yes."

"Why do you trust him now?

Sebastian took a deep breath and sighed. "Because he is meant to serve me. He will pay for his crimes. Some day."

"Come home, Sebastian." Tears fell from Amara's eyes. "At least my daughter can grow up knowing what her father looked like. Even if he is just a story to her." Amara took her daughter back and started toward the door. "I love you, Brother." She winked and left the office.

The following morning was bitter and snow clouds were on the horizon. Sebastian mounted his horse alongside Dani, Jon, Valirus, and a group of soldiers. Candor joined the group and Sebastian nodded to Frey, who had promised to keep watch over the castle grounds in his absence. They took to road into the forest, across the town, and into the valley before reaching Sun Shadow late the next evening.

It was silent. Even in normal conversation, the soldiers' voices were low. The fires flicked embers into the sky and kept the camp warm in the prairies south of NorthBrekka. Sebastian laid back against a stump with Dani resting against his chest. Valirus smoked a pipe with Jon. Candor scribbled in his journal, causing Sebastian to narrow his eyes for a moment.

"What are you writing?" Sebastian stared at Candor's fast-moving quill strokes.

"Everything." Candor stopped writing and searched his bag until he pulled out a new ink well. He pressed the tip of the quill to his tongue, then dipped it in the ink. "Your journey, Nephew. It is worth writing into history." He turned to a clean page. "You are the last dragon god. This war will scar our nations in a way our future generations could not possibly understand unless I write it down as it happens." He began to write again.

Dani wrapped Sebastian's arm around him. "He's right. It is important for the people who live on after us to know what molded them into the society they live within." He turned to look at Sebastian. "You are Chaos, and your legend will live on, forever." Dani laughed. "Whether you like it or not."

Sebastian smiled, closed his eyes, and leaned back. "Why doesn't everyone try to get some rest? We arrive in Oyster Cove in a few days' ride, then we sail for Hast."

A cold, rainy night rolled across Blackport Bay as Sebastian and company rode into the harbor town on the tip of the peninsula. The glow from the lanterns along the long pier where the Hetta sat waiting for its long journey to Hast. Along the boardwalk, where shops and cafes had already closed for the night, were drunken sailors and townsfolk crossing the path to homes, bars, and alleyways between buildings. Music came from a sizeable tavern on the bay as Sebastian passed by on his way to the large manor in the center of town where the City Master lived.

Jace met them on the road and took the lead. "The others have not arrived yet. I left the harbor in East Bay early. The others will be here by time to sail." He marched up the steps to the sea-battered oak door to his family home. He glanced over his shoulder at Sebastian, then grasped the knocker and pounded it against the wood three times. Locks shifted and bolts creaked as the door gently opened. A young girl appeared, smiled, and then jumped into Jace's arms. "Hello, sweet Sister." Jace squeezed her tight. "Is Father home?"

She nodded fast. "He is expecting you." Her hands began to shake when she saw Sebastian. "And him. I mean, Your Majesty."

"Thank you." Sebastian reached for her hand. He leaned over and kissed the tip of her knuckle. "You are all grown up."

Magdeline blushed and curtsied. "Your soldiers." She looked around the crowd. "There is room at the inns. There is room for the few of you here."

Sebastian walked over to Valirus. "Go on. Take the others and get some food and sleep. We are safe here tonight."

"My brother has struck Oyster Cove before." Valirus scanned the town and noticed the town folks nearby, watching them. "They are scared. This town has no defenses against an attack. Us being here is dangerous for them."

"Lay low. Stay inside. Eat and go straight to bed. All of you." Sebastian started to back away. "We still need a map to Hast. It is here in Oyster Cove. I will get the location from Jace's father."

"He doesn't like you." Valirus crossed his arms.

"I don't care." Sebastian turned and walked to the house. He was the last through the door when Magdeline closed it. Sebastian watched her crank a wheel that braced a bar against the wrung that connected to the locks.

She closed the curtains tight and took a lantern from the table. "Follow me, Your Grace."

They walked through a massive family room with cozy-looking couches in front of a roaring fire. In the dining room, a table large enough for a small army lay perfectly placed as the crystal glasses twinkled under the candlelight. The ornate windows overlooked the bay, where Sebastian saw Dani sitting on a windowsill, watching the lighthouse signaling boats coming in from a late night at sea.

Down a long hallway, through a decorative archway and two glass doors, was a man sitting at a fantastically handcrafted desk in front of broad windows that overlooked the same view from the dining room, and the others faced the sea. Sebastian looked at paintings of the family over the years until he stopped at the ones where Jace was no longer there.

"Your Majesty," Lord Astra said. "We have much to discuss."

Sebastian sat facing Jace's father. Dani joined them in the room and took a seat by the windows as Jace sat by Sebastian. Magdeline appeared with a kettle and teacups. She poured a cup and handed it to Sebastian, then set a plate of biscuits on the desk. "Dinner soon," she said. "But I thought you would be hungry now." She bowed and went to Dani with another cup. Sebastian took a sip of his tea.

"King Maxen." Lord Astra started. "He came here and destroyed everything. Our markets, the farms . . ."

Sebastian squeezed his eyes shut, remembering how when they first arrived in Oyster Cove, they came directly into the upper district. The outlying areas were gone due to Maxen blasting them to rubble. "He will pay for his crimes against this city. Oyster Cove falls under my protection, and I failed you."

"You were gone!" Lord Astra's voice got louder. "You were gone too long, Your Majesty."

"I had no choice. If I didn't leave, I wouldn't be able to defend this world from Maxen and, now, Hydros." Sebastian raised from his chair. "I am sailing to Hast, but I need something from you. The coven told me this is the only place on earth that has the map."

"Your uncle knows the way." Lord Astra sat back in his chair.

"I want the map." Sebastian gritted his teeth and noticed his golden scales form across his skin.

Lord Astra reached into his desk drawer and pulled out a key. "This is to a lockbox on the market square where the harbor meets the sea. It is at the marina in the Harbor Master's office. I will send word that you are coming in the morning." Lord Astra sat up straight. "I am an old man, Your Majesty. My people rely on you, as much as I hate to admit. But you care about my son, and that means a lot to me." He paused and cleared his throat.

Jace's face lit up and a smile cracked across his serious face.

"Jace is a good boy. Loyal, even to those who don't deserve it. Like his own father." For the first time all night, Lord Astra gently smiled. He turned back to Sebastian. "Make sure my son comes home."

Sebastian reached out to shake Lord Astra's hand. "I am going to end this once and for all. When we leave these shores, you will be at peace. Never again will Erras face the cruelty of Maxen Bolin." Sebastian felt a pit in his throat. "No matter what I have to do." His eyes stared over Lord Astra's shoulder and out the window facing the sea.

"Dinner!" Magdeline popped her head in the doorway. "I heard that you hate fish, Your Majesty, so I had the cook bake chicken instead. I hope that is alright."

Sebastian laughed. "It's perfect, thank you."

They enjoyed a meal as Sebastian was lost eavesdropping on Jace and his father's quiet conversation. Dani chatted with Magdeline about Midrel Istan, and Sebastian enjoyed his meal while staring at the distant light of the torches lit near the Hetta gangway.

The next morning, the sun peaked bright over the sea. Sebastian told Dani he was going to retrieve the map and would meet them back at the house for the breakfast that Magdeline had demanded they stay for. Jace joined him on the road where fishermen were up early, preparing their boats for another day at sea. The seagulls rested on the smooth water's surface and bugs bounced along the bay until fish popped up for their meal.

Sebastian stopped and stared at Jace for a moment. "I know you cared for Petra, and I am sorry it turned out the way it did. I just need to know if your head is in this. I can't lose you, Jace."

Jace bit his lip, then cleared his throat. "She lied to me... She betrayed us. Trust me when I say that I am with you." He gritted his teeth. "I will help you end Maxen's entire dynasty."

"Is it wrong to say that I am relieved?"

"What do you mean?" Jace's eyes grew wide.

Sebastian set his hand on his hip and sighed. "I never trusted her. She may have fooled us, but there was always something off."

"You should have told me!"

"You seemed so happy." Sebastian grabbed Jace by the shoulders. "I thought it was just me. Jace, you are a great man. You can have any woman you want. Petra was not the one for you." He started back on the pathway toward the harbor. "Actually, there is one woman who would love a loyal man to keep her in the comfort she deserves."

Jace followed with raised eyebrows and his head slightly to the side. "Playing matchmaker already, are you, Your Highness?"

"Jace, do you like children?"

Jace narrowed his eyes. "Are you talking about Amara?"

"She would be a good wife to you."

"She is beautiful and kind, but it's too soon for both of us."

Sebastian let out a chuckle. "It will be months before we return home."

Jace smiled. "She might find someone before we return."

"You are ridiculous." Sebastian laughed. "Are you alright? Seriously."

Jace put his arm over Sebastian's shoulders. "Yeah ... I'll be fine."

They walked along the boardwalk to where the piers shot out to the larger boats and ships. Sebastian stopped at the sight of the Hetta being loaded with cargo as the fog settled back out to sea. Jace led them down to the marina where a large house sat at the end of a long fishing pier. He pointed. "That is the Harbor Master's house. His office is right up front. He should be in by now."

Sebastian and Jace walked down the pier, catching the eye of several fishermen that were gossiping—likely about the sailors making too much noise. There was a younger man standing by the railing with no fishing pole, dressed in finer garments one would normally find in Oyster Cove. As they walked further down, there was another. Sebastian furrowed his eyebrows but shook his head and kept walking. They arrived at the white-and-blue-painted front door. Jace knocked. "Harbor Master Hardin." He knocked again. Jace pushed the door open. The lamp in the office was lit, but there was no one inside.

"The lockbox." Jace pointed to a trunk on the floor in front of the desk.

Sebastian took out his key and opened the trunk. There were piles of small folded maps, but one sat in the pile, rolled and twined closed. Sebastian opened it, revealing a large map of a vast ocean extended east from Erras. Nothing more than islands stretched a far distance until the other end of the map where a massive island marked *Hast* lay.

"This is it?" Sebastian looked it over again. "The coven said this map is desired by many. All we have to do is sail east?"

"Ridiculous children's tale of the most sought-after map in the world. People don't sail to Hast because people are afraid of the place." Jace took the map and rolled it tight. "Let's get back before my sister finishes prepping breakfast."

"What's to be afraid of?"

Jace stopped at the door before opening it. "I don't know. No one will tell me. They say to let the place be lost to the rest of us." A rumble in the next room stopped Jace from finishing his speech. "Harbor Master Hardin, is that you?"

A loud rustle filled the hall. Sebastian rushed to the scene where some plates had been knocked off the serving cart. Then, he saw a man on the floor. Jace darted past him and knelt by the man on the floor. A glint of steel caught Sebastian's attention. "Jace, look out!"

A man with a sword appeared in the hall. He swung his sword at Jace's head but was met with Sebastian's blade. It was the face of the young, finely dressed man at the dock. "You," Sebastian grunted and gripped the man's neck. His skin flared with glowing scales and lightning danced across his forearms.

The man laughed and then screams filled the streets. Sebastian ran his sword through the man's heart and ran outside to see the town under siege by mindless soldiers in flashy armor. "Altanians." Sebastian groaned. Jace darted down the pier, shouting that he had to protect his sister. Sebastian's heart sank. "Dani," he mumbled and followed after Jace.

Altanian soldiers chased the townsfolk down the streets. The people jumped onto boats and backed them out of their docks as quickly as they could catch the wind. They came across three soldiers cornering Valirus and Jon. Sebastian conjured flames that danced along his fingertips and formed into fireballs aimed at the soldiers' heads. Jon and Valirus ducked just as a powerful gale slammed the soldiers into the side of a shop and knocked them to the ground.

Down the street, buildings shook and fires erupted. A shop exploded and wood debris scattered and littered the streets. Windows burst, sending shards of glass in every direction. Sebastian saw a pair of burly fishermen locked in a fistfight with two Altanian soldiers. Sebastian hurried in their direction but saw the soldiers gut the men with ease, then continue into the town.

"Is King Maxen here?" Jon asked.

"I'm not sure." Sebastian unsheathed his sword and made his way toward scared and running citizens. "But we have to protect these people first, then we can find out answers to the difficult questions."

Jace took Sebastian's side as they marched down the streets of Oyster Cove and cut down every Altanian in their path. They followed the road until the site of the City Master's mansion came into view. Jace grabbed Sebastian's arm. "T-the d-door," he stuttered.

"Dani!" Sebastian darted to the manor. The door had been broken and kicked in. The house lay in shambles, with paintings and trinkets broken and littered on the floor. The banister was broken away from the stairs and a small fire had formed in the kitchen where a frightened cook hid under the table. Sebastian bent down and addressed the young lady. "Where is the City Master? The others?"

The girl shook her head and cried.

"It will be alright. Come with me." Sebastian reached out his hand, but the girl shook her head again and pointed over Sebastian's shoulder. He turned to see a soldier waiting for him. Their swords clashed loudly in the little kitchen. The soldier kicked Sebastian in the chest, sending him crashing into the table. "Run upstairs and lock yourself in your bedroom," he told the girl. Sebastian climbed to his feet and engaged with the man again. Their blades crossed and collided back and forth. Sebastian shoved his flaming palm into the soldier's chest and sent him into the roaring cooking fire. The soldier shrieked, and Sebastian shoved his blade through the Altanian's open mouth.

He found Jace and followed him up the stairs, throwing open every door. Jace found Magdeline, the young cook, and his father hiding in the study. Sebastian continued down the hall until he came to a locked door. He kicked hard, sending pieces of wood flying as he stepped into the room. Suddenly, the room fell cold as winter, and he saw white glowing eyes and a hand reaching for him. "Dani!"

The room warmed. "Sebastian!" Dani fell into his arms. "I thought you were—"

"I know." Sebastian held him tight. "Your father's soldiers are ripping the city apart."

"What about my father?"

"I don't know yet." Sebastian led Dani to the study. "Listen, everyone." Sebastian closed the door quietly and took a knee. "I am going to lead the people out of the city. Head to NorthBrekka. My sister will house you all while she sends people to repair your home." He peeked out of the window and looked down the main city street. There was no one running, and he could no longer hear screams. "If Maxen is here, I cannot risk the lives of the innocent. Follow me and do not ask questions." His eyes locked on Lord Astra. "No arguing. Let's go."

Sebastian poked his head through the barely opened door that gave view of the hallway to the bedrooms. He listened, but the house was seemingly empty. He flicked his hand for the others to follow and placed his index finger over his lips. They crept down the old staircase with the shattered banister. Broken debris littered nearly every step. Sebastian stepped carefully but others weren't so nimble. "Jace, you sound like an elephant coming down the stairs."

"Sorry." Jace tiptoed the best he could. His heavy feet clopped down every stair until he set foot on the lower floor. They walked outside, realizing the streets were as silent as the house. "Where has everyone gone?" Jace stepped into the street. "Where are our people, Sebastian?"

Magdeline began to sob. "They aren't... dead, are they?" She buried her face in her hands.

"No, of course not, my girl." Lord Astra wrapped his arms around his daughter. "Right, Your Majesty?" He sneered.

Sebastian rubbed his shoulders and followed Jace into the shattered harbor town. "We shall see." He peered through broken windows and opened doors. Jace entered a few shops along the way. They passed from the market square to the larger homes and down to the remainder of the outer city. In the daylight, Sebastian noticed the remnants of where the trade and fish market once sat. The shiplap buildings were gone and the carts of wares were no longer there to greet travelers entering and leaving the city.

All that remained were fence posts and pieces of stone floors. Sebastian stopped and turned to the others, who wore defeated frowns across their faces.

"Maybe they fled to Sun Shadow," Jace said.

Sebastian glanced over his shoulder, then marched back toward the center of the city in the market square.

Dani ran to catch up and grabbed his hand. "What are you doing?" His azure eyes shined under the bright sun.

"Stay close to me, my darling." Sebastian took a deep breath and shouted, "Citizens of Oyster Cove, come forth. You are safe."

"What if the soldiers hear you?" Dani's hand was shaking as it rested against Sebastian's chest.

Before Sebastian could answer, there was a rumble from the next street over. Sebastian and Jace unsheathed their swords and stood before the others. They waited until a young couple came jogging toward them. Then, Valirus and Jon. Sebastian sighed and put his sword away. "Where are the rest of the townspeople?"

Faces popped out from every corner, in windows, and from behind planters. The people of the city joined in the market square. Chatter and questions filled the air. Lord Astra addressed his people while Sebastian paced the area looking for soldiers. Once he'd made his way around, Jace announced Sebastian's plan. "His Majesty, King Sebastian, has graciously offered his homelands to you while Oyster Cove is repaired. Leave everything behind and make way to NorthBrekka immediately."

Jace and Lord Astra immediately broke into deep conversation. Sebastian started walking down the street until he heard Dani shout, "Sebastian, where are you going?"

The town fell silent and their attention turned to their king. Sebastian turned. "I don't have all day. Either you follow me to the edge of Oyster Cove and leave, or you stay here and find out if King Maxen is in the city."

Sebastian led the people to the border of Oyster Cove where the lowlands turned into prairie and rolling hills. He waited for them to meet with the NorthBrekkian soldiers who had come from Sun Shadow to guide the people north.

Sebastian and Dani turned back down the road. "Back to the ship." Sebastian led the way.

"Sails." Jace darted down the street. "It's the others."

Sebastian squinted his eyes until the tattered old sails and mossy ghost ships came clear on the horizon. They crossed the old market and through the housing corridor. They walked along the path to the marina where the Hetta awaited. Sebastian glanced at Dani but was met with three soldiers who burst from the door of a shop. He grasped the hilt of his sword and stepped forward. "Where is your king?" he growled.

The soldiers did not speak. They moved their heads and hands in unison and reached for their swords. "He is controlling them," Dani whispered. Sebastian reached for Dani as he stepped out before a soldier. Dani pushed Sebastian's hand away. "Don't touch me, my love." His eyes turned white and his skin paled. The winds increased with an icy blast as Dani reached his hand forward. The soldier reared his sword back and swung, but froze in place as Dani's hand connected to his cheek.

The soldier shook and fell to his knees. Dani gripped his neck. "Where is my father?" His voice was eerie. Dani's lips turned blue and his skin grayed. "Where is he?" he shrieked.

The soldier jerked violently and screamed, "King Maxen resides in Hast." Then he fell dead at Dani's feet.

The streets filled with Altanian men who all wore the same blank stare with swords in their hands. Sebastian and the others stood with their backs to one another, ready to fight their way to the Hetta. The crash of iron followed by blood splattering the street lasted until the sun began to set. Valirus's staff gave light to the fast-darkening streets and black water as there were no townsfolk to light the torches that night. They cleared the square and followed Jace to the docks.

Past Jace's home was a bright, roaring fire at the marina. Ships blazed violently on the water's surface. The boardwalk to the long pier on the farthest point began to burn. Sebastian urged his people forward before the path fell to ash into the sea below. As they started across the water crossing, they heard footsteps fast approaching from behind. Sebastian spun around to see dozens of Altanian men charging at full speed. "Run." Sebastian's voice was calm but shaky. They darted across the boardwalk until the wood began to shake dangerously from the stomping legion of soldiers behind them.

Sebastian stepped back and peeked over his shoulder at the incoming armada while guarding the others from the soldiers. One of the ghost ships turned toward the bay where he stood. Sebastian smirked and summoned a gust of wind that crashed into the fast moving soldiers, sending them flying back. Sebastian reached his arm to the sky and shouted as a bolt of lightning violently struck the boardwalk in between him and the Altanians.

"Run!" A distant voice came through the storm clouds.

Sebastian turned. "Kristoff?" The ghost ship swung portside, too close to the beach. The ocean floor rumbled as the bottom of the ship scraped the sand. Across Oyster Cove were hundreds of Altanian soldiers pouring through the streets, all sprinting for the boardwalk. Sebastian shoved the others toward the burning water crossing. They dashed through the fire and made their way to the last pier where the NorthBrekkian soldiers waited, firing arrows to protect the ship's crew from the Altanians.

As his people climbed the gangway, Sebastian stopped and turned to the fast-moving soldiers. Then, the ghost ship ruptured to life as a dozen cannons fired on the city. Sebastian boarded the Hetta and brought the wind to the massive black sails.

"A little help, Brother." Kristoff shouted from the starboard side as the Hetta crept to sea. "We kind of got beached saving your lives."

Sebastian laughed and walked to the rear of the Hetta. He raised his arms and stretched forward. His lungs filled with the smell of salt and sea as he filled his chest and released a deep breath. The sea rose along the bay, putting out fires on the harbor and the ships, allowing Kristoff and his ghost ship to escape.

CHAPTER THIRTEEN

The Power of Wind

The Midnight Sea turned from its usual black shade to a deep blue after days of sailing east. There were no signs of land, islands, or life anywhere. Just a choppy, open sea lust with ample wind to carry the ships quickly. Nights had passed before Sebastian spotted a chain of small islands in the near distance. He directed Jace and the crew to anchor nearby as he looked over his map.

"They are unnamed. Perhaps uninhabited." Sebastian boarded the row boats to shore along with Dani and Jace. On the beach, they waited for the Order to join them.

As soon as Kristoff's boots touched the sand, he sprinted to Sebastian. "I've been waiting a week to do this." He embraced his brother in a quick, snug hold.

"You are brilliant." Sebastian playfully pushed Kristoff away.

"Well, technically, it was Viktor's plan. I just executed it."

The rest of the Order encircled Sebastian. Candor stood by Sebastian's side and said, "I suggest we rest here for the night. Catch as much fish as we can store. There is nothing else out there until we reach Hast."

"I agree." Sebastian nodded and told the Order to direct the crew to cast fishing lines and scout the island for water and fruit. "Candor, can I speak with you in private?"

They took a walk into the palm forest as the others started their duties for the evening. Sebastian slowed to address Candor. "Everyone keeps telling me that Hast is unimaginable. That it is unlike anything I could prepare for, but you are the only one who has been there. I have people and loved ones to protect, including you. What are we sailing into, Uncle?"

Candor turned in every direction and glanced up at the sky before squeezing his eyes closed. "Nephew ... you won't understand until you see it. All I can tell you is that you are greatly in danger, and I mean more than the fact that your mortal enemy has the stone that was made by witches to kill you."

"Thanks for the reminder, Uncle." Sebastian rolled his eyes. "I need to know what I am facing so I can train."

Candor's eyebrows raised. "I suggest you practice your water powers, Your Majesty. I know it is your weakest attribute."

The ships and crews departed early the following morning for the long stretch across the open sea. Candor and Dom joined Sebastian on the Hetta to help with training, and Barron boarded to work with Dani.

A few days later, late in the morning, Sebastian lay belly down across the bowsprit and concentrated on the sea as it was cut by the ship's bow. Sebastian jumped when he heard a tap on the deck behind him.

"There is no time to be lazy." Valirus's voice echoed through Sebastian's head. "Get up. You have a lot to learn."

Sebastian growled and crawled back to the deck to join Valirus.

"You're getting a little old to be throwing fits." Valirus swatted him with his staff.

"And you are too old to be picking fights with me." Sebastian unbuttoned his coat and dropped it to the deck. "Alright, I am ready, old man."

Valirus gripped his staff tight and stamped it onto the deck. It sparked and a sharp gust of wind threw Sebastian on his back. "Idiot boy."

"Ouch." Sebastian held his stomach and stumbled to his feet. "That wasn't necessary."

"No," Valirus said. "But it was fun . . . for me."

Sebastian trained for hours over rough seas as he tried to deflect waves from crashing into the ship. His muscles burned and ached with every movement of his arms that broke the water apart, allowing the ship to pass. "I can't do this forever, Valirus."

Candor sat on a crate next to Sebastian and bit into an apple. He looked up at the dark clouds growing above. "You must know that this storm is only the beginning. Wait until we have no wind to push the sails."

Sebastian stopped and stared at Candor. "Did you say no wind? How did you manage to get there with no wind?" The sky darkened and Sebastian threw his hands up in the air. There was a loud rumble and the splash of a wave on the deck. Valirus cursed and scolded him, but Sebastian stared at the wheel where Jace and Dani stood, soaking wet.

"You need to learn to focus!" Valirus finished his rant.

Sebastian ignored him and went back to Candor. "How did you do it? How did you get the Hast without wind?"

Candor scoffed. "I am a witch, Nephew. We have our magic."

"Yes, but you're not very good at it..." Sebastian winked and turned back to the storm that started to calm to a light rain. He flicked his arms out in front of him and directed the wind to push their sails faster into the clearing afternoon sun that lay ahead.

Dom sat with his back against the mast. As the sun began to break through the clouds, he took water to an exhausted Sebastian, who sat down panting in the misty rain. Dom wrapped his arm around Sebastian's shoulders. "I hope you know that you are not in this alone. The Sinook will always serve you. I will always serve you."

"Dom." Sebastian's voice was hoarse. "When this is over, I am returning to Adurak."

"I already know."

"I want you to come with me." Sebastian's heart fluttered and his face flushed. "But... I know you will never leave The Far North."

Dom chuckled. "I want to see this Adurak, but you are right. I won't leave my home. You must promise me that you won't disappear. Erras is still your home."

"How could I ever leave you, Dom? You are my best friend."

The next morning, Sebastian sat up slowly in bed with stiff, sore arms. He reached next to him to feel an empty space where Dani would normally lay. Clothes sat neatly folded on the armchair by the window. Sebastian limped over and pushed open the porthole's curtain to see the sun starting to rise over the ocean ahead of the ship, meaning they were still heading east. He dressed and walked out to the deck where Dani and Barron were discussing something quietly and making hand gestures.

Jace nodded from the wheel. "Good morning, Your Majesty."

Sebastian joined his side. "Have you slept?"

"Yes. I relieved the soldier on duty last night just before those two came out." His eyes gestures across the deck.

Sebastian tilted his head when Dani and Barron took each other's hands. "What are they doing?"

Jace shrugged. "Something about amplifying their powers. I guess it is what the Blackbirds did. I don't know. I stopped listening to Dani after about four words escaped his mouth."

Sebastian sighed and walked down to the deck to watch from a close distance.

Dani picked up an old book and flipped through a few pages. "Here it is. I told you that you were standing wrong." He pushed the book in Barron's annoyed face. "See how the picture shows it?"

"Alright, Dani, I get it." Barron slapped the book away. "To be fair, there are supposed to be more of us."

"What's going on?" Sebastian interrupted.

Dani looked up from the book. "We are trying to learn how to use our powers to help you. This book Barron found in the castle talks about how Dragon's Blackbirds were amplifiers for his power."

"Where did you find this book about Dragon?" Sebastian took it in his hands.

"It was in a trunk in the locked closet in the library." Barron shrugged. "I was curious and got nosey and discovered all kinds of Father's things in there, but that book stood out amongst all."

"Maybe he was learning about Dragon when he found out about my powers." Sebastian looked over at Dani and Barron, who were still practicing their magic. "You two look like you're trying to hold hands." Sebastian laughed. "I'm starting to get a little jealous."

"Disgusting." Barron dropped his hands to his sides.

In the book, there were notes that were labeled *Dragon's Reminders*. He flipped through the pages and read the notes Dragon had added himself. "Who is Ryu?"

"Who?" Dani looked at the book.

"There are notes that mention someone named Ryu being his strongest amplifier."

Dani shook his head. "I have no idea. I assume he was a Blackbird."

"Yes, but which one?" Sebastian thumbed through the pages more but couldn't find any more notes by Dragon.

"No one knows anything about Dragon's Blackbirds outside of what's in this book." Barron paced. "I have looked everywhere for more information. I have talked to the Sinook, King Lucian, even Frey, but the only information anyone knows is about as much as we know."

"And that's barely anything." Sebastian closed the book.

"No, but I do have something for you." Dani took Sebastian's hand and led him to the captain's quarters. "I thought it was time you started dressing like the King of Kings and not the King of NorthBrekka. You no longer rule in the north, my love, you rule over all." He opened a trunk and pulled out pieces of new armor, boots, and a coat.

Sebastian ran his fingers across the rich dark leather. He held the coat up to his nose and took in the scent while admiring the intricate craftsmanship of the black boots. "This is amazing." He looked up at Dani. "You are amazing."

Dani slipped his arms around Sebastian's neck. "You deserve the best of everything. I only wish for you to realize how lucky I am to have you."

Sebastian kissed his lips and laid him on the bed, climbed on top, and cupped Dani's cheek in his palm. "It is I that is lucky."

That afternoon, Sebastian gathered the others and invited them to the captain's quarters to discuss strategy. Candor explained if they took their ships to port in the western harbor, there wouldn't be soldiers posted. "The harbor was devastated in a hurricane and the people decided it wasn't worth it to rebuilding. It is cold in northern Hast. Not many people reside in those parts."

"I'm not afraid of winter." Sebastian nodded. "Continue."

Candor found some parchment and began drawing a map of the route from the north to the tower, marking every populated area and identifying shops they could lay low in if needed. "There is a group of people called the Unrahli. They were the natives before outsiders came. They built the town of Oranu . . . That is, until the gods arrived . . ."

"Wait." Sebastian held up his hands. "The gods? In Hast?"

Candor's face turned red and his eyes widened.

"When were you going to tell me?" Sebastian's voice got loud.

"I wanted you to see it for yourself, Your Majesty. But yes, Hast was named as such because it means 'the Isle of Gods.' The natives called it Na'Huk." Candor hesitated for a moment. "They are not fond of the gods, but they will help us."

"Lovely." Sebastian sat back in his chair. "More people that hate me."

"Yes, but they will choose you over their current option."

"And why is that?"

"Because they know you will leave when you are done." Candor's face was serious, then he cracked a smile.

Nights passed with clear, starry skies and calm seas. Sebastian practiced every waking hour with Valirus, moving the water, breaking the water, freezing the water, and whatever else Valirus shouted for him to stop complaining and do. Sebastian was exhausted. He sat with his back against the railing of the ship and rubbed his sore shoulders.

Valirus sat on the crate and stared with bloodshot eyes. "I know conquering water is not easy for you, but I must say, you are doing remarkably well."

Sebastian lifted his head and narrowed his eyes. "Did you just compliment me?"

Valirus let out a laugh. "There is not much more I can teach you. I believe time will continue to be your teacher from now on."

"But Valirus, I need you."

"I am with you until you win this war and we go home." Valirus crossed his arms. "Then, I believe I would like to retire to my keep in Lastorum, if you don't mind."

"I have decided I will rule from Adurak. It is the only place I feel I belong."

Valirus tilted his head to the side. "What about NorthBrekka, your family, your home?"

"Trust me, Valirus. I will place the crown on Nadya's head and take my rightful place in Midrel Istan. To me, Adurak is my home."

Valirus took a deep breath. "If it is what you want, then so shall it be."

"You sound like you don't want me there?" Sebastian smirked.

Valirus rolled his eyes. "I think you are connected to Adurak in a way you don't quite understand just yet."

"And what does that mean?" Sebastian sat up.

"All in good time, Your Majesty . . . Also, the thought of having you around all the time is exhausting."

The next morning, Sebastian came out from his quarters to a loud and bustling crew. On deck, there was no breeze and no movement of the ship. Sebastian walked over to the railing to see all his fleet were dead in the water, merely bobbing on the glassy surface. "This must be what Candor was telling me about. No wind . . ."

"What are you going to do to fix that, Sebastian?" Jace stepped down from the wheel.

Sebastian raised his eyebrows and looked around at all the staring faces on the deck. "Right, I make the wind . . ."

He hurried to the rear of the ship and stood facing the sea behind him. Off his starboard side were the ghost ships waiting. He climbed to the upper deck, stood upon the aft, and gazed across the deep blue waters of the calm and unstirred ocean. The horizon shimmered under the piercing sun, and the air was stifling. The idea of summoning enough wind to push a fleet across the sea was something Sebastian could never imagine was possible.

"Everyone take their positions." Sebastian's voice was calm and silky, but loud enough to echo across the motionless space. He squeezed his eyes closed and whispered to himself, "How the hell are you going to pull this one off?"

The men shouted across the deck until they could relay the message loud enough for the closest ship to hear. Sebastian spun around and tilted his arm to the sky behind the fleet. Lightning cracked and thunder bellowed to the west. As the smell of salt water brushed gently through the air, Sebastian reached one palm forward. Clouds rolled in with a dense haze and a humid drizzle. The deck of the Hetta shook with the sharp claps of thunder after a luminous display of lightning striking the sea.

Sebastian turned to Jace. "Hold on." A gentle breeze transformed into a fierce gust, billowing the sails of his fleet with newfound vigor. The once-stagnant ships now surged forward, cutting through the waves with unprecedented speed. Sebastian stood at the helm of the Hetta; his eyes focused on the distant horizon.

Jace gripped the wheel tightly and watched Sebastian over his shoulder. Dom protected Dani, while Candor and Valirus braced themselves on the bow. There was a rumble and an eerie silence from the west. The rain came and the air impeded the wall of deep-blue sea that towered in the near distance. "Uhhh, Sebastian." Jace's voice was shaking.

Sebastian looked over his shoulder. "That was not my intention." He turned to face the west and stretched his arm out, palm up as if asking the storm to take his hand. "But if I am to master water powers, then I guess now is the time."

The waves swelled and the ships lifted as the sea rose. As they crested the peak, Sebastian spun around, spread his arms as wide apart as he could, and brought his hands together with an earth-shaking concussion. The ships fell as fast as the water could drop. Sebastian's skin burned and cracked as scales etched into his face and chest. His scream shrieked through the skies. His arms dropped to his sides and he braced himself with ropes of the rear mast sails.

As they fell down the waterfall of tidal waves, the Hetta's black sails burst open wide as they passed into the steadying ocean that lay ahead. The fleet lunged forward with the strength of hurricane-force winds pushing them against the once-motionless sea.

Chapter Fourteen

The Isle of Hast

The early hours of the night cooled as the stars reflected off the water's surface. Sebastian stopped guiding the wind, and the ships slowed to a crawl. He stretched his tired arms and made his way to his quarters where Dani lay in bed reading. Sebastian dragged his feet and fell face-first onto the blankets.

Dani set down his book and pulled Sebastian's head onto his lap and brushed his hair back with his fingertips. "Are you hungry?"

"No," Sebastian mumbled. "Just tired. I don't know if I can do this much longer." He wrapped his arms around Dani's waist. "If I have to keep this up, I won't have any strength left by the time we reach Hast." Sebastian was comfortable and warm. He felt his head dropping until he fell fast asleep nestled warmly in Dani's embrace.

In the morning, Sebastian climbed onto the aft of his ship and took a deep breath before conjuring the wind. Even as his muscles burned, he pushed the ships through late morning when Candor came to take the wheel from Jace. "How much further does this dead sea last, Uncle?"

"When we reach the Statues of the Hidden Shores, our weather misfortune will change and you will face another obstacle which is crucial to the entrance into Hast. You will understand when you see it."

Sebastian clenched his jaw. "I am seriously tired of you telling me that I will see it when we get there." He pivoted back to his place and abruptly raised his arms. The wind howled between the fleet and pushed the day forward. Mid-afternoon, Sebastian sat with a steady wave of his arms.

Dani leaned against the rear mast with Sebastian and watched the armada that trailed in their wake. He propped up on his knees and put his hands on Sebastian's lap. "Can I try something?"

"Try what, my darling?"

"Well." Dani checked over his shoulder, then swiveled back. "Barron and I have been practicing a lot, and I think we might know how to help you."

Sebastian tightened up his posture and narrowed his eyes. "I'm not entirely sure I trust my life in Barron's hands, Dani."

"That is why I came up here alone." Dani cupped Sebastian's chin. He leaned in and whispered, "Let me help you."

The hair on the back of Sebastian's neck stood and he felt a chill shoot down his spine. Dani's hot breath on his cheek made his heart race and the blood rush through his body. He pulled Dani's lips to his and kissed him deeply until he forgot about the wind.

There was a flutter from falling sails and the humidity returned. Sebastian ran his fingers down Dani's chest and opened his shirt to stroke his bare torso. He kissed Dani again, then sat up straight. "Why is it so hot?" The lowered sails caught his eye. It took every ounce of strength for Sebastian to lift his arms again.

"Your Majesty..."

"I got it, Jace." Sebastian waved his arms and pulled the wind from the west.

Dani pulled Sebastian to his feet. "I am going to try something. Just focus on your power over the wind." His eyes turned white and he reached out to place his hand on Sebastian's shoulder.

"Sebastian, no!" Jace shouted from the wheel.

"Quiet, Jace." Dani's voice was stern and strong.

"You could kill him, Dani." Jace protested.

"I can do this." Dani returned his hand to Sebastian's shoulder.

Barron stepped onto the platform and lifted his hands to the sky, and the sun turned black. "Focus on the wind, Brother. Nothing else."

Sebastian stared into the darkness, and the air got cold and quiet. A thunderous gust burst the sails of the fleet wide open, and the hull of the Hetta argued against the pressure. "Hold together, girl," Sebastian mouthed to the ship. As Barron allowed the light to slowly return, Sebastian could see massive statues far across the horizon. Dani's lips turned blue, and his white irises and pale skin frightened Sebastian in a way he didn't quite understand.

Barron stood stoically with his arms spread to his sides and his eyes closed. He exhaled a deep breath and lifted his head to meet Sebastian's face. He clenched his fists tight, and the darkness turned so black that Sebastian felt disoriented and confused.

There was a rush of wind and a shiver, then an intense warmth when the light began to return. But when the light returned, it was night, and the moon was full. Barron opened his palms and spread his fingers, and the moon turned as red as freshly spilled blood. He dropped to his knees choking for air.

Dani yanked his arm away from Sebastian, his white eyes returned to their beautiful sky-blue shade. He stumbled and fell backward against the mast. "Wait ... How did we make it so far already?" His head faced the upcoming statues.

Barron coughed and came forward. "I have learned that when I turn day to night and vice versa, time is really shifting the world around us. We had to hurry or else we would have missed the moon."

"That's unbelievable." Dani looked at Barron, then Sebastian. "To travel through time is—"

"Unfortunately"—Barron coughed even harder than before—"to do so shortens my life."

"So you risked your life to get us to Hast on time." Sebastian stared at Barron for a long moment.

Barron nodded and walked over to the railing to see the statues better. Sebastian took Dani's hand, pulling him along to the deck where the others stood with their heads tilted up at the stone faces of two men. One appeared young, while the other one was an elder man. Both were armed with stone swords and shields, forever watching the southern sea. The younger of the men was slender with long hair and a piercing gaze that Sebastian could not help but stare at.

Dani squeezed his hand. "That statue kind of looks like you."

Candor came to stand next to Sebastian. "This is the gateway to the Isle of Hast. There is no other way in but through here."

Sebastian peered through the entry. Between the statue sat jagged rocks and rushing, low water. "We will never make it through that."

"Remember what I said about the Red Moon?" Candor held up his index finger. "Just wait for the tide, Your Majesty."

"Why can't we just go around?"

"You will see along the way that there is no way around." Candor pivoted on one heel and gasped. "It is time."

Sebastian turned to see the ocean begin to swell. Soon, the entry waters appeared as the rest of the sea, with a rim of rocky hills surrounding the path. He raised one arm and invited the wind to push the sails once more.

The silence on the deck was uncomforting as they drifted between the mountainous statues, yet nothing felt quite as eerie as what lay ahead. Sebastian marched to the railing, his hands gripping the mahogany tight. Shattered hulls, cracked masts, and tattered sails were scattered among the exposed rocks. He checked behind the Hetta for the other ships that all sailed gently through the mass water graveyard and into the canyon ahead. The narrow river wound through the sawtooth mountains that stood high above the water's surface.

As they rounded the last bend, fat raindrops fell onto the deck until the sky released a fury of rain onto the fleet. They floated away from the mountains, then Sebastian ran to the bow and stared straight ahead. "Uncle," he shouted. "Is that—"

"Hast. Yes, Your Majesty."

The island in the distance was wide enough that Sebastian could not see the end of either side across the horizon. It was too far to make out the city, but the open waters allowed the ships to line up side by side on the approach. Candor guided Jace toward the western side of the island before they could be detected from the land. The rain finally stopped when the sun began to go down.

"We dock at the tail and make our way across the serpent's back on our way to the tower. That is surely where we will find Maxen and Hydros."

Sebastian sat on the railing across from the next ship, where Viktor and Kristoff begged him for stories about his adventures. Meecah was stationed at the wheel and smirked at the story about when he was on Padora. Sebastian told stories of his adventures in

NorthBrekka, finally revealing all the shenanigans he'd gotten into in The Break when he was younger. When he told the story of his and the alpha wolf's first interaction, Dani gasped and said, "She could have eaten your face off, Sebastian."

"Well, she didn't." He continued to another story about when he got lost and ended up crossing into The Far North by mistake and was taken captive by Sinook guards before they learned he was King Ivan's son. He looked at his brothers and a sinking feeling filled his heart. "I am sorry I never took you both with me. I just left you guys to deal with everything while I was too selfish to care."

"Yeah." Viktor interrupted. "You left us with Barron. Therefore, you owe us, big time."

Sebastian burst out laughing. "And what exactly do you want, Brother?"

"Land." Viktor's eyebrows raised. "A big house and some land to raise my family." His face turned red. "Seville . . . She is pregnant."

Sebastian's mouth stretched into a wide smile. "So, that is why she did not wish to come with us."

"That was my idea, not hers," Viktor said. "I will return to Adurak with you. After all, I serve the true king. But I want a place of my own with some horses, and maybe cattle."

"Anything else?" Sebastian laughed. "What about you, Kristoff."

"I already have everything I want." Kristoff patted the rail of his ship.

"King Lucian offered you a position in his armada, with your ship and all."

Kristoff's face lit up. "I may consider it." He tried hard to cover his smile.

Sebastian heard tapping approach from behind.

"Shouldn't you be practicing, Your Majesty?" Valirus's voice was serious, deep, and bored.

"I figured if there is a chance that I may die on that island, then I should spend my final hours with my brothers." His eyes shot over to his husband. "And Dani, of course."

"You're not going to die." Dani went over and sat next to Sebastian. "I don't care what I have to do to make sure you don't."

"Alright." Barron stood and walked toward the stairwell. "This conversation is making me nauseated with all this family love and bonding. I am going to bed."

"Not so fast," Sebastian said. "I said I wanted to spend my time with my brothers. Are you not my brother?"

Barron kicked his toe into the wood and let out a laugh. "I want nothing from you, Sebastian. After everything I have done to you, and to them." He nodded at his brothers.

"Barron, I—"

Barron walked away quickly, disappearing below deck.

Sebastian jumped off the railing to follow Barron.

Dani grabbed his arm. "Let him go. He is sick. I don't think he has much time left." He stood and rested his head against Sebastian's chest for a moment. "But you have to consider the fact that Barron has renounced his name. He no longer wishes to be a Drake. To him, you are the king, not his brother, and after everything the two of you have been through, I think that is the best thing for both of you." Dani peered around all the staring faces. "I think we should all get some sleep before we reach Hast tomorrow." He gripped Sebastian's head. "Come to bed with me."

Sebastian followed Dani to their quarters and locked the door behind him. His eyes flickered up and down as Dani took off his shirt and moved his hands to the fastening on his pants. Sebastian's eyelashes were wet from tears, and his coat was soaked from the rain, yet he stood frozen, entranced by Dani slowly disrobing under the candlelight. His milky skin glistened from the mist outside and his cheeks were rosy from the chill. Sebastian wrapped his fingers around Dani's throat and dragged his body to meet his own.

He lifted Dani's chin and kissed his lips. Dani pushed the wet coat from Sebastin's shoulders until it dropped heavily to the floor. Sebastian yanked his shirt from his body, picked Dani up, and set him on the edge of the table. Their lips tangled in twisted romance and the taste of wine. Sebastian dropped his pants to the floor and kicked them away. Sebastian kissed Dani's neck and wrapped his arms around his chest before bending him delicately face-down onto the table.

As the last few candles still flickered, Dani fell against Sebastian's chest, and they stayed there until the light was gone and footsteps from the deck became quieter. They fell asleep to the sound of the smooth ocean and the scent of a salty breeze.

The wee hours of the morning arrived and the sun had yet to peek from over the horizon. Sebastian stood at the wheel and enjoyed the silence. The sounds of sails catching the wind from an armada in tow calmed his nervousness about seeing Hydros again. The dark sky turned a deep shade of violet with a hue of orange over his starboard side, and to the east. Ahead, a flicker of fire came from the shadowy embankment.

"Land, straight ahead, Your Majesty," a soldier shouted from the crow's nest.

"Awaken the others," Sebastian commanded another soldier and steered the ship toward the light.

The soldier rushed to the underdeck and began shouting. There was a thunder of boots on wood planks and the rumble of men coming up the stairs.

"Start lowering the sails." Sebastian ordered. "We are close."

The faint sight of an old town came into view as the sun poked above the horizon, turning the dark sky into copper that made the sea appear to be on fire. Candor joined Sebastian on the upper deck.

"I thought you said these docks were unmanned." Sebastian pointed. "There are torches lit ahead."

"It must be the Unrahli." Candor squinted at the distant harbor. "Don't worry. They will listen to me."

The sun lit the sky enough for Sebastian to see the remnants of a fishing village. He steered the Hetta where Candor instructed, to an old battered pier with an uncrossable boardwalk. "We will have to row ashore. Let's not get too close." Sebastian's voice was calm and confident.

Dani appeared from the captain's quarters and rubbed his eyes as the sun shined bright against his face. He ran to the bow where Valirus and Barron stood, having a conversation Sebastian could not hear. Jace appeared at Sebastian's side. "Let me take the wheel. You go get ready for whatever is about to happen."

Sebastian marched down to the main deck and started toward the bow when a sharp thump hit the hull of the Hetta. He stumbled but caught himself on a cargo crate, then ran to the rail. "Did we hit a rock?"

Another blow slapped against the bottom of the ship, sending some of the crew stumbling once again. Sebastian gripped the rail and held himself in place, staring over the edge into the water.

"Sebastian!" Jace said. "What is that?"

Sebastian stood straight and gawked at the sea below. A light push slapped against the starboard side as something emerged just barely above the water's surface. Only part of a tail broke free and revealed itself. Sebastian watched as it swam away. "What the hell is that?"

The others ran to the railing and looked in every direction, but the creature was gone. Jace brought them to a stop not far from the shore and shouted for the men to lower the boats and drop the anchor. He stepped onto the aft and waved for the other ships to do the same. Sebastian sighed as he gazed painfully at the shore. Then, Dani grabbed his hand and pulled him along. They climbed down the ladder and into the boats and rowed toward the harbor.

Soldiers leaped from the boat and dragged it to shore. The crunch of their boots was noisy as they crushed shells and sand with each step. Candor walked past everyone else. "Keep moving. We want to be at the village of Oranu by nightfall. There is nothing else before there, so it is best to keep moving."

They left the beach and walked into the empty harbor town. Sebastian turned his head back and forth, taking in the ruins of a village built from clay and rock. He looked for people and poked his head into windows, looking for supplies. Viktor and Kristoff went ahead with Candor to scout the road ahead. He heard Dani laughing and turned to see him and Barron chatting. Jace walked quietly by his side as they crested a hill and saw what lay ahead.

"Candor," Sebastian shouted. "There is no cover here. We will be spotted from leagues away."

Candor backtracked to Sebastian. "No one is watching these lands. I promise you that."

"What happened here?" Sebastian looked around at the vast, empty land. Only weeds grew on the seemingly endless stretch of northern Hast.

"It was all burned to the ground many years ago." Candor took a deep breath and scanned the island. "It's best to keep moving." He turned his head back and forth quickly before he resumed walking ahead of the others.

The afternoon became late and Sebastian slipped away from the others to follow a herd of deer he saw earlier in the day. Dani chased him down and scolded Sebastian for leaving by himself.

"We are hungry. I am going to get us a deer." Sebastian lowered his body. "Get down," he whispered.

The herd stopped across the way and nibbled at the patches of grass. Sebastian took an arrow from his quiver and readied his bow. He held his index finger over his lips and glanced at Dani. He took a knee and pulled back on the bowstring until his thumb rested against his cheek. The deer were blind to him in the thicket, with his bow ready to fire. He took a deep breath, then his fingers released their grip on the tail of the arrow. The arrow whooshed through the air and pierced into the shoulder of the innocent creature in the field.

The herd pranced away in fear as the animal dropped to the ground. Sebastian bounded from the brush and marched across the way to collect his kill. Before he descended the hill into the prairie, a massive shadow cast across the tall waving grass. Sebastian's head fell to one side as he made out a head, a body, a face, and then the tail he recognized from the ocean. His mouth fell open and he lifted his chin to the sky. The creature swooped down and landed on the field where the deer lay dead.

Sebastian froze in place and could not blink. The creature turned its enormous, scaly body, and its face stretched toward where Sebastian stood alone in the field. He looked over his shoulder to see Dani still behind the thicket at the top of the small hill. He looked back to see the beast step forward, its eyes locked on his. Sebastian felt his body get hot and his skin burn. His fists filled with flames and he growled, "Dragon."

The dragon's scales were a deep shade of blue and its wings were webbed. It sniffed at Sebastian, then turned back to the deer and roared with an intense freezing wind. It chomped on the deer and spread its wings open wide, then, with a tremendous gust, lifted into the sky and flew away to the east. Sebastian sat down and gasped for air. He heard Dani come running from the hill.

"My love." He fell to the ground and wrapped his arms around Sebastian. "Was that ... a dragon?"

Chapter Fifteen

The Story of Dragon

Sebastian said nothing, just nodded his head and he heard screaming from over the hill and the sound of thundering footsteps coming fast. Soon after, his brothers were excitedly running over the hill, shouting about the dragon.

They built a fire and soldiers went to hunt. Sebastian sat down next to Candor and offered him water. "I know you wanted to get to that village tonight, but I don't foresee that being possible."

"There was a reason that we needed to make it to Oranu." Candor's eye never turned away from the fire.

"Did you know about the dragon?"

"Yes."

Sebastian sighed. "And you couldn't warn me?"

"Oranu would have given us protection from the beast. You could have been killed."

Sebastian's veins felt as if they were on fire. "Why didn't you tell me!" he shouted.

"I told you . . . you have to see it for yourself."

Sebastian stood. "What else are you hiding from me?"

"A lot." Candor stopped talking and refused to make eye contact with Sebastian.

The next afternoon, they made their way through the empty village of Oranu and to the far reach of the grasslands. The land turned into plateaus as they came upon a deep valley where a town lay ahead with a gateway that sat wide open. The label at the top read "Sector One."

As the night came, they entered the town and wandered down the quiet street. There was music and loud chatter ahead, and a roaring bonfire that flickered above the buildings. Sebastian caught the eye of an elderly woman sitting in a chair by her front door. She put down her pipe and stood quickly. "He is here." Her voice was hoarse. She walked backward down the street toward the noise.

Sebastian started to talk, but Candor took his arm and stopped him. "She is Unrahli. She is terrified of you." Candor let the woman disappear into the crowd as they approached the square where the fire burned.

Sebastian stopped. "You know these people, Uncle. Advise me."

"I will speak with one of the elders." Candor pointed to a grand stage built across the square where two elderly men sat. "They will give us a place to stay and food. For now, stay back here, keep your hood up, and stay in the shadows." Candor patted him on the shoulder and made his way through the people who danced merrily to music.

Sebastian breathed in the scent of cooked meat. His stomach growled loud enough for Jace to come to him with a sack of food that soldiers carry as they march.

Jace passed him a handful of biscuits. "You haven't eaten all day. Take them."

Sebastian pulled up his hood, leaned against a shop's outer wall, and shoved a piece of food in his mouth. He locked his eyes on Dani, who slipped next to him. "Are you alright, darling?" Sebastian offered Dani a biscuit.

Dani smiled and took one. "I have read about dragons from the olden days when Dragon ruled on earth, but I thought they died off when he died."

"This must be why Hast is kept secret from the rest of the world. A dragon..." Sebastian huffed out a laugh.

People passed Sebastian and the others in the street. Some stared too long as Sebastian pulled his hood down and Dani buried his face into Sebastian's chest. There were whispers, but no one spoke to them.

Meecah appeared out of nowhere on Sebastian's other side. "I believe I know these people."

Sebastian's eyebrows peaked. "How?"

"The Unrahli were created by a tribesman from Padora. He was my ancestor, and he married a woman from a place that no longer exists called Unrahli."

Sebastian turned his head to one side. "What happened to it?"

"It sunk." Meecah shrugged. "There was a hurricane, and the island was gone when the storm died. It used to be connected to Padora by a sandbar. So, when my ancestor joined the Unrahli and married their princess, they left on a ship they built from palm wood and clay. We never knew what happened to them."

"They are here and they want to kill me." Sebastian lifted his hood a bit to show Meecah he was smiling. "That kind of reminds me of someone."

Meecah laughed. "I already apologized for trying to kill you."

Sebastian caught the eye of Candor as he weaved through the crowd and made his way down the street. "What did the elders say?"

Candor tucked against the building. "They want to meet you. Present yourself to the people."

"No." Jace interrupted. "These people want the gods dead. The gods took over their homeland. They don't trust him."

"Meecah, you will accompany me." Sebastian took his hood off and stepped into the streets. "Maybe you can talk some sense into these people."

"I am coming." Dani's voice was loud and demanding.

"And me." Jace stood by Dani.

"Anyone else?" Sebastian looked around at his people.

There were gasps and whispers when Sebastian pushed through the groups of people. The music quieted down and stopped when he stood before the bonfire. The Order was scattered throughout the crowd, and everyone stared until the shouting came from a rustle in the onlookers. The elders stood and hurried from the stage. They pushed past Sebastian and halted at the sight of Meecah.

She glanced at Sebastian and back to the elders. "Unrahli people. My name is Meecah, and I am the Princess of Padora." The crowd gossiped louder. "I believe our kinds were once family."

One of the elders bowed and nodded graciously. "Princess, your presence here is a gift." He squeezed Meecah's hand, then pivoted sharply around to face Sebastian. "But he is not welcome here."

"Elder, if I may." Meecah gestured toward Sebastian. "I did not trust him once either, but he proved himself to be valiant and loyal. He is the King of Kings—"

"We do not worship kings here." The elder got close to Sebastian. "Especially not the Heir of Dragon."

"I promise you—" Meecah started.

"He is not welcome here. The rest of your pack may stay, but not him."

Sebastian sighed. "I thought you wanted to speak with me. Yet, you want me to leave." He felt his face get hot. "Well... which one is it?"

Candor bounded from the crowd. "Elders, please allow me to explain."

"We only needed to see his face. To make sure he is truly the Heir of Dragon. He must leave." The elder spat. "He brings death everywhere he goes."

"Fine," Sebastian spoke loudly. "I will leave. The rest of you stay and get a meal." He backed away toward the road.

"No." Dani shouted from the crowd, but then he shrieked.

Sebastian spun around and saw Dani being pulled back into the crowd. "Leave him!" he shouted, but Dani disappeared into the people. Sebastian spread his arms wide and slammed his palms together, causing the earth to shake. Everyone stopped and backed away, releasing Dani.

Valirus helped Dani to his feet. "If Hydros didn't know you were here, he does now. We should get moving."

"Hydros." The elder spoke loudly and clearly. "He will destroy Na'Huk with the King of Men by his side."

"That is why I am here." Sebastian's voice grew softer. "Hydros is my brother. I will stop him, and you can have your homeland back." He addressed his men and set off down the road that out of town.

They climbed up into the highlands late the following day as the warm afternoon turned into a chilly evening. Sebastian saw bright lights in the near distance. His body felt warmer than usual and the hairs on his arms stood. His skin flecked and glowed but quickly returned to normal as he climbed the last hill. At the summit, a site of architecture Sebastian had never seen covered the landscape ahead. A tall gate with the label "Sector Two" on top stood closed.

Sebastian pushed his people forward. Candor joined his side and demanded he lead the way from there. The homes on the outside were mud and clay structures built with trunks and leaves of palm trees. The people sat on the side of the road, not speaking, only watching. Candor held up his hands and waved here and there. He looked over his shoulder at Sebastian. "Something is not right here."

The people of the outskirts all stood in unison and followed. Dani took Sebastian's hand and said in a soft voice, "They are being controlled by my father."

Sebastian sped up to catch up to Candor. "We have to get out of here. Maxen has them under his control."

Candor kept moving at a steady pace. "Just keep moving. If we do anything irrational, King Maxen will notice."

"They are following us." Sebastian looked behind him. "It's creepy."

Candor grabbed him by the collar. "I am serious. Keep moving."

The townsfolk were within feet of the rear of the accompaniment. A man with a blank stare reached out and put his hand on Meecah's arm.

"Don't react!" Sebastian said.

"Walk faster." Candor hurried toward the next section of the city, which was divided by a wall and a massive oak gate. "Inviticus. I hope you are home." Candor's voice sounded shaky but loud.

A young man appeared in the lookout at the top of the gate.

"Drop the gate, boy." Candor's voice raised a bit louder. "Hurry!"

The gates cracked and the locks snapped. Smoke billowed from the chains as the gate dropped, making a loud thud on the ground.

"Run." Candor sprinted toward the opening.

The entranced man grabbed Meecah and threw her backward onto the ground. Sebastian spun around and strung an arrow in his bow. He fired the shot—it stung through the man's eye—then scooped Meecah in his arms as Jace stuck his blade through the next man's chest.

"Both of you, go!" Sebastian set Meecah on her feet and pushed her along with Jace. Fire burst in Sebastian's hands. He pulled his arms to his gut and thrust forward, both palms out as fire roared from his outstretched arms, igniting those who were near. Sebastian spun around and sprinted toward the open gate, where only a few of his people had made it.

The townsfolk dashed after them with the same empty gaze across each face. Some held weapons of iron rods, knives, and pitchforks, while others attacked empty-handed. Carts and firepits were knocked over, sending embers shooting into the sky. Boiling water flooded the streets as cauldrons were flipped off their pits. Sebastian found Dani cornered by two men and a woman. All had iron pikes pointed at his throat.

Sebastian lunged forward but felt a sharp pull on his leg, then he crashed onto the ground with a painful thud. "Dani!" He shouted but saw Dani's skin turn pale. His sapphire eyes turned white and his hand stretched before him. Dani set his hand on each man, and one at a time they fell at his feet. Sebastian kicked the man who'd knocked him down in the gut and thrust his sword through his chest.

They stood in the center of the road. The town had fallen silent and there was a distinct smell of death looming in the air. Bodies lay in the street, but not one of Sebastian's people died that day. Voices carried from the gate to the next sector of the city.

Sebastian grabbed Dani by the arm and sprinted toward the gate just as a hoard of townsfolk came from the shops, alleys, and homes. Sebastian unsheathed his sword and stepped backward. He scanned over the faces of people who were citizens of Hast, but his eyes fell upon one who stood out more than others, with shining metal armor and the distinct red and gold uniform.

"Dani." Sebastian stared at the soldier in the crowd, and then another like him appeared. "Altanian soldiers are here."

"I thought my father left them in Erras." Dani stared at the same soldiers Sebastian had seen, only now, more had appeared. They packed into the town, and the royal army of Midrel Istan glistened in the sun. The townsfolk, still entranced, marched at the front of the line, and the Altanian soldiers followed. "We should run." Dani pulled on Sebastian's arm. "Come on, Sebastian!" Dani gritted his teeth and pulled hard, but Sebastian did not budge.

He was frozen. His skin began to burn and his eyes seared like they did the first time they turned red. Scales glowed and etched across his skin.

Candor's voice carried from behind. "Your Majesty, stop! You'll kill innocent people."

Dani clenched onto Sebastian. "You have to run away. Please come with me." His mouth fell open and a tear ran down his cheek. His hand slipped off of Sebastian's arm and he turned toward the gate. The oak gate began to lower. Sebastian summoned the wind and threw Dani forward to where Barron was waiting to pull them through the gateway.

Sebastian ran fast with hands barely ripping at his coat as he slipped through to the next sector, and the gate slammed closed behind him. Shouting came from the other side, where Maxen's army could go no further. Sebastian rested with his hands on his hips and his head tilted back. He tried to ignore the voices of the others for just a moment. After a few deep breaths, he opened his eyes and scanned across the new township they had entered.

Townsfolk hustled up and down the streets. Sounds of a noisy marketplace came from over a hill and the air was filled with the aroma of cooking meat. Sebastian felt sick to his stomach. "I am starving." He held his stomach. "Candor, are these people friendly?"

"Yes." Candor smiled and nodded. "They are not under King Maxen's spell. It sounds like business as usual as the day begins to come to a close."

"Then we should get moving." Sebastian sniffed the air. "That smell is divine. I must find out what it is."

Candor laughed. "That would be a Hast specialty." He signaled for the others to prepare to depart as he led the way down the road toward the lights.

"Yes, but what it is?" Sebastian walked fast to catch up.

"You will find out soon enough."

Sebastian stopped walking and crossed his arms. "Why do you always say that? Is everything here a surprise? You could have warned me that there is a damned dragon on this island."

Candor shrugged. "Surprise!"

"I hate you." Sebastian rolled his eyes and followed his uncle up the hill.

The people of this sector of Hast were vibrant. The women wore dresses of pink and yellow, and the men mostly wore hues of white and blue. The market bustled with energy; smoke from spit roasts billowed from behind vendor carts. Money was exchanged quickly from hand to hand as goods were wrapped and carried off. As the accompaniment stepped into the market, the crowd did not stop. They did not stare. They continued working, talking, laughing, singing, and carrying on with their day. Sebastian smiled. It was the first time in a long time that his presence had not silenced a crowd.

"Spread out but stay close," Sebastian ordered his people. "Let's find something to eat and a place to rest." He reached out and stopped Candor from walking away. "How much further until we reach the tower?"

Candor clenched his jaw. "If we leave at first light, we can make it to the tower by tomorrow night. However, once we pass into the next sector, Hydros and Maxen will know we have arrived."

Sebastian started to ask what would happen in the next town, but decided he didn't want to hear Candor tell him that he would find out soon enough. He found Jace and Dani craning their necks over a fire pit next to a cart that was selling sausages and cuts of meat, chicken, and fish.

In the fire sat a pig on a spit. Vegetables were pinned to its body along with different types of fish. The cook took some of the meat on a plate and shredded it, then unpinned a fish. He chopped its head off and added the fish meat to the pork along with some carrots and passed it to Sebastian. The cook bowed. "For the king."

Sebastian eyed the plate, specifically the fish. He was hungry, but his stomach turned. "I hate fish." He blurted out without thinking.

The cook set the plate down on the cart and stared at Sebastian with a stoic glare. Before Sebastian could speak again, the cook nodded. "They say Dragon hated eating fish too." He turned and cut some more pork and vegetables from the roast. He poured a red glaze over the meat and passed the plate to Sebastian. "No fish."

Sebastian stared at him for a moment, then reached for the plate. "What do you know about Dragon?"

"All in good time, Your Highness." The cooked bowed again.

Dani took a piece of pork from Sebastian's plate and put it in his mouth. "Wow." His eyes grew wide. "This is unbelievable!" He turned to the cook. "Can we have more of that?"

Sebastian stared at Jace. "What do you think he meant by 'all in good time'? Why is no one telling me anything?"

Jace shook his head. "This place is odd. This whole island is quite incredible, but also kind of scary."

"How would a cook know what Dragon liked to eat?" Sebastian took a bite of his pork. "This is delicious." He spun around to find Dani loading up his plate.

The cook was grateful for the amount of gold Sebastian paid him for the mountain of pig meat Dani was shoving in his mouth. He bowed and kept trying to offer more food, but Sebastian suggested feeding it to someone that is hungry and in need instead. They went about visiting different parts of the marketplace. Dani snuck away to see what others were selling. Jace and Sebastian appreciated not having to constantly plan and plot for what was to come. Instead, they enjoyed the music from young boys and girls sitting on the ground with baskets filled with coins at their feet. Sebastian nodded at Jace to give the children money.

A tug came at the sleeve of Sebastian's coat. He turned and had to look down. A little girl was holding a plate of pork from the cart before. Her little blue eyes looked weepy, but she managed a smile. "Thank you, King Dragon." Her voice was soft and sweet.

Sebastian watched the little girl hurry away. "This place is getting weirder by the minute." He saw a blacksmith on the edge of the marketplace and decided to go pay him a visit. There were swords and axes for sale. Sebastian picked up an arrowhead and examined it closely. The arrows in his quiver were worn. He set his bow on the table and picked up several arrowheads from the blacksmith's table.

"Ahh," the blacksmith said. "You fancy a bow over iron, I see."

"A blade is best in close combat." Sebastian ran his fingers across the edge of a sword. "But if the score can be settled by the distance a bow can send an arrow, then yes, I prefer a bow to iron."

The blacksmith stood on the other side of the table and stared at Sebastian. "It makes sense, knowing that Dragon preferred a bow as well."

A woman popped out from behind the forge. Her black curly hair stuck straight up and streaks of gray showed at her roots. "It's true." She touched Sebastian's face, his hair, clamped his biceps with her hands, and patted his chest. "Dragon is in here." She rested her palm over his heart for a moment, then disappeared behind the forge again.

Sebastian paused for a moment and then purchased his arrows. "I'm not . . . Dragon." He backed away from the blacksmith's table. Jace joined his side once again as they found some of the others chatting with the locals by a fountain. Sebastian's eyes darted in every direction. "Did I mention that this place is odd?"

Jace ogled the townspeople. "It's almost like they are all obsessed with Dragon."

"Yes, but why?" Sebastian looked all around. "Where is Dani?"

"I guess the answer to your first question would be: all in good time." Jace smirked. "Secondly, Dani is at the cheese cart, stuffing his face."

"All in good time." Sebastian shook his head. "If anyone says that to me once we leave this island, I will run them through."

"Damn," Jace said. "I was planning to make it my new catchphrase."

Sebastian grinned and narrowed his eyes. "I'll have the crypt keeper carve your plaque to say, 'Here lies Jace Astra. He died because he pissed off the king.'"

Jace rolled his eyes and started walking toward where Meecah and Samir were tasting brightly colored candies. "I'm going to go get fat now. Would you like to join me, Your Majesty?" He bowed lower and more vibrantly than one would typically bow to a king.

At the dessert merchants' tables, Sebastian found Dani with a plate covered in pink puffed pastries and purple marble-sized candies. "How are you still hungry?" He couldn't help but laugh.

Dani crunched a purple candy between his teeth. "Indulge for once, my love." He picked up a pastry and put it up to Sebastian's mouth. "Eat this."

Sebastian tasted fresh berries wrapped in a flaky shell and a delicious crème filling. "Is all of the food here this good?"

Dani had a mouthful but nodded.

A woman passed an apple tart to Sebastian. She placed it in his hand. "It was King Dragon's favorite treat."

Sebastian stared at her with his head hanging slightly to the right. He wanted to ask her how she knew that but took a bite of the tart instead. His eyes shot open wide and his mouth stretched into a smile. "It might be my favorite as well."

As the evening fell late, Sebastian, Dani, and the others followed Candor toward the inn so they could rest. Down a dark street, Sebastian saw a large building with a book engraved on the door. He raised his eyebrows and stared for a moment, but followed Candor across the way.

Sebastian sat in bed and watched Dani wash himself in the small tub in the corner. He laughed at Dani's belly, swollen from gluttonously devouring every kind of food that he could fit in his mouth. Dani threw a towel at him and continued his bath while Sebastian's mind wandered back to the building across the street until Dani dried his body.

"I think that is a library across the way." Sebastian stared at Dani. "I need to find answers, and I think I might find them there."

"Answers to what?" Dani crawled into bed and laid his head on Sebastian's chest.

"Everything." Sebastian drifted into deep thought. "They seem to almost admire Dragon. Several people mentioned his name like they have known him for centuries." He kissed Dani's forehead. "I have to try."

Early the next morning, Sebastian slipped out of bed and left the inn. The streets were filled with a thin layer of fog, and a mist fell from the low clouds overhead. The lanterns in front of the library remained lit through the rain. Sebastian crossed the street and stopped when he noticed the iron cases that held the glass around the lanterns. They were forged into the shape of dragon claws clasping each corner of the light.

Sebastian bit his lip and climbed the steps. He pushed open the door and poked his head inside. "Hello?" No one responded. The inside smelled of old parchment and wood burning from the two monolithic fireplaces that sat directly across from one another on opposite ends of the library. There were velvet couches and chairs stretched out in all places so anyone could read in a comfortable area. Sebastian started to understand why Tomas had loved the library so much. It was quiet and still a little dark. Sebastian saw the sun starting to shine through the sheer curtains. He walked down the aisles, unsure of what he needed to search for.

He touched the spines of some very old, tattered books in hopes that one would call to him and selected one from each rack until his arms were full. The mahogany tables were as long as the king's dining table in Castle Drake. Sebastian set the books down and looked around some more. He found a candle and lit a flame at the tips of his fingers. He reached down to light the candle but noticed someone in the corner of his eye. A man stood hunched over, gripping a cane with a shaking hand. He clutched a book under his arm and his eyes were barely open, but he stared nonetheless.

"Sir." Sebastian approached him. "My name is—"

"Your Majesty," The librarian mumbled, then set the book on the table. "I knew you would come." The old man turned down an aisle and slowly clopped away until he disappeared around the corner of a shelf.

Sebastian stared at the book on the table for a moment, then pulled up a chair. He touched the cover gently. The leather was old and thick, and some of the pages were loose. Sebastian opened the cover. The first page was written in a messy hand, much like Sebastian's own. He flipped through the pages until he saw the name Dragon.

Sebastian read aloud, mumbling, "Ryu feared my death, and as my powers grew stronger in time, I started to fear death myself. When I built NorthBrekka, I called for my Blackbirds to come home to me. Of course, my dear brother Ryu was the first to arrive by my side. He was always there for me." The page ended.

He flipped through more of the journal, reading over entries that spoke of war strategies and talked about how much he missed Ryu. Sebastian understood that these entries were written by Dragon himself. The pages were very old and quite delicate. He carefully turned each one and stopped when he noticed the word *Adurak*. "I never wanted to stay in Erras forever. Adurak was my home. I loved it there, and my father forced me from the one place that I had ever felt safe. I was angry. So, I built NorthBrekka as my empire, and I will fight every man, woman, or child that tries to take it away from me."

Sebastian sat back and stared out the window and watched the sun come up. He thought about how all the townsfolk proved that he was much more like Dragon than he'd thought. It started to get bright inside the library. Sebastian thumbed through the pages and read more of the passages. He quietly read the words aloud. "He is gone. My brother. They took him from me. He was my everything. I will destroy them. I feel nothing. I will make them fear me."

The library door creaked open and a bright light filled the entry. Dani appeared with the glow of the sun's rays bouncing off his ivory skin. He came over to the table and sat down. "Did you find something?"

Sebastian passed over the journal. Dani grabbed it and opened it quickly. Sebastian set his hand on the book. "It is Dragon's journal. All his secrets are in there."

Dani read some of the pages aloud until the door opened again. Valirus stepped into the foyer. "Your Majesty, if we wish to make it to the tower by nightfall, we must push forward."

Sebastian nodded and went to find the librarian. The old man was dusting a bookshelf around the corner from his table. Sebastian held the journal up. "Can I keep this?"

The old man looked at the book and smiled at Sebastian. He only nodded and then returned to his dusting. Sebastian stuffed it into his pack and hurried outside to meet with the others.

The morning turned to midday when they arrived at the next gate, labeled "Sector Three." Candor stepped forward and went up to a tiny window. He turned to Sebastian. "I do not know if King Maxen has taken these people's minds, but once we cross the threshold of sector three, the tower is notified and scouts will announce our arrival. We will need to move quickly and keep an eye on everything."

Candor opened a trap door in the gate and shouted, "Filonias Hinkle."

Sebastian's mouth dropped open, but he closed it fast and turned his head to one side. He listened for the sound of locks opening and chains cranking, but none came. A cold breeze came from over the wall, which carried an eerie wheezing sound.

Candor cleared his throat and shouted louder, "I said, Filonias Hinkle."

It was quiet. The wind began to howl over the wall. Sebastian gripped the hilt of his sword tight. A loud pop made everyone jump. Dust flew from the hinges, and the grinding of rusted chains echoed down the street. The gate lifted slowly and a man near Candor's age appeared from the other side. A blast of wind gusted through the opening.

The man held onto his hat and waved his arm. "A storm is brewing. Follow me inside."

Sebastian and the others hurried to follow the stranger into a nearby dwelling. He stopped to take in the look of this new sector of Hast. The homes stood tall toward the sky and were packed in along a winding pathway through the town. Sebastian instructed his soldiers to scout the area and then followed the Order into the man's home. Inside the man's home was artwork lining both walls along the narrow entryway. He followed the hall down until he found Dani standing inside an extravagant parlor room.

Sebastian found Candor and the man sitting in armchairs by a fireplace.

Candor gestured for him to sit. "Your Majesty, this is Filonias Hinkle, my oldest friend." He winked at Filonias.

Filonias sat straight in his chair and stared into Sebastian's eyes. "It's uncanny how much you look like him. Only his face was more ... innocent."

"You mean Dragon." Sebastian opened his pack and pulled out the journal.

Filonias immediately reached for it. "How did you come by this?" His eyes shot open as he sniffed the spine.

"It was in the library in sector two. The librarian gave it to me."

"Did you read it?" Filonias glanced over some of the pages, then snapped it shut. "I am not worthy to read his words." He passed the journal back to Sebastian. "And no one from sector three would ever pass into two. Or one, for that matter. We live here and they live there, but that is not what I invited you inside for. Has your uncle told you about the place Dragon sailed to when he was exiled?"

Sebastian stared at Candor. "My uncle has told me nothing. He keeps saying that I will find out soon enough."

"Well now is that time, Your Majesty. Heir of Dragon. I will tell you about your legacy."

Trays of fruits and meats came into the parlor along with brightly colored drinks of all kinds. "I want to know everything." Sebastian took a drink and sat back in his chair.

Filonias nodded and took a sip from his glass. "When Dragon was exiled from Erras by his own father, he tried to sail home to Midrel Istan." Everyone in the room looked up at Filonias. He looked back at all the glaring faces. "You all really know nothing, don't you?"

"No one knows anything about him," Sebastian said. "All his stories were erased and he was dragged as being a genocidal maniac."

"Well, he is that and more." Filonias continued. "He got lost at sea and ended up on the wrong side of the world. Instead of Midrel Istan, he found Hast. Unfortunately, upon his arrival, the Unrahli were violent toward our god. But he managed to break them and push on until he found the rest of us. The people immediately bowed to a god, for they had never seen one. They thought he had come to Hast to answer their prayers. Dragon was our king, our leader. He lived out the remainder of his life here in that tower until the day he died." Everyone sat closer and listened as they enjoyed the food.

"So, that is why everyone knows all of Dragon's favorite things or how he likes his food." Sebastian narrowed his eyes. "Go on."

"It wasn't just that he lived out his life here. He built a world here. He and his dragons." He paused to see Sebastian's reaction.

"I saw the dragon when we arrived on Hast."

"Yes, that dragon is one of his. She is very old and is the last one. There are no more eggs, no other dragons to mate her with. She is the very last one. The people here understand Dragon so well because—"

"No, Filonias." Candor held up his hands. "I protest against you mentioning this."

"You will tell me." Sebastian looked from Candor to Filonias.

Filonias stared at Candor for a moment, then cleared his throat. "The people of Hast know everything about Dragon because they were alive when Dragon lived." Filonias stopped talking and looked into Sebastian's eyes. "Do you understand, Your Majesty?"

"No." Sebastian was confused and angrier than he was when Candor had kept secrets from him the whole journey. "I do not understand. So, you are telling me that all those people out there are hundreds of years old?"

"Yes. Around three hundred, to be precise." Filonias sat back and crossed his arms.

Sebastian rubbed his forehead. "How?"

"In those times," Filonias said, "Dragon had a legion of gods, Blackbirds, and witches. When his power became too strong for the rest of the world, he was exiled, but we, the people of Hast, accepted him as our king. And to reward us, his coven of witches cast a spell on the island so we would always be protected from the rest of the world. But we were cursed with being forced to live forever."

Sebastian took a moment. "This island is not well protected if it allowed King Maxen to invade it with his soldiers."

"He is a sorcerer and he brought one of the two of our gods."

"Hydros is my brother, and he is—"

"The dead Prince Tomas." Filonias nodded. "We know, but the spirit of Litha lives in him still, although—"

"Although what?" Sebastian's face got hot. He wasn't sure what Filonias would say.

"We don't believe Dragon was the villain in this story." Filonias stared at Sebastian. "He was just a boy ... in love."

"But all the massacres, the violence."

Filonias nodded. "That was him, alright. But I believe he wasn't right in the head after the death of his brother, a Blackbird they called Ryu. That is when Litha pushed him into war. She had her reasons for turning on her own kind."

"What were her reasons?" Sebastian's voice was lower and he saw no one else in the room at that moment except Filonias.

"They abandoned her ..."

Sebastian had a sharp pain in his gut. He remembered Tomas being angry with him for abandoning him when he sailed to Midrel Istan.

Filonias cleared his throat. "Hydros has the Oscura. In the olden times, Dragon gave Litha the Oscura for safe keeping because he wanted the only person who could end his life to be her."

"Did she?"

Filonias smiled and picked at his nails. "Dragon died in the arms of the woman he loved."

"She killed him," Sebastian whispered.

That night, Sebastian sat up in bed. "Do you think Hydros wants revenge against me for abandoning him?"

Dani was reading Dragon's journal by the fireplace. "I fear more that he will try to use you for your powers like Litha did to Dragon." Dani closed the book and climbed into bed. "Do you not see it? Hydros wants to rule over the world. Litha was angry and wanted to rule over all. Dragon was seduced by her."

"I won't let him consume me, Dani. I promise." Sebastian kissed Dani's lips. "Tomorrow I will go to him. But tonight, I am with you."

In the morning, the accompaniment met in the streets and faced the tower in the near distance. It was quiet. In sector two, the townspeople were out early setting up their market wares and cooking goods. But in sector three, the people did not seem to awaken too early. Sebastian led the group across the township. Ahead, there was a massive, open stone courtyard. There were no guards ahead, no people, not even birds or cats.

"This isn't right, Sebastian." Jace walked closely by his side.

"The Tower of Dragon." Candor started forward on the path. "That tower technically belongs to you, Your Majesty."

The tower was enormous at its base, surrounded by stairs that led to double doors in the front that overlooked the city. The courtyard had palm trees lined along the path that circled around the tower completely. Sebastian craned his neck and looked at the top, but the sun flashed in his eyes. He turned to see his people surrounded by Altanian soldiers.

All of his people, including Dani, were pushed to their knees with swords to their throats.

The Altanian soldiers outnumbered his own by double. A tall, blond-haired knight with a massive iron longsword in one hand stepped forward. "King Sebastian... King of Thieves," the knight taunted. "Remember me?"

Sebastian narrowed his eyes. He recognized the smug look of a conceited knight he'd once seen in Altania during the joust. Sebastian clenched his jaw. "Let them go."

The knight smirked. "Mmmm, let me think about that one... No!" He cleared his throat and stepped closer to Sebastian. "My name is Sir Roki Dinora. When I am through with you, they will call me the Dragon Slayer."

Sebastian stood up straight, meeting Sir Roki eye-to-eye. "Let them go." His chest filled with a fiery sensation and the glow of scales etched across his skin.

"Do you think I am afraid of you?" Sir Roki's smile was manic, but it was clear he was not under Maxen's control.

A cackling laugh filled the air followed by a loud pop. Petra stood next to Sir Roki with a wide smile across her face. "Welcome home, gorgeous." She winked at Sebastian and then turned to Sir Roki. "My father said don't kill him." She backed away toward the Order.

Jace jumped to his feet and shoved the soldier away. "Petra, please—"

She burst into a loud laughing fit, interrupting Jace. The soldier kicked him in the back and knocked him to the ground. Out of the corner of his eye, Sebastian saw Sir Roki rear back his sword and charge at him.

Each man squared off, with iron crashing into iron ringing through the still air. Sebastian reached his sword back as far as his arm could stretch, then brought it crashing down onto the blade of Sir Roki. The knight groaned as he struggled to fight back against the strength Sebastian displayed against him.

Sebastian glanced over to Dani, who was being held down by a man holding a knife to Dani's throat. He huffed angrily and threw his weight into the next strike, which was blocked once again by Sir Roki. He threw his arm forward and a blast of icy wind shot from his fingertips. Sir Roki flew backward into the tower steps and dropped his sword. Each step Sebastian took echoed against the smooth stone of the ground beneath his feet. He scooped up the sword and gripped one in each hand.

Roki climbed to his feet and screamed before charging at Sebastian and knocking him to the ground. Roki reached his elbow back and threw his fist squarely into Sebastian's jaw. The sting made Sebastian dizzy. He turned his head to see Dani scream but felt a sharp sting in his ribs as Roki stood over him and kicked him in the side repeatedly until Sebastian rolled out of the way. He took a deep breath and climbed to his feet. Sebastian felt the familiar burn lighting up as his dragon scales danced across his skin.

Sebastian raised his arm before him. "You cannot defeat me." A powerful, hot, burning sensation filled his entire body. Sebastian dropped open his mouth as a flame shot from his throat. "Let them go, Petra!" He marched toward her.

Sir Roki picked up his sword and stood waiting for Sebastian to strike. "You will have to get through me if you want her." He laughed with an evil grin across his lips.

"You don't want that." Sebastian sheathed his sword and pulled his hands together to form a fireball in his fist. The fire shot from his outstretched arm and crashed into Sir Roki's armor, knocking him on his back. Sebastian conjured lightning in the palm of his hand. "You didn't think you were going to win, did you?" Lightning streaked across Sebastian's chest, down his arm, and through his hands that met Sir Roki's exposed skin.

Sir Roki shook uncontrollably and spit blood as Sebastian refused to release him. His body twitched and he choked up vomit until he could no longer hold himself up. Roki fell and jerked violently on the ground until his own blood spilled from his eyes, nose, and mouth. Sebastian smiled and spun around to save Dani and the others from their captures, but the courtyard was empty.

Chapter Sixteen

The Tower of Dragon

Nothing could describe the pain Sebastian felt. He fell to his knees and screamed until his voice broke. An intense storm brewed above the tower as Sebastain displayed the full force of his anger before anyone who was watching from above. "Give them back!" he shrieked at the front doors. "I know you are in there, Maxen. Let them go or I will destroy everything you have built. I will destroy everything!"

No one answered. The tower doors remained locked and Sebastian was trapped in the courtyard alone. He slammed his shoulder into the door repeatedly until he felt a painful snap and fell on his back. The pain in his arm was minimal compared to the fire in his heart. Sebastian climbed to his knees and threw his head back, and with a loud, maddening scream, Hast began to shake dangerously. Sebastian heard a loud crack followed by an explosive shift as the ground around him split in two.

The doors to the tower swung open. Sebastian tilted his head and slowly stepped one foot in front of the other until he stood across the threshold. No one stood in the doorway—not a guard in sight, nor anyone for that matter. Inside was cold and everything was sterile, odd, and too perfect for Sebastian's liking. He turned his head back and forth until he reached the center of the tower. On the floor was a massive dragon, carved and painted into the stone. The blend of red and blue in its scales caught Sebastian's attention. Not two dragons, but one.

The tower was silent, but a hum came from the west corridor. There was a cage in the wall held by chains that disappeared above. A small man sat in the corner of the cage with his hand on a crank. "Going up, Your Majesty?" His serious voice carried into the hall.

"Where is up?" Sebastian stood at the opening. "What is this thing?"

"Up is where you are supposed to be." The man gestured for Sebastian to enter. "This is called a lift. I believe it was Dragon himself who came up with the idea. He hated all those dreadful stairs."

Sebastian stepped inside as the man closed the gate and sat down in front of the crank. "Did you know Dragon too?"

"There are many here who have had the pleasure, but I, however, was not alive when the spell was placed on the people of the island." The man started to turn the wheel and the lift ascended into the darkness of the tower. With nothing more than a small lantern, the man whistled happily in his seat as he turned the crank around and around.

Sebastian watched above, expecting a light to come from the part of the tower where he would be let out. The lift slowed and creaked as they reached a dimly lit corridor.

The man opened the gate. "I think you will find who you are looking for straight ahead." He pointed at a set of black double doors embossed with dragons.

"Thank you." Sebastian stepped out of the lift and walked toward the doors. The torches flickered as he approached the carvings. He leaned his head against the door and listened for sounds on the other side, but heard nothing. The doorknobs were in the form of dragon claws. He reached out his hand, and the door fell open heavily without a sound. Sebastian stepped inside and his heart skipped a beat.

His eyes darted to Hydros standing with his back against the wall and a drink in his hand. The door slammed closed behind Sebastian. He looked back quickly, then turned to face Maxen.

"Welcome to Hast, Your Majesty."

Sebastian narrowed his eyes. "King Maxen Bolin. The man that just won't seem to die."

"You would miss me." Maxen bowed.

"Enough." Hydros's voice was deeper than Tomas's. "Chaos." The sound escaping his lips stung Sebastian in the gut. "Brother." Hydros's head tilted to the side. "We are brothers, right?"

Sebastian scowled. "We were brothers. When you were Tomas."

"The spirit that was broken." Hyrdos looked at himself in a mirror that hung next to the fireplace. "Tomas left this body so I could thrive. Just as you should do for Chaos. Let Sebastian die."

Maxen laughed and backed out of the room. Sebastian ran to the door as it closed. He pulled on the knob, but it was locked. He smashed his fist into the door but turned when he heard Hydros's eerie voice from across the room.

"We could be brothers again."

Sebastian felt an icy touch on his neck. His head turned slowly until his gaze met bright blue, sapphire eyes.

Hydros was inches from his face. "Join me," he whispered and leaned forward until his lips brushed against Sebastian's.

"Get off me!" Sebastian shoved him back.

Hydros grabbed his arm. "You belong here. This place was built for Dragon and Litha. They are the reason you and I exist."

"No, we exist because of King Ivan and Queen Shauni." Sebastian pushed Hydros's hand away. "They are our parents. Dragon and Litha are the reason we are cursed."

"Cursed?" Hydros tilted his head. "This is not a curse. We are the most powerful beings on earth."

"And you don't see a problem with that?" Sebastian interrupted. "No one should have this power. It should have ended when Dragon and Litha died."

Hydros sat down with his drink. "They wanted it to live on for a reason. Imagine what you are capable of."

"I know what I am capable of—"

"No, you do not." Hydros stared intently at Sebastian. "Trust me. If you let Chaos take control, you would fully understand just how powerful you are."

"I won't do it."

Hydros sighed. "Not even to save them."

Sebastian's heart sank into his stomach. "Where are they?"

"Safe." Hydros pointed at the door. "King Maxen is tending to them now."

"No!" Sebastian ran to the door. "You can't let him near Dani."

"Oh yes, his son. Your lover." Hydros stood and walked over to Sebastian. "He is instructed to not touch them. Any of them."

"Let me out."

Hydros grabbed him by the shoulders. His fingers brushed across Sebastian's cheek. The Oscura rested on his ring finger.

Sebastian jerked backward and kept his eyes fixed on the ring. "That belongs to me."

"No, actually it belongs to me." Hydros twisted the ring on his finger. "I don't plan to use it on you unless you deserve it." He grabbed Sebastian's arm. "Join me, or regret your decision for both you and Dani." His voice cut through Sebastian like glass.

"Don't threaten me." Sebastian's body ignited with a hot, tingly, burning sensation as the sound of thunder rumbling came from outside. Through the window, he saw clouds forming thick over the island.

"That's it, Chaos." Hydros stood close to Sebastian again. "Come to me."

Sebastian pulled his arms back and slammed them forward into Hydros's chest. With a blast of wind from Sebastian's hand, Hydros crashed into the floor. "I will never join you."

Hydros leapt to his feet and shouted, and his hands wrapped around Sebastian's throat. His blue eyes shined brighter than before and his face etched with the same scales Sebastian has seen on his own skin.

A tear dropped down Sebastian's cheek, and then he started to choke. His body was too cold and his muscles felt frozen solid. Every movement struck painfully. His lungs felt as if they were on fire as he struggled to take a breath. Sebastian reached out and touched Hydros's face. Fire flicked from his fingertips like flint being lit, but his powers were failing him, and Sebastian felt limp.

He stumbled and his legs shook as his body turned from hot to cold and his head spun. Sebastian struggled to remain on his feet, and yet the fire in his gut forced him to try. Sebastian raised his arm like he would when he summoned a fireball in his fist. A flame flickered but quickly diminished. Sebastian stared at his fist in disbelief.

Hydros pushed him to his knees with the Oscura rested on his finger. "I won't kill you now. I want you to feel the consequences of your decisions." A blast of freezing air hit Sebastian hard, and suddenly, he couldn't move.

Hydros whistled and two men barged into the room. One threw Sebastian over his shoulder and carried him out. He struggled to hold his eyes open, but soon everything went black.

Chapter Seventeen

Whatever I Want

Sebastian woke up in a warm room with one small window. His body was still too weak to move easily on his own, but his stomach turned suddenly. He crawled over to where a bucket sat in the corner and threw up repeatedly until the door flew open.

"Let me go!" came a shrill from the hall.

Sebastian sat back against the wall. The vile laugh and hideous smile of King Maxen burst through the door. He had black hair gripped between his fingers as he dragged Dani into the room.

"Look at him, son." Maxen threw Dani to the floor. "Look at what has become of your husband."

"My love." Dani's voice was light and cracked. "What happened to you?"

Sebastian couldn't speak; he merely stared at Dani. His weakened body lay limp on the floor, and no matter how hard he tried to fight, he remained where he was dropped.

"Hydros is a lot more powerful than you thought, isn't he, Your Majesty?" Maxen's face was proud, with his head held high and his chin pointed upward.

Dani jerked free and ran over to Sebastian. He scooped Sebastian's head onto his lap. "Fight back, Sebastian. You are stronger than both of them."

"Get back over here!" Maxen tapped his staff on the floor, which sent a blast of light that lifted Dani and threw him backward. He tumbled back to Maxen's side. "Hydros has the stone and he will use it to destroy our King of Kings. Even if I have to make him do it." Maxen grabbed Dani by the arm and backed out of the room.

After hours had passed, Sebastian saw the outline of Hydros enter, and then his face came clear as the door closed behind him. Hydros sat on the floor next to Sebastian and rested his hand on his torso. An icy sensation burned in Sebastian's chest. He began to scream, and then it was as if everything was suddenly crystal clear. Sebastian felt lighter, less angry and more prideful. His fears and worries seemed to have vanished and he began seeing Hydros in a different light.

"What did you do to me?" Sebastian glared at Hydros.

"Chaos, God of Fire and ruler of all. Just as Dragon before you, you are the guardian of this world. It is up to you whether the power lives or dies." Hydros twisted the ring on his finger. "Obviously we all want it to live, but your definition of the perfect world and mine are much, much different."

"What do you want from me?" Sebastian was feeling powerful and strong. He sat up and faced Hydros. "I will not kill innocent people in order to rule. Dragon was wrong for what he did."

"Was he?" Hydros raised one eyebrow. "Or was he simply defending himself against a world that feared him?" He paused and pointed to Sebastian. "Isn't that exactly the same thing you have been doing all these years?"

"I am not like him!"

"You are exactly like him!" Hydros grabbed Sebastian by the arms.

Sebastian felt a familiar icy sensation travel across his body, only this time, his muscles started to feel strong again.

"Join me, Brother." Hydros's voice mimicked Tomas's soft and quiet tones. "Stay here and rule the world with me."

"Why do you trust Maxen?" Sebastian snarled. "He is the one who killed you."

"King Maxen is merely a pawn." Hydros grinned. "You see, Brother, I am using him. And once I finish using him, then I will kill him."

"Does he know that?" Sebastian raised his eyebrows.

"What would be the fun in that?" Hydros stood tall and reached his hand out to Sebastian.

"What you are doing is wrong."

Hydros pulled his hand back and shook his head. "No, it is what is meant to be."

"Don't start with the prophecy, Brother." Sebastian climbed to his feet quickly. "I am done with this forsaken prophecy. I am not Dragon ... I am Chaos, and I am my own person. And I will never join the team that wishes ill upon innocent lives."

"Fine." Hydros backed toward the door. "Do it the hard way." He opened the door and Maxen came inside. "Do to him whatever you wish. Torture him. He seems to like that. Just don't kill him. I want every remnant of Sebastian destroyed and the true God of Fire to emerge. Make it happen, or else." Hydros left the room with a quick flutter of wind following.

Maxen smiled wide and stomped toward Sebastian. He twisted the black stone atop his staff until it lit up bright. "We're going to have lots of fun." He grabbed Sebastian by the throat. "What's the matter? Still weak?"

Although he felt his body grow stronger, the process still had him in limbo. His legs held him up but he could barely use his arms, and his head throbbed horribly. Maxen clenched his collar and dragged Sebastian from the room and into a corridor of stairs.

"Whatever I want." Maxen repeated what Hydros had said. "Well, right about now, I want you to take a nasty tumble."

Sebastian barely had a moment to react when he felt a foot plant into his chest. The hard stone pierced into his ribs and spine with every turn as his body rolled down the stairway until it slammed hard onto a landing between floors. He growled painfully and struggled to sit up. Footsteps thumped down the steps until the sound of metal-tipped boots clinked against the same landing he lay upon.

"Whatever I want." Maxen's voice echoed through the tower. He reached down and yanked Sebastian to his feet by his hair and dragged him along the remaining steps. The boom of music came from down the stairs. Maxen pulled Sebastian to the ground floor and into a magnificent hall adorned in deep blood-red stone carvings of dragons. Between each statue was a man with a wide timpani drum and a mallet in each hand.

The grip on Sebastian loosened when he was tossed helplessly onto the floor. His body ached to the bones, and even that wasn't deep enough to describe the way he felt. The pounding of the drums made his head spin, but he still climbed to his feet and stood face-to-face with Maxen. "You will never break me."

"Oh, but I will try and try again." Maxen cupped Sebastian's chin in his hand. "You are not strong enough to stop me. It has been my destiny since birth to end the line of gods, just as my ancestors strived for in the past."

"And failed." Sebastian finally regained most of his arm strength. "The Bolin kings before you were driven mad by hate. That is why your brother sought a better life for his children and kept them away from the blood feud your ancestors started."

"My brother was a traitor." Maxen paused to listen to the drummers bang their timpanis in unison. "Do you know what they are playing, Your Majesty?" He paused for a moment. "It is the war drums Dragon marched to when he went to war against Ansel Bolin in Erras. The war in which he went mad and was exiled here to this island."

Sebastian glared at Maxen but listened to the rhythm that filled the halls of the tower. The drums were empowering, and the stoic expressions of their players inducted ferocity that sent Sebastian into a fighting stance. "You think you are strong enough to take me down." He flicked his hand, gesturing for Maxen to battle him. "Fight me ... one last time. If I live, my people, and my Dani, are to be set free—"

"And if you lose?"

"Then the entire world will fall with me." Fire burst in Sebastian's fists. "But ... I won't lose."

Maxen brandished his staff and the gem shined bright, lighting the tower from the floor all the way to the twin spikes that rose from the peak. "Let's take this outside."

Sebastian nodded and led the way to doors that opened up to a courtyard on the brim of sector three. As he stepped into the sun, horns blasted from above on a balcony high above his head.

Maxen laughed. "Since the days of Dragon, these people have lived lives separated from one another for the greater good of the survival of this island. But allow them to blend together, and ..."

The roar of madness breaking out into the streets of Sector Three sent chills through Sebastian's spine. He turned to face Maxen. "Is this what you wanted? For those people out there to rip each other apart."

"Since when do the gods care about anyone but themselves? That is why Dragon became so powerful. The people cast him away to this godforsaken island where nearly everyone is as old as the age of Dragon itself. It's time they join their ancestors. Let them destroy one another while I destroy you." His staff lit up as bright as the sun and Maxen crashed it into the stone ground before him. It created a blast of wind so powerful Sebastian's body was ripped away from its footing and swept across sector three to land in the center of the town where folks from sector two were raiding the homes and shops of the people of sector three.

There were screams, cries, and desperate calls for help coming from all around. Sebastian knelt on one knee and gasped for air. There was a loud burst, and suddenly Maxen appeared merely a few feet from him. "That's a new trick, sorcerer."

"A good sorcerer never stops training." Maxen stopped and looked down at Sebastian.

Sebastian smirked. "You sound just like your brother."

Maxen took a deep breath. "You are going to pay for that." His hand reached down and took a bundle of Sebastian's hair and pulled him to his feet.

Sebastian forced his palms into Maxen's chest, causing him to stumble back a few feet. "You do know that my brother is going to kill you when he is through using you." He lit a fireball in his hand. "That's if I don't kill you first." Sebastian let out a scream and engulfed his arms in fire before sending a burst of flames crashing into Maxen's armor.

Maxen spun around, clenched his staff, and swung, sending a beam of light that knocked Sebastian into a merchant's cart. He looked up in time to see Maxen enchant the black and gold stone. His menacing smile stretched wide as a laugh escaped his mouth. "I can't wait to see what this does to you." He blasted a spell at Sebastian, narrowly missing him as Sebastian rolled out of the way.

The townsfolk of both sectors three and two stopped robbing one another long enough to see the fight. Their mouths gaped open at the sight of Sebastian with his etched glowing scales and fire wisping from his fingertips as he strolled casually over to Maxen. He lifted Maxen's chin with his index finger and stared in his hazel eyes. "You cannot defeat me, so let me do the honor of making your death a fast one."

An echoing pop bounced around the town square and the blue-haired empress appeared beside her father. Her evil smile and glass, cutting voice was always certain to be noticed. "My love." She chanted and stroked Sebastian's cheek and then set her hand on Maxen's shoulder.

Sebastian threw his arms forward and a gust of wind threw Petra to the ground. "You will not disappear with him this time, traitor."

"Once a traitor, always a traitor." Petra smiled and shrugged. "How is my sweet Jacey?"

"Much better without you." Sebastian slowly stepped over to where she still lay on the ground. "I should have done this long ago." He clutched his sword and pointed the blade at her heart. He poked through her skin, and blood spilled down her breast, but a horrible pain shot through his body. He dropped the sword and fell to his knees, screaming. Maxen held his staff, his magic crippling Sebastian's body. Petra reached out, took her father by the arm, and took Sebastian's hand with the other.

With an uncomfortable pinch and a snap, Sebastian opened his eyes to the marketplace of sector two. He looked around as the citizens gathered their wares and scurried away quickly. Sebastian turned to Maxen and Petra and let out a loud snarl as fire built up in his throat. Sebastian stamped his foot, causing the ground to quake dangerously, sending merchant carts toppling over and shop windows shattering.

There was a loud pop and Petra was standing inches from him with her lips too close to his. "All you have to do is join us, and all of this will stop." She pecked her lips against his.

Sebastian let out a haughty laugh and clapped his hands together. Suddenly, a thunderous cadence broke out across Hast. The island split between Sebastian's feet. Petra fell back and scurried away, but he waved his arm fast from side to side and a massive gale shot from behind him, sending Maxen and Petra through the shop behind them.

Sebastian stretched his neck and back and calmed his breaths as the cracks stopped forming on the ground around him. The shops and homes were crumbling and battered from the elemental force Sebastian had inflicted upon them. He turned toward the road leading to the tower. Sebastian dashed through the remainder of sector two and into three, where buildings had been destroyed by the looters. Fires rang throughout the sector, and the townsfolk scampered through the streets in a panic.

The tower stood tall even through the raging storm overhead. Sebastian glanced at the top, then pushed the doors open where the drum line still waited for the champion to return. As he entered the hall, the men bowed their heads and finished their war drum ballad. Sebastian turned to the same stairway he'd tumbled down from above. Instead of climbing, he descended into the lower rooms where he assumed the dungeons would be located if the tower had such a place.

The corridor below the main floor was well lit, with multiple candelabras hanging on the walls. But as he entered a widened room that was cold and smelled wet and dirty, he saw dark holes in the walls. "Hello." Sebastian's voice echoed through the room. "Dani?" He looked closely at some of the holes, but could not see any faces. As he got close to one, the face of an old woman who seemed to be screaming appeared out of nowhere. Sebastian stumbled and tripped over the rocky floor. He fell and turned his head when he saw something moving in the corner of his eye.

"Dani?" The faint image of his black-haired, blue-eyed husband waving frantically caught his attention. Sebastian rushed over, but Dani shook his head fast and held up his palms. His voice was so muffled that Sebastian thought there must be a spell keeping the prisoners inside their cells. The opening seemed clear, with a hint of a shimmer Sebastian could see if he turned his head just right. Dani's mouth was moving, but Sebastian could only hear a faint mumble.

"I can't hear you, my darling." Sebastian pointed to his ear and shook his head. He held up his index finger and then reached it toward the opening. As his fingers touched the spell, Sebastian cried out and pulled his hand back—his fingertips were black.

"No, not a curse." Sebastian held his hand tight against his body. "How the hell do I do this?" He looked around at all the other cell doors. "Where is Valirus?" He sighed. "It doesn't matter if I can't hear him."

"Sebastian." Dani's voice was loud and clear.

He turned his head to see the invisible shield had turned red. Sebastian reached out, but Dani held up his hands again.

"No! Don't touch it again. See?" Dani touched the spell and it popped and snapped. "I think it reacts differently for everyone, because Meecah touched it earlier and she hasn't been able to move ever since." Dani pointed across from him where Sebastian could see the faint figure of Meecah laying on the floor.

"Meecah." Sebastian hurried over to her cell. "Are you alright?"

"I'm fine." She still lay in the same position but could speak clearly. "Now, go find Valirus and get us out of here before I tear myself apart to get out of the prison."

"Sure thing." Sebastian stood and peeked into the cells around her.

"You should hurry," Dani said. "My father comes in to check on us every hour."

"That won't be a problem." Sebastian continued peeking into the cells of his order. "I left him and your sister implanted into a building somewhere over in sector two."

"What happened out there?" Dani tried hard to watch his every move.

"They turned the people against each other."

A loud thud came from a cell close to Sebastian.

"Tell me that they did not open the gates." Candor's voice was weary. He slammed into the barrier once again.

"Yes, they did, and why do you keep trying if it didn't work the first time?"

"He's been doing it all day," Dani said.

"Valirus!" Sebastian looked around in every direction.

Candor gasped. "He is right above me." His finger pointed up to where some of the cells were high up on the walls with no steps to get to them.

Sebastian stared at the distance between him and Valirus's prison. He paused for a moment and thought about how Valirus would tell him to stop being an idiot and think. Then, he remembered how the coven used steps they'd created to climb in and out of the canyon in Safareen. "I'm going to try something."

Sebastian closed his eyes and pinched his thumb to his middle finger. He opened his left hand and clenched his fist, but the tower shook angrily and the ground below his feet trembled. Sebastian stopped and shook his head. "No, not like that."

"My love," Dani said. "You never learned your earth powers in this way. You could bring the tower down on top of us all."

"I can do this. Trust me."

"I do trust you." Dani sounded scared.

Sebastian whispered, "I promise I won't hurt you." He closed his eyes and felt an odd flicker spread through his arm and down his hand. His fingertips felt as if they were touching the stone wall itself, only he grabbed for air and pulled his arm back. The tower rumbled again, but a step protruded from the wall, then another, and then finally one just at level with Valirus's cell. Sebastian put his hands on his hips for a moment and laughed. "I can't believe that worked."

At the highest step, Sebastian saw into Valirus's cell. It was pitch black. Sebastian could only make out a faint image of an old gray-haired man.

"We have done this before." Valirus sounded amused. "Remember?"

"I'm starting to think you enjoy prison." Sebastian looked around. "How do I get you out? And can you get everyone else out?"

"Do you remember freeing me in Mosisle Dur?"

"Yes." Sebastian nodded.

"The spell on the map?" Valirus came closer to the barrier.

"Oh." Sebastian twiddled his thumbs. "For fuck's sake. I didn't memorize it."

Valirus choked as he let out a laugh. "Think, Your Majesty. And hurry. Even if my brother is incapacitated, that doesn't mean Hydros won't come to check on things after that earthquake."

"I can't concentrate with you rambling." Sebastian covered his ears. He took a breath and opened his mouth. "Twenty knots and thirty-three clicks." A loud pop echoed through the room. "Wait," Sebastian said. "This spell knocked me unconscious for weeks."

"You have no choice." Valirus stated.

"From the wings of birds as dark as night, a curse will break, and the birds take flight." Sebastian stepped down to the floor and squeezed his eyes close and crouched to the ground. He remembered the horrific pain that came from reciting that same spell in the Adurakian prison. But this time there was no pain, only a tap on his head. Sebastian looked up to see Valirus towering over him.

"Get up, idiot boy." Valirus mumbled something quietly as his staff lit up with a soft purple glow. His voice grew steadily louder and louder as a gust of wind rushed into the dungeon. He shouted and gripped his staff tight between his interlocked fingers. "Release them!" Valirus shouted and there was a loud bang. "Hurry!" Valirus started to guide the Order from their cells. "Before Hydros discovers our escape."

"Get to the ship." Sebastian commanded. He pulled Dani against his chest and kissed him deeply. "Go to the ship with the others. Lead them, Dani."

"No, I won't leave you behind. Come with me."

"I have to end this." Sebastian looked around at the watchful faces. "I think I know how to, but I need you to get out of here. I will find you. I swear." He kissed him again.

"I love you," Dani whispered.

Sebastian pressed his forehead to Dani's. "I love you too, my darling." He gasped and pulled away. "Now go. All of you!"

"I won't leave your side." Jace finally climbed down from his cell. "You can't ask me to leave you alone here."

"Jace, go with the others. Protect Dani as you would me."

Jace stood by Sebastian's side and puffed his chest. "I am your hand. I will not run away and leave you to fight your brother alone."

Sebastian turned and grabbed Jace by his upper arms. "I need you to do this for me, Jace. They need you. You are the commander of my army and protector of the people. As your king, I ask of you to guide our people back to the ship, set sail, and protect Dani with your life. Do you understand me?" His face burned and his throat felt as if he'd swallowed lava. "I will find my way home."

"Alive." Jace's eyes watered. "Do you understand me? Alive."

"I swear." Sebastian rested his forehead against Jace's for a moment and took one last glance at Dani, then turned to Valirus. "If you could give me one last piece of advice, what would it be?"

Valirus's face was solemn and his head hung low. "Do not let this be the end for you." He set his hand on Sebastian's shoulder. "Remember that you are more powerful than them. And don't be stupid."

"Thank you for making me understand that my powers are not a curse. Not really." Sebastian cracked a smile. "Now get out of here." He rushed from the dungeons up the stairs to the higher rooms of the tower where he knew he would surely find Hydros waiting for him to arrive.

His legs burned from the steep climb, and a windy howl came from the next landing above where he stood. Sebastian stopped at the flat space on the steps and looked through the wide-open archway and the dimly lit, cavernous room that sat on the side of the tower. Wind whipped through the room as the entire outer wall was open to the outside air. The room reminded Sebastian of his castle in

Adurak and how many of the rooms did not have outer walls, allowing the fresh air to draft inside.

Sebastian ran his fingers across the old wooden desk that sat near a small fire pit by a stained glass window. Unlit torches lined the walls where Sebastian could barely make out words etched into the stone. He lit a fireball in his palm and set the torches aflame. The room brightened to a yellow glow and the words came clear. On one wall read *Aero,* and the other wall read *Sigura.*

The howl of wind quickly changed to an odd noise Sebastian was unfamiliar with. He furrowed his eyebrows and spun around, but saw nothing. He walked along the length of the room toward the balcony where the gentle grumbles came from. Sebastian reached his hand out for the dark curtain that waved gracefully as the breeze rushed through. He passed through and nearly fell backward.

"Dragon." Sebastian stared. "You are a dragon." He clutched the curtain and slowly backed away, but the dragon jumped up to its feet and slowly stepped toward Sebastian. She lowered her head and sniffed as Sebastian kept his pace toward the door. When he nearly made his escape, the dragon slapped her tail down behind him, blocking him from running away.

Sebastian squeezed his eyes closed and gripped the hilt of his sword. When he opened his eyes, the etching of glowing scales danced across his skin in the familiar tingling sensation it always made. The dragon inched its massive head toward him. He could see the shimmering blue of her eyes and the deep azure of her scales under the glow of the torches. She reached her nose out to Sebastian and nudged his chest, and he stumbled back and fell against her tail. She growled and scampered over to the side of the room under the name Sigura.

"Is that your name?" Sebastian pointed at the carving. "Sigura." He turned to the other wall. "There was another dragon. Aero."

Sigura let out a moan and lowered her head to the ground. Sebastian walked over to Aero's side of the room, where a saddle and armor were displayed on the wall. "He died," he whispered. Sebastian made his way back to Sigura, but she let out a roar and ran for the balcony and bounded into the sky.

He watched the open sky from the edge of the terrace. From there he could see the entirety of the island and how the sectors that had been closed off from one another were now wide open as smoke billowed from buildings across the town below the tower. The people could be seen running through the distant streets. He couldn't help but look in every direction for Dani and the others fleeing the city. Sebastian craned his neck to the north and saw that Hast really was shaped like a serpent and that the ocean divided the land and nearly reached the base of the tower. "Right at the snake's neck." Sebastian remembered Candor's words.

Sebastian body burst with adrenaline as he darted up the narrow, winding stairs inside the centuries-old tower. Each step brought him closer to the inevitable confrontation with his brother, the one he had trained alongside, the one who had once been his closest ally and his best friend... The only person among the Drake family who truly understood him.

The torchlight flickered against the cold stone walls, casting dancing shadows that mirrored the tumult within Sebastian's mind. Memories of shared laughter, long hours of practice, and a bond that had once felt unbreakable clashed with the looming conflict ahead. With each step, the weight of their impending battle grew heavier. His brother, once noble and true, had succumbed to the icy grip of his dragon god, twisting his purpose and threatening the realm they had both sworn to protect.

Sebastian's grip on the hilt of his sword tightened. The clash seemed unavoidable, the resolution of their differences now reduced to a duel within these age-worn walls. As he emerged onto the upper platform, the sight of his brother standing tall and unyielding met his eyes. There was a fleeting recognition, a glimmer of the sibling he had known hidden behind a mask of ambition and darkness.

"Here we are again, Chaos. Brother. King of Kings." Hydros laughed. "Whatever they all call you... No. To me, you are just Chaos. My brother." His voice calmed to a whisper. "My equal."

"Don't you dare compare yourself to me, Hydros." Sebastian's face turned hot and his gut burned with anger, but as he stared down his brother, a searing pain stretched across his spine from top to bottom. The room was filled with a bright white light. Sebastian's body hurt like it had never before. His breathing was difficult and his vision fell blurry.

A shriek of laughter seemed to come from far away and then a loud pop made it clear to Sebastian that he was no longer alone with Hydros. "Petra." He groaned and shook his head.

The soft, porcelain-like hand of the blue-haired empress rested against his cheek. "Hello, my lover." She giggled and then slipped out of the way as Maxen proudly stamped into the room with his glowing staff in hand.

"You can leave now Petra." Maxen jerked his head toward the door. "Return to Altania and await my ships." He commanded the clearly upset Petra. Maxen turned his attention to Sebastian at the very moment Petra disappeared from the tower. "You didn't think you won back there in the marketplace, did you?" Maxen puffed his chest and crossed the room until he stood between Hydros and Sebastian. "If only my ancestors could see me now." His head passed back and forth between the two gods. "Once upon a time, Dragon and Litha faced King Ansel in battle."

"And King Ansel succumbed to their power." Sebastian gritted his teeth. "There is no man alive more powerful than me." His skin ignited in the fiery scales he was too familiar with. Sebastian's breaths came in ragged gasps, his chest heaving with a mixture of fury and despair. The clash with his brother had ignited a storm within him, a tempest of emotions that threatened to consume reason and restraint. The desire to hurt, to lash out and destroy, surged within Sebastian. His grip on the sword tightened, his knuckles turning white. The image of tearing Maxen apart, rending the source of his pain and anger, flashed vividly in his mind. Something inside him intensified more than he had ever felt. His head felt as if it were going to burst open, his scales shined bright, and the searing sensation returned to his eyes. Sebastian growled and raised his arms wide.

Sebastian's erratic feelings came together to form an unadulterated, primordial force. He summoned crackling lightning bolts that danced in the air, arcing and pulsating with unbridled power, an act motivated by a combination of wrath and a desperate attempt to put an end to the fight. He unleashed the scalding energy at Maxen with a low groan. The energy surged, bringing with it blinding brightness and terrible thunder that echoed throughout the tower.

 Maxen hardly had time to respond before he was taken aback by Sebastian's unexpected display of power. The crackling bolts slashed out, casting a fierce, dazzling illumination over the area between them. The smell of ozone and the roar of electricity filled the chamber for a brief moment. The lightning crackled and sizzled, licking at the opportunity to seize Maxen again, but he ducked and the lightning crashed into Hydros. A short, agonizing cry escaped Maxen's lips as the remaining energy singed his garments, leaving burn marks.

Sebastian watched as Hydros covered his face with his cloak and emerged from the attack unscathed and looking volatile.

Hydros gripped his hands together and rubbed his palms as a cold breeze wafted across the top of the tower. The air became startlingly cold and Sebastian's teeth began to chatter. Hydros summoned a hail of icy fragments that shot in Sebastian's direction with a simple hand gesture that controlled the elements.

Due to his own exhaustion, Sebastian was in no position to respond quickly. His battle skills and instincts came into play as he tried to dodge the hail of frozen projectiles. With a quick maneuver, he avoided some of the incoming shards of ice, but others grazed him, leaving his leathers pierced with sharp, icy daggers.

The already-tense battleground became even more turbulent as a result of the elements colliding—the biting cold of the ice against the crackling intensity of lightning and fire.

Sebastian summoned a roaring storm to surround the tower. "We will all die if you do not surrender to me right now, Hydros."

"I am already dead, so to speak." Hydros smirked. "Remember?"

Sebastian shouted and darted for Hydros, meeting him with a force of fire against Hydros's ice. The room lit in a dazzling display of elemental light and the tower shook dangerously against Sebastian's force. As Sebastian sent a fiery blast of wind at Hydros, an icy blizzard engulfed Sebastian, and both gods were sent flying apart across the room. Sebastian crashed into a desk and strained to catch his breath as he climbed to his feet and hurried across the room toward Hydros.

As the elemental battle stalled, Maxen used his powerful magic to take advantage of the pandemonium. He called forth his glowing black and gold gem, and with a sweeping motion of the hand that had a grip on his staff, Maxen released a burst of evil energy, guiding it with an accuracy refined by his arcane expertise. The black strands twisted through the unstable air straight toward Sebastian in the midst of the elemental whirlwind that surrounded him.

Sebastian ducked quickly, and Maxen's spell crashed into an unintended target.

Maxen relaxed his hold on his staff, waltzed over to an unconscious Hydros, and ripped the Oscura from his finger. "All that power." He stared intently at the ring. "And it can be brought down with something so simple. So delicate."

The Oscura, a legendary stone of immense power rumored to hold the capability to end the life of the God of Fire, pulsed ominously as Maxen, fueled by his malevolent intentions, placed it upon his finger. The stone was ethereal as it pressed against his skin, giving the room a sinister light. There was a growing sense of impending dread in the air, as if Maxen's own intentions were being resonated by the evil energy of the stone.

A shiver went down Sebastian's spine as he saw the Oscura on Maxen's finger. The circumstances became more serious and the stakes became extremely high. The confrontation was already explosive, but the stone's sheer presence, which had the power to take his life, gave it an overwhelming sense of urgency and danger. A mixture of resolve and malice shined in Maxen's eyes.

"Are you prepared to die?" Maxen's voice carried throughout the tower.

Sebastian's anger grew rapidly as he saw Hydros's body still sat limp on the stone floor. Although he was no longer Tomas, Sebastian still felt love for Hydros in his heart. He knew he had to end his terrible reign so that Tomas could rest peacefully, but seeing him like this was overwhelming. Sebastian fought with the horrid thoughts that filled his mind.

Amidst the disarray, Sebastian started to change—a merging of his human and dragon essence. The dragon that had lain asleep inside him awoke in response to the dreadful situation. He caught his reflection in the mirror on the wall; his eyes blazed otherworldly, capturing the ferocious resolve and tenacity of the old creature within. A surge of energy shot out of him. While his powers had seemed to reach their peak before, this was different, and Sebastian felt overwhelmingly more violent than he had ever felt before.

Sebastian's form changed dramatically as the internal conflict raged. An ageless, primordial force that represented unadulterated and everlasting might filled his body and boiled his blood. Sebastian discovered that the ancient dragon strength, when combined with his own volition, created a unique force when his human and draconic essences blended together.

Maxen whispered to the Oscura, and the stone turned from a sleepy black to shimmering onyx. Sebastian raised his eyebrows, understanding that the Oscura was controlled by magic. Maxen backed away and turned his attention to Hydros. "First, I will end him." He reached down and gripped a fistful of Hydros's hair. "You only thought I was working for you, monster." He laughed in Hydros's face and yanked him to his feet, snapping Hydros awake.

"Traitor!" Hydros shouted. He balled his fists and wrapped his arms around Maxen.

Maxen let out a loud shriek and shoved Hydros away, revealing a sheet of ice that had formed across his torso. The already turbulent battlefield became even more unpredictable as Hydros's energies collided with Maxen's sorcery.

The room crackled with a cacophony of clashing elements. Maxen's dark energy, the searing cold of Hydros's hand, the roaring fire of Sebastian's protection, and the clashing sounds of opposing elements filled the room. As Hydros diverted his energies, the confusion increased, and the combat shifted to include all adversaries in the room. Still possessing the dragon's inner strength, Sebastian was forced to deal with not just Maxen but also Hydros's unexpected interference.

Sebastian could feel the intensity of Dragon's power consuming him. He battled his thoughts of destroying Maxen and Hydros, or ending Maxen only to save Hydros so that he could give him the peaceful death Tomas deserved. Blood was smeared across the stone walls—a somber reminder of how fierce the battle had become. Maxen, the once-powerful sorcerer, stumbled feebly. He doubled over and leaned painfully against the wall. His strength faltered him and he lost his balance as the elements burst around him, colliding and erupting with intensity so magnanimous that Maxen cowered to the floor and covered his head.

Sebastian and Hydros fought viciously, throwing each other around like rag dolls and painting the tower red. Maxen silently approached, his hand outstretched toward Sebastian as he whispered again to the stone, which lit up brighter with every word. Sebastian threw Hydros aside and let out a horrendous shriek. The tower shifted and shook. The sky turned a dark, stormy gray, and rain began to stream down in icy pellets that click-clacked against the tower's stone floors.

"No more fighting." Sebastian held his arms out before him. "This is the end...for all of us." His voice was deeper and more gruff than usual. He let out a monstrous scream and the storm exploded into fury. The tower creaked and groaned and swayed with the intense winds that came from the sea.

Both Maxen and Hydros attempted to approach him but were thrown into the wall once again by a blast of wind.

"I said we will end this now." Sebastian turned toward the split in the island and reached one arm forward. "I will eradicate this world of our powers once and for all," he snarled as a thunderous force left his body and plummeted to the ground below.

All of Hast jerked and cracked. Walls that had encompassed the districts tumbled to dust and buildings collapsed under the force of a massive earthquake. There was a sudden calm that invited Hydros and Maxen to climb to their feet.

"Is that all you've got, Brother?" Hydros's icy voice shot through Sebastian like poison. "You are weak." He spun around and punched Maxen hard in the throat and ripped the Oscura from his finger. He laughed maniacally and wore a joker's smile. Hydros placed the ring on his index finger and reached for Sebastian's throat. "One touch... that is all it takes." His fingers nearly scraped Sebastian's scaly skin as he stumbled back to avoid Hydros.

Sebastian roared and spread his arms apart before Hydros could reach him. Suddenly, the island jarred dangerously, sending the tower into a furious sway in the sky. Sebastian knew the tower would fall. He stood and watched as the island cracked even further and the sea rushed to fill the empty space until it hammered against the base of the tower. The sound of rock and glass shattering below their feet was deafening. As the tower fell to the side and split apart, Sebastian saw that Hast had become two islands and the tower that sat dead center had been broken in half.

He ripped Maxen away from the wall and punched him repeatedly in the face. "Your ancestors would be disappointed in you." He walked toward the edge where the balcony draped over the waiting sea below. "You will never hurt Dani or anyone again. You are disgraced and stripped of your crown along with the Bolin bloodline that will end forever at the death of your brother and son. They are the last of your line, and you are dead." Fire blazed in Sebastian's fists as he screamed and shoved his palms into Maxen's chest, sending him backward over the edge and to his doom. The tower jerked, and suddenly both he and Hydros were falling to the sea below.

Sebastian thought about Dani as his feet finally left the floor of the tower. He watched Maxen fall fast. His screams filled the air and his staff slipped from his grip and smashed into bits on a falling piece of tower flooring. Maxen cried out in hopes that his power would save him, but as he recited a curse as loud as his voice would carry, a statue that once graced the top of the tower crashed into his body, and all that could be seen of Maxen was blood spraying from all sides of the stone before it splashed into the sea.

As he fell, Hydros locked his shining blue eyes onto Sebastian's with a look of innocence. All he could see in that moment was the innocent, kind face of Tomas. No shimmering scales and no icy fury to consume him, just the pale, brown-haired, quiet boy who Sebastian loved more than anyone else in the whole world... his brother... his twin, falling fast until his body was swallowed by the ocean below.

Sebastian closed his eyes. He thought about how his death would create peace in the land and how everyone he loved would now be safe without Maxen, Hydros, and himself living there. A tear dropped from his eye as he wanted nothing more than to kiss Dani one last time. "I love you, my darling," he whispered before he closed his eyes and waited for his body to collide with the water below.

He knew he was close and took a deep breath. He waited for whatever was to happen next, expecting to feel himself be encompassed by saltwater before being knocked unconscious and then drowning. Sebastian heard a shrill roar before he crashed onto a hard surface. His eyes still closed, he ran his hands along the scaly body that had saved him. Sebastian opened his eyes and felt the forceful wind whip through his hair. He was clutched onto the back of a great blue dragon. "Sigura!" He cheered.

Chapter Eighteen

The Flight of the Dragon

The Isle of Hast lay in shambles. Sigura found an open space to land near the harbor where the Hetta had been docked when they arrived. The ships were gone, and Sebastian couldn't help but smile knowing his people, especially Dani, got away safely before the destruction ensued. He turned back to peer across the island where a tower once could have seen in the distance. His heart sank at the thought of Tomas's body being lost to the sea and that he couldn't take him back to NorthBrekka to rest with family.

He sighed and slowly approached Sigura, hoping she wouldn't fly away. Her eyes were heavy and her groan sounded pained. Sebastian stood before her and stared into her deep eyes. "I'm sorry I destroyed your home, but you are now free to live anywhere you wish to go."

Sigura lowered her head to Sebastian's level and bumped him with the tip of her nose. She growled, revealing a whirling blue flame in the back of her throat.

Sebastian took a step back and shielded his face with his arm. "Don't set me on fire." He peeked one eye open and met Sigura's gaze. He'd expected her to be ready to eat him, but instead she closed her mouth and lowered her shoulder to the ground. "I said you are free." Sebastian backed away. "Go! Fly away."

Sigura let out a gentle roar.

Sebastian held up his arms. "I said fly away." He waved his arms. "Get out of here."

The dragon stamped her foot, making the ground shake. She stared at Sebastian and lowered her wing to the ground once again and let out a grumble from the back of her throat.

"No." Sebastian shook his head and turned to walk to the empty harbor. "Leave. I don't need a pet dragon." He paused and looked out over the sea. "I need my ship." His voice was quieter than before. "Dani," he whispered, but then the ground shook again. Sebastian spun around, ready to scold Sigura, but she was sitting in place with her head craned toward the city.

The rumble was from footsteps coming hard and fast. Sebastian walked back to the road and stood by Sigura's side. "What do they want?" He watched them come in the hundreds, a crowd of Hast citizens that Sebastian had learned once served Dragon.

Filonias appeared to be leading the people to Sebastian. He walked further forward and stopped when he was close enough. "Before you leave." Filonias approached Sebastian. "We must ask of you one last thing." He passed Sebastian a handkerchief. "You are bleeding, My King."

"I am the one who destroyed your homeland." Sebastian interrupted. "I will send men to rebuild once I return to NorthBrekka."

"No, no." Filonias held up his hands. "You see, Your Majesty, our God of Fire. All we ask of you is that you release us."

"Release you?" Sebastian looked around at the crowd with furrowed eyebrows and a clenched jaw. "King Maxen and Hydros are gone. Lost to the sea. You are free of their tyranny." He turned back to Sigura, but was stopped when Filonias set his hand on Sebastian's shoulder.

"Perhaps you misunderstood." Filonias gestured to the people of Hast. "We ask of you to break the curse that is set upon us... You are a curse breaker, aren't you?"

Sebastian looked at the massive number of islanders that swamped the entirety of the harbor. "There are so many of you. It would take me ages."

"Not to worry." Filonias reached his palm out toward Sebastian. "Take my hand, My King."

Sebastian placed his shaking hand in Filonias's. "I don't understand."

"We understand..." Filonias waved for the crowd to come close. "You only have to do what you would normally do to break someone's curse."

"But." Sebastian pulled his hand away. "Does this mean you will all die? And what about those who aren't cursed?"

Filonias nodded his head. "We have lived a very long time. Hundreds of years have passed, and we have waited for our Dragon to return to us—and he has, in you. Please understand that Dragon was not a monster. He was our king, our god, and he was a good man who lost his path. But you, Sebastian Drake, can be the change the world needs. And don't worry about the others. They will rebuild Na'Huk the way it was before." Filonias gripped his hand again. "Free us and go rule the world the way Dragon had always wished for it to be ruled. In peace..."

Sebastian's eyes teared up. "Thank you for your knowledge and kindness. I hope you rest well, my friend." He closed his eyes and felt his body intensify with a sharp pins and needles sensation, shaking him to his core. The power shifted through his gut and into his chest until it traced down his arm and a glowing light met Filonias's hand. He stared into the old man's eyes and watched as his delicate smile began to vanish and he could see through his body to the other people of Hast, who all vanished with a gust of wind.

The harbor was empty. Sebastian stood alone with Sigura, who watched his every movement. She lowered her shoulder, fanned her wing onto the ground, and groaned once again. Sebastian took one last look around and hurried over to the dragon and climbed onto her back. She kicked off from the ground and lifted high into the sky. The now scarcely inhabited island sat lonely with smoke billowing from all around.

They drifted over the sea and through the clouds as a light rain fell, soaking Sebastian's coat. The warm air felt nice on his aching body as Sigura began to descend from high in the sky. Sebastian gripped her scales as tightly as he could as she dived toward the waiting sea. The wind bit at his skin painfully until Sigura spread her wings wide and a sudden jolt had them soaring just above the water's surface.

Ahead, the towers that had invited Sebastian's ships into the ring of Hast's outer realm lay waiting, but Sebastian caught a glimpse of black sails through the fog. "Follow those ships." He pointed straight ahead. The ghost ships came clear and Sigura let out a snarl as the heads of Sebastian's soldiers turned and cheers were heard from all around. Sigura let her wings glide with the breeze as they came alongside Kristoff's ship. Sebastian noticed their confused and impressed faces and couldn't help but laugh.

As they came up to the Hetta, Sebastian locked eyes with Jace, whose mouth dropped open wide. All that could be heard was Jace's voice screaming, "He's alive!"

Jace left the wheel and ran across the deck. "Dani, you might want to get out here."

Sebastian climbed to one knee as Sigura balanced her flight to match the speed of the ship. He scanned the faces of everyone on board until he heard a gasp and someone running through the staring men. Sebastian's heart skipped a beat. "Dani!"

Dani's bright blue eyes lit up the cloudy sky. He held a hand over his mouth and wiped a tear from his cheek. "How ... What?"

"I have no idea what I am doing." Sebastian patted Sigura. "Get me closer, girl." He patted her neck. Sigura drifted against the port side of the ship, giving enough room for Sebastian to leap onto the deck. He watched Sigura lift off and fly just above the highest mast. A pair of skinny, pale arms wrapped around his neck.

"I thought I had lost you." Dani sniffled.

Footsteps came quickly across the deck. "He's been panicking the entire time since we left." Jace joined them. "I thought I was going to have to toss him overboard."

Sebastian stared at Jace in disbelief and then held onto Dani tighter, whispering into his ear, "I told you that I would never leave you ... that I would always come back to you."

"I saw the tower fall." Dani's voice cracked.

Valirus pushed Jace out of the way. "Go and steer through the tide before we are stuck in Hast another day." He turned to Sebastian with a scowl on his face. "What did you do? Tell me everything."

Sebastian went to the center of the deck and sat on top of a crate. Barron came up from downstairs looking more pale and tired than he had the time in Castle Drake when he lost his mind and tried to kill his entire family, including beating Sebastian bloody, leaving him scarred and dying on top of a frozen lake.

Barron sat next to Sebastian and leaned over to whisper, "I need to speak with you in private after we return home."

"You look unwell." Sebastian stared at Barron's hollow cheeks and beady eyes. "Brother, tell me what is wrong."

"In due time." Barron shifted himself to face the rest of the others. "Tell us your tale. What happened in Hast?"

Sebastian turned to the waiting faces, including Dani, who sat on the deck below his feet with a proud smile on his face. Over Valirus's shoulder, he could see Sigura drifting gently along as the other ships hovered and the people on board gawked at her greatness. Sebastian nodded to the dragon. "Her name is Sigura. She was alive when Dragon ruled in Hast. I believe she was his dragon. If the stories are true, and Dragon was born in Adurak, then that is where I belong. There is a reason I feel connected to that land, and once we return to NorthBrekka, I will set everything straight with the kingdom before my departure to my new home." He sighed and stared at Sigura, with her graceful glide. "I will take her with me. It can't hurt to have a dragon around." He shrugged.

"My love." Dani interrupted. "The dragon is amazing, and I have some things that I collected from the library before we left, but we can talk about that later. What happened to my father?"

Sebastian squeezed his eyes closed as he thought about the blood and how Maxen's death was gruesome and well deserved. "He is dead."

Dani clenched his jaw tight. He fell to his knees and slowly lifted his head up to meet Sebastian's eyes. "How?"

"When the tower collapsed, he fell . . . We all did. He was killed by the falling debris. Sigura saved my life."

Dani paused for a moment and then sat up straight. His head fell to one side. "What about—"

"Hydros fell. I watched him die all over again." Sebastian choked back his emotions as his chest suddenly burned and his face got hot.

Sebastian continued his story of everything that had happened before the tower. Hydros begging him to join him and sending Maxen to torture him when he declined. The battle in the marketplace and how Maxen had opened the sector gates to allow the townspeople to go to war with one another.

"That must have been catastrophic for the people of Hast." Candor shook his head. "What about the Unrahli . . . Filonias?"

"They're all gone, Uncle. I lifted their curse."

"You what?" Candor's voice got loud and he moved too close to Sebastian.

"They asked me to do it!" Sebastian held up his arms in defeat and then started to pace. "The last thing I wanted to do was kill any more people. But they asked me to set them free." His voice lowered. "There was nothing left for them there."

Candor backed away and joined the others as Sebastian finished telling them the story up until his arrival on Sigura's back.

That evening, while the others slept, Sebastian sat on the deck and read a book that Dani had given him over dinner. It was an account from one of the town elders about Dragon's history. The author noted himself as a caretaker in Moonlight Palace who'd followed Dragon's father and watched Dragon's rise to power. As he read on, Sebastian started to admire the person Dragon was as a boy.

Dani came out of the captain's quarters wrapped in a blanket and sat down next to Sebastian. He nodded at Sigura. "How long can dragons fly without rest?"

"I have no idea." Sebastian wrapped his arm around Dani. "You didn't happen to swipe a guidebook about how to raise dragons, did you?"

"It never crossed my mind." Dani snuggled close. "Although I did wonder what happened to the dragon we saw in the fields."

"He used to have two of them." Sebastian opened the book and searched for the pages. "There were two dragon keeps in the tower. One was marked 'Aero' and the other 'Sigura.' The book says the dragons were brother and sister."

"I wonder what happened to Aero." Dani laid his head on Sebastian's shoulder.

Sebastian let out a light laugh and continued with his book as the story of Dragon became more and more relatable. "All this time I have told everyone I am nothing like Dragon, but from what I read, Dragon was desperate to save his people ... the gods. There used to be so many." He flipped through the book some more.

"My father said my ancestors destroyed most of the gods." Dani wore a blank stare. "And over time, they all just died off. Once Dragon died, the line just stopped."

"Until Tomas and I were born." Sebastian closed the book. "I don't believe the world needs gods to survive. I think when my time ends, the line will end. But then, there is Liliana."

Dani sat up straight. "Do you think she is a goddess?"

"I feel something strong when I am near her. But perhaps it is just because she is Tomas's daughter."

"Or," Dani said, "maybe she is a goddess, and the line remains."

Chapter Nineteen

The Ruby Dagger

The ships arrived at the icy shores of the East Bay Harbor early on a cold morning in NorthBrekka. Sebastian climbed down the gangway and stepped foot on his home ground, a sigh of relief with every step. The Order joined him as they ascended the cliffside until they reached the grounds of the watchtower, where a stable of horses awaited their riders. Sigura rested on the snowy field as guards watched from the tower courtyard in fear.

"Don't worry, gentlemen." Sebastian made his way through the guards on his way toward the watchtower doors. "She won't eat you ... I don't think so, anyway." He went inside and walked over to the fire to warm his hands as his order came in. A group of maidens scurried about and went to prepare breakfast for the crew. Sebastian sat down and read more of his book while waiting for the food to be served. He heard everyone's quiet conversations and the whispers about his stories that the others hadn't gotten to hear.

"Are you alright?" Meecah's voice startled Sebastian. "You seem ... sad."

"I can't believe it's all over. Finally." Sebastian set his book down. "I finally get to just rest and live my life." He put his arm around Meecah. "I'm not sad. And neither should you be."

"I'm happy, My King. I do have a surprise to share with you." Meecah took Sebastian's hand. "Samir and I are having a baby." She patted her stomach.

Sebastian smiled wide and pulled her tight. "I'm so happy for you both."

"We are going to settle in Dunebar."

"At least you will be close so I can visit my niece or nephew." Sebastian nodded to her stomach.

They had breakfast, took their horses, and set off through the East Bay Pass. Once they passed the caves, the wolves joined their journey on the way to the castle. The courtyard was filled with townspeople awaiting the arrival of their king. Sebastian looked over his castle and his kingdom as they descended the road to the gate. Nadya and Amara stood on the steps before the entrance to Castle Drake, along with their children and Sara, who stepped up to join them. The people bowed as Sebastian passed, and the courtyard gates closed as the last horse crossed through.

Sebastian climbed down from his saddle and stood in the center of everyone. "Our enemies are dead. Peace has finally come to these lands. May we be thankful, for tonight, we feast!" He went to the door and kissed Nadya and Amara, then stopped before Sara, who looked at him oddly, then wrapped her arms around his shoulders.

"Welcome home, Brother." She kissed his cheek.

"Barron ... he seems ill. You should go to him." Sebastian looked over his shoulder at where his oldest brother waited with Viktor and Kristoff, who were helping him down from his horse. As Sara trotted away, a roar came from the sky above.

Sigura flapped her wings and landed on top of the castle walls as the crowd of Erras citizens gasped and moaned in excitement and fear. Sebastian ran out with his arms open wide. "She won't hurt any of you. Do not fret." Sebastian marched over to face Sigura. "Go hunt. You can rest in the fields by the lake." He nodded down the mountain. "I don't know why I am talking to you. It's not like you can underst—"

Sigura roared and lifted from the wall and flew down toward the lake. "Or maybe she can." Sebastian turned and went inside his castle, straight to his father's office, hearing Amara and Nadya shouting questions about the dragon to him. Jace and Dani quickly explained, which let Sebastian slip away to be alone.

The days passed with celebrations, and stories of the old days went by. Sebastian finished reading all the books Dani had taken from Hast and started to gain an understanding of what kind of person Dragon truly was. He wrote a letter to King Lucian and sent it home to Safareen with Candor after a long discussion about what the coven would do now that war was over. They all agreed to spend their lives in their canyon just as they always had done before. But before they departed, Frey came to have a discussion with Sebastian.

"I believe it's time we have one last conversation before my time here is over." Frey sat across from Sebastian. "You are the spitting image of her, and I considered her my daughter." A tear came to his eye. "She was so beautiful."

Sebastian tilted his head. "You never did explain to me how my mother, the Princess of Safareen, was allowed to run away to live with a coven of witches."

Frey laughed. "The king knew he couldn't tame her. She was a wild one. They once thought that she perhaps inherited the Dragon's curse, but he couldn't keep her from coming to us. No matter how hard he tried." Frey sighed. "She was so loved by all. When the news spread that she died giving birth to the King of the North's child, the Safarian people were broken. That is why they revolted against the north. Your parents died so that you could live. Your father knew that the only way to force you to rise into your power was to induce as much pain as you could tolerate."

"Wait, stop. You're wrong. My father didn't want me growing into my power."

"You are wrong." Frey grabbed his shoulder. "Your father knew the only way NorthBrekka could survive was for him to fall and for you to rise in his stead. He believed in you so much. He would be proud of what you've become, and your mother, I know, has been watching over you since the moment she left this earth. You are not cursed, Your Majesty. The prophecy may have been true, but you are no monster."

"But the prophecy was wrong." Sebastian shifted in his seat. "I never committed genocide."

"No?" Frey raised one eyebrow. "Did you not put to rest much of the population of Hast?"

Sebastian's mouth dropped open. "Oh no . . ."

"Don't fret, my dear boy. It was not in vain. You set things right, and the people love you for it." Frey hugged Sebastian and said his final goodbye before retreating to say his farewells to the others.

The next morning, Sebastian went down to the tomb chambers to say goodbye to his ancestors, his father, and Cyrus before preparing to depart for Adurak. He stopped at the plaque that read Cyrus's name and rested his hand and forehead against the wall. "You will always be the first man I ever loved. And I will love you until the day I die. I swear. I only hope that you are free, just like we always wanted for each other."

He walked over to Tomas's broken tomb and rested against the debris. "I'm sorry I couldn't bring you home, Brother. Please forgive me for not being there for you. I will never forgive myself for what happened to you."

Sebastian went to his father's burial place and knelt. "I'm sorry I called you a coward. It must have been a hard decision to end your own life for me. I promise to do what is right by our people, and I will continue to lead this world to peace. No more war, Father. Not as long as I am breathing."

After a moment, he went over to his mother's resting place. Sebastian knelt down and touched the wall, behind which rested her tomb. "I wish I could have gotten to know you. I don't even remember your face or your voice, but I know I would have loved you so much." He wiped a tear from his eyes. "One day we will meet again, and I can't wait to wrap my arms around you for the first time."

Sebastian said goodbyes to his stepmother and his brothers and sisters who died before, then went off to seek Barron. In the cold and bitter war room, Sebastian found Barron sitting on the edge of the table alone.

Barron turned his head to greet him. "Thank you for coming."

"Are you going to tell me what is happening to you?"

Barron let out a huff of laughter. "Sebastian, I am dying."

Sebastian sat next to him, noticing Barron's face was wet from tears. "Dying? Because of your powers..."

"I started feeling unwell after the first time I used my powers." He pulled a thin book from his pocket. "It's a book of the Blackbirds." Barron passed it to Sebastian and opened it to the page where it explained the story of the Blackbird that once held Barron's powers. "When he used his magic, it weakened him. But when he kept using his powers to save Dragon, it killed him."

Sebastian looked over at Barron. "So, by using your powers to save me—"

"My life is ending, Brother. I am in pain. I'm tired. I brought you here to ask that you end my life." Barron reached into his coat and pulled out the ruby-encrusted dagger that he had stabbed into Sebastian's leg, and the same dagger that Cyrus had driven into his own chest.

"I can't do that."

"Yes, you can." Barron pushed it into his hand. "I only have a few days left. Sara and my son will travel back to their village and return to their lives there. She has accepted my fate just as I have." Barron took Sebastian's hand. "It is only right that I die by your hand. I deserve it after everything I have done." Tears poured down his cheeks. "I murdered so many people, and I don't know why I did it. I was so angry, so jealous, for nothing... And I am sorry for scarring you. But I ask of you to end my life. Please." His shaking hand pulled away.

Sebastian gripped the dagger tight. "Here, now?"

"Yes." Barron smiled. "This is your favorite room in the castle. It's only fitting you get closure before you leave NorthBrekka for your new throne." He took a deep breath. "I wish I could have seen Adurak. I'm sure it is beautiful."

Sebastian's chest burned and his face was soaked in tears. He fought against unleashing his emotions of hurt and anger toward Barron as he remembered the faces of his dad and stepmother, along with the youngest of the Drake siblings whom Barron had buried alive. Barron's arm slipped around Sebastian's back and pulled him in for a hug for the first time Sebastian could ever remember.

"I love you," Barron whispered.

Sebastian gripped the dagger tight, pulled away, and shoved it into Barron's chest. "I love you too, Brother. Rest well. I promise to send you to our ancestors' waiting arms." He laid Barron on the table and held his hand until it went limp and the blood had spilled from his body.

The funeral was in Castle Drake on a dark and stormy evening. Sebastian spoke in front of all and told stories of Barron when he was still a sweet and innocent child, before he was a murderous witch. As he regaled the good times, the crowd laughed and cried, and the night fell into silence in the castle once all had gone off to bed.

The following morning, Sebastian called for a meeting of the townspeople and all of Erras who wished to come to the crowning of the new King and Queen of the North. As the weeks passed, all who could come gathered in Castle Drake, including King Lucian and the Safar. Sebastian stood before all.

"As you all know by now, I will be leaving to spend my days in Adurak, where I belong. But with NorthBrekka being the capital of Erras, you need a leader. Therefore, I crown my sister, Nadya, and her husband, Jon, as the new King and Queen of NorthBrekka." Sebastian walked over to the two thrones where his sister and Jon sat waiting. He placed their crowns upon their heads and turned to the crowd. "All hail the King and Queen of the North!"

The crowd erupted in cheers and chants, and the feast began to arrive on the tables in the hall. Sebastian turned back to Nadya. "I always planned to leave this place to you. You are the only one worthy of that throne. The best of us all."

Nadya stood, her eyes flooded with tears. "You better not disappear forever, Brother. Regardless of what you believe, your people here still need you."

"I will visit often, I swear."

Finally, Sebastian went down to where Dom and his wolves sat outside in the garden on the bench where Sebastian had been born.

"I wish you would stay." Dom looked at Sebastian with tired but teary eyes. "I can't imagine not seeing you anymore. You mean everything to me, Sebastian."

"Please Dom, come to Adurak with me." Sebastian begged. "I need you. I've always needed you."

Dom smiled and shook his head. "I love you so much, but this is my home, and this is where fate leaves me. Erras and The Far North will not be the same without you in it."

"No, it won't." Sebastian sighed. "It will be better. I promise to come home as often as I can stand to sail. Besides, I am feeling a little emotional leaving home once and for all."

"I thought you would run from this place as fast as your legs would carry." Dom laughed.

"So did I." Sebastian wrapped his arms around Dom. "So did I." He pulled away and held Dom's hands in his own. "I will miss you the most."

Chapter Twenty

Goodbye Erras

Sebastian gathered his order in the courtyard on the morning of departure. As the horses circled and everyone said their goodbyes, Jace hopped down from his horse and ran toward the castle door where Sebastian stood saying farewell to Amara and her daughter. Sebastian tickled Lilaina. "I can't believe how much she looks like Tomas."

"I miss him, Sebastian." Amara cupped his cheek. "I don't want my daughter growing up not knowing what her father looked like." She glanced over Sebastian's shoulder. "That is why I want to come with you to Adurak."

Jace plowed his way between Sebastian and Amara and put his arm around her and the baby. "I invited them. I hope this is alright, Your Majesty."

Sebastian smiled and embraced all three of them. "Nothing would make me happier."

As the accompaniment made way through the gates and started toward the East Bay Pass, Sebastian stopped and turned to his castle.

For the first time, he felt painfully regretful for leaving his home. He wanted to go back and stay, to live with his family, both dead and alive, and rule the world from NorthBrekka as it was always intended to be, but Sebastian knew he did not belong there. He never had, just like Dragon had never belonged there either. Only this time, he was going to fulfill Dragon's final wish that he was never able to carry out: to return to Adurak and live his life in his homeland with the person he loved. He took one last look and whispered, "Goodbye."

The Hetta set sail as the armada of ghost ships followed. Viktor decided to join Sebastian in Midrel Istan, and Kristoff still planned to sail the seas once he crossed the map with his family one last time. Amara and Jace were already planning their wedding, and Samir and Meecah couldn't wait to get back to Dunebar and start their own family. Sigura left East Bay with the ships and soared high above the Hetta as they crossed from the Midnight Sea into the open waters of the southern part of Erras.

They traveled across the seas until they entered the familiar Sea of Glass, where they stopped at the port in Lastorum and Valirus, Meecah, and Samir left the accompaniment.

Valirus stopped before walking down the gangway and rested his hand on Sebastian's shoulder. "I still expect to see you often. You still have much to learn, Your Majesty."

"I look forward to it, my friend." Sebastian wrapped Valirus into a hug, which felt both awkward and pleasing. He said his goodbyes and well wishes to Samir and Meecah and promised to come visit Dunebar when the baby arrives.

The ships made port in Adurak's harbor at the feet of The Creed. They ascended the mountains and followed the pathway down until Sebastian caught sight of his palace on the river in his perfect mountain city. His heart raced and his body flooded with excitement upon finally being home. The smile across his face was too much to conceal as he followed his people down into the prairies across the valley floor and to the fountain that sat between the castle and the town.

The citizens of Adurak awaited his arrival as music played and dancers performed in the courtyard. Sebastian had never seen such merriment in his time in Midrel Istan and learned that word had spread that Maxen was no longer alive. The people cheered and brought massive trays of food of all kinds for their king to try. The streets were decked out in vibrant banners and decorations, reflecting the joy that was in Sebastian's heart.

He felt loved and at home as he was reunited with his family and friends. He developed a close bond with the City of Thieves and its inhabitants and they grew to embrace him as the one true king. He felt he had rediscovered his position in the universe at that instant, one of pure joy and belonging.

The moment Sebastian and Dani found themselves alone in the grand halls of the castle, it was as if the world outside had faded away, leaving just the two of them amidst the echoes of history and the whispers of the past. With a shared glance, an unspoken understanding passed between them, deepening their connection in ways words couldn't describe. In the quietude of the castle's private chambers, their love bloomed like a garden in spring.

Their love story had weathered storms, embraced joys, and wove itself through the fabric of time. In this moment, the air was fragrant with passion. Their gazes lingered a little longer, and their touches spoke volumes, resonating with an indescribable depth of emotion. Their love deepened, not just romantically, but in a profound, soul-stirring way. It was as if the very essence of their beings were intertwined, enriching and elevating each other. In the silence and solitude of the castle, they built upon their love, making the walls resonate with a timeless kind of affection, strengthening the foundation of their marriage.

"I will love you until the end of time, Dani."

Dani smiled more powerfully than Sebastian had ever seen. "And I will always love you."

Sebastian fidgeted for a moment. "I'm sorry about your father."

"I hated my father."

"I know." Sebastian interrupted. "But all the same . . ."

"What happened to Petra?" Dani said.

Sebastian tilted his head and remembered Maxen's last order to his daughter. "She's in Altania. Your father sent her there."

Dani rolled his eyes. "She will surface as soon as she hears we have returned."

"And she will be dealt with, Dani."

Dani closed his eyes and sighed. "Maybe she doesn't have to die, Sebastian."

"She doesn't have Maxen to hide behind anymore. We will see how powerful she is when she surfaces. But if she challenges me—"

"No, let me deal with her. Please, my love." Dani's face was serious with not even a hint of a smile, and his sapphire eyes were ghostly, almost white, as they turn when Dani gets angry.

"If that is what you want." Sebastian reached out to touch Dani's face. The night was ended after they made love in their warm bedroom that overlooked the flowing river which was once an empty canyon.

A month had passed in Adurak, and the land of Midrel Istan was quiet. Sebastian traveled to Lastorum with Viktor and Dani following. Kristoff had already set back out to sea, taking word back to NorthBrekka that the others had made it to Adurak safely. It was a beautiful spring day and the valley below The Creed flocked with deer and wild horses grazing along the river. The hot sun started to make Sebastian's neck burn until the light was blocked. He peered up into the sky to see Sigura flapping her wings above them, blocking the sun.

The low mountains that encompassed Lastorum came into view as they crossed near where the fog market had once sat. Dani stopped his horse and climbed down to stand by the lakeshore. The old tattered bridge that once led a way into the grasslands from the swamp was now mostly submersed under the shimmery surface of the formerly dry lake. Sebastian joined him as Viktor walked the horses to get a drink.

"Are you alright, my darling?"

Dani wore a smile that was cheerful and almost comical as the fog settled gently against the water's surface. "It's hard to forget that place, but I am happy to see it underwater." He let out a simple laugh.

"If only the fog would stop coming so you could forget it was there altogether." Sebastian knelt and tasted the water. He spit the water out. "Don't drink that. It's awful."

Dani burst into laughter. "Did you know they used to mine gold here back in the olden days? I read about it in one of those books.

There was a whole map of Midrel Istan that shows how different it once was here."

"I never really like gold much." Sebastian started back to his horse. "We should move on. Valirus is waiting, and I don't feel like getting hit with his staff this time."

"Good luck with that." Dani laughed and followed.

Viktor came riding up by their sides. "I like it when he hits you." He winked. "Don't look at me like that, Sebastian. You deserve it." Viktor kicked his horse and dashed away, with Sebastian and Dani following.

They arrived late one afternoon as the mountains cast a shadow on the land around them. They climbed through the hills until they reached the flat valley floor with a massive fortress built into the mountains below their feet.

Viktor shoved Sebastian out of the way and stared in awe at the intricate carvings on the rock. "What is this place?"

"It's Lastorum." Sebastian straightened his coat and shrugged.

"I know that, but this isn't just some wizard's underground castle..."

Dani walked past them both on his way to the stone doors ahead. "It was once the land of the air gods."

Viktor raised one eyebrow. "How does he know everything?"

"That's easy," Sebastian said. "He is smarter than you and me. Now come on." He hurried to catch up.

They descended the stairway into Lastorum's great halls. A group of guards waited at a doorway that Sebastian had never entered in all his time at the fortress before. They followed the men across the threshold and into a cavernous room with only torchlight along the walls to lighten their path. Sebastian heard voices echo farther down the hall where a set of old oak doors lay lazily open. The guards moved aside, and Sebastian led the way to the room beyond.

The room was bright, but not because of fire. A shining white light beamed from the top of a long staff in the grip of a gray-haired old man. "Valirus." Sebastian crossed the room and stopped upon the sight of someone he did not expect to see. "How did you find this one?" Sebastian bent over and looked into Petra's bright blue eyes. She appeared to be in a trance. Then Sebastian stepped back, and his foot kicked over a candle.

He picked it up and lit a flame on the tip of his finger to relight the wick. Sebastian stepped back to see Petra was sitting in a circle of candlelight. Her lips were moving, but her words were quiet. Sebastian slowly approached and listened to her chanting.

Petra wore a flowing robe adorned with mystical symbols, and her hands moved gracefully through the air as she chanted ancient words. The room hummed with an otherworldly energy, and Sebastian couldn't help but awe at the sight before him. The words of the spell were unfamiliar to Sebastian, a blend of archaic languages and mysterious incantations that sent shivers down his spine. The candles' flames flickered as if responding to the enchantment, casting eerie shadows that danced across the room's walls.

Petra stopped chanting and fixed her eyes on Sebastian as she became aware of his presence. A definite tension filled the air in the room, and for an instant, it was as though time had stopped. Petra's penetrating blue eyes revealed a depth of mystery that suggested there were magical forces at work.

He held his hand over her mouth. "Shh. Do not talk yet. Just sit there and shut your mouth. Understand?"

Petra nodded. Dani walked into the room and stood directly in front of her, not speaking, only turning slightly more pale than his normal skin tone. Petra locked eyes with her brother but did not speak, and Sebastian pulled his hand away and stood straight.

Valirus cleared his throat. "She kind of fell into my keep—literally." He stood by Sebastian's side. "She is hurt. Her powers have been damaged since the death of my brother." Valirus paused and took a deep breath before looking at Sebastian. "Which we will discuss later." He turned back to Petra. "She tried to disappear after being caught sneaking toward the harbor where a few of the ghost ships are ported. She was trying to steal one."

"And go where?" Sebastian turned to Petra. "Where were you going to take one of my ships?"

Petra stayed silent. She shook her head fast and her eyes were wide open and locked on Sebastian. Her shoulders shook, although she struggled to conceal her fear.

"You can speak now." Sebastian's voice was calm and soft.

"I don't know." Petra blurted. "I don't know where I would go and how I would even sail a ship on my own, but I didn't care. I am alone in this world, Your Majesty. I have nothing."

"That is your fault, Petra." Sebastian lowered his head and got inches from her face. "I offered you a home and a family, and you betrayed us. It got Dom's daughter killed. If he ever finds you, and trust me when I say he is searching for you, he will tear you apart limb from limb."

"I know." Petra's voice trembled and a tear ran down her cheek. "I'm sorry."

"You don't get to apologize to me!" Sebastian gripped the arms of the chair. "You betrayed my family, me, and . . ." Sebastian sighed. "You betrayed Jace. You don't deserve to live on this earth."

"Your Majesty." Valirus set his hand on Sebastian's shoulder.

"Are you suggesting we trust her?" Sebastian rested his hands on his hips. "Tell me you are joking, Valirus. I will not stand for it."

"You don't need to trust her." Valirus held up his hands. "Just give me time to figure out what to do with her. She shouldn't die for her father's faults."

"I won't keep her location from Dom. I will send word to him, and he will come."

"Let him come." Valirus shrugged and sighed. "He won't find her."

Sebastian felt his body get hot and his chest burn like a fire blazing within. He wanted to scream at Valirus, but a hand fell into his that turned him calm again.

"My love," Dani said. "Valirus is right."

Just then, there was a thundering sound from above, and the fortress beneath the mountain shook. Sebastian looked around. "What was that?"

"Please tell me that was just your dragon." Valirus looked at the ceiling, which rumbled again.

"Sigura is hunting today, so it is not her." Sebastian backed toward the door. "We need to get up there fast."

"Let me help." Petra jerked, trying to free herself from her bounds.

"You just sit there and be quiet."

"Your Majesty, I can help!" Petra jerked her arms again.

"We don't have time!" Dani took a knife from his belt and cut at Petra's ropes. "She will take me first just to prove to you that she won't drop us into the ocean or something."

"Dani." Sebastian clenched his jaw and gritted his teeth. "Fine... She can take me first."

Petra stood and walked over to Sebastian. "Hold still, Your Majesty." She grabbed him by the arm and closed her eyes.

Sebastian felt like the wind had been sucked from his lungs and his body was being ripped apart, only to open his eyes and see the stone courtyard above the fortress.

Petra turned to disappear but hesitated. "Sebastian, watch out!" She grabbed his collar and pulled him to the ground just as a massive wall of water crashed over the mountains and down onto Valirus's home.

As the water rushed away, Sebastian stood and pulled Petra to her feet. "Go back to the others, warn them, and bring Valirus here first. I might need his magic." Sebastian started toward the path that broke between the mountains. He had only traveled through that way once before. As he walked, he heard Petra reappear with Valirus and Dani in hand, and then she was gone again. Sebastian kept his heading as they hurried to join him, along with Jace and Viktor. He turned and looked back and saw Petra staying behind. "Is she going to run away, Valirus?"

"She can't." Valirus laughed. "I have a spell on the fortress keeping her tethered to the grounds."

Sebastian was about to speak until a loud rumble came from ahead. "Everyone get down!" He cuffed his arms around Dani and fell to the ground, holding his body over his. The water rushed down onto them like rocks had fallen from the mountains and buried them under their weight. It cleared away fast and moved across the valley, leaving them soaked.

Chapter Twenty-One

The Sinking Island

They arrived at the end of the road where the path stopped at the harbor. A storm billowed out to sea and the waves crashed angrily against the bluffs. Sebastian hurried down to the ports where two of his ghost ships were being pounded by the nasty weather.

"It's just a hurricane." Dani walked out to the end of a short dock.

The ground jerked and trembled as a loud rumbling sound came from out to sea. "That was no hurricane." Sebastian ran toward the other end of the harbor, where the hillside rose from the sea and a lighthouse shined from above. They ran as fast as they could as another wall of water approached the land. The waves smashed hard into the side of the mountains and spilled over the summit to the other side, where Lastorum waited.

At the entry to the lighthouse, the keeper watched from the bottom floor through a window. A stout ginger-haired man with a long beard stood looking out ahead in fear. He turned and noticed Sebastian standing in the room and immediately bowed. "Your

Majesty!" He shuffled back to the window. "It is a miracle." He pointed.

Sebastian came to the window and immediately raised his eyebrows. He backed away. "How do I get up to the top?"

The keeper pointed toward a door in the corner of the room. Sebastian darted away and rushed up the stairs. The twisted stairwell made his head spin, as he couldn't wait to see the rest of what had appeared in the window. The others followed him, all shouting about what it could be.

Sebastian slipped through the door outside the top of the lighthouse. The thunderous booming thrashed on as the sight of what was to come appeared. "Is that . . ." Sebastian tilted his head to the side. "Is that an island?"

Dani gasped. "That is the kingdom of water. It was in one of those books. Midrel Istan had four kingdoms of elemental magic. Adurak was fire, Lastorum was air, and then there was the water kingdom, which was sunk long ago. They said it stretched across much of The Sea of Glass."

"So why is it rising now?" Sebastian watched as the mass of land nearly touched the edge of Midrel Istan.

"Sebastian." Viktor appeared next to him. "Are you sure Hydros died when he fell in Hast?"

"He couldn't have survived that . . ." Sebastian squinted his eyes as the island finally stopped rumbling and sat flush with the tip of the outer edge of The Creed.

"He is the God of Water, and sort of undead." Dani reminded Sebastian.

Sebastian stared at Dani from the corner of his eye and then turned his sights back to the island as the skies began to clear. A figure appeared on the piece of land that kissed Midrel Istan.

"I'm going." Sebastian turned and hurried down the stairs of the lighthouse and darted onto the pathway heading south. As the others caught up, Sebastian turned and stopped. "Follow, but keep a distance. If that is Hydros, I don't want to risk your lives."

"Don't start this again." Viktor groaned and stayed by his side. "Always the hero, Sebastian."

"Fine, I warned you." Sebastian bounded toward the new land that joined his. As he made his way up the cliffside, he could see more clearly the man who waited on the other side. The lands barely kissed one another where the man stood. Sebastian stopped when he was toe to toe with his brother. A crack where the lands collided was the only thing dividing the two gods from one another.

"Good afternoon, Brother." Hydros grinned. "Happy to see me?"

"You should have died." Sebastian felt a well of emotions flood his body. A thick fog began to form on the island.

Hydros looked over his shoulder and back at Sebastian. "Come with me. All of you." He started off into the fog.

Sebastian followed, making his way across the unknown land that was still wet and covered in corals of all colors, urchins, and barnacles. "You are killing ocean life, God of Water," Sebastian taunted. "This island was meant to be below the sea."

"I just thought you should have a full understanding of the world you wish to rule. Join me, and I will help you discover endless possibilities." Hydros continued as the fog began to break up.

The path led down an intricate walkway until it circled inside a massive courtyard before a beautiful manor. Sebastian followed Hydros inside into a foyer filled with bioluminescent coral. It illuminated the surroundings with a gentle, dreamy glow, and the walls seemed to pulse with the gentle rhythm as if they still were underwater.

Hydros stopped and turned. His face looked different, almost gentle and shy. Almost like it was Tomas, except for the soft blue lines shimmering across his skin. His scales were the only thing that differentiated him from the real Tomas. "Brother... These lands were built by the gods. Back then, there were many, now it is only us two. The last of us all."

"Tomas's daughter could be gifted. Your power could spread to her." Sebastian joined him in the middle of the room. "I will ensure she will be raised properly and trained if so. I will see to it myself."

"She will not be like us. The powers of the gods died out on its own, with fewer and fewer of us being born." Hydros grabbed Sebastian's hand. "We were a mistake, you and me. The powers were to die with Dragon and Litha, but in a lasts-ditch effort, they concealed their powers into a prophecy meant for two who carried their blood. Twins. Us."

"But there is only one problem." Sebastian stopped Hydros from continuing. "You are dead. You cannot rule in this world if you are dead. Therefore, it is only me who wields the power... Let me help you rest."

Hydros backed away. "I am a phantom. Only death himself can come for me."

Sebastian turned his head to Dani. "I just happen to know a reaper."

The shining blue of Hydros's eyes were bright against the moonlight that cast through the broken ceiling. "Him! He is the one who brought me back from the darkness."

"And he will be the one who puts you back there." Sebastian stepped aside as Dani came forward.

"Are you sure about this?" Dani looked up at his husband with a tear in his eye. "I know what he means to you."

"He may wear Tomas's face, but he is not him. Brother or not, he cannot stay in this world. He belongs in the afterlife with our family."

Hydros stepped between them and faced Sebastian. "You and I would be more powerful together. Imagine what we could do."

"I don't need you to make this a better world." Sebastian backed away and glanced at Dani.

Dani's eyes turned white and his skin paled. He reached out and rested his hand on Hydros's shoulder.

Hydros riled and screamed, then fell to his knees. His head shot up to Sebastian as his blue eyes turned brown and his scales disappeared. "Sebastian." His voice cracked.

Sebastian stared into the desperate eyes of his brother. He wanted to run to him, and he wondered if it were a trick, if Tomas had even been dead to begin with. "Dani, stop."

Dani gasped. "What? Do you have any idea how hard it is to take the life of a god? I can't just stop."

Hydros began to drift away, but in a violent jerk, his brown eyes flashed blue and he screamed. Ice formed in his outstretched hand as he drove them into Dani's chest. Dani flew backward into a post and his limp body slumped to the floor.

Sebastian's heart pounded painfully and his head spun. He lunged to Dani and picked him up off the floor only to see the ice spreading across his chest rapidly. Dani choked for air and tears fell from his face. The island shifted violently as Hydros stood and laughed.

"You had your chance and you made your decision." As Hydros lifted his arms, the manor shook and the ground began to drop. "Now you will die."

Sebastian scooped Dani up and dodged a falling part of the ceiling. Valirus stopped and turned to block an attack of icicles from

Hydros's outstretched hand. "Valirus," Sebastian shouted. "Run! He is sinking the island."

The waves slammed into the side of the island as Sebastian sprinted toward the border of Midrel Istan. They whipped through the fog, but a sudden drop in the island's elevation threw them all to their knees. Viktor crashed into a piece of coral that stuck in his leg. The thundering tidal waves returned to smashing into the harbor. Sebastian watched a massive burst of water sail high above his head and fall directly onto his ghost ships, leaving debris and the shell of a ship littering the beach.

Viktor screamed, yanked the coral from his calf, pulled himself to his feet. "Go, Sebastian. Run! Don't wait for me, all of you." He limped along slowly.

The island dropped to where the ocean began to breach to the surface. The ground became slippery as they struggled to reach The Creed. The sight of the mountains came clear through the fog as the water caused them to splash with every step. A tremor caused the ground to shift uneasily and the island tipped a little to the side, causing Sebastian to nearly lose his balance. With Dani in his arms, he fought to keep his footing, but a loud roar echoed from above.

Sigura soared above and dived to the sinking island fast. Her landing was thunderous, and with each step, the land revolted and sank faster. The water was up to Sebastian's knees and the border was still so far away. Sigura lowered herself.

"Get on." Sebastian shouted to the others.

They stared at each other and then at the dragon.

"You don't get to think about it, just go!" Sebastian ordered.

They all ran to the dragon and climbed onto her back as the water rose above Sigura's legs. Sebastian laid Dani down and held on tight to Sigura's scales as she lifted, nearly knocking them all off. They rose high into the sky and Sebastian watched the island disappear underwater.

They flew high above The Creed until the town of Adurak came into view and the firelight filled the darkening sky. Sebastian held Dani tight. He took a deep breath and set his hand on the ice that covered Dani's torso and throat, which restricted his air. Sebastian's body got hot and his hand glowed bright. Slowly, the ice steamed and broke away, sending Dani gasping desperately for air.

"My love!" Dani breathed heavily. "Wait, are we flying?" He sat up too fast and lost his grip on Sigura's back.

"Easy…" Sebastian pulled him against his body.

Dani rested his head against Sebastian's chest. "What happened to Hydros?"

"He sank the island with us on it. If it wasn't for Sigura, we would have drowned."

"That means he is still out there." Dani tightened his grip and Sigura began to descend near the castle. She dropped into the massive open field between the mountains and the castle and lay on the ground to let everyone off. Viktor slid down first, cursing painfully and holding his leg.

Dani climbed down next and ran to help Viktor while Valirus hopped down, leaving Sebastian last. Sebastian patted her back. "Good girl." He climbed down and ran to Dani as Sigura dashed across the field and rolled in the grass.

Inside the castle, Sebastian helped Viktor along through the atrium and across the stream to a sitting area. He dropped him onto the sofa and checked his badly bleeding leg. Pieces of coral stuck through, and Viktor's bone could be seen through the torn flesh.

Jace came down from upstairs and stopped at the sofa and looked at Viktor. "What happened? What is this in your leg?"

"Coral." Sebastian stepped away. "It's a lot to explain, and now is not the time." He went to tend to Dani as Jace and Amara tended to Viktor's wounds.

Sebastian patted Viktor on the shoulder and led Dani toward the stairs. "I think we are going to go get some rest."

The following morning, Sebastian stood on the terrace next to the river and watched the ships pass from the sea toward the ports in Dunebar. Valirus slipped to the edge and stood by his side. Sebastian glanced over at him and then back to the river. "I need your advice."

"I suggest you do something Dragon had to do in his most desperate time of need." Valirus sighed. "If there are any others left out there."

"What do you mean?"

"Your Blackbirds. Call them home."

"But Dani is the only one."

"Wrong." Valirus interrupted. "I sense others . . . I have for some time now."

"I probably shouldn't have killed Barron."

Valirus laughed. "It was terrible timing, but I understand why you did it. Besides, Barron was dying. An illness was going to take him regardless."

"Then who can the others be?"

"I don't know, but you must call them." He nodded. "You know the chant. Close your eyes and let your voice fly."

Sebastian stood on the edge of the river and took a deep breath as his eyes closed. He opened his mouth and chanted, "Blackbirds, fly." A gust of wind soared down the river, and his voice could be heard echoing in the far distance.

"Again!" Valirus's voice was loud and stern. "Use your voice, Sebastian. Call them home!"

Sebastian straightened his back. "Blackbirds . . . fly!" The words resonated and a flash brightened the sky and, in a burst, spread out like the sun and shined across from Adurak, then across the world.

Valirus smiled and started to laugh. He clapped his hands. "I believe you have finally sealed your prophecy, Your Majesty. You have gone full circle. The world is now yours." Valirus bowed and backed away.

Sebastian stared across the river and to the north, thinking about whether or not anyone would actually come, or if it had even worked. A noise came from the doorway. Sebastian kept his stare ahead on the horizon. "Valirus, what if you're wrong?"

"He's not wrong." The voice did not belong to Valirus.

Sebastian spun around. "Dani."

Dani was stark white and his eyes were a ghostly gray. As he made his way toward Sebastian, his color returned and his haunted eyes turned their magical shade of blue. "Now we wait for the others."

"Do you believe there are any more left?"

Dani nodded. "I feel it in my heart."

Chapter Twenty-Two

Blackbirds, Fly

Summer was quickly approaching in Adurak, and the townspeople decorated the market and the town square in celebration of Dragon's Day. Sebastian had only recently learned about this holiday from one of the books Dani swiped from the library on Hast. After calling his Blackbirds, Sebastian had waited patiently in his castle on the river nestled against the cozy comfort of The Creed. He read every book he could find on Dragon, the gods, or the history of Adurak. Dani delivered a stack after lunch.

Sebastian laughed. "Where did you get all of these?"

"Hast." Dani picked a book from the pile and forced it into Sebastian's hands.

"How did you—"

"Read that one." Dani pointed. "You will like that one."

Sebastian sat back and opened the book. He learned that Adurak was not only the birthplace of Dragon, but the capital city of all the god's kingdoms in Midrel Istan. But Dragon was born on a late spring day. He claimed his rightful place among the god's royalty and was the first in hundreds of years who was gifted dragon eggs that hatched. The people adored him and declared his birthdate as a day of celebration in Adurak.

Now, the town was adorned in red banners with black dragons stitched on them. Red and gold ribbons decorated lantern posts and shop patios. Meats, pies, cakes, and a vast variety of ales were being prepared in taverns and on market streets. By the fountain in the castle courtyard, they prepared an arena for swordsmen and swordswomen to battle before all to become champion. Travelers arrived from all over Midrel Istan. Sebastian couldn't help but watch their faces, wondering if any were his Blackbirds.

Jace and Amara walked out to the courtyard and stood by his side. Amara held Liliana in a light yellow blanket and tickled her ribs as Liliana giggled uncontrollably.

Sebastian smirked and eyed the child. "Can I hold her?" He stared at Amara awkwardly.

Amara smiled. "Are you sure? She is heavy and is walking now, so she squirms."

Sebastian sighed and held out his arms. Amara passed Liliana over to him and he held her at eye level. He stared into her deep blue eyes and studied her face as if waiting for something to happen. Liliana stared back, calmly chewing on the corner of her blanket as she studied her uncle's face.

"Sebastian." Jace interrupted. "What the hell are you doing?"

"Just checking." Sebastian kissed Liliana on the cheek and passed her back to Amara just as Dani came to join them.

"Checking the child for goddess potential, Sebastian?" The voice was not Dani's.

Sebastian knew the voice, but was confused. He stared at Dani for a moment until Dani pointed over his shoulder and started to laugh. Sebastian slowly turned and raised his eyebrows high. "Dom?"

"I heard your voice in the wind..."

Sebastian's face dropped, his shoulders slumped, and his heart pounded. "Wait... You are a Blackbird?"

Dom shook his head. "How did I not know this before?"

Dani ran over and held Dom's hands. "Which one are you?"

"What do you mean?" Dom looked at Dani then at Sebastian.

"There are different Blackbirds," Dani said. "In the time of Dragon, there were four. They used to say one Blackbird for each elemental-god king or queen. I would be the Blackbird of fire. That could be why I am so attracted to you, Sebastian. I believe Barron would be aligned with the element air, and Dom would be earth, depending on your powers. Perhaps water."

"So that means there is still another one out there." Sebastian shrugged. "Or they are dead."

"They would have come by now." Dani's voice was low.

Sebastian stepped forward. "Dom, can you show me what you can do?"

"Not here." Dom looked around.

"Come with me." Sebastian headed away from the castle and into the open field outside of the town. They slipped into a corner of the prairie that was blanketed in light from the nearly full moon above. "Show us."

Jace and Dani watched and waited, and Amara stood a little farther back than the others.

Dom stared into Sebastian's eyes and raised his arms up as the grass around their feet grew fast until the blades scratched against his hip, encompassing them both in the foliage. Dom raised one eyebrow and flicked his wrist as the grass quickly wrapped itself around Sebastian's leg, like a snake. "It's funny that my powers have to do with plants, because where I live, everything is frozen. Plants do not grow there."

Sebastian thought about Icefall and then his eyes shot wide open. "Your mother's atrium. It was warm and filled with plants."

Dom laughed. "She knew the whole time." The ground gave way to vines that curled elegantly around Dom's fingertips. He ordered the vines to dance and weave in elaborate patterns. When he touched flowers, they opened up in a kaleidoscope of colors that reflected the splendor of the natural world.

The earth came alive beneath their feet, and the air was filled with the delightful scent of blooms. With a smile, Dom invited Sebastian to see his abilities in their entirety. Dom coaxed the plants to grow and form themselves into intricate shapes with a gentle wave of his hand. Branches intertwined to build arches that presented a living, organic scene.

"You are incredible, Dom." Sebastian stared at him with awe. "It explains why we were always so close." He laughed. "I have earth powers too, but usually I just break everything."

"You do like to destroy things, Chaos, God of Fire... But it explains why my mother always said that you and I were bonded."

"I will always love you, Dom. You know this. Welcome to Adurak. Come and enjoy this day of Dragon." Sebastian backed away to take Dani's hand. "We should get back to the festival. I want to watch the fights."

They enjoyed the food and music as performers from all over pulled Sebastian and Dani into the circle of dancers. The festival grounds were alive with energy, and they were encompassed in a world they never knew existed. The true City of Thieves came alive just as the stories tell of the days past. They marveled at the intricate dragon-themed lanterns that illuminated the evening sky, casting a warm glow over the lively scene. Street performers captivated the crowd with fire-breathing displays and acrobatic feats that left both Sebastian and Dani in awe. They partied deep into the night until horns blew loudly across the town.

"Let the tournament begin!" the announcer shouted. The dancers cleared into the crowd and Sebastian and Dani went to the sitting area set up for them on the steps of the castle where they could watch the fighters up close.

With great anticipation, the sword fighters arrived, their weapons gleaming in the moonlight, and charged into the makeshift arena. The two front-runners confidently stepped forward and brandished their swords. As they circled each other with their eyes fixed on one another, the sound of steel crashing reverberated in the air.

Sebastian leaned forward, his eyes narrowing with concentration, and Dani gasped at the skill and agility on exhibition, commenting back and forth with Viktor. With a grace that bordered on ballet, the sword fighters executed every stab and parry with deliberate precision. The audience cheered and applauded as the fight progressed. Driven by the enthusiasm of the onlookers, the warriors continued with unyielding strength. Their swords clashed, sending sparks flying, and the tension in the arena increased with every second that went by.

The fighters, locked in a final exchange of blows, delivered a sequence of strikes that left the audience breathless. As the swords clashed for the last time, one of the fighters emerged victorious, standing tall and proud, and was crowned the victor.

Summer was already hot and dry as Sebastian trained with Valirus in the higher points in The Creed. They climbed to the summit of Mosisle Dur, where the mountain prison waited quietly and Sigura slept all the way at the bottom. Sebastian focused on his most difficult powers: water. He knew that if he wanted to defeat Hydros, he had to practice day and night. He stood high on the edge of Mosisle Dur with his arms outstretched toward the choppy sea.

The wind tousled his hair as he focused his energy, channeling the ancient powers that flowed through his veins. The rhythmic sound of crashing waves echoed in the distance, providing a natural backdrop to his practice. He experimented with shaping the waves, guiding their movements with subtle gestures of his hands. The sea responded to his command, dancing in harmony with his intentions. The sun dipped below the horizon, casting a warm glow across the water. Sebastian continued his practice, pushing his limits and exploring the extent of his powers.

He thought he had a grasp on how to control water, but his hands began to shake and ache uncomfortably. He dropped his arms and the waves fell, crashing into the waiting water below.

"Focus," Valirus taunted.

"I am focusing!" Sebastian snapped. He struggled with water manipulation. It angered him, and he wondered if Dragon too had trouble with water. He shook his arms and stretched them back to the sea.

"Balance, Your Majesty. Control." Valirus's voice was rhythmic.

"How do you balance water?" Sebastian's voice cracked. "Seriously, a little advice would be good right now." A tidal wave raised high in the sky, yet dropped quickly, causing a thunderous roar in the sea below that awoke Sigura. A growl came from the cavernous prison behind Sebastian, followed by the flapping of wings. The dragon flew from the entrance and drifted just over the cliffside. Sebastian locked eyes with Sigura, and he felt a fury rise in his chest. He extended his arms one last time as his golden scales etched across his bare skin.

The wave rose higher than before in a perfect harmony of natural mastery. The moon rose overhead, casting a silvery sheen on the water. Sebastian, now more attuned to the ebb and flow of the sea, continued his training, knowing that the mastery of his water powers would unlock a world of possibilities. He moved the wave out to sea and let it disappear as fish skipped off the surface. Sigura dove into the water before the fish could disappear.

Sebastian burst into laughter as she dived beneath the water's surface. "If all else fails for me, at least Sigura can cause a ruckus." He paused and stared out to sea. "I know he's out there watching me right now. I can feel his presence." He clenched his jaw and stepped away from the edge.

A loud thunder of water and the swift flap of dragon's wings flying high above the water's surface rang over the mountains. Sigura bounded toward the town of Adurak as Sebastian and Valirus descended Mosisle Dur.

"But, he will have to leave the water in order to get to me." Sebastian walked fast.

"He could surface anywhere, just as he did before." Valirus kept pace, but his steps slowed as he began to get winded.

Sebastian turned to face the castle that slowly came into view off the side of the mountain. "Come on. I need to get home . . . quickly."

"I agree." Valirus quickened his pace. "How is Dominic coming with his training?"

Sebastian laughed. "He's already a master. I swear, everyone is much more talented in their craft than me."

Valirus laughed. "That's because they are all practicing more than you."

"That's not nice."

They returned to the castle to see Sigura rolling in the high grass that Dom had formed in the prairie. Sebastian couldn't help but stand and watch as Dani and Dom laughed and had fun into the late hours of the night.

The following afternoon, Sebastian stood on the terrace, concentrating hard on the rapidly flowing river at his feet. Dani and Valirus were out in The Creed with Dom and Jace while the townspeople went about their usual daily routines. Sebastian closed his eyes and extended his hands before him. In his mind, he visualized the element of water—its fluidity, its power, and its ability to shape and cleanse. He felt a connection with the essence of water, drawing inspiration from the rhythmic flow of the world around him.

His palms tingled with a faint sensation, and he slowly opened his eyes. Before him, a small, shimmering orb of water hovered in the air. The translucent sphere glistened in the sunlight, capturing the hues of the sun. Sebastian marveled at the manifestation of his abilities. He experimented, manipulating the water with subtle gestures. Ripples danced across the surface, responding to the unspoken language between Sebastian and the element. It was a delicate waltz of control and harmony.

He sighed and let the water fall back into the river and turned to go inside the castle, but a splashing noise caught his attention. The low rumble of a voice stopped him in his tracks. Sebastian spun around and saw Hydros emerge from the water and stand, dripping wet, on the terrace of Moonlight Castle.

"I am here to offer you one last chance to join me." Hydros slowly inched forward. "It is for your own good and for the good of your people."

"The good of the people?" Sebastian tilted his head.

"You and I both know what you will do to them." Hydros interrupted before Sebastian could speak again.

"Leave my lands or suffer the consequences." Sebastian was calm. He was not fazed by Hydros... He only wanted to keep his kingdom safe from the wrath of the water god. Sebastian turned to walk inside but felt an icy grip wrap around his waist. The sky turned gray and a bone-chilling wind gusted through from the mountains. Cracks and pops deafened the usual solemn sounds coming from the city. Sebastian watched as the river succumbed to Hydros and froze over completely until it stopped flowing.

Sebastian unleashed a fireball at Hydros, knocking him onto the frozen river. Sebastian's breath formed clouds in the freezing air as he extended his arms, summoning his water powers with a focused intensity. He marched onto the icy surface as Hydros surged a glassy shard of ice in his direction. A clash between fire and ice started to unfold.

As the first droplets of water spiraled from Sebastian's fingertips, Hydros responded with a surge of frosty energy. The river beneath their feet groaned and shifted, releasing the pent-up power of the frozen waters. The combatants circled each other, their movements graceful and deliberate on the slippery surface.

Sebastian conjured whirling currents of water, creating a shield that shimmered with liquid resilience. Hydros, undeterred, crystallized the water into sharp, frozen blades that hung in the air, ready to strike. The dance of elements intensified as the battleground became an arena for the manipulation of water and ice.

Sebastian, feeling the chill seeping through his defenses, tapped into his inner reservoir of power. With a focused determination, he transformed the surrounding ice into a series of ice spikes, rising from the ground with deadly precision, nearly nipping at Hydros feet as he skipped around each one with precise movements. Hydros retaliated with frozen tendrils that snaked toward Sebastian.

With a swift move, Hydros unleashed a surge of freezing energy, overwhelming Sebastian's control over the water. The icy force encased Sebastian in a crystalline prison, leaving him immobilized and at the mercy of Hydros. Sebastian struggled within the confines, his breath visible in the frigid air. Hydros, victorious, paced before the trapped fire god. He laughed and poked at the ice with the Oscura on his finger. Hydros stroked Sebastian's cheek, allowing the stone to graze his skin. "I am not ready to kill you yet. I still have hope for you. For us." He twitched his hand and the ice beneath his feet melted. Hydros disappeared and did not resurface.

Sebastian screamed as his body ignited in flames and the ice shattered into a steaming mist, yet the river could no longer hold him. He gasped just as the frozen river turned to liquid and his body fell into the rapidly flowing current, pushing him to fight to swim to the shoreline. His hand gripped the edge of the castle's terrace. Sebastian strained to pull himself to dry ground, but he was weak, and his grip would not hold much longer. A hand slipped around his wrist and yanked him onto the atrium.

"Jace." Sebastian gasped for breath. "Thank the gods." He panted.

"We leave you alone for not even an afternoon and you get in trouble." Jace joked and wrapped a blanket around Sebastian. "What happened? I arrived in time to see Hydros glance over at me, and then slip into the river."

"He almost beat me." Sebastian clenched his jaw. "I have to end this, Jace. Before he does end my life and comes for all of you."

The morning of the summer solstice arrived, and as the city was preparing to celebrate the birth of their king, a messenger came from the harbor town to the south of Adurak that had recently been built, where the Hetta and the remaining ghost ships lived in port. Sebastian donned his leathers and dressed his belt with knives and axes. The letter read that there was something odd happening out to sea and fishermen have reported unusual creatures hiding in the reefs off the ocean shelf not far from the harbor.

Sebastian did not know what to expect to find out there, but knew if something lurked on his shores, Hydros could be behind it. He was calm, with a rested demeanor and level head. Sebastian's fingers gracefully intertwined with the buttons on his coat until he was poised and ready to ride. He stood before the mirror and admired his slender yet strong body, fully dressed for a battle with the only other god in existence. His red eyes shined bright as the morning sun cast a heavy glow through the windows. Dani had already dressed and gone down to the great hall for breakfast. Sebastian brushed back his hair and tied it up before marching down to meet the others.

Voices echoed from down the way. Sebastian stopped and listened, only making eye contact with the guard who stood by the door with a smirk on his face.

"Good morning, Your Majesty." The guard nodded.

"What are they talking about in there?" Sebastian peeked through the partially open door.

"Your husband has his theories." The guard laughed. "He said there once was an underwater kingdom filled with people. Is that true?"

"There is an underwater kingdom, but I know nothing of any people, only Hydros." Sebastian pulled open the door and sighed. "Wish me luck."

He slipped inside quietly and snuck across the room, seemingly unnoticed, until Valirus shouted, "Good morning, Your Majesty."

Sebastian grinned and sat at his table next to Dani, who was already eating. Sebastian watched him devour every bite as if it were his last. "Hungry?"

"Always." Dani smiled and went back to his pancakes. "Eat. We don't know when we will eat again."

"Yeah..." Sebastian paused and looked around the room. He scooped some eggs onto his plate and took a biscuit from the tray. "I'm bringing Sigura."

"The dragon... You don't know what she is capable of."

"We are going to find out, aren't we?" Sebastian's voice was louder than it should have been. He noticed Dani sit back in his seat and narrow his eyes at him. People in the hall, including his brother and Jace, stopped to stare. "Sorry. I didn't mean to shout. But yes, Sigura is coming. We have a small army and we don't know what awaits us out there."

"Let the dragon torch the sea kingdom." Jace held up his glass. "If they have risen to the surface world, let her enjoy a nice meal."

Sebastian slowly shook his head. "We don't know if there are actual sea people and if they want war with us."

"Sebastian is right." Dani interrupted. "They might be peaceful. If they exist."

"Or," Viktor said, "they might be working for Hydros. He is their god, after all."

Sebastian held up his hands. "Alright, everyone calm down. If there is a kingdom of sea people, they will have to come to shore if they wish to fight. If they charge our shores, we will fight, and so will Sigura."

"She is a water dragon." Viktor paused and looked around. "What if she turns on us for Hydros?"

"She belonged to Dragon." Sebastian's voice grew more serious than before. "Sigura was one of the two last dragons to ever grace this world. And now, she is the last one remaining. She senses Dragon in me; therefore, she is loyal to me."

Dom returned to the castle after having spent his morning high in the mountains, watching over the sea. He rushed into the hall, sweating and breathing hard. "Sebastian..."

"Dom, rest for a moment." Sebastian gestured to the empty chair next to him. "Are you alright?"

"It's hot here." Dom took the towel from the table and wiped his face. "From the overlook, I could see a ridge raised along the horizon. It forms a complete circle around the harbor." Dom clenched his jaw. "He has your ships blocked in."

"What do you mean, he blocked us in?"

"You have to see it to understand." Dom reached for some food. "I can't begin to describe it. It's like a piece of land has risen, and it has enclosed the bay."

"Then I suggest we ride for the harbor." Dani shoved another pancake in his mouth and stood as he chewed and swallowed. "Quickly." He hurried out of the hall.

Sebastian raised his eyebrows and stood. "Eat, Dom. Then join us in the courtyard."

Chapter Twenty-Three

The Sea of War

Sebastian led the march through The Creed and into the pass that made way to the harbor. They stopped at the overlook to rest before the path gave way to the steep descent into the mouth of the bay. He hopped down from his horse and stood at the edge of the cliffside. The Sea of Glass was typically so clear that he could see the ocean floor and the reef from atop the mountain. But this time, something interrupted the balance between land and sea. Sebastian didn't speak, just stood stoically and with a calm heart, as he knew only Hydros could be responsible for this.

Dani and Jace joined his side, and both merely gasped at the sight. With its magnificent spires rising above the water's surface, the sea kingdom had emerged from the abyss. The architecture was unlike anything he had ever seen, with iridescent towers that shimmered in the sunlight and were decorated with coral and seashells.

From the cliff, Sebastian saw that the kingdom was intricately designed with patterns reminiscent of the tides and the dance of sea currents. Under the surface, schools of vivid fish dipped in and out of the underwater arches, weaving a living tapestry of color. The underwater songs echoing from beneath the sea made it clear there were in fact people living in the depths. The appearance of the water kingdom was that of a mystical place that had suddenly appeared in front of him, beckoning him to discover its secrets.

Sebastian shook his head. "Hydros is down there somewhere." He marched to his horse and climbed onto his saddle. The others hurried to catch up, and Sebastian started the downward climb to the shore below.

In the harbor town, merchants unloaded spice, silks, and rare items from far-off regions as ships of all shapes and sizes were anchored in the harbor. A distinct and seductive environment emerged with the aromas of seawater and a blend of exotic foods filling the air. The buildings were decorated with vibrant banners and flags that bore the symbols of powerful families and trade guilds. The waterfront was dotted with taverns, market stalls, and shops that catered to the needs and preferences of merchants and sailors.

Sebastian walked along the longest pier, where the Hetta bobbed in the calm water. He climbed aboard and crossed the deck without slowing or hesitating. He wasn't even sure if Dani and the others had followed until he heard their footsteps on the boards. Sebastian climbed onto the bowsprit and cast his eyes straight toward the barely emerged island. "Hydros!" He shouted. "I'm here. Come off your island and fight me."

There was no noise, and the whispers and melodies from below the water's surface disappeared. The air fell still and eerie, even the birds that typically swarmed the bay found a place to land. Sebastian leaned out over the edge of the ship, and suddenly there was a jolt in the earth followed by the loud bellow of a group of horns sounding an incoming battle. But the horn blasts did not come from the harbor.

Sebastian spotted a line of men emerge and stand on the outer ring of the island that protruded from the sea. They held their horns high and played a harrowing tune as others appeared just below the water from the ocean's depths. The hues of their shimmering, iridescent scales reflected the sunlight's play on the waves. Fins spiked from their backs as they lurched forward into the bay, swimming fast toward the harbor. The sirens moved in unison as they neared the coast, doing a smooth dance that appeared to match the tide's beat.

The song of the sirens reached the ears of those on land. It spoke of secrets revealed, of underwater worlds, and of aquatic mysteries. The sound was both enchanting and ethereal, weaving a spell that captivated the hearts of those who listened.

The soldiers lowered their weapons and their shoulders slumped. Sebastian looked back toward the island with one last hope of seeing Hydros before returning to the people who had finally reached the shallows. As they stepped free from the water, their scales turned into skin and they transformed into people like any of the others who stood on Midrel Istan. The soldiers stood as if in a trance as the sirens raised their weapons in the air and drove them through the hearts of each soldier protecting the harbor town.

Sebastian raised his sword high and shouted toward the army waiting to charge the bay and ride into battle. A loud, thunderous eruption bounced off the cliffsides that encompassed the harbor and the rumble of horse hooves came from the hollows of The Creed. "Dani, Dom, I want the two of you to stick together. Now go and help the people get out of the harbor, quickly!" Sebastian watched them take off from the ship and down the pier.

Water and magic clashed with a monstrous force, sending cracks of energy streaming through the air. Using their enchanting abilities, the sirens called forth currents and let loose a torrent of water that rushed in the direction of the town. Soldiers armed with swords, shields, and bows rode in and bounded through the army of sirens who brandished weapons of their own design. The waves heightened and began to rip apart the harbor as if it were made of straw. The once-vibrant marketplace was reduced to rubble, with merchandise strewn among the debris and its stalls toppled over.

The sirens navigated the battle with grace using the sea to their advantage. Although they were not gods, they had evolved to the sea and learned to call on its help in times of need. Their tridents sliced through the air with deadly accuracy, and their scales reappeared to deflect arrows and knives. Among the debris, the villagers who struggled to avoid crossfire sought safety in The Creed.

Sebastian caught sight of Dani climbing over a pile of broken wood from the distance of the aft of the Hetta. Dom followed, and together they wove their powers through the armies of sirens. Dani moved ahead with his inherent ability to control death. His abilities, cloaked in an aura of darkness, set him apart from both the sirens and the soldiers. Dani reached his hands out before him and a darkness shrouded him as his hand touched each siren who crossed him. Sebastian watched many fall to their deaths upon a simple stroke of a finger, while Dom used the roots of thorned plants to choke any enemy who neared him.

Dom twisted the sand around the torsos of sea soldiers and squeezed them until they slumped into death. He raised his hands, and the ground underneath him pulsed back in response. The sand started to rise and stir, solidifying into the shapes he chose. Compacted sand walls rose to protect the soldiers and townsfolk, acting as a temporary shelter against the sirens' onslaught.

The sirens paused and set their eyes on their fallen soldiers, then sounded a loud shriek that caused the ocean to ripple dangerously. But the emergence of another boundless army of the sea did not keep Sebastian's attention—it was on the footsteps coming from behind him. Sebastian spun around to face Hydros.

The majestic dragon with scales that gleamed like blue azure descended from the jagged peaks of the mountains. The sky came alive with the beating of leathery wings as the massive beast circled above, frightening and inspiring awe in the sirens. With a thunderous shriek, Sigura let loose a torrent of burning flames that kissed the heavens. Smoke plumes rose into the air as the flames crashed down upon the sea, transforming the water into steam. The battleground became chaotic, and the sirens scurried around in fear.

A group of sirens gathered around a circle and chanted in an antiquated, melodious language. A wave came from the horizon fast and grew taller as it flowed into the bay and threatened Sigura's stance. She let out a roar, and a blue flame shot from her throat. The dragon's icy breath collided with the tidal wave, but the force of the water sent the icy shards directly into The Creed, as well as back to Sigura. She shrieked and fell to the shore. The sirens donned their weapons and prepared to strike the dragon down.

Sebastian screamed, his voice echoing across the bay, sending Sigura into a thrashing fight, snapping at the sirens as they moved too close. He turned back to Hydros. "Let's finish this." He unsheathed his sword.

"Are we still using swords to fight, Chaos?" Hydros smirked as ice formed from his open hand into the shape of a blade. "But if you insist."

"Do you really think ice will stand up to fire?" Sebastian sheathed his sword and spread out his fingertips before him as fire and lightning danced between his palms. "Tell your people to yield, and I will not destroy their home world. They did not have to be involved. It is just me against you."

Hydros laughed. "You are so naïve. Your human side is strong, but it weakens the dragon god burning within."

"The dragon and I work together." Sebastian interrupted. "Chaos and I are one person, and that makes us much more powerful than you could ever dream." He looked out at the harbor. "Command them to stop or my men will destroy them."

"They willingly came to fight." Hydros raised one eyebrow. "They follow me, and if I am to battle on land, then so will they."

"Then," Sebastian said, "they will die." He pulled his arms together in a tight ball against his gut and shot forward, blasting Hydros flat onto his back. "Jace, Valirus. Ready the ship."

Hydros hurried to put out the fire on his coat.

"For what?" Jace looked around. "We can't go anywhere."

"We're not leaving, Jace." Sebastian stamped his boot on Hydros's throat and held him to the boards. "Bring the Hetta around to the starboard side."

Valirus came to Sebastian's side. "Are you suggesting we fire on our own port?"

"It's already in ruin. Valirus, go to shore, warn the people to evacuate the harbor immediately!" Sebastian spun around to the soldiers who waited on board to protect their king. "Ready the cannons."

The men rushed down the steps below deck, and the rumbling of cannonballs sounded above. Sebastian knelt and gripped Hydros by the throat. "One last time. Make your people yield or they will suffer the power of my warship."

"Join me and they will follow you. Chaos, let's rebuild the realms of the gods. The water kingdom was once magnificent. A place where the people left the land and adapted to the water to keep themselves safe from the horrors of war. But now they want to come back to the land, and Adurak was once a part of their home."

Sebastian narrowed his eyes. "Adurak was the kingdom of fire. Not water."

"How do you think Litha, a water goddess, and Dragon, a fire god came, to find one another?" Hydros smiled. "They lived among one another, in Adurak."

"Your people attacked mine." Sebastian stood and held onto a rope hanging from the mast. "Do you define that as wanting to share the land with the others?" He watched Dani and Dom run toward The Creed and saw Valirus shouting from the base of the pier, signaling for all to retreat.

Hydros watched the shore come directly before him as the Hetta turned slowly into the shallow bay. The sound of the canons being loaded into the portholes echoed from below deck. Hydros's eyes cast across the shore. "My people will never stop. I instructed them to decimate Midrel Istan if Chaos refused to accept his birthright. If you won't be on our side, you are too dangerous to live."

Sebastian held his arm in the air as a swirling storm cloud flickered and thundered overhead. "You can save them." He stared into Hydros's blue eyes. He waited for a response, anything, but Hydros said nothing, only watched the shore. Sebastian took a deep breath. "Fire!"

The Hetta surged to life as the blast of twelve cannons simultaneously fired on the harbor town. The shoreline exploded in black smoke and fire. Sebastian squinted, trying to see if any of his soldiers were caught in the fire, but all he saw was the people of the sea kingdom retreat toward the water and swim fast, straight for the ship.

"Umm, Sebastian." Jace pointed.

Sebastian's body ignited in stinging pain as his golden scales etched across his skin. The storm overhead furiously spun like a cyclone ready to fall. The winds brought icy air and freezing rain that pelted his face. "Tell your people to yield." Sebastian demanded.

"You murdered their kind. Now they are coming for you." Hydros stepped back and spread his arms apart. "But they will have to wait their turn to tear you apart." Hydros held his hands out to the ocean, drawing moisture out of the atmosphere and shaping it into jagged pieces of ice. He shot an arsenal of ice projectiles in Sebastian's direction in an instant.

Sebastian ducked and twisted through the icy onslaught and blasted lightning from his fingertips as he fell to the deck. With a bright flash and a deep growl, Hydros was struck hard in the chest and fell to the deck. With his sword shining in the moonlight, Sebastian drove forward. Hydros threw his arms up to cover his face as a barrier of ice formed to deflect the slashing blade. The sound of metal on ice shattered the night. Hydros drew in the water from the sea and shot jets of icy water in Sebastian's direction, but Sebastian summoned a wall of fire with such speed that the water heated and turned to steam.

Hydros reached back and pulled moisture from the sea. He threw his arm forward, sending a blast of freezing rain that covered the deck in a layer of frost. Sebastian was encased in a blanket of ice that squeezed his body so tight he could barely catch his breath. Hydros created a water vortex that swirled around him and dropped the temperature of the air to a painfully bitter cold. Sebastian summoned the heat within his body, and the ice started to fracture. He broke free of the frozen prison with a burst of scorching fire. Sebastian marched over and punched Hydros hard in the face, sending him stumbling, and all his powers diminished.

Sebastian felt the pain of fire swirling in his chest. He was viciously angry as he stepped to the railing. The sirens surrounded his ship. Their melodies drifted through the breeze. Sebastian's soldiers all looked around and lowered their weapons. Sebastian ran before them. "No. Don't listen to them."

Jace dropped his sword and walked away from the wheel toward the rail. He tightened his hand on the mahogany and set his foot on the ledge.

"Jace, stop! Don't listen to it. They are tricking you!" Sebastian's heart raced as he ran over to stop Jace from diving over the side. As he grabbed Jace's collar and pulled him down, he heard a splash. He looked over the side as one of his soldiers dived into the water below. "Stop!" Sebastian screamed so loud a massive bolt of lightning struck directly into the center of the bay and ignited a fury of lightning and thunder across the sky. The bitter winds threw the other soldiers back onto the deck.

Hydros stumbled to his feet and stopped to watch the sky turn bright white, then a soft grayish blue as snow began to fall from the clouds. Sebastian looked over the rail and shouted. "I am Chaos, God of Fire and the King of Thieves. I will protect my lands from force by any means necessary. However, it is not my wish to destroy your kind. We can have peace if you just leave. Or you can stay and freeze to death. Make your decision now."

The sirens stared up at Sebastian and then at each other. A woman spoke quietly to a siren male. She stared into Sebastian's eyes and tilted her head as if she were staring into his soul. She lowered her chin and then nodded to the man next to her. The man swam forward further than the rest and bowed his head gently. He gestured for his people to swim away. Sebastian watched the people of the sea kingdom retreat out to sea, disappearing over the ring of the island.

Hydros's face turned red and his scales shined brighter than before. He gritted his teeth and snarled. "You have no right to command them!" Ice formed across the deck of the Hetta.

Sebastian turned to Jace. "Get the ship back to the dock. Hurry!"

Jace shouted for the crew to adjust the sails as he ran to the wheel.

The ice covered much of the surface as it crept up the railings. The glaze wrapped around the base of the wheel. Jace furiously shouted for the crew to move faster as the wheel became difficult to turn. The sails turned solid as the wintry weather encased the cloth surfaces. The Hetta was stuck floating directionless in the open bay as the wheel was entombed in ice.

Sebastian tackled Hydros to the deck and smashed his fist into his jaw repeatedly. "Why won't you just die!" His eyes snapped open and he stopped punching. "Only Dani can end you..."

Hydros thrust his icy fists into Sebastian's chest, sending him writhing on the deck as the ice clenched around his throat and chest, just as it had done to Dani before. "You can't kill me, but I can kill you." He twirled the Oscura ring that still rested on his finger. "Your Blackbird is far away. He can't save you."

Sebastian squeezed his eyes shut and strained to breathe through the encasement of the ice around his body. He gasped and stared into Hydros's crystal blue eyes. "Blackbirds, fly." His voice cracked but carried loudly over the bay. "Blackbirds, fly!" Sebastian flexed his chest muscles and shoved his arms through his frozen prison and slammed his palms into Hydros's chest, sending him flying backwards into a mast.

He crawled to his feet and snarled. "You don't belong in this world." Sebastian reached his arms out and summoned a gust of wind so powerful the sails of the Hetta snapped open wide, sending ice shattering onto the deck and the sailors diving for cover. The ship lurched toward the dock. With the wheel still frozen, the Hetta whipped around until they smashed through the pier and crashed into the land itself. The crew stumbled to the ground and Sebastian shouted, "Get out of here, all of you! Jace, you as well."

"Absolutely not." Jace started.

"There is nothing you can do here." Sebastian shook his head. "Please go. My niece needs a father." He turned and saw Hydros sneaking in his direction. "Jace, get out of here. That's an order." Sebastian balled his fists and searing pain shot across his skin as fire shot from his fists.

Jace climbed onto the landmass and ran toward the harbor as the air got colder and it started to snow heavily, dropping fat snowflakes everywhere.

Sebastian drew his arm back as far as he could reach and slammed his fist forward, sending a bolt of lightning across the deck of the Hetta. Its white and blue blinding light scattered in every direction and snared everything in its path until it clapped against Hydros's cheek.

Hydros faced the deck of the ship on his hands and knees and breathed heavily. A thick vein stuck out on his neck and he clenched his hands into fists and pounded them into the boards. "Enough of this." He climbed to his feet and grasped the Oscura ring in his fist. "If you wish to ignore your fate, so be it, but you will die, and then I will force your precious Blackbird to revive you, so when Chaos returns to this world, he will rule with an iron fist, just as Dragon did before him."

"You won't win this war. You see, Chaos and I live together in harmony, making us stronger than you. Stronger than everyone." Sebastian summoned a powerful fire blast that nearly toppled Hydros over the edge of the rail. With his sword in hand, he summoned flames that danced along the blade. He lunged at Hydros, the heat from his attack sizzling in the moist sea air.

Hydros summoned an ice shield to stop the oncoming fire. The collision of fire and ice released a plume of steam. "When will you realize that fire never mixes well with water ... it often diminishes the flame." He winked. "But I will let you try again." Drawing strength from the surrounding sea, Hydros increased the force of the water, sending waves crashing against Sebastian. The ship quivered against the force of the icy water; the railing that was already broken from the crash splintered and popped as the Hetta scraped against the land.

Sebastian encased himself in flames as the water crashed on top of him. The deck became engulfed in billowing white smoke, making it difficult to see Hydros. In the midst of the haze, Sebastian maneuvered with swift precision and shot lightning from the cover of the screen he crept through. But as he reached out to grab Hydros, a horrible pain shot through his shoulder. He looked down to see an icicle impaled through his body and hot blood streaming down to the deck. His hand wrapped around the ice and fire formed in his fist, which melted the icicle. Sebastian slouched and clutched his shoulder and cried out as Hydros held onto his injured arm.

Hydros smirked. "Look how easily you get hurt." He paced across the deck. "Bleeding, writhing in pain ... so vulnerable. Stop being weak, Dragon."

Sebastian's eyes shot open. He stared at Hydros with a fury of fire building within. "My name is Chaos." He screamed and fire formed in the back of his throat.

Hydros stumbled back and stared at Sebastian oddly with his head tilted to the side. "Weak, but evolved." His voice was as icy as the wind. "Your kind shouldn't exist. You are a mistake in the gods' creations. A freak. Powers that are so chaotic that they cannot coexist with the world around them. The apocalypse. That is why the world turned on him." Hydros stood face to face with Sebastian.

"You are not the King of Kings . . . You are the King of Everything, and that is too much power for any man to wield. But not too much for Chaos alone." He smiled and spread his arms wide apart. A wall of water rose from the bay and surrounded the ship. "I'm going to end this now."

Hydros mumbled something Sebastian couldn't understand, but then the black stone on Hydros's finger lit bright.

Sebastian's chest ached horribly at the sight of the Oscura being activated to kill him. He peered over his shoulder for Dani, but the sound of rumbling caught his attention. A swirling typhoon formed above his head. He thought about his water training with Valirus, but not even being called an idiot was going to save him from this situation. The force of the water would certainly crush him on impact. Sebastian raised his arms and invoked his natural ability to control fire. He created an intensely hot, spinning vortex of wind and fire that wrapped around above him.

The Hetta creaked and popped as the raging winds of the storm barreled down upon it. The sails ripped as they fought against the gale force. The masts threatened to snap in two as they swayed dangerously. Sweat dropped from Sebastian's brow as he kept channeling his furious defense against the unrelenting onslaught of wind and water.

Sigura descended from the skies with powerful beats of its massive wings. The air around her body shimmered as its scales glinted in the mist. Sebastian and Hydros shoved one another away and turned their eyes to the fierce dragon bounding through the storm toward the deck of the Hetta. Her foot had barely landed on the wooden planks when the ship shifted to hold her weight.

She wrapped her wings around Sebastian as Hydros shouted a mighty groan and the storm intensified, sending icy shards pelting into Sigura's scales. She roared and a blue flame shot from her mouth. Hydros raised a shield of ice just as the fire blast reached him. He stepped through the melted slush, his boots thumping with every movement. Hydros bravely approached the dragon. Sigura snapped and raised her wings as she gathered up the intensity to blast another fireball at Hydros.

She dropped her jaw open wide and reared back, but with a flash, Hydros slung his palms forward, sending a massive icicle straight down Sigura's throat. Sebastian shouted, "Sigura!" But the dragon screamed out a cry and lowered her head. Her powerful jaws snapped the icicle into pieces. "Fly away!" Sebastian said. "Go help Dani." The dragon opened her wings wide and lifted from the deck, causing the ship to rock uncontrollably. Sebastian tumbled and fell to his back.

"You can't beat me." Hydros's voice was higher and strained. The fog cleared and Hydros stood twirling the Oscura on his finger.

Sebastian kicked away and tried to scurry to his feet, but a loud call came from behind. A howl he recognized as the Sinook warriors' battle cry. "Dom . . ." He smiled. "Blackbirds, fly."

A long vine extended over Sebastian's head and wrapped around Hydros's weaponized grip, shattering the ice. Dom appeared at his side as the tree he'd conjured retracted back to the land. "You called?" Dom laughed.

Sebastian embraced Dom tight. "What took you so long?" Sebastian looked over his shoulder toward the land. "Where is Dani?"

Dom pointed in the direction of Hydros, where Dani stood before him, ghostly white and reaching for Hydros's cheek.

Sebastian's mouth fell open. "How did he get here so fast?"

"The branch." Dom winked.

Sebastian wanted to run for Dani, scream, anything, but he felt frozen in place as Dani's hand nearly touched Hydros's skin. When he managed to take one step forward, Hydros's arm reached back and then crashed into Dani's chest. Sebastian's body ignited in flames and he lunged for Hydros.

Sebastian concentrated on his powers, focusing like Valirus always told him to. The flames around him whipped furiously. He aimed a single blast of intense fire toward Hydros. The flames surged forward, guided by Sebastian's control.

Hydros waved his arms and conjured an ice barrier that shrouded his body. The flames collided with the icy defense, creating a dramatic explosion of elements on the ship's deck. Steam hissed and billowed into the air as the heat sought to overcome the cold, and the deck rattled dangerously at the severe rumbles of thunder.

Sebastian slapped his palms against the ice barrier that protected Hydros from his attack. He gritted his teeth as flames engulfed the frozen coffin, causing it to shatter into pieces.

As Sebastian stumbled away, exhausted from the fight, he rushed over to Dani and scooped him into his arms. "My darling."

Dani gripped Sebastian's arms and buried his face into his chest. "Let me finish him."

Sebastian nodded and helped Dani to his feet.

"Look out!" Dom shouted.

Sebastian and Dani spun around quickly, but Hydros swung his arm back and slapped Dani hard, knocking him to the deck.

Hydros whispered to the Oscura and a bright light shot from the ring in every direction. He smirked and reached for Sebastian. "Not even you can survive the power of the Oscura." He laughed maniacally and clenched his ringed fist. "Die, Sebastian Drake. King of Everything." The Oscura hissed and shined brighter, then a horrid crack popped as the stone shattered to dust and a powerful magic burst to life around them.

Sebastian's body intensified and his powers ignited, calling for all his elemental gifts of fire, earth, air, water, and spirit to come together. An aura surrounded him as the blackened glow of the Oscura's remnants still drifted in the air. Sebastian waited for his death as he locked eyes with his brother one last time. He heard Dani's voice screaming his name. The boundless display of elements danced around his body until the Oscura's magic shined purple and wisped like smoke. It floated for a moment and then shot all of its powers directly into the heart of Hydros.

Hydros stumbled backward and gasped for air as he slowly fell to the board of the Hetta and the shimmer of his blue eyes and icy scales disappeared. His eyes turned brown and his features softened to the sweet, gentle Prince Tomas Drake. His body fell to the deck, limp, and his dead stare brought Sebastian to his knees.

"Tomas." Sebastian cried and held his brother in his arms. "I'm so sorry."

Dom came over quickly and took what was left of the Oscura from the ring. A tiny pebble of the once-beautiful black stone that had the tiniest fine crack through its body. "It backfired." He held the pebble for Sebastian and Dani to see. "What do we do with it?"

"Toss it into the sea." Sebastian looked out as the typhoon broke apart and sent a wave of surging water to crash into the water kingdom. "Far out to sea, where no one will ever find it."

"But, my love, we are trapped." Dani pointed at the island ring.

Sebastian stood and walked over to the edge of the Hetta and faced the water kingdom. He held up his hands and focused, determined to master his water powers once and for all. An unusual cold sensation took over, different from the usual fire in his belly. He shivered against the wintry winds whipping in from the sea. Sebastian took a deep breath, spread his fingers apart, and pushed as the earth started to shake tremendously. The island nation that was once submerged completely in the depths of the Sea of Glass disappeared once more.

"No one is ever to go searching for that island. Let the people of the water kingdom live their lives in peace." Sebastian watched as the land disappeared and the bay was open once again. "I want to take Tomas home, to NorthBrekka. He deserves to rest among our ancestors."

As the sun fell below the horizon, casting a warm glow on the wreckage, Sebastian vowed to rebuild the tiny harbor town and breathe life back into the already shaken land of Midrel Istan. His silhouette against the twilight sky embodied the spirit of hope rising from the ashes. The war-torn city on the bay may have fallen, but in that desolate moment, a new chapter awaited—one of reconstruction, resilience, and the determination to rebuild the pieces of the shattered world around him.

Chapter Twenty-Four

The Rage of the Sea

For Sebastian, the trip back to Adurak was a dismal one. Tomas's corpse weighed heavily on him, both emotionally and physically. The streets of the City of Thieves were quiet as the townsfolk came out to watch as the procession of soldiers and their king returned to the kingdom. Each thud of a footstep was a reminder of the hollow spaces left in Sebastian's heart as he walked alongside the wagon carrying Tomas's body. With cautious and heavy feet, Sebastian made his way through the prairie, his face covered in a mask of grief. The simple cloth that hid Tomas's lifeless body against watchful eyes whipped delicately as a breeze washed down from the mountains.

The townspeople, those who had survived the onslaught, emerged from the shadows to witness the return. Faces etched with sorrow lined the path, their eyes reflecting the shared pain of loss. A solemn hush settled over Adurak as they paid their respects to the fallen. The only sound was from the dragon's wings as she gently landed in the prairie.

Sebastian stopped in the town square next to the fountain and turned to the gathering crowd. He looked down at Tomas's body and back at the people. "This man was not our enemy." He stopped when a rupture of voices erupted.

One man stepped forward. "My brother was a soldier in your army, Your Highness. He was killed by one of the sirens."

"I understand," Sebastian said. "We have all suffered loss on this day." He paced before the crowd with his hands interlocked. "But this man... was my brother. His life was celebrated in Erras before he was brought back from the dead"—he glanced over at Dani—"and became his god form, Hydros." Sebastian heard a gasp over his shoulder. He turned to see Amara walking from the castle doors with Liliana in her arms. Her face turned red and tears fell down her cheeks.

Jace hurried forward to stop her. "No, Amara!"

Amara shoved Jace away. "He is my husband. My daughter's father..."

"He is gone, Amara." Sebastian stepped toward her. "Tomas will finally rest."

Amara narrowed her eyes. "This is the second time you have brought him home to me wrapped in a sheet in the bed of a wagon."

"Amara," Sebastian whispered. "Please, just listen." He stepped back and turned to the crowd again. "This man was my twin brother, and he was the best of both of us. Hydros was a god filled with anger, like Litha, his predecessor. Do not take out your anger on my brother. Nor the sirens, for they only know to follow their god of water."

"Then who do we blame?" a woman yelled. The crowd broke into a rumble of conversations.

"Me." Sebastian stood with his back straight and head held high. The crowd silenced. "You heard me." He stared at the people's shocked faces. "My name is Chaos, God of Fire. Disaster and death follow in my wake. I don't ask that you all follow me, but I promise each and every one of you"—he turned to the Order, Valirus, Amara, and Dani—"and all of you, that if you choose to follow me, we will build a new world, just as Dragon wanted before he turned evil. My enemies are defeated. Now we can live our lives freely, just as I always wanted."

Amara took Sebastian's hand. "You are our king. We will follow you until the end of time." She knelt and lowered her head. The townspeople followed until all were on one knee, including Dani.

Jace knelt but kept his eyes on Sebastian. "One day, you will learn that we are all on your side. Always have been."

Sebastian's body ignited with a happy sorrow that overwhelmed his emotions. His eyes filled with tears and he reached his hand out for Dani. "Then let's work together and create a world where we can be proud to call our home."

In the months that followed, the harbor town was rebuilt and Adurak was alive with the noise of commerce as ships passed through from the sea on their way to Dunebar and to the fish market that had opened for business along the river. Travelers from the villages came to Adurak to trade and buy wares, even those who traveled from as far away as Altania. Sebastian had Tomas's body encased and prepared for departure on the Hetta for NorthBrekka.

That afternoon, Valirus rode in from Lastorum with news to share. "Your Majesty, may I have a word?"

Sebastian was in the war room with Dom, Jace, and Dani, where they were planning their trip back north for the summer. "Valirus! Will you be joining us to NorthBrekka?"

"Afraid not." Valirus took a seat. "I just thought you should know I am transporting Petra to Runeheim tomorrow."

Before anyone could speak, Dom stood fast. "Petra!" He rushed over to Valirus. "You will bring her to me so I can avenge my daughter's murder."

Sebastian grabbed Dom by the arm. "Petra did not kill Torra."

"She helped him!" Dom shouted. "She helped King Maxen attack my people." He grasped his chest. "They took her from me." Tears fell down his face. "She was my everything."

Sebastian pulled Dom tight against his chest. "I know you want vengeance, but that is not who you are, Dom. Your daughter would not have more blood spilled in her name."

"Petra needs to be punished." Dom turned back to Valirus. "Allow me to face her."

Valirus held up his hand. "She will be returned to Runeheim, where she will be imprisoned in her own fortress. She will never see another face and never hear another voice. That alone is enough punishment for her crimes."

"How can you ensure her entrapment?" Dom asked.

Valirus grinned. "I will cast the spell myself. A very old one written by the ancient witch cult of Runeheim in the days of Dragon." He sighed. "It was created to imprison Dragon if his powers were to ever grow too strong."

Dom raised an eyebrow. "But it didn't work."

"That is because they were killed before they could use it." Valirus shrugged. "But it will keep her in Runeheim for all eternity with nothing to keep her company but her own manic thoughts."

Dom backed away. "I still wish to speak with her."

That evening, Sebastian, Dani, and Dom trekked to the river bridge crossing in the southern borders of Adurak. An accompaniment of soldiers waited with a carriage that sat on the road facing west. Valirus opened the carriage and pulled Petra from inside. Dom stood so still it was as if he had stopped breathing. Petra's hands were bound and Valirus held his staff tight in his fist as he sat her on a boulder.

Dom walked over and knelt before the former empress. He didn't speak for a moment, only glared into her sky-blue eyes. He squeezed his eyes shut and chanted a song in the ancient Sinook language. "*Sinah, ilbrek, diloyn, uwil.*" He clenched his jaw and sat back. "Blue-haired witch. I curse you to a life of eternal damnation." He held a stone in his hand and slapped it between his palms. The stone lit up in a bloody shade of crimson, and a rune glowed against the surface. "*Sinah, ilbrek, diloyn, uwil!*" he shouted and pressed the rune into her chest.

Petra screamed and doubled over. "You bastard!" she snapped furiously.

Dani stepped forward but was pulled back by Sebastian.

"What is he doing to her, Valirus?" Sebastian couldn't take his eyes away from the magic taking place before him as he held Dani tight against his body.

"He is casting his pain onto her." Valirus watched Dom work. "The pain of losing his daughter. It is a pain that Petra will endure every single day for the rest of her life." He turned to face Sebastian. "The Sinook are full of surprises, aren't they?"

"I didn't know he could do that." Sebastian watched as Dom finished and climbed to his feet. As Petra groaned, she leaned back, and the sight of the burning flesh on her sternum mirrored the rune on Dom's stone.

Dani broke free and rushed over to his sister.

"Those books Dani took from Hast had a lot of Sinook secrets." Dom stood by Sebastian's side. "I still have much to learn." He winked at Valirus.

Sebastian laughed. "How many books did Dani steal?"

"He had us all carrying them to the ships." Dom smiled and rested his hand on Sebastian's shoulder. "I like Dani. He is good for you." He turned to Valirus. "Thank you for letting me avenge my only child."

Dani sat before Petra and held her hand. "My only wish is that we could go back in time and love each other like brothers and sisters should. I know we will never see each other again, but you're still my sister, and I love you."

Petra did not speak, she only stared through emotional tears.

Sebastian knelt before Petra. Her usual pretty face was weathered and tired. She truly was defeated and broken to nothing... a feeling he didn't favor, no matter how terrible she had been. "I exile you from my lands and will allow you to roam the mountains of Runeheim until your death. You will be given nothing, only your life. No go and find your peace." He stood and walked over to Valirus. "Good luck, and I will see you when winter falls in the north."

Valirus bowed his head. "May your journey be merry and bright. Come home to us, Your Majesty."

Sebastian nodded and backed away toward his horse. "I always will, my friend."

The sun hung low on the horizon as Sebastian, clad in weather-beaten attire, stepped onto the creaking deck of the Hetta. The ship, though scarred by the recent war, stood ready to set sail once again. Sebastian's eyes swept over the vessel, noting the repairs hastily made by the remaining crew members. The salty sea breeze carried with it a mix of melancholy and determination, a reflection of the journey that lay ahead.

Sebastian's gaze lingered on The Creed behind them and whispered a silent farewell to the place that had shaped his life and brought meaning to the prophecy he wished to forget. The ship's anchor rattled as it was hoisted aboard, signaling the beginning of a journey back to NorthBrekka. As the crew prepared for departure, the rhythmic sounds of the sailors' work echoed against the wooden hull. Sebastian stood at the helm, his hands gripping the worn wheel with a mixture of determination and sorrow as Tomas's casket was loaded just after the cargo.

Viktor, Dani, Jace, and Amara with her daughter joined him on the deck as Sebastian summoned the wind to carry them out to sea. The massive black sails opened wide and the Hetta edged forward on the long way to Erras with Sigura flying along through the clouds overhead.

After a few days out at sea, Sebastian leaned over the railing and watched as the water churned under the ship's wake. The familiar sound of footsteps on the hollow deck came closer and closer. A pale hand rested next to his on the rail. Dom's presence was always comforting to Sebastian.

Dom opened his palm and held the last piece of the Oscura. "I think we are far enough out to sea."

Sebastian smiled and pinched the stone between his fingertips. "It is hard to believe this little pebble can kill me."

Dani appeared by his side. "That is why you need to cast it overboard . . . for good."

Sebastian looked at the Oscura one last time. He brought the stone to his lips, kissed it, then threw it into the thrashing sea.

The days at sea passed with an uneasy tension hanging over the Hetta and its crew. Even Sigura flew low, hovering close to the surface of the water until the sea became angry in the near distance. The initial optimism that had fueled their departure from Adurak was tested by the relentless fury of the sea. The sky darkened ominously, and the winds began to howl with an intensity that hinted at the approaching squall.

Sebastian, standing steadfast at the helm, squinted against the driving rain as he surveyed the swelling waves. The ship pitched and rolled with the unpredictable rhythm of the storm, each wave threatening to engulf them. The once-resolute faces of the crew now bore expressions of concern, their hands gripping the rigging as they worked tirelessly to secure the ship against the hurricane.

The hurricane unleashed its full force upon the Hetta, causing the vessel to groan and strain against the battering waves. The crew, soaked to the bone and clinging to their positions, struggled to maintain control. The ship heaved and dipped at the mercy of the tumultuous sea. Sebastian barked orders over the howling wind, his voice cutting through the thunder as he directed the crew to reef the sails and brace for impact. The sailors moved with practiced urgency; their movements were synchronized in a desperate attempt against nature's wrath. He saw Sigura dodge and weave around waves as she was determined to stay close. Sebastian ran over to the rail. "Sigura, fly away. Get out of here before the storm takes you."

She snapped and moaned. Her eyes were saddened as she stared at Sebastian. He nodded and opened his mouth as his voice flowed through the air. "I can handle this. Go and save yourself. I will see you on the other side of the clouds."

Sebastian watched the swirling clouds overhead as Sigura disappeared into the storm. He reached his hand out and tried to break the storm apart, but the hurricane was a furious fighter. Lightning arced and connected to Sebastian's outstretched hand, and the ship's hull stretched to withstand the storm. The waves surged, surrounding them, promising to rip the ship in two. Sebastian left the wheel to Jace and ran to the center of the deck.

As the Hetta battled against the relentless fury of the hurricane, a haunting sound cut through the howling wind—the mournful wail that the crew dismissed as a trick of the storm, a manifestation of their exhausted and battered minds. But as the eerie melody grew louder, its ethereal quality pierced through the roar of the wind.

Sebastian strained to see through the thick mist that enveloped the ship. The crew exchanged bewildered glances as the song seemed to beckon them from the heart of the storm. "The sirens." His voice carried, echoing into the wind.

Chapter Twenty-Five

Guardians of the Sea

The ship sailed further into the eye of the storm, the waters thrashing with the fury of the hurricane. The sirens' song reached its crescendo, each note resonating with an otherworldly power that seemed to defy the laws of nature. As the Hetta teetered on the edge of surrendering, Sebastian, his mind clear despite the hypnotic pull, shouted orders to his crew.

He widened his stance and closed his eyes. Sebastian took a deep breath and pulled his palms together as if he were praying. He lowered his head, and with a sudden jolt, threw his arms apart in a thunderous motion that rattled the ship's deck. Sebastian directed his energy toward the heart of the hurricane. The storm, now confronted by a force beyond comprehension, wavered as if in a celestial duel. Sebastian's powers manifested in a display of light interwoven with the turbulent currents of the storm.

As his power intensified, his body ignited with the burning fire that pitted in the depth of his belly. He let out a loud roar and fire escaped from his lips. The earth shook, and the storm spit out cyclones between the tidal waves. A reverberating echo came from the sea below the ship. The shrieks turned into a unified wave of melodic sound that encompassed all of the ship with its grace and beauty. The sounds grew louder, carrying a deafening bellow into the sky. Sebastian slapped his palms together and spread his arms apart fast and wide, and a booming force bounded free from his body.

The sirens' song was all that could be heard as the storm struggled to fight back against the force of a god and the people of the sea. A loud crack silenced the song, and everyone watched as the hurricane split in two and the waves fell. As the Hetta sailed through the eerily calm of the dying hurricane, the enchanting melody of the sirens lingered in the air. Sebastian, sensing a mysterious presence, stood vigilant on the deck, his eyes scanning the surrounding mist. He marched to the railing and looked over the side. Soon, from the depths of the calm sea, the sirens emerged, their forms illuminated by a soft, otherworldly glow. He backed away quickly as they began the climb up the port side of the ship.

The sirens, with flowing hair that seemed to dance with the wind and eyes that held the ancient wisdom of the sea, rose from the water onto the ship's deck. Their voices, once distant and haunting, now took on a soothing quality, like a lullaby whispered to a weary traveler. The crew, still recovering from the storm's assault, watched with wonder.

A man adorned in silvery garments that stuck closely to his body and black, pin-straight hair hanging down his back stepped forward further than the others. The same man Sebastian had watched leading the people of the sea away from the war in the harbor. He bowed his head and opened his mouth. "God of Fire. You carry a power that commands even the most evil of things in this world. What purpose brings you to these treacherous waters?"

"I am traveling to Erras, my homeland, to take my brother to his final resting place."

The siren raised his eyebrows and turned as a woman stepped forward from the others. The man fell to his knee as she passed to stand face-to-face with Sebastian. She walked with elegance as her thick, dark hair bounced in the breeze. "Hydros, God of Water. We sense him." She looked to the stairway to the cargo hold. "My people have lived in these waters since before man walked on the land. Our god was the eldest of all the gods. His powers lived in your brother, but they also live within you." She placed her pale bluish skin against his chest. "Our role in this world is to guard the seas. Yours is to guard the earth. And together, we will work to keep our nations free. Travel peacefully, King of Everything."

Sebastian watched her back away for a moment. "Wait." He stepped toward the woman. "What may I call you?"

The woman bowed her head. "Queen Indicia Ama, and we are the siren clan of all the seas. And we follow the one true king." She nodded at Sebastian before commanding her people back to the sea. "Safe travels, Sebastian Drake. We will meet again very soon." She winked before diving from the rail.

Sebastian watched as the sirens and their queen disappeared into the deep once more. The clouds were still heavy and gray and the rain continued to fall, but the hurricane was diminished, its stormy arms traveling out to sea and far away.

"Jace." Sebastian's voice cracked. He cleared his throat and took a deep breath. "Jace!" His voice was powerful and clear.

Jace came to join his side, but his face showed a bit of fright as he stared at the sea with wide eyes and a gaping mouth. "Sebastian... What the hell just happened?"

"Everything." Sebastian laughed. "Don't you see it, Jace?" He nodded at the sea and then the sky. "Sirens. Hurricane." He pointed at himself. "The only living god." His eyes averted to Amara and Liliana emerging from the captain's quarters. "Perhaps."

Amara sighed. "Don't start that again, Sebastian."

"It is possible." Sebastian reached down and took Liliana's hand and followed the brown-haired girl with blue eyes over to the rail to stare out at the sea. "Jace!" He said with a sharp snap in his voice. "Command the men to sail. We have a long way to go before we reach Safareen."

"Safareen?" Jace walked up to the wheel. "Not NorthBrekka?"

Sebastian smiled. "I will have a crew take Tomas to Castle Drake, but first, I need to pay Lucian a visit. I believe I will throw a ball for the turn of summer. That means I must invite the family. The coven, the Safarians. If I am this King of Everything, then I want the world united as one new order. No more fighting. My days of war are over."

Liliana squeezed Sebastian's hand and smiled before running back to Amara. From the clouds behind them, Sebastian saw Sigura catch up to the Hetta as she soared just above the highest mast. They sailed for weeks before the call from the crow's nest alerted Sebastian to land on the horizon. The Hetta gracefully crossed the sea with its sails wide open, holding onto every last bit of wind that soared across the open water. The port of the desert city of Safareen blossomed with life as the Hetta passed by fishing ships along the way into the harbor.

Sebastian stood on the bow and nodded at the fisherman as they knelt in his passing. They pulled up to port on a long pier, and the crew stowed the sails as Sebastian took Dani's hand and departed from the ship. The thump of their boots on the boardwalk made Sebastian smile as he breathed in the hot, dry air. As they walked along the fish market, Sebastian wrinkled his nose up at the scent and walked faster until he saw the road to the castle come into view.

Built of worn sandstone, the castle stood majestically against the backdrop of the never-ending desert and a seemingly endless ocean. Sebastian could see elaborate sculptures on the castle walls that told tales of long-gone civilizations. The heavy wooden doors creaked open, revealing a cool, dimly lit interior that provided a welcome relief from the scorching heat outside.

Inside, the air was filled with a faint scent of incense, and the sound of his footsteps echoed through the spacious hallways. As Sebastian's eyes adjusted to the dim light, he stopped to admire the bright mosaics and elaborate tapestries. The castle had a sense of intrigue and history that made him wonder what secrets it might hold. He reached out and ran his hand across a painting of a woman with long, dark, wavy hair and deep brown eyes.

Someone cleared their throat. "That was your mother."

The voice made Sebastian jump. "Lucian." Sebastian smiled and embraced his kin.

"I have never seen a painting of her." Sebastian stared at the features of her face.

"You look just like her." Lucian looked at the painting and back at Sebastian. "What do I owe the pleasure? Is there peace in Adurak?"

"I need to speak with you." Sebastian got straight to the point.

As lunch was served in the hall, a feast large enough to feed Sebastian's crew, Lucian and his wife joined Sebastian at the head of the room. "A lot happened the last time I left Erras."

"Yes." Lucian sipped his wine. "I hear you defeated both Maxen and Hydros in Hast."

"So I thought." Sebastian raised one eyebrow. "Maxen was killed in Hast. He was human. He fell from the top of the tower. He was crushed by falling debris... but Hydros." Sebastian paused for a moment and then went on to tell the tale of his brother's arrival in Lastorum by raising a sea kingdom from the ocean floor. He explained the story about the sirens and the battle in the Adurakian harbor, only for Hydros to end his own life with the cracked Oscura. "Oh, and I also found a dragon." Sebastian coughed.

Lucian dropped his fork. "A dragon?" He laughed and looked at Dani, and then back at Sebastian. "You're not joking right now, are you?"

Sebastian shook his head. "She is real, Lucian. She is here, if you would like to meet her."

Lucian couldn't eat fast enough before he was on his feet and following Sebastian out into the stadium where Sigura had decided to land. The steep stairs were cracked and worn ever since Sebastian had been brought in to battle in the tournament.

"Did you ever think to fix the steps?" Sebastian joked.

Lucian grinned. "No. I tell the sailors the stories of your battle here. I show them the damage to the stadium, then they stay in Safareen and drink, eat, and shop for their wives before returning to sea. They all admire you very much."

"Where are they from?" Sebastian cautiously made it to the bottom landing.

"All over the world." Lucian paused and stared at the dragon, awestruck and still. "She is beautiful."

"Her name is Sigura." Sebastian walked to the center of the arena where the dragon waited patiently. "She was born to Dragon. She belonged to him."

"Wow," Lucian gasped. "She's been out there this whole time and no one has seen her."

"After Dragon died, her spirit died with him, and there she remained in the tower on Hast."

Lucian slowly crept forward. "How tragic."

Sebastian admired Lucian. He was young, and last in line for the throne. His father left the throne to Lorna in his will before his death, but she chose to marry Roman, and then she joined Maxen but died soon after. Sebastian's mother, Shauni, died giving birth to Viktor. Lucian was only a child when he succeeded them all and was leading the Safarian army at the age of twelve. But unlike his father, who despised NorthBrekkians, Lucian was a curious soul who reminded Sebastian a lot of himself.

After Sigura decided she was finished being ogled by Lucian, she spread her wings and lifted into the sky. Sebastian sat on the bottom of the steps and sighed. "She probably went hunting. I apologize in advance for her frightening your people."

Lucian laughed. "Things could use a little shaking up around here. It's been too quiet."

"Well, for the first time in only the gods knew when, the world is at peace." Sebastian smiled. "It will probably get a little boring from time to time."

"Until the next man claiming to be all mighty rises against you." Lucian stared around the arena.

"Well," Sebastian said. "Until that happens, I would like to ask you and your lovely wife to join me in NorthBrekka for the summer solstice. There will be a ball."

"A party for your birthday..." Lucian raised his eyebrows. "You don't strike me as the type of man who enjoys a party."

"I don't." Sebastian shrugged. "But I have a hidden agenda and I wish for you to come."

Lucian nodded. "I would be honored. How about we ride north, together. The Safar have the fastest horses in Erras."

Sebastian stood and rolled his eyes. "Yes, I have heard the harrowing tales of the Safar."

"From your father." Lucian followed Sebastian up the stairs. "You should come back to Safareen and stick around a while. I think you would like it here."

"I'd actually like that." Sebastian stopped and turned to Lucian. "Only if you agree to come to Adurak for a time."

"Agreed." Lucian pushed forward. "I want to see the whole world someday but as a king, I am sort of, tied down."

"Nonsense." Sebastian reached the top of the stairs. "Because you are a king, you are allowed to do whatever the hell you want. Take it as a word of advice from me."

Lucian laughed and smiled. "Yes, I heard you have a new title. King of Everything." His eyes darted around the stadium. "I hope you find your happiness. You of all people deserve it the most."

A few days passed and Sebastian and his accompaniment headed north from Safareen with a small army of Safarian soldiers and King Lucian and the queen. Late in the afternoon they arrived at the canyon where the coven resided. The warm hugs from Frey and Candor made Sebastian feel more and more at home with his family with every second passing. He explained to him that he wanted them to come to NorthBrekka to celebrate the solstice and without hesitation, the coven cheered with acceptance.

"We would never miss the opportunity to celebrate our king's birthday." Frey took Sebastian's hands and led him over to a table to eat.

The evening set in the canyon and everyone settled in to sleep before the long journey through the seemingly endless desert they would face in the morning.

Chapter Twenty-Six

The Masquerade

The journey through Erras was long. Sebastian sent a crow with word to NorthBrekka that he would be arriving as the accompaniment pushed forward until the familiar sight of the mountains of The Break came clearly across the horizon. Sebastian's heart pounded with anticipation as he approached NorthBrekka, the land he once called home. The journey had been long, filled with memories and emotions that surged within him like a tumultuous river. Years had passed since he last laid eyes on his castle.

The towering peaks of the mountains stood proudly against the sky, and the forests whispered tales of ancient secrets. As he rode closer, the imposing silhouette of his castle emerged on the horizon, perched atop a hill like a guardian watching over the realm.

Sebastian's mind was flooded with memories of days gone by— of laughter echoing through the halls, the clinking of armor in the training yards, and the warmth of the hearth in the great hall. The castle held stories of triumphs and challenges, of friendships forged and alliances broken.

As he approached the gates, he couldn't help but smile. The castle, once a symbol of his authority and legacy, now stood as a silent witness to the passage of time. He dismounted from his horse and walked through the gates, the gentle thumps of his footsteps resonating through the courtyard and through the castle doors.

The air was filled with a sense of nostalgia. Sebastian passed the grand staircase, and continued down the corridor, each step carrying him closer to the heart of his memories. The halls were adorned with tapestries that depicted the history of NorthBrekka, telling the story of his family and the kingdom they ruled.

As he rounded the corner into the great hall, he heard giggling come from the throne room. As he approached the oaken doors, the sight of two boys playing a game in the center of the room came clear. He walked into the room and the young men jerked their head's up in unison. They jumped to their feet. "Uncle Sebastian!" They cheered and ran into his waiting arms.

"You're home!" Nadya's voice echoed through the room. She rushed over and hugged her brother tight, then yanked Viktor into her arms. "My beautiful brothers." A tear ran down her cheek. "I am so happy you are both home."

"We are home for the summer." Sebastian looked around the throne room. "I need to talk to you about—"

"He wants to throw a ball on his birthday." Viktor blurted before Sebastian could finish. "Sorry." He covered his mouth and laughed. "It's just not like you at all."

Sebastian rolled his eyes and started to speak before Nadya leapt into his arms unexpectedly. He winced as a sharp pain shot through his back, but he smiled and hugged his sister tight, then slapped Viktor on the back of the head. "Mind your business, Brother." Sebastian turned back to Nadya. "I want to have a meeting with all city leaders that we know about." Sebastian nodded to the door as

Lucian walked in. "I've already collected the Safarians and the coven, and I sent a messenger to Oyster Cove."

Nadya held up one finger. "A ball? You want to have a ball on your birthday?"

"I know," Sebastian said. "It's completely disgusting of me." He started to explain himself but a loud roar echoed through the air and shook the castle walls.

"What was that?" Nadya hurried over to her children. "Sebastian?"

"That is Sigura." He clenched his jaw. "She is a dragon."

Nadya's oldest son gasped and he jumped to his feet. "A dragon?"

"I told you I have a lot to explain." Sebastian looked around at everyone filtering into the room. "I need you to call a meeting. Where is Jon?"

"On a hunt," Nadya said. There was another loud roar and the sounds of shouting came from the corridors.

Sebastian sighed and ran to the castle front doors. In the courtyard, Sigura stood on her hind legs with her wings flapping fast, knocking men to the ground. A group of soldiers waited at the gate, trying to calm their horses as the dragon continued to banter. Sebastian squinted "Jon?" He glanced at Sigura as she rear her head back and dropped her jaw. "Sigura, no!"

The dragon dropped her head and lowered to the ground. Sebastian went to her side and shouted for the men to file into the courtyard. As the soldiers rode in, the familiar sight of a former Sinook leader and now King of NorthBrekka hopped down from his horse and ran over to greet Sebastian, only stopping suddenly when Sigura shifted.

"He is our friend." Sebastian told Sigura and turned to Jon. "It's good to see you."

They embraced as the sound of horns sounded from the castle towers. A rumble of horse hooves came steadily from the mountain pass to the west. Jon looked at the dragon, then back at Sebastian. "Ask your pet not to eat my men, Your Majesty." He laughed. "I got your message and called upon the Sinook to come with haste."

Sebastian patted Sigura on her wing and watched for the men and women of The Far North to come. That evening, after dinner, everyone gathered in the hall to say goodbye to Tomas one more time. Nadya had brought children from the village down the mountain to sing a harrowing song as the prince passed into the heavens and joined his ancestors. After everyone had traipsed off to bed, Sebastian snuck down to the tombs and found the place where Tomas's body had been once again laid to rest.

He kneeling and rested his hand against the stone. "Tomas ... I swear on my life that you will never be disturbed in your peace ever again. Jace and Amara have fallen in love. He will be a great father to Liliana, I promise, and I will be there for her as well, and of course, I will care for Amara." He leaned back against the wall and told Tomas the story of Hydros and how it broke his heart to fight his own brother. A tear fell down his cheek. "I had to watch you die all over again." Sebastian turned and rested his forehead against the stone. "When I join you in the heavens, I swear to you that I will be your servant." He laughed and wiped his tears away. "After everything I have put you through ... please rest, Brother. I love you. I always have and always will. Until we meet again." Sebastian kissed the tomb and stood.

Sebastian spoke to his father and his mother, and even his stepmother, telling them all the stories of his adventures, about the dragon, and about the last battle against Hydros. He told them about how he learned about Dragon and how he realized he was more like him than he thought."

Weeks had passed when the great hall filled with people, leaders, and soldiers from all over Erras and Midrel Istan. Sebastian stood in the bedroom he and Tomas once shared and sifted through the clothing in the closet, looking for the jacket Tomas wore on the last birthday they spent together. He held the leather in his hands and took in the faint scent of Tomas's favorite fragrance that he swore all the ladies swooned over. Sebastian wrapped the coat around his body and slid his arms into the sleeves, realizing the coat was too tight against his broad shoulders. He slipped the coat off and hung it back in the closet as the bedroom door opened and Dani slipped through with a box in his hands.

Dani set the box on the table and opened the lid. "I didn't have time to have someone make you an outfit for the masquerade, but I managed to put something together."

"Did you say, masquerade?"

Dani nodded. "Nadya insisted. She said it would be fun." He dropped a mask onto the table next to the elegant black coat. "Get dressed. The ballroom is filling up with guests."

Sebastian noticed Dani was not dressed. "What about you?"

"It's a surprise." Dani winked. "I have to get ready." He ran to the door. "Hurry up and dress." Dani disappeared down the hall.

Sebastian's stomach knotted as he stepped into the grand ballroom. The air filled with the enchanting melodies of the orchestra and the soft rustle of elegant gowns and tailored suits. The room was bathed in a warm, golden glow, courtesy of the candle lit chandeliers hanging from the high ceiling. The masquerade ball was in full swing, and the guests, adorned in elaborate masks and lavish costumes, twirled gracefully across the polished dance floor. Sebastian marveled at the opulence of the event, taking in the rich tapestries, gilded mirrors, and towering flower arrangements that adorned every bit of space in the room.

He held the mask in his hand. An intricate silver creation adorned with feathers and jewels that concealed his identity, adding an air of mystery to his presence. He couldn't help but feel a sense of liberation as he blended into the sea of masked faces, leaving the outside world behind.

As he strolled through the crowd, the soft strains of classical music beckoning him, Sebastian caught the eye of a mysterious figure across the room. A masked stranger, their blue eyes locked in a silent invitation to dance. With a nod, Sebastian made his way through the swirling dancers, eager to meet the mysterious person from across the room. Sebastian, clad in a midnight-blue velvet cape, exuded an air of sophistication and charm. A black leather corset hugged his frame perfectly, adorned with subtle silver embroidery that glinted under the soft glow of the candlelight. A crisp, white silk shirt peeked out from beneath the corset, fastened with a silver and onyx-studded button.

Dani wore a deep purple suit garnished with silver embroidery and a long flowing coat. His mask was darkened with black bird feathers that made the starry blue in his eyes sparkle bright. As they danced, the two moved in perfect harmony, their connection evident in every step. The soft rustle of fabric and the rhythmic tapping of shoes merged with the melodic strains of the music. After they were both tired and dizzy, the call for the feast sounded from the great hall. Everyone gathered to eat and the rumble of conversation filled the room.

Nadya arrived at the table and took her mask off. She was holding the hand of a young red-heading child that was not her son. "Remember him?"

"Boy." Sebastian shook his head. "I hate calling you that. I can't believe you are so grown up already."

"He is very smart." Nadya smiled and patted his hand. "But, we think it is time for a proper name. He is ready."

Boy stared at Sebastian with the same goofy grin he always wore when he first met him in Safareen.

Sebastian tilted his head. "Wait, you want me to choose?"

Boy nodded.

"Meecah said that the whole village gets to decide. What happened to that?"

Nadya laughed. "Boy requested you name him."

Sebastian sighed and looked at Dani for help but Dani just nudged him. "Alright, fine." Sebastian stared at boy. "If I were to have a son of my own, I would have named him Alexsander. Therefore, that is what we will call you."

Once the food was gone and desserts were served, Sebastian stood before all and cleared his throat. "In all my journeys I never imagined one where I would be standing before all of you, as your king. I have had the pleasure to see things most others could never dream and to meet people unlike anything anyone had ever seen. I used to despise my life. I ran away all the time, never listened to my father, I was the most unruly of all twelve of my siblings, and I genuinely had an entire plan to disappear once and for all . . . to be free from my royal bonds and live a life in a land of my own creation."

Sebastian paused and looked at the many faces of people from all walks of life. "I always thought being king meant I was bound to a throne, like my father. He was sad and lonely despite all of us running around making his life hell." The crowd erupted into laughter. "But my father was a prisoner in NorthBrekka, just as many kings before him. I always was taught that NorthBrekka was a land of peace and community but as I have learned over the years, I was wrong. NorthBrekka was built out of the rage of a king that was named, Dragon. This nation was violent, war ridden, and unwavering in keeping the north a sanctuary from the power of the kingdoms in the south, and from faraway lands. I never wanted any of it. When I was crowned and my life changed during war times with my brother, Barron, I wanted to die. I hoped and prayed to our gods to take my life over and over again."

He stopped and noticed the tears falling down Dani's cheeks. Sebastian straightened his back and continued. "But one day, I found a reason to keep going. I realized that I was the only person that could change my fate and I refused to be bound to a prophecy. I found love ... hope. I discovered my powers and how to use them to do great things, not just destroy. I know I have taken so much from so many. I have leveled kingdoms, and killed loved ones. But from this day forward, I swear to you that we will create a world together. All of us. A world where we will live in harmony. The time of war is over. Our enemies are defeated. Now it is time to rebuild."

The crowd whispered to one another until the candles in the chandeliers above their heads flickered.

Chapter Twenty-Seven

A Sinook's Revenge

Sebastian narrowed his eyes. "That was odd." He shook his head. "As I was saying."

The walls rumble gently. Dani took Sebastian by the arm. "Was that Sigura?"

Sebastian shook his head. "No, she is in The Far North hunting."

A loud cackle echoed around the ballroom followed by a loud pop. A women in a long-feathered cape appeared before Sebastian; her blue eyes complimenting the azure shade of her hair.

"Petra?" Sebastian felt his heart race. "How did you get here? You are supposed to be—"

"Trapped in Runeheim for all eternity?" Petra's voice was high pitched and cold. She lifted a velvet sack from the floor and reached her hand inside. "Did you really think an old man's magic is stronger than the most powerful witch on earth?" In her hand was the strands of tousled gray hair. She lifted it completely from the bag and held her prize high for all to see.

The crowd gasped and women shielded children's eyes. Sebastian's heart pounded painfully against his bones and the fury of the dragon's curse ignited within as golden scales danced across his skin and cinders wisped away from his skin. His eyes lay fixated on the lifeless head of Valirus that Petra gripped tight in her hand. His chest rose and fell fast with every breath. He wanted to scream, attack, do anything that would inflict the most amount of pain possible onto her, but he stood frozen in his place, unable to muster the strength to avenge his teacher.

Dani shrieked and charged at his sister. "How could you?" His voice was sharp and carried over the crowd. "He was the last family we have."

"And what did family ever do for me?" Petra set Valirus's head on the ground. "Better yet, what did family ever do to you?" She gracefully strided across the floor toward her brother. "You were raped, beaten, and tormented your whole life and yet you still want to defend the people who oppressed you."

"Valirus was kind to me. He loved me!"

"Wrong!" Petra shouted. "He is the reason our father sold you. With all his helping you learn your powers ... if he would have just left well enough alone, you wouldn't have murdered our mother."

"That was an accident." Dani cried. "Valirus did nothing wrong. He was only trying to help me."

"Of course ... help Dani. Everyone wants to help Dani. Save the sweet, innocent little one from the wrath of his big mean father." Petra rolled her eyes. "But not once did Valirus try to help me."

"Perhaps not." Sebastian stepped between her and Dani. "But I did. I believed in you. I saw good in you and you betrayed me, you betrayed my family, my people, and now you come here, for what?"

"Revenge." In a daring move, Petra summoned spectral forms, shadows that twisted and writhed as they advanced towards

Sebastian. The fire god responded with a blazing aura, incinerating the ethereal entities that dared to approach. The battle between light and darkness unfolded in every corner of the ballroom. Petra hurled curses and dark tendrils of magic, while Sebastian responded with torrents of flame that danced with controlled chaos. The ballroom became a battleground of opposing elements—fire and shadow weaving through the air, each seeking dominance over the other.

Sebastian conjured pillars of fire that soared towards Petra, illuminating the ballroom in a mesmerizing display. Petra, agile and cunning, dodged and weaved through the inferno, her dark magic countering the searing heat. The clash of fire and shadow cast a surreal glow over the once-elegant surroundings.

The grandeur of the ballroom transformed into a scene of violence. Furniture and decorations became caught in the crossfire, with shadows contorting and flames leaving scorch marks on the luxurious surfaces. The temperature in the room rose dramatically as Sebastian's fire clashed with Petra's dark sorcery.

As Sebastian tried to shake off the dizziness a hand appeared before his face. He looked up and saw the long, blonde-haired Sinook warrior standing beside him.

"You should have let me kill her in Adurak." Dom, clad in Sinook warrior attire, wielded a gleaming blade with mastery. Petra, determined and resolute, conjured her dark powers, ready to unleash them upon Dom. The air crackled with tension as the adversaries locked eyes, each aware of the stakes in this battle. Dom's sword crashed into Petra's dark magic, creating sparks of energy that illuminated the grand ballroom. The fight unfolded with intensity as Dom's Sinook warrior skills countered Petra's arcane assaults.

Dom's resilience and strategic prowess became evident as he anticipated Petra's movements, countering her spells with swift and calculated strikes. The Sinook warrior's determination to protect and conquer drove him forward, each step bringing him closer to victory.

Petra, realizing the tide turning against her, summoned a final surge of dark energy in a desperate attempt to reverse the outcome. However, Dom, drawing strength from his Sinook heritage, channeled his focus into a powerful strike that breached Petra's defenses.

Dom smiled and marched three paces to reach Petra. He gripped her throat in his hand and jammed his sword into her stomach. As she choked and stumbled back, Dom pushed the word further into her gut, causing blood to pour from her mouth.

Her body quivered but Dom's voice was relentless and fierce. "You are the reason my daughter is dead and therefore; I relieve you of your life and your suffering. Now go and join your father in the darkest pit of hell for which you came from."

The ballroom was silent. Jace took a deep breath and fixed his shirt and jacket. "Well, Your Majesty, now what?"

Chapter Twenty-Eight
The King of Everything

On the rooftop platform of Castle Drake, a place where Tomas was once a prisoner at the hands of Barron, stood Sebastian. He breathed in the last of the warm summer air before making the long journey back to Safareen and on to Adurak. The platform was a chilling reminder of where he came from. Of a time when his journey first began, being dragged away to the frozen lake in The Far North and Tomas being tortured and left to starve in the cold, alone, without his twin to protect him.

Sebastian fell to his knees and cried into the palms of his hands for a moment, then he stopped suddenly and focused on the pain. The sky darkened and thunder rumbled over the peaks of the mountains. Lightning licked the platform beneath his feet and tapped along the stone walls of the castle around him. Bolts crashed into the castle grounds, sending soldiers running for cover. The summer air turned hot and the earth shook. Sebastian stood as his scales shimmered gold and his belly burned with the fire of a thousand dragons.

The vibration of flapping wings came from above The Break as Sigura landed roughly on the side of the castle and set a foot on the platform. She faced Sebastian and roared. Sebastian jumped and the storm broke apart, and the sun peeked through the clouds once again.

Sebastian panted and looked around. He walked to the edge and peered at the grounds below where a wagon filled with hay was on fire and men shouted, trying to blanket the fire. He turned back to Sigura and nodded. "Thank you for bringing me back." He crept toward the waiting dragon. "You are the last connection I have to my past. I need you, Sigura. I promise to keep you safe if you promise to do the same for the world around me. Keep me from becoming this apocalypse."

Sigura placed another foot on the platform and lowered her shoulder to the stone floor. Sigura grinned and ran over, climbed on, and Sigura lifted fast into the sky. They rode over the mountain and into the town of Shadowmire. Shop keepers, merchants, and the townspeople ran inside as the dragon gently landed in the center of the village.

Sebastian climbed down and footed into the Inn. "Grimmel?" He shouted.

Grimmel came from the back room, his shaggy red beard hung down to his pot belly and his massive fists were balled. "Who is shouting?" His voice was angrily loud.

"Whoa, it's just me." Sebastian held up his hands.

"Your Majesty!" Grimmel's tone changed quickly as Mikhail, Grimmel's son and NorthBrekka's blacksmith, came from the back. "I see you have brought your dragon." Grimmel pushed past Sebastian and went outside. "She is truly magnificent." He glanced at Sebastian. "Fancy a game?"

Sebastian smiled. "Absolutely."

The three men sat at a table as Grimmel dealt cards. His wife came out and made them sandwiches and brought a pitcher of ale to the table. Sebastian had to pause between hands to check on Sigura as the occasional screams came from the courtyard outside. As the afternoon passed and Sebastian was drunk, they sat with their cards in hand, staring seriously into each other's eyes.

"Let's see what you've got, Your Majesty." Grimmel raised an eyebrow.

Sebastian clenched his jaw and looked at his cards. He had three stars which was difficult for any hand to beat, but he did not hold the bird card, which automatically made the holder a winner. He carefully placed down his hand and looked up in time to see Grimmel throw down his hand in frustration.

"How do you always win?" Grimmel slapped his hand on the table.

"It's not over." Sebastian turned to Mikhail.

Mikhail shrugged and eyed his father before dropping his cards one by one, revealing he had nothing good. Sebastian eyed the terrible hand and then heard Grimmel laugh. Sebastian looked up at Mikhail to see a wide smirk on his lip and a card pinched between his fingers with the face toward Sebastian showing a small black bird inside a cage.

Sebastian dropped a coin purse on the table and pushed it over. He reached out and shook Mikhail's hand and then Grimmel's before standing. "I am returning to Adurak. I don't know when I will return but hopefully I will see you both again someday." He walked over and hugged Grimmel's wife. "Thank you for always keeping your husband from beating me to a pulp."

He took a last look around at the Inn and said his goodbyes to the innkeepers before making his way to Sigura. Sebastian took in the sights of the tiny mountain village that he loved so much as a boy.

He bit his lip and climbed onto his dragon and directed her to Stormfire Lake where he remembered Dom said he was going to catch fish before trekking home to Icefall. Sigura landed in the tall waving grass in the field next to the lake and Sebastian hurried over to the shoreline where Dom and the other Sinook enjoyed swimming and fishing on the hot afternoon. Sebastian didn't have to say anything to get Dom's attention.

Dom ran to meet him and embraced Sebastian before words were exchanged. "I know you're leaving and I don't know when or if I will ever see you again." Tears fell down Dom's cheeks. "But I wanted to tell you that I love you. And I will miss you more than you could possibly know."

"Dom." Sebastian wiped her tears away. "This isn't goodbye forever. I will be back and you can come to Adurak anytime you want." His throat tightened as he tried to hold back his emotions. "I've always loved you, Dom."

Dom smiled and took a deep breath. "We are heading home this evening after the ceremony."

Sebastian nodded. "Then we will make this night special for us all."

That evening, all gathered in Castle Drake for one final farewell to Tomas, and to all the loved ones lost. The people gathered with flowers and sage and walked in a line across the great hall, each leaving their gifts for the dead on the king's table. Families who had lost ones to war announced their names as they bowed to Sebastian.

The air was heavy with the fragrance of incense, and soft candlelight flickered, casting dancing shadows on the aged stone walls. The attendees, clad in a myriad of traditional funeral attire from various cultures, reflected the global nature of the event. Some wore dark suits and veils, while others adorned vibrant garments representing their heritage. The sound of hushed conversations in different languages created a hum of diverse condolences and shared grief.

As everyone took their seats, Sebastian stood before all. "Tonight is not for us... it is for them. I will save you the silly speeches tonight. But I must say that I am truly grateful to have all of you here on this day to celebrate those who we loved and lost. No matter where we come from, no matter who we choose to call a friend, and no matter our differences, we are all here, united as one, just as it was always meant to be. Now let's mourn our lost and have some fun!" He smiled, but then the hall doors burst open wide.

The crowd stood and gasped, looking around quickly and whispering their suspicions. Sebastian marched down from the king's stage and started toward the doors as Queen Indicia Ama led the sirens into the hall.

Nadya and Jon quickly joined Sebastian. Nadya grabbed his arm. "Do you know her?" She gripped a dagger in her fist and Jon's hand rested on the hilt of his sword.

Sebastian stepped between both his family and the sirens. He smiled at his sister and turned to Indicia Ama. "I was not aware you traveled so far from the water or else I would have invited you myself."

The siren queen came forward and took Sebastian's hand. "We came to mourn our lost as well, King of Everything."

Nadya came to Sebastian's side. A sweet smile stretched across her mouth. "Welcome, to NorthBrekka." Her eyes twinkled under the candlelight.

"You must be Queen Nadya Drake." Indicia Ama placed her hand over her heart. "It is nice to see another strong woman leading a kingdom."

Sebastian cleared his throat. "Shall we continue the ceremony?"

As the night progressed, Sebastian found himself alone in the war room watching out over the village in NorthBrekka's valley. The creak of the door opening broke his meditation. He spun around and saw Nadya come in and shut the door.

"So, I guess this is it . . ." Nadya's eyes flooded with tears as she spread her arms wide and engulfed Sebastian.

"Why does everyone keep saying goodbye to me like it is the last time?"

"Because we know how you are." Nadya cupped his cheek in her hand. "I know you will come back and visit, but I also know that know that you have finally got everything you've ever wanted, that you will slip away from the world." She bit her lips as the tears fell once again. "Please don't disappear forever."

Sebastian shook his head and pulled her against his chest. "I swear I never will." She held her as she cried into his arms. "I love you," he whispered.

"So." Nadya pulled away and straightened up, wiping her eyes quickly. "About this siren queen. How?"

"Hydros." Sebastian smiled. "They were here to mourn him. The God of Water. Our brother. They knew him differently, but they still loved him the same."

"Can they be trusted?" Nadya asked.

"They are loyal to the gods. If you ever decide to leave this castle and come to Adurak, I will call a meeting so that the two of you can get to know one another." Sebastian shrugged. "I know you need more lady friends."

"Well, you took Amara away from me."

"Well..." Sebastian paused. "She is going to marry Jace so she moved to Adurak." He glanced at Nadya. "Come for the wedding. It will mean the world to her."

"I will be there."

That night, as the others went off to bed, Sebastian walked to the castle gates, with Dani in hand and Dom by his side. The Sinook took to their horses and Dom reached out for one last hug and then another to Dani.

"I will see you both when the north thaws." Dom squeezed both of their hands tight. "I look forward to spring in Adurak."

"I'll see you when the ice thaws." Sebastian embraced Dom one more time before the High Priest of Erras joined his Sinook warriors and took to the road west.

The next morning, Sebastian waited in the courtyard early in the morning before the sun came from the east. Sigura landed by his side. He stared at his castle with a heated sorrow filling his belly.

Dani emerged from the castle doors with Nadya and Jon following with Jace, Amara, and Liliana trailing not too far behind. The soldiers and members of the Order who were returning to Adurak mounted their horses. Lucian and the Safar gathered in the courtyard and prepared to depart along with Queen Indicia Ama and the sirens.

The sirens bowed to Sebastian and took to the road onto the EastBay Pass. Indicia Ama stopped before Sebastian. "I will be there to greet you on your return home, King of Everything."

The sirens departed and the Safar led the march away from NorthBrekka. Sebastian said one last goodbye to Nadya, Jon, and the children and noticed Sigura leaning her shoulder to the ground.

Sebastian sighed and turned to Dani. "Want to ride with me?" He nodded toward Sigura.

Dani smiled. "More than anything!"

They mounted Sigura and lifted into the sky and the accompaniment made their way down the mountain toward the southlands. The journey back to Safareen was long and with the heat of the end of summer, the riders were worn and weathered. Sebastian said goodbye to Frey and Candor and the coven at the canyon, then made way to the harbor where the Hetta awaited.

As everyone boarded the ship, Sebastian embraced Lucian. "I hope to see you as well in the spring. The wedding." He nodded toward Jace and Amara. "I think you will like Adurak. It reminds me of Safareen in a lot of ways."

Lucian smiled and nodded. "Did you know that Safareen was built by Dragon?"

"How—" Sebastian tilted his head. "Let me guess, it was in one of Dani's books."

Lucian laughed and nodded. "I will see you in the spring, Nephew."

The Hetta departed Safareen and sailed across the seas until the sight of the Adurakian harbor town they named New Hope, came into view. Townspeople worked hard to rebuild the fish markets and piers damaged in the fight. The sirens helped the shopkeepers and the Harbor Master raise walls and move materials needed to make homes and stores as they were before. Sebastian was glad to be greeted by Queen Indicia Ama and the others as he stepped foot on the pier where the Hetta Horizon would rest until its next sailing.

As they descended the final pass through The Creed and into the prairie lands before the township of Adurak, Sebastian breathed in the cool wintry air blowing down from the mountains. He thought about NorthBrekka and how they were most likely buried in snow at this point in the year. They made their way to the castle where maidens bustled around quickly, decorating the halls of Moonlight Castle in Yule decorations. Sebastian kissed Dani's cheek and headed outside.

Nothing could take the smile from Sebastian's face as he wandered through the streets of Adurak, enjoying the sounds of his city coming to a close for the night and the songs of celebrations happening all around. He walked into The Fat Angry Crow and sat down at the bar, his eyes darting to the painting on the wall of the plump woman who was the inspiration for the name of the tavern. Sebastian laughed and enjoyed a drink with the townspeople. He listened to their stories and shared some of his own before heading back to the castle.

Sebastian watched the lights of the town dim as darkness fell over the valley. The stars twinkled bright in the sky above and the moon was nearly full, casting a ghostly glow across the castle. He was at peace. His heart was full and he was truly happy. Sebastian thought about the ones he lost over the years, but mostly about the loved ones he still has ... and about Dani and how much he loved him with his whole heart. Sebastian wanted to give the world everything. He wanted to truly wear the name, The King of Everything.

Ten Years Later

Sebastian watched over the city of Adurak as a soft summer breeze drifted across the castle. He was proud of the world his people built. Adurak stood as the capital of Midrel Istan, just as it did when Dragon was a child. The city boomed in commerce and trade from land and sea. Roads were built connecting Feldor Bay directly to Dunebar where boats would travel down river to Adurak, bringing new and old friends to the King's city.

Sebastian had a memorial built in Lastorum in honor of Valirus, and turned the mountain fortress into a training center for soldiers. Meecah and Samir had three children and took over the governorship of all of Midrel Istan. Viktor went back to NorthBrekka to help Nadya when Jon passed a few years before. Viktor and Seville had two children and owned land in both Midrel Istan and Erras. Lucian and Dom made a trade pact and worked together to provide food and goods to all of Erras. Dom visits Adurak often, but can never stay too long due to the winters of The Far North.

The world had turned into the story, once written by Dragon, on how the world would thrive and live in harmony. A guide to the perfect civilization between humans, gods, witches, and sirens that Sebastian followed to the letter. He had grown to admire the person Dragon was in his past and wanted to finish the work he hoped to start one day, but never did.

As he breathed in the salty water of the river, the girlish laugh of an adolescent girl broke his focus. Sebastian laughed and watched his prodigy closely. "Liliana, you are never going to learn properly if you're just playing around all the time."

"Oh come on, Uncle Sebastian." Liliana rolled her eyes and groaned as she climbed to her feet. "Okay, have it your way ... as usual." She turned to the river and lifted her hand as a stream of water hovered and turned into a ball that spun in mid-air."

"What else can you do with that?" Sebastian asked.

The ball of water turned in the shape of a pike with a sharp pointed end and froze as it rested in Liliana's hand. Sebastian rested his hand against its shaft and looked into Liliana's eyes. "Remember one thing. With this power comes a great responsibility and people are going to expect a lot from you." The pike melted against his hot touch. "Your father never let it consume him. Even when he transformed, he was still the kindest person I ever knew. Be like your father. Be the good this world so desperately needs."

One evening, Sebastian and Dani lay naked on their bedroom terrace that overlooked the river. Wrapped in silk blankets, they made love under the moonlight until neither could spare another breath. Dripping in sweat, the lovers held one another and stared into the starlit sky. Sigura let out a whining roar as she flew over the castle and disappeared into the western ridge of The Creed.

"This is everything I have ever wanted." Sebastian kissed Dani on the forehead.

"You finally have the freedom you always dreamed of." Dani rested his head on Sebastian's shoulder and closed his eyes. "And I will always love you."

Sebastian kissed Dani's lips. "Forever."

THE END

About The Author

From living in 16 different states to traveling around the world, Rey Wicks utilizes her knowledge of adventure and travel to write the epic quests appearing in her fantasy novels. "People always ask me how I keep up with such lavish world building in my books, and I have to tell them that it's because every world and every city I have written into one of my novels has been a creation based on a place that I have either lived or visited and loved (or hated). That way I never forget."

Rey Wicks has been writing since she was 15 years old when she published her first song and won an award as a rookie songwriter. After that, Rey often was found writing poetry in one of her many little notebooks. She even was known to have a few cute little horror stories scratched away in journals. Now, Rey writes in many genres and has multiple projects coming up in the genres of fantasy, sci-fi, and poetry.

Milton Keynes UK
Ingram Content Group UK Ltd.
UKHW022040131124
451149UK00015B/1553

9 781959 860518